SISTERS OF THE FROZEN VEIL

Part One of Shadowed Kings
Book Eight in the Pantracia Chronicles

Written by Amanda Muratoff & Kayla Mansur

www.Pantracia.com

To our brothers and sisters.

Dustin, Tyler, Miriam & Emily.

♥

The Pantracia Chronicles:

Prequel:
Dawn of the Thieves

Part 1: The Berylian Key Trilogy
Book 1: *Embrace of the Shade*
Book 2: *Blood of the Key*
Book 3: *Unraveling of the Soul*

Part 2: A Rebel's Crucible
Book 4: *Ashes of the Rahn'ka*
Book 5: *Pursuit of the Hawk*
Book 6: *Heart of the Wolf*
Book 7: *Rise of the Renegades*

Part 3: Shadowed Kings
Book 8: *Sisters of the Frozen Veil*
Book 9: *Wings of the Eternal War*
Book 10: *Axiom of the Queen's Arrow*

Visit www.Pantracia.com to discover more.

Prologue

Winter, 2590 R.T. (recorded time)

Screams shattered the silence, but the girl's cries stirred nothing in Giffran's gut.

He lifted the crimson-filled vial, tilting it in the light. "How much are you taking from her veins?"

"Ten vials each day." Felina's voice held the same reluctance it had before. "And giving her the same amount in serum, but she's in considerable pain."

"Pain is expected." He narrowed his eyes at his underling, catching the hint of empathy in her gaze. "She's not a person, Fel. Remember that. She's a weapon and will be the key to Feyor's future."

"Yes, sir."

The girl's cries faded from the other room, where she must have lost consciousness.

"Where are you giving the injections?" Giffran picked up the parchment from his desk, which outlined the stages each Dtrüa endured in fulfilling their potential.

This subject had shown significant improvement over the years in her tolerance of the serum made for her. They'd mixed the grygurr blood with panther blood, adding a serum concocted by Feyor's highest ranking Art practitioners.

"Only the spine, now." Felina's tone hardened. "We had little success with the other areas, as much as we tried." She twisted her hands together in front of her hips, as if the process still bothered her.

She'll learn its necessity.

He returned to his papers but couldn't read a single word before Felina interrupted.

"Is your meeting with King Lazorus soon?"

"It is. I'm headed there now. He's here to inspect our progress. Is there any other news you have to share?" Giffran flipped the parchment to the first page and read the girl's intake notes.

> *Name: Unknown*
> *Sex: Female*
> *Age at commencement: Four*
> *Subject resistant to sedation, recommend Varanithe Danilisca poison to aid in transition. Blindness incurable.*
> *Predicted term: Ten years*

Giffran touched the Varanithe Danilisca blossom he kept fresh on his desk, its pearlescent petals like satin. Its scent hovered in the air, deceptively sweet for a bloom so poisonous.

Only two more years before we'll know if it worked.

Felina again interrupted his thoughts. "Our original timeline seems accurate, though she's gaining some attention from the other Dtrüa who've completed their transitions. She's getting stronger, endures the treatments better. We have yet to force her to shift, as her obedience still needs work, but her belief that we are saving her life is increasing. That *is* what we are doing, is it not? They informed me she had a rare illness that would have killed her had we not intervened."

"Of course it's true." Giffran sighed. "An orphan on the streets would surely have perished by now." He tucked the parchment under his arm and nodded at Felina. "Excellent work, keep it up. I want her shifting next year into full form. Her training must commence immediately after her transition finishes."

"Yes, sir."

Giffran strode out of the windowless room, climbing the stone stairs until daylight greeted him through tall windows overlooking Feyor's thick forests. Snow blanketed each pine, untouched over the wilds.

Anticipation roiled in his stomach before he quelled it with a huff.

"Lord Giffran." The king's baritone voice echoed behind him, and he turned to face his ruler.

"Your majesty." Giffran bowed low, pausing before rising. "I trust your journey was pleasant?"

King Lazorus scoffed. "As pleasant as a bumpy carriage ride in the snow can be. Though let's speak farther from prying ears. The snow is perfect for that, is it not?"

"Of course, your highness. I brought the paperwork on the subject you're interested in." Giffran offered it, but the king waved a hand.

"Leave it. I want your thoughts, not your notes."

Annoyance bubbled in his gut, but he nodded and dropped the parchment onto a nearby table. "Lead the way, my king."

Lazorus turned, striding through the dank hallways at a brisk pace. As he approached one of the heavy oaken doors, it opened before he needed to lay a finger on it. The dark armor of one of the king's personal guards shimmered in the sunlight.

The chill air permeated Giffran's scholarly robes, but his blood heated at the sight of ruby scales. Chains shuddered as the wyvern's head snapped towards the door, a guttural hiss curling over its snout.

Giffran jumped back, eyes wide on the draconi. "Nymaera's breath."

"Oh, yes. I failed to mention we were bringing you a toy. This is Keleshna." Lazorus raised a brow at him, daring him to complain. "Our trainers are still struggling with teaching these beasts anything beyond the basic. Thought you could try your hand."

Giffran's hands brushed the cold stone behind him. He'd backed into the wall without fully realizing it, unable to pry his gaze from the chained beast. "My king, with all due respect, we are unequipped to handle a... a beast of this size. The white one is not finished her transition... And we have no guarantee she will succeed in taming it once she has."

"Failure is not an option, Lord Giffran." The king tilted his head as he gazed with admiration at the draconi. "And do come up with something better than *white* one."

It hunkered down on its hind legs, claws at the bend in its wings scraping the stone.

As the king turned his attention back to Giffran, his gut turned to acid under the hard steel blue stare of his ruler.

"We... we don't name them, your majesty. It's too... personal."

King Lazorus scoffed. "This is a very personal matter. These *Dtrüa* will make all the difference in the coming war with Isalica. They will save many Feyorian lives."

"War?" Giffran balked, the word more vile than the experiments he oversaw. "But we're not—"

"It's coming." The king's eyes darkened like storm clouds. "We *will* be ready for it. And you *will* train this wyvern. Name those who will be our saviors in the years to come. But this one..." He pointed at the building, his tone lowering. "This... white one, the one who will tame Keleshna. You must never let her know how important she is." The king glanced at the beast as it snapped its jaws. "This beast belongs to my son, and I want her fully trained and as docile as a kitten by his thirteenth birthday in six years."

Giffran nodded. "We shall do our best, your highness."

Chapter 1

Winter, 2596 R.T.

"I heard he's handsome. Even more handsome than Master Yelisen."

Serna giggled, but kneaded her dough more fiercely after Katrin scowled at her.

"He's not married, yet." Jelisa wiggled her eyebrows at Katrin. "You can't possibly be as uninterested as your face suggests."

"You really think an acolyte like you would have a chance with a prince?" Katrin threw her ball of dough onto the table, flour splattering onto her apron. "His visit is just a temporary annoyance."

Jelisa hummed a tune, picking up the front of her apron and dancing in a circle before dipping into a curtsy. "And he's welcome to whisk me away to a life of royalty and pampering."

Serna wiped her hands and skipped to Jelisa, joining her. Her airy laugh echoed against the hard stone of the temple kitchen. "Can I come with you as your mistress?"

Katrin pounded her fist into her dough, shaking her head as she cupped water from a bowl to offset the dryness.

They're so distracting. And foolish.

"Of course, my sweet." Jelisa spoke in a sing-song voice. "I shall bear his children, but you will always own my heart."

Katrin rolled her eyes. "You two better stop before—"

"What is going on here?" Mistress Melean's voice shattered the playful air in the room, and the dancing acolytes jumped apart.

They bowed their heads, clasping their hands in front of them.

Katrin, dough stuck between her fingers, hurried to do the same.

The priestess stalked over to Serna. "See that the place settings are arranged properly and then you can take the scraps to the hogs."

Serna dipped her head again, locks of her red hair falling from her bun. "Yes, Mistress Melean." She scurried from the room, leaving her dough on the counter.

Katrin held in her annoyed sigh.

I suppose I'll have to finish her bread now, too. So much for extra reading time before the feast.

"And you." Their priestess turned to Jelisa. "There will be no *dancing* in my kitchen, especially when there is an abundance of work to be done before our distinguished guests arrive! Would you rather empty chamber pots?"

"No, Mistress."

"Then finish your chopping quickly so I may forget your indiscretions. Why can't you follow Katrin's example? Her dough is a mess, but at least she's trying." The priestess huffed and spun on her heel, stalking from the kitchen.

Jelisa lifted her gaze once their superior disappeared into the next room. "You've been here three months, and you're already her favorite." She looked at the dough sticking to Katrin's hands and laughed. "Even if your dough is a *mess.*"

Katrin frowned. "I wouldn't have *messed* it up if it wasn't for your silliness." She turned back to the table, pinching more flour. She flipped and rolled her dough, the muscles in her arms aching from the hours of making bread.

Jelisa returned to the cutting board beside her, resuming her work on a pile of carrots. She nudged Katrin with her shoulder. "You need to lighten up sometimes. You're too serious."

"I'm dedicated to my studies." Katrin balled her dough and added it beneath a large cloth to rise with the rest of the prepared loaves. She moved to take up Serna's unfinished work.

"You can be dedicated to your studies and still enjoy life." Jelisa tilted her head, catching Katrin's gaze. "What's the point, otherwise?"

Katrin sighed, tucking a piece of onyx hair that'd fallen from the messy bun at her neck behind her ear. Flecks of dough stuck to her cheek. "I don't want to be an acolyte forever."

"You're only eighteen!" Jelisa nudged her again. "You'll be an acolyte for at least another seven years."

Five if I work hard enough.

Katrin shrugged and eyed the doorway to the kitchen. Her thick linen dress stuck to her skin in the heat from the ovens. "I just hope this visit from the prince is over soon. I could do without all the priests and priestesses fussing all day long."

Jelisa rolled her eyes. "Yes, please. Let's get this rare exciting time over with so we may resume the monotony of our mundane lives." She laughed. "You are a unique breed, Katrin."

"To our royal guest, Crown Prince Alarik Rayeht. May your family's honorable rule continue for generations to come." High Priest Krek lifted his goblet of wine, and the hall followed suit.

They had extended the tables for the temple's higher ranking members to accommodate the prince and two of his elite guards, while the rest dined with the acolytes on the main floor. His impressive company of twenty guards and ten dedicated staff made the room more claustrophobic than usual.

Prince Alarik grinned beneath his thick, short beard, darker than his chestnut hair. He rose from his seat as the high priest sat and the room quieted. "Your generous hospitality is much appreciated. Our staff are some of the most talented people I've met, but there's something exceptional about fresh baked bread, is there not?"

The people in the hall laughed.

Jelisa elbowed Katrin and whispered, "He already likes you and doesn't even know it."

Katrin batted at her, her cheeks heating. "I'd still rather be studying."

Their low conversation earned a glare from one of the prince's nearer guards, whose ocean blue eyes met Katrin's.

She bowed her chin, kicking Jelisa under the table.

"Ow," Jelisa whined.

"I bid everyone to enjoy this feast, and I look forward to meeting more of this temple's dedicated wardens tomorrow." The prince lifted his wine and drank before sitting.

The annoyed-looking guard sitting with the acolytes rolled his eyes before drinking, too. He ran a hand over his dark beard, much the same as the prince's.

"Too bad the priests will monopolize the prince's time, and we won't get a chance to talk to him." Belfor, another recently transferred acolyte like her, leaned over the table towards Katrin until his robe collar nearly touched his food. "I was hoping to ask him more about the conflicts at the border and whether he thinks Feyor will back down or continue pressuring us into war. He's the military's royal liaison, you know, and I have some ideas that could help our front line."

Jelisa shook her head and muttered into her wineglass so only Katrin could hear. "Can't organize his books, but he's ready to lead an army."

"I'm sure your ideas are great, Belfor." Katrin gritted her teeth to hold in her laugh. "But the prince certainly has a whole army of people already giving him ideas to deal with the conflict."

"Damn Yorries, always pushing their luck at our borders." Jelisa gulped her wine. "Say, mister." She gestured her mostly empty glass to the grumpy guard who'd eyed them. "Have you seen any of the fighting at the border?"

Katrin's eyes widened.

Of all the brash... By the goddess, Jelisa.

One of his dark eyebrows twitched, and he set his goblet down. The discontent in his gaze diminished. "I've seen enough of it." His bass voice made Katrin's stomach quiver. "Though it's more honest than this political horse shit." He gestured to the prince and priest.

Jelisa choked, and Katrin narrowed her eyes.

"That seems awful disrespectful to say of the throne you're loyal to." Katrin had hardly touched her meal, resting her hands in her lap as she stared at the guard.

To her surprise, the man laughed. "The throne should be stricter where it sends funds. Endless border disputes and unfounded religion seem like a waste of time."

"Excuse me?" Katrin's veins heated.

The guard gestured to her. "No offense. I'm sure you're a very talented priestess." He rose from his seat, patting a fellow guard on the shoulder before whispering in his ear.

"I'm not a..."

The other man nodded, and the two of them strode out of the dining hall towards the courtyard.

Jelisa's eyes widened at Katrin. "He thought you were a priestess!"

"That's what you got out of that?" Katrin sputtered, glaring after the man's back as he vanished. Anger spurred her legs to straighten as she stumbled out from the bench seat. She tugged on the hem of her skirt to free it, pulling down her sleeves from where she'd shoved them up.

Her friend caught her by the wrist with a playful expression. "Chasing him already? He's better looking than the prince, even if he is a little broody. Careful, Kat."

"He can't just say things like that and walk away." Katrin twisted her hand gently from Jelisa. "And I don't care how handsome his face is."

"It's his voice, right? Have you ever heard such a deep tone? Gods, I could listen to him recite the—"

"Jelisa..." Katrin hissed, but the memory of his voice made her spine tingle. "Don't let them take my plate. I'll be back, and hopefully, so will my appetite."

Padding quietly to the end of the row of tables, Katrin pursued the disrespectful guard towards the temple's center courtyard.

The two men stood near the center of the Art-warmed outdoor space, the one Katrin had been talking to speaking in low tones to the other. His comrade nodded and walked away, re-entering the temple on the opposite side. Shoulders relaxing, the lone guard tilted his head back to look at the sky.

The sunset turned the stormy clouds to a deep orange, coloring the large snowflakes before they melted on the translucent shield protecting the temple's gardens. The aroma of blooming night jasmine mixed with the sweet scent of the rich greenery.

"I demand an apology." Katrin approached the mosaic walkway at the center.

Tension returned to the man's shoulders as he faced her. "Of course you do."

"You make light of the two domains our country holds most dear, and the two closest to my heart. As you are a crown elite, I might forgive your ignorance of the temples, but would have expected more respect for the military."

His expression flattened, any semblance of humor leaving his eyes. "The monarchy has no business being involved in the temples. In taking children from their homes to be raised by strangers and forced into beliefs not their own." When she opened her mouth to interrupt him, he stepped closer and held up a finger. "No. You came to me, so you can hear what I have to say before you make more demands."

Katrin pursed her lips, glaring.

"I am not ignorant of what the priests and priestesses do here, but I don't think it belongs on our charted path. Which, by the way, we've taken so many times that I recognize the individual trees. Nothing happened each other time, and nothing will happen this time. Except more wasting of the prince's precious time."

"Well, then I *apologize* for granting you a night off the snowy ground and a fresh meal in your belly."

He barked a laugh and threw his hands up. "I *like* the snow." He studied her. "You did make some amazing bread, though. I'll give you that."

Katrin's shoulders loosened, his laugh and compliment weakening her more than expected. She glanced up and sighed. "The north courtyard is open to the elements and may better suit what you'd enjoy. I can show you, if you'd like."

And maybe then I can convince you that not all you believe is true.

"Might I learn the name of my generous guide, Priestess?" He tilted his head, a lock of deep brown hair falling over his forehead.

"Katrin." Her chest seized. "And I'm just an acolyte."

"All right, Priestess." He grinned.

She scowled through the instinct to smile at him. "And your name?"

"Matthias." He nodded at the dining hall. "Don't you have a meal to finish and a friend to return to?"

"I work in the kitchens. I can get a meal later if I'm hungry. You won't find the north courtyard without me." Katrin turned towards the halls, glancing over her shoulder at his charming face.

"Ah." Matthias smirked. "So you're the one I should talk to when the prince gets hungry later. Gods know he hardly has a chance to eat during these things. So many people pestering him."

"I'm certain Jelisa would be happy to assist in that matter. Especially if it meant getting to meet him." She slowed until he walked beside her, passing through the darkened hallways side-by-side.

The Art radiated in pale light from the alcoves spaced five feet apart within the wood-paneled walls. Katrin reveled in the dull hum of power that constantly surrounded her. The priests at this temple seemed far more open about using the Art than her previous home.

The guard quirked an eyebrow. "You're not interested in meeting his *royal highness* yourself?"

Katrin laughed. "Hardly. I wish he'd continue on his way so my studies of the Art can continue without more interruptions. You speak of children taken from their homes, but most of us find peace and joy here. We're not prisoners, not like in Helgath."

"I shall let him know his company isn't as welcome as he thinks." Matthias chuckled, his heavy fur-lined cloak swaying behind his broad form.

"I'm sure he hardly cares about a lowly acolyte's opinion of him."

"You'd be surprised."

Katrin narrowed her eyes and shook her head. "There are far more important things that should be on his mind. Like the conflict at the border. It is not something that can be taken lightly. Not with the growing tension and skirmishes."

"You know, if you're not careful, I might think your only interest in me stems from my connection to him."

"Oh, I have little faith in your ability to sway him, either. The prince will do what he believes to be right, regardless of what a soldier or an acolyte might believe. He was born into that right, unlike us." Katrin slowed as they neared the end of the maze-like hallways that led to the north courtyard. She gestured to the locked wooden doorway ahead. "As promised."

Matthias stepped ahead of her before pausing. "Are you not accompanying me to further argue why this place isn't as bad as I believe?"

She lifted a single eyebrow.

"Are you still waiting for my apology?" He crossed his arms.

"It would help."

Matthias laughed again, and the deep sound made her shiver. "I apologize for upsetting you, Priestess. I'm not sure which is more surprising. That I'm standing in a temple without loathing life, or that the reason for it is my conversation with one of its inhabitants."

Katrin's stomach fluttered as she reached for one of the cloaks hanging beside the door. Pulling the warm fur over her shoulders, she tied it. "Perhaps you've never tried talking to us before? We're people, just as you or the prince himself."

Striding to the courtyard door, he flipped the latch and opened it to a gust of icy mountain air. "On the contrary, I have." He walked outside, holding the door open for her. "My lady."

Katrin's cheeks flushed, and she tried to recall the last time someone had held a door for her. The guard's formality struck her as odd, though enchanting. She stepped into the snow, shadows from the temple roofs looming over the white blanketed courtyard. Clusters of flakes fell together, vanishing in the banks of snow beside the cleared walkway. A thin layer of slush coated the cobblestone, and Katrin carefully stepped over it.

Matthias shut the door, the wind ruffling the mottled fur around his shoulders. "You like it here, then?"

"I do." Katrin turned to him as they made their way to the center of the courtyard. Her nose twinged at the cold, but it felt good in her lungs. "I only transferred to this temple a few months ago. Before, I was closer to Mecora. But I like the snow, too. And now I'm closer to my brother, and I'm hoping I may see him soon. But my studies are my priority."

"I didn't think acolytes could have visitors?"

Katrin snorted, steeling her face from showing her horror at making the sound in front of him. "Rules like that haven't existed for decades. Besides, there are accommodations made for family serving in the military."

"Where is your brother stationed?" Matthias stuffed his hands in his pockets, snowflakes clinging to his windswept hair.

"The border." She reached back to loosen the knot in her hair, pulling it around her neck to keep her skin warm. "He's serving with the 134th Battalion, which has been at the front of a lot of those skirmishes I mentioned earlier."

Matthias lifted his chin. "A highly respected unit. I understand your defensiveness of the military, now. That's the same military encampment for which we are bound. Perhaps I'll have the pleasure of meeting your brother."

Katrin smiled. "Then I hope you might tell Liam I miss him." Her eyes burned as she thought about the years that had passed since she'd seen her brother.

"You should tell him yourself. Your studies will always be there, but with family..."

"The border seems hardly the place for an acolyte right now. Besides, until I become a priestess, requests to leave the temple are rarely granted. He's the one who'd have to gain leave to come here. Several more years..."

The corner of his mouth twitched. "If only you knew someone with royal connections."

Katrin shook her head rapidly. "I would never ask that of you."

"If the prince doesn't help those he can, what good is he?"

She laughed. "Why in the name of the goddesses would you actually want me along after tonight? That's what you're suggesting, you know. You'd have to put up with me far longer than just a day. I got the impression you wouldn't like religious company."

Matthias grinned. "I like those who challenge me. Though, if you'd rather wait out the years in these stuffy halls..." He shrugged. "I can't even pretend to see the appeal."

"Better than sleeping on the ground." Katrin brushed her hair back behind her ear and tugged her cloak tighter.

His eyebrows rose. "Who said I sleep on the ground?"

"A cot, then. I have a bed. With a mattress."

Something playful danced in his eyes. "A mattress, too? Unexpected luxury in the temples."

"I share the room with four others..." Katrin glowered, but a smile touched the edge of her lips. "Hardly luxurious."

Matthias crossed his arms, tilting his head. "But there is so much more beyond these walls."

The light from the hallways within flickered against the tightening leathers at Matthias's chest. His biceps were bulky, far more than any of the priests in the temple. A soldier in his prime.

She opened her mouth, but nothing came out.

The door they'd entered the courtyard from clicked open, and Matthias stepped back.

Another one of the prince's guards stood in the archway. "You're needed."

Matthias straightened. "It was a pleasure, Priestess."

"Acolyte." She managed a mere whisper. Lifting her hand, she gave a dazed wave.

The guard turned from her, dipping his chin before striding to his comrade, and they both disappeared inside.

Katrin stared at the ajar door, counting her frozen breaths. Her entire body tingled in a way she'd never experienced, and her gut felt like a beehive swarmed within.

What just happened?

She looked up at the darkened sky, snow catching in her eyelashes. Blinking them away, she let the flakes cool her heated skin.

Chapter 2

Matthias walked down the hallway, Riez next to him. "That's what you pulled me away to tell me? We're here a few days. The high priest's requests can wait until tomorrow. If he thinks a little wine in my belly will increase the temple's budget, he's got another thing coming."

Riez snorted, followed by his spine straightening. "I don't think you've indulged in nearly enough wine tonight. This will be your last chance to relax before the border."

"I can't relax in a temple."

"Looked pretty relaxed outside, just now."

Matthias frowned at his guard. His friend. "I got distracted." Pausing, his thoughts drifted to Katrin. "Wine is a good idea. Has Micah had enough fun playing prince today? We can go over tomorrow's agenda while we drink."

Ruiz chuckled. "Micah is never done having fun. I'll let him know to meet you in our chambers. Are you sure you don't want to take the grand room and stick him with us for the night?"

"I don't want to take any chances. This close to the border, we can't risk anyone learning that I'm using my stand in." Matthias touched his finger where he usually wore his signet ring.

He grew up with Micah, and the man was another brother to him. The physical similarities granted him the role of prince in necessary circumstances.

Except he gets to drink wine and fool around while I get stuck with the real work.

Matthias waited in the front room of the chambers provided to him and his men, savoring the solitude and dark whisky. He'd poured glasses for his four crown elites. They knew the truth of his identity, but encouraged the rest of the troop acquired in Omensea to believe Micah was the true prince Alarik. The crown guards who'd been privy to his secrets had been sent home to Nema's Throne on a posting change.

The door opened and Riez returned, the other three in tow.

Micah strode to Matthias, claiming one of the whisky glasses. "I'm sorry I agreed to your rules, now, *my liege*. Did you know not all priestesses are celibate?"

The prince frowned. "How, exactly, do you know that?"

"Don't worry so much. There's a married couple here. How were you thinking I'd know?"

"Married doesn't mean they have sex." Riez lifted a hand. "First hand knowledge with my old lady."

"Maybe if you stopped calling her *old*." Matthias smirked.

"Actually, I spoke to the couple." Micah nodded. "People will answer anything when a prince is asking."

Matthias groaned. "You give me the worst reputation."

The men refilled their glasses and sat at the round table Matthias had laid the military documents on.

"Are you going to remember my instructions for the discussions tomorrow?" The prince motioned to his double.

Micah pushed his empty whisky glass aside, preventing Stefan from topping it up. "No more for me. I'll remember."

At least he knows when to put the job first.

Matthias pushed a stack of several documents over to his stand in. "We already know the high priest wants an increase in his budget from the monarchy. The arch priestesses back home keep reminding my father how imperative this temple will become with the war because it specializes in healing. While I don't disagree with the sentiment, we have to be careful how much more we give them. The gold we granted them years ago to find a solution to Cerquel's Plague resulted in nothing. We can offer them a four percent increase in crown funds, but if he pushes, you can take it to six. Understand?"

Micah wrote the numbers down, nodding at each instruction. "And if six percent doesn't satisfy him?"

"Too bad." Matthias leaned back in his chair and put his boots on the table. "Tell him the border is costing us a fortune. It'll work because it's true. Damn Yorries are relentless."

Barim poured more whisky into Matthias's glass and sat next to him. "I heard you were talking with a priestess earlier. Does she know who you are?"

Matthias shook his head and laughed. "She's an acolyte. And with the things she said, she definitely doesn't. No need for concern."

Too bad she's adamant that I'm a prick.

"What should I tell the high priest if he asks to increase the recruitment rate to this temple?"

Bile rose in Matthias's throat. "No. They take enough people."

"Recruitment is still voluntary..."

"Still no. What else is on the agenda?"

Micah cleared his throat. "He also has concerns about protection, should Feyor breach the border. Since most members here are healers, they can do little to protect themselves and the temple itself."

Matthias gritted his teeth, imagining Feyorian brutes slamming down the doors and slaughtering the temple's inhabitants.

Katrin's face appeared among them.

"Tell him he'll have military support should the situation at the border worsen." Matthias frowned at the surprised looks from his guards. "What? I'm not heartless."

Riez coughed. "Should we send word to prepare an emergency battalion out of Omensea?"

Matthias nodded. "All right."

"Is that all?" Micah scribbled the last of his notes. "I will go over these again in the morning before we get started."

"That's all." Matthias downed the rest of his glass. "Enjoy the next few days. There's no feasts or whisky at the border."

Chapter 3

"Did you see when he smiled?" A sigh accompanied Serna's question as she leaned into the dough in front of her.

"I spoke with him today," Jelisa wiggled her eyebrows, and Serna gaped.

"You *what*? When? Why is this the first I'm hearing about it?"

Katrin's eyes rolled back so far she thought she'd see the blazing hearth behind her. "Can we *stop* gossiping about the prince? He's not *that* good looking."

Both women faced her and frowned.

"Oh, yes, of course. Jelisa..." Serna faced the other. "How was the weather today?"

"A little cloudy, but the sun sure broke through those clouds... when I *personally* delivered a meal to *the crown prince of Isalica!*"

Serna squealed, bouncing up and down with their giggles. "I still get to be your mistress, right?"

Katrin threw her kneaded dough onto the table, flour puffing into the surrounding air. "This is why Mistress Melean always gets so angry with us. We'll never get these rolls rising in time for breakfast if you two keep flitting about." She waved her hand, little flecks of dough still stuck between her fingers.

Jelisa stuck out her bottom lip. "Why must you ruin my happiness?"

"Because despite being two years your *junior*, I'm clearly the more responsible of us." Katrin turned, transferring her dough into one of the large proving baskets before moving to the next ball.

"Or the more *boring*," Serna muttered. "What happened after you chased that guard last night, anyway? You didn't come back for your dinner and neither did he."

Katrin's cheeks heated, her spine straightening as Matthias's face entered her mind. Then the bulging of his tunic when he'd crossed his arms. His deep voice. She shivered. "Nothing. We talked. He... sort of apologized."

"And...?"

"And nothing. He's an arrogant ass who thinks he knows what's best for me without even knowing me."

As much as she told herself the same words over and over, she couldn't push away the desire to see him again. Speak to him. Learn more about what his promise of life beyond the temple could look like. To train with a healer who worked directly with the crown prince was an opportunity few ever received.

Jelisa hummed, bumping Katrin's hip with her own as she placed her proving basket beside Katrin's. "So why are you smiling?"

It altered into a frown as Katrin turned from her friends, feigning the need for more flour as her cheeks heated. "I'm not."

Silence settled as the other two had a wordless conversation.

"I think you should—" Jelisa stopped short when the hallway door swung open, spinning to face who she must have assumed was the priestess with the way her face deadpanned.

"Apologies for the interruption." A familiar deep voice made her insides quake. "I'm looking for the whisky... or any liquor, really." He spoke slowly, too slowly. Like the two women were staring him down.

Katrin could imagine their wide eyes and vacant grins.

Ridiculous.

Her spine straightened as she tried to convince her heart to slow. Brushing flour from her apron, she turned to give the crown elite an unamused quirked brow. "Not enough already provided in your private quarters and the three-hour feast?"

Matthias stiffened and crossed his arms. "The stash is empty, and the prince is requesting more, if possible. Will you demand an apology for this, as well?" A playful glint danced in his eyes, daring her to argue with him.

She pursed her lips and mimicked his arm cross and posture. "Do you often get sent on such trivial errands for the prince?"

Amusement crossed his face. "I offered." His gaze traveled to her friends before returning. "A change of scenery is welcome after spending the day stuck in small rooms with only *men*."

"If we'd known, we'd happily have taken another bottle to the prince." Serna licked her lips, her eyes wandering down Matthias from behind, lingering on the crown elite's muscular body without his knowledge.

Katrin's stomach twisted.

The guard looked at Serna, a charming smile replacing his smirk. "If it is a task you will find pleasure in, I'm sure he'd appreciate the bottle from your hands more than mine."

Jelisa beamed as Serna's gaze hovered at Matthias's chest and arms, her eyes glazing over as if she hadn't even heard the guard speak.

The knot in Katrin's stomach doubled.

She's looking at him like he's a piece of meat.

"Seems like you have this handled, Kat." Jelisa elbowed Serna, who gasped and swatted at her friend. "And we'll find the prince a fresh bottle."

Katrin started, eyes going wide as she looked at her departing friends. "What? You're leaving?"

Oh, don't you dare, Jelisa.

The two exchanged a look, and Serna nodded with a foot on the first stair. "We should finish our... other chores, after, anyway."

They are terrible liars.

Before Katrin could yell at them not to leave her, they disappeared up the stone corridor, leaving her and Matthias alone.

The guard held her gaze, his smile dimming to a thoughtful look that unsettled her.

Her fingers played with the hem of her apron as she busied herself by returning to the table near the crown elite, grabbing a fresh ball of dough. Watching him from the corner of her eye, she chewed her lip. "I'm sorry about those two. They're just..." She sighed, blowing a strand of black hair from her face.

Matthias waved off her apology. "It's nothing." He stepped back from her, his arms still crossed. "I don't wish to intrude. Unless you're open to having company?"

The way he said it, her heart skipped. "I don't mind." She said it before she even fully realized she'd opened her mouth.

The guard hesitated before leaning on the wall, his sword sheath tapping against it. "Do you have much work to complete tonight?"

Looking at the pile she'd almost completed, she refused to acknowledge Serna and Jelisa had somehow finished their batches despite their games. Though they'd left her with all the cleaning. "Nearly done with the preparation for the morning, but there's always more to do in this kitchen." She set to kneading another ball, her arms pleasantly aching from the exertion. Narrowing her eyes, she met his ocean-blue ones, but refused to fall into their trap. Clearing her throat, she pushed the heel of her palm into the dough. "So, how's the political horseshit?"

Matthias coughed on a laugh before it turned into a rumbling chuckle. "You're different from the others here, you know that?" He huffed, but his smile faded. "Exhausting, honestly. It's been a long day. The men are looking forward to a drink and soft bed."

"You talk about them like they're yours." Katrin narrowed her eyes.

The guard shrugged. "Feels like it, sometimes, since I've been with the prince the longest."

A strange tickle touched her stomach at the mention of the crown prince. She looked to her dough, kneading it harder into the tabletop as she tried to swallow the questions she wanted to ask Matthias about the one he served.

Jelisa would never let me live it down if she knew I actually cared.

Slamming the dough again, she watched him from her peripheral vision. He spoke so casually about the prince. It was strange to consider just how powerful Matthias himself was in his position. And how far she truly was from it as an acolyte.

Clearing her throat, Katrin tucked the dough beneath as she dropped it into its basket. "You must keep busy, then. I'd think you'd like a chance to relax at a place like this temple."

He let out a short huff. "There are many places I enjoy going for relaxation, but this... this is *not* one of them." His tone had softened, but a smirk lingered on his face. "Couldn't you tell last night? I do apologize, genuinely, this time. I have difficulty being in places like this, but my words were harsher than necessary."

A warm shiver ran up her spine as her lips curled into a smile. "At least you're able to admit it. Some men wouldn't, or bother to try." Turning out the last bit of dough, she remained trapped in his gaze until the tip of his sword tapped against the wall behind him as he pushed away from it.

He walked further into the kitchen, collecting a clean rag and dipping it into a wash basin before wringing it out.

Katrin slowed in her work. "What are you doing?"

Matthias approached the dirty countertops and cleaned. "If I'm here, I may as well help." As he progressed across the counter, he replaced lids on jars and returned them to their shelves.

Katrin kneaded faster, suddenly desperate to be done so she could stop him. "You really don't need to. It's my responsibility."

He scoffed. "If I hadn't come in here looking for liquor, you'd have two others helping. So the way I see it, I'm making up for sending them off." Glancing at her, he smiled, retying a sack of flour.

Katrin rolled her eyes. "As if they could stop gossiping long enough to pick up a broom." Hastily, she rounded her loaf and deposited it into the final proving basket. Shimmying sideways along the counter, she reached to take the cloth from his hand.

Matthias lifted it away from her. "Whoa, now. Get your own."

A tension rose through her, straightening her spine as she glowered at him. "Just give it to me. You don't need to clean. You're a soldier, not a cook."

A playful grin touched his lips as he hid it behind his back. "Maybe I like cleaning. Like Kitchens. This might just be my favorite room in this temple."

Katrin lifted a brow, nearly reaching around him for the cloth again, but put her hands on her hips instead. "The kitchens? Really?"

"Why not?" Matthias tilted his head, looking closer at her eyes.

"Please reference my previous statement. Soldier." She poked his chest and instantly regretted it. He hardly moved with the prod, his body solid beneath her touch. Her heart leapt into her throat as her eyes deceived her and looked at the muscles of his arms and chest.

A flash of recognition crossed his face, and his jaw flexed. "Can't a man be more than one thing?"

Katrin dropped her hands to her side, pushing them beneath the edge of her apron in a desperate need to control them. "I'd like to think so, but our society doesn't seem to condone such things. We are what we are. You're a crown elite." She chewed her lip and looked down. "And I'm just an acolyte."

Matthias lifted his empty hand towards her, hesitating only briefly before using a finger to lift her chin. His voice lowered, and he whispered, "We are never *just* anything. You can always be more."

All she could hear was her heart thundering in her chest. The kitchen seemed to vanish in a haze with his gentle touch. It made her want to believe him. "How do you do that?" She'd considered nothing else, but her mind suddenly jumped in impossible directions without her permission. To places someone like Matthias would see. To Matthias's suggestion that she didn't need to stay at the temple.

"Do what?" He touched the front of her chin with his thumb before lowering his hand.

She watched him stretch his hand, suddenly craving to hold it. The fleeting feeling swirled before she urged it away to focus on his question. "Be something else. Have the courage to try."

A smile twitched the corner of his lips. "Faith, I suppose, as ironic as that is, coming from me. You have faith that when you take that unknown path, it will lead you somewhere new. Somewhere different.

Somewhere that could be better, or could be a disaster, but you'll never regret taking the chance because at least you tried. I'd never trade my cot for a mattress, because I've never found adventure amid throw pillows."

Katrin met his eyes, and it sent her stomach fluttering again. "I don't know if I can do that."

Matthias hummed. "Well... You're wrong. And... rather filthy." He raised the cloth and swiped it over her nose. "Do you get *any* flour in your dough?"

She pushed his hand, confused by her own fingers as they tightened against his palm. "I was being serious. And yes, of course I do. If I recall..." She realized she hadn't pulled away, and he'd dropped the dirty cloth to the ground as his fingers curled around hers. "You rather like... my... baking?" She narrowed her eyes where her hand rested in his, evaluating what it meant and why it made her whole body tingle.

"Is that a question?" He quirked a brow, rubbing his thumb over the back of her hand.

Taking a shallow breath, she couldn't find the words as his touch continued. The sparks it sent through her made the kitchen seem far hotter than it was, and her mouth went dry. "I..." She pulled her hand from his and took a slow step back. "I think you should go."

Matthias straightened, his smile disappearing. Stooping, he picked up the fallen cloth and placed it on the counter. "As you wish."

She felt frozen as he walked past her, and she urged her eyes to stay on the third stone of the hearth's arch while he crossed the kitchen. When he hesitated at the bottom of the steps, she spun towards the counter and snatched the rag before rushing back to the basin. Plunging her hand and cloth into the cold water, she considered dumping the entire thing over her head when she couldn't stop herself from watching him from the corner of her eye.

His footsteps disappeared up the stairs, and suddenly the kitchens felt horribly empty.

Chapter 4

Barim's snores echoed through the room, and it felt as if they shook Matthias's bed. He'd been staring at the ceiling for hours, hoping sleep would come, but his mind still whirled.

Battle strategies. Paperwork to order more troops. How best to use the 134th, who he'd heard of even before Katrin.

They'd been one of the more self-reliant of the border troops, with far fewer casualties in the skirmishes.

Too many casualties, regardless.

Matthias rolled onto his side, staring at a speck on the wall.

Could Katrin's brother be one of those that died, and she just doesn't know yet?

Flashes of the fiery acolyte's face rippled across his closed eyelids, and a smile twitched on the side of his lips. The anger in her eyes. The challenge to what he said. It was refreshing.

Despite his crown elites being more friends than personal guards, they still rarely went against what he said.

Yet, that night, he'd done something wrong. Thinking about the rest of his problems kept him from analyzing where he'd made a mistake in his conversation with Katrin. One moment, it'd felt like they had a connection, and then next... she'd asked him to leave.

Another thunderous rattle of Barim's snores made Matthias wince.

I'm not getting any sleep in here. Should have listened to Riez and made Micah stay in here.

Quietly rising, he drew his cloak over his shoulders but left his sword. He laced his boots and crept out of the room, welcoming the fresher air away from the other sleeping men.

I wonder if I could find that courtyard again.

His stomach rumbled.

Or the kitchen.

Unease settled in his gut at the thought that Katrin might still be there. Hoping she'd gone to bed, he strode down the silent hallway, reveling in the peace even if he was still within temple walls. Usually the temples never slept, but he suspected even the early rising priests slept more soundly after the luxurious feast.

Matthias paused in his descent down a curved stairwell to peer out the dark window.

Moonlight shimmered off the snow, creating shadows between the trees that swayed in the early morning breeze. The sun would still sleep for hours, promising him he still had time to try again after a walk.

He leaned forward, looking along the side of the building, and noted the plumes of smoke rising from the northern wing.

Must be from the kitchens. But Katrin never mentioned needing to cook tonight.

Descending the rest of the stairs, he took the north hallway and left the dormitories. He passed classrooms and smaller libraries, closed-door offices and sitting areas with tall windows. If he didn't know better, he'd think he walked the halls of a university in Nema's Throne.

Rounding a corner, the smoke he'd seen earlier touched his nose, but it didn't bring the scent of cooking with it.

Furrowing his brow, he pushed through the next set of doors that led to the northmost rooms. The air thickened, and he coughed, raising his forearm over his mouth. "What the..."

Speeding his pace, he turned another corner and touched the next door. He jerked his hand off with a hiss, looking at his bright red palm. "Shit." Lifting a boot, he kicked the door open and leapt back when flames surged from within.

Matthias's back hit the wall as he gaped. His mind spun, and he used his boot to close the door again. The leather came away blackened.

How long does it take for a fire to get this big?

The prince gulped and backed down the hallway, arm still covering his mouth.

Too long for me to prevent it.

"Fuck." He turned, sprinting the way he'd come and taking the stairs to the dormitories two at a time.

Please let her be safe in bed.

On his way past Micah's door, he pounded a fist on it, then continued to the room he shared with the others.

Bursting inside, he coughed again. "Get up. All of you. Up!" He retrieved his sword as the men rolled, finding their feet with relative speed.

"What's going on?" Barim rubbed a hand over his face.

"Temple's on fire, and it's too late to do anything about it." Matthias snatched the blanket from his bed and threw it at Barim. "Cut that up for masks."

"You didn't set it, did you?" Riez smirked, but wiped the expression at the prince's glare.

Stefan pulled on his boots before reaching for his blade.

"Stefan, start banging on people's doors. Barim, go find the high priest and get him to help with an evacuation plan."

They both nodded, and Barim ripped the fabric with his bare hands before he threw scraps at each of them. Stefan vanished through the dark doorway, and the sound of his fist pounding on doors began.

"I'm here." Micah stumbled into the doorway, rubbing his sleep from his eyes. Matthias's family sword hung at his side. It'd been a gift from his father on his sixteenth birthday, and the prince missed feeling it at his side when Micah played the part.

"Good. There's a fire in the north wing. Micah, you work with the rest of our crew to set up a shelter outside. Riez, go where you're needed. A lot of the older priests will need help." Matthias pulled one scrap of blanket from the few he'd caught and tied it around his nose and mouth.

Micah stepped into the doorway to avoid the priests suddenly whizzing down the hallway. "Aren't we in a temple full of Art users? Can't they—"

"Healers, remember?" Matthias stuffed more scraps of fabric into his tunic pockets.

"Shit." Micah tied the mask into place.

As they rushed to alert others of the fire and aid in evacuations, chaos descended on the temple. Organized chaos. People raced to fill buckets and assist others in making their way outside, where Micah's shelters quickly took form.

Matthias searched the crowds for the only other face he knew, but had yet to confirm Katrin's safe escape. Despite urging himself not to get hung up on one person, he growled.

A young woman dodged the crowds, water sloshing from a bucket in her hands.

Katrin's friend from the kitchen.

She yelped when Matthias snagged her upper arm.

"Is everyone from your dormitory accounted for?" He dipped his head to catch her gaze. "Are you missing anyone?"

The girl shook her head. "I'm not sure. I didn't stay long enough to make sure everyone left. We have to put the fire out." She shoved the bucket against him. "Take this to the library. We can't let the flames destroy it."

"The fire is too large to stop at this point."

"We have to try. We have to save what we can."

Matthias looked down at the bucket in his arms as the girl raced off, and he huffed. "Saving some books. Not exactly what I had in mind." He whirled around, meeting the gaze of a man carrying an armload of texts. "You. Where is the library?"

The man spun to him, wide-eyed, his face dirty with soot. "North-west corridor, left at the statue of Loman Ord."

Matthias resisted rolling his eyes as he took off in that direction, careful to keep the water from sloshing out. Rounding the corner at the god's statue, he skidded to a halt as he stepped into the library.

Shelves towered up the walls for several floors joined by wrought iron spiral staircases. At one side, the walls blazed, flames licking into the arched ceiling. Scholars and acolytes scrambled to unload the shelves, carrying out their precious books in batches.

Too many people are still in here, and this is all kindling.

The ceiling cracked, and Matthias covered his head when the fire above burst across the wooden beams, raining ash and embers through the library.

People screamed at the explosion, taking shelter beneath shelves while others fell from precarious perches on ladders.

"Get outside!" Matthias grabbed the closest person and shoved them towards the exit with one hand.

Several hurried past him, arms loaded with tomes.

These people are insane.

The shouting stopped, overpowered by a calm, clear voice. "We mustn't lose the work preserved here. You, go get another bucket. May Shen Tallas slow the flames!"

"Lunatic," Matthias mumbled.

An acolyte, no older than fifteen, snatched Matthias's bucket from his hands, scurrying towards the study desks, already partially alight.

"Master Yelisen, we can't continue this!" Katrin's voice came from between book shelves, and relief washed through him that the fire hadn't claimed her. "We should be grateful for the texts we have saved and let Eamane have the rest."

She should be outside already, not trying to save the kindling.

Matthias stalked across the room to the two arguing. "You need to get out of here." He looked from Katrin to the priest, refusing to let the awkwardness of their previous conversation affect his tone. "The structure is failing. You're out of time."

Katrin coughed, pulling on the priest's arm even as he climbed a step stool to yank books from the upper shelves.

He dropped them into the waiting arms of more acolytes beneath him. "No, not yet. There's too much knowledge to be lost." He shoved Katrin away so he could take another step up.

She stumbled back with a huff, colliding into Matthias's chest.

Matthias steadied her with hands on her shoulders, moving her to the side and quickly releasing her. "There are too many lives to be lost!" He grabbed the crazed priest by the arm and jerked him off his step stool.

Yelisen wrestled free of Matthias, wedging his step stool between himself and the prince. He grappled for more books, ignoring the crackling beams above them.

Katrin shielded her mouth and nose with the crook of her elbow, coughing into it. She pushed her palm against the chest of a young man trying to assist. "Get out! Leave them!"

Pulling two strips of fabric from his cloak, Matthias pushed one into each of their hands. "Cover your faces."

Instead of taking the fabric, Yelisen collapsed against the bookshelves, pulling fallen tomes into his lap.

Choking on the smoke, Katrin seized the fabric and hastily tied it into place over her messy hair. She pushed harder against the insistent line of acolytes. "Just go!" She waved her hands at the group as Riez sidestepped around her.

Riez bumped his shoulder into Matthias's. "Problems?"

"He's lost it." Matthias motioned to the priest who sobbed in a heap against the shelves. "Get him out."

Riez, though shorter than the prince, could lift any of them and had performed the feat on more than one occasion. "You got it." He wrapped his burly arms around the frantic priest and hauled him up and towards the door.

Katrin's hand closed on his arm, her dark, almond-shaped eyes meeting his. "Thank you."

Matthias took her hand to lead her out of the library. "Can we—"

The remaining ceiling splintered, and he looked up. A wide beam struck a bookshelf on the third floor, jarring it free from the wall. It lurched forward, falling towards them.

Do I jump? No. The shelf is too wide. It won't hit us if we...

Sucking in a breath, Matthias yanked Katrin into him and knelt, curling his body over her small frame.

The wooden shelf crashed into the ground and nearby wall, a barrage of books slamming into his back. The wall prevented the shelf's entire weight from hitting him, but it buckled and pushed into him hard enough that he had to brace himself to keep from squishing the woman he protected.

In the stillness, only Katrin's breath penetrated the chaos. It tickled his throat, a faint whimper escaping her.

"I've got you," he murmured.

She pulled her face away, the mask dislodging. Her hands touched his chest while she met his eyes. "I know. Are you hurt?"

"I'm..."

The shelf groaned and cracked, thudding onto his back and forcing him forward. Both his hands met the floor, arms shaking with the effort of holding its full weight.

You made the wrong call, Rayeht.

Katrin's hands shot up beside his head, palms pressed to aid in lifting the weight from him, her shoulders tightening.

He gasped, meeting her gaze mere inches away. Ash marred her smooth skin, flecks of debris caught in her eyelashes. Yet, a determined expression remained on her face, tainted only with concern for him.

She's a brave one.

Matthias's surroundings shook again as Riez and Barim lifted the shelf off them, heaving it to the side with a grunt.

Katrin let out a sigh, but the following inhale turned into a cough as she pulled her mask back into place.

Riez seized Matthias's arm and hauled him to his feet as bright spots danced across his vision.

"Is everyone out?"

"Looks clear. Except you two." Barim released Katrin as she straightened her sooty dress. "But fire's spread to the main hall. Can't get out that way, now."

Katrin grabbed Matthias's wrist, tugging. "Follow me."

Heat blasted against his face and he raised an arm, following her lead with his two guards close behind. He coughed, pressing the torn material closer around his face as his eyes burned from the smoke. His back ached like a dagger protruded from his flesh.

Moving quickly, Katrin held tight to his wrist, leading them into a corridor opposite of the exits he knew. The temperature cooled as the architecture shifted to stone. "Watch your step." Her shoes tapped on the steps as they descended below the smoke line.

Matthias's boot caught on an uneven edge and he grunted, pain shocking through his back as he stumbled.

Barim caught him by the arm, concern etched over his features. "How far, priestess?"

He's overreacting, it's not that bad.

Hurrying across the worn pantry floor, she plucked a lantern from a hook by the cold fireplace. She lifted the hood of the lamp and, with a gesture of her finger, an ember sparked to life.

The lamp's hood snapped back into place as the orange glow pierced through the haze of smoke.

"Not too much further." Her gaze passed over Matthias, studying his face. Her eyes, red rimmed, spoke her worry for her. "But we'll have to climb out."

Matthias stumbled again and cursed when his guard righted him.

"He needs to stop soon." Riez grabbed the prince's other arm, supporting his weight with Barim. "Climbing is out of the question."

"I can climb." Matthias doubted the words even as he said them, the muscles in his legs tingling. He tried to straighten his spine and gasped, buckling forward again. "All right, I can't climb. And my feet aren't working properly."

Fear touched his stomach, and he cursed himself for not using his connection to the Art earlier.

It does me no good now.

Katrin rushed to the large tables. "Bring him here." She pushed bowls and containers holding various food stores off the edge, and they smashed on the ground. "Matthias." Her voice sounded strangely calm. "Are you feeling any tingling in your legs?"

His guards hauled him towards the table as he growled, agony spiking through his thighs. "Some. And I can't feel anything in my toes."

Riez scowled. "We need one of our healers. We had two with us. Show me the way out."

"If his spine is fractured, it can't wait. Every moment we allow to pass, the less possible it is to heal." Katrin tugged her mask down around her neck, the air breathable even if it still tasted like smoke. "I need to do something now. Give me his cloak." She hoisted a bag of flour onto the table, pushing it towards the end.

Flour?

Barim pulled Matthias's cloak free of his shoulders. "There's not much blood, at least."

Riez held the prince next to the table and stared at Katrin. "I can't let you do that. We have procedures in place if... if one of us comes to harm. He's too—"

"We don't exactly have time for your procedures." Katrin scowled, snatching Matthias's cloak and bundling it tightly on the head of the table. "Now help me lift him. We have to get the pressure off the injury or it'll get worse."

Matthias groaned as he leaned on his guards, lowering himself onto his back on the table. His breath quickened, the tingling expanding up his legs. When Riez opened his mouth to argue again, the prince shook his head. "Let's get this over with. I trust her."

"Put that sack under his knees." Katrin pointed as she adjusted the cloak beneath his head and shoulders. Her fingers brushed his jaw. "Does it still hurt?"

Barim slid the flour into position, and the pain faded, his back no longer straining.

The prince cleared his throat. "If this doesn't work..."

"None of that, Matthias." Riez clutched his hand. "You've been through worse."

Katrin sidestepped down the table, her eyes locked on Matthias's abdomen. "I need to touch his skin. Help me with his tunic, please."

"Why? Our healers don't need contact." Riez frowned.

Matthias tried to work the buttons of his tunic to no avail. "Did the prince and Stefan make it out?"

His guards hesitated before Barim solemnly nodded. "They're safe."

Katrin pursed her lips as she unfastened his tunic. "Tunic. *Please.*" Despite the polite word, her tone sounded angry. "Or do you want him paralyzed? I'm still a novice at healing, and skin contact helps me refine it. This is too important to try without it."

Matthias glared at his men "Help her, damn it!"

Riez and Barim huffed and let go of their reservations enough to unfasten the front of his tunic, pulling the material away from his chest and stomach.

"Shit. Is that normal?" Riez pointed to his midsection, but Matthias couldn't lift his head to look.

"Move." Katrin shoved Riez's shoulder, moving to the head of the table. Running her hands down the sides of his neck, she slid them onto his chest, long strands of her black hair escaping to tickle his cheeks as she shut her eyes.

The room spun, and Matthias closed his eyes, focusing on the sound of her breathing.

Don't let me die in a temple.

"I'll find the exit and get Merissa just in case." Riez's voice moved farther away.

Her palms heated his skin, a faint golden glow penetrating his eyelids. Her breath remained steady as she slid her hands up to his collar, between the layers of his tunic and his back.

A twinge sparked where her fingers were, vibrating down his spine.

He opened his eyes, watching Katrin's face where she bowed over his. With her lips parted, her breath grew uneven as she took a shuddering inhale. Her nails dug into his skin as his entire body ached.

Searing heat cascaded through his back, igniting his connection to the Art.

Matthias cringed and growled, gritting his teeth against the pain.

She's going to know.

Coils of Katrin's power mingled with his, regardless of how he tried to prevent it. Gentle, but confident, her Art directed his energies around the invisible injury. Agony ebbed like the ocean's tide, hitting him in great swaths as she worked. His muscles quivered, then her energy vanished so abruptly it left him feeling empty.

He blinked as Katrin let out a slow breath and collapsed.

Barim rushed for her, but only caught her head before it hit the stone. He laid her down as Matthias urged his core muscles to help him sit.

His ribs screamed, but when his toes wiggled in his boots, his fear subsided. Swinging down from the table, he knelt next to Katrin and tapped her cheek. "Hey. Wake up."

Her eyelashes fluttered, a rosy complexion just visible on her pale cheeks through the soot. She groaned and touched his wrist, her grip surprisingly strong for how weak she must have felt. "Did it work?"

"I think so. I can feel my feet again."

"I'm sorry I didn't have energy for the rest."

"You did great, Priestess."

Something thudded against the ceiling above them, the distant crackling of the fire surging as a billow of smoke erupted down the stairwell into the storage room.

Coughing, they pulled their masks back into place.

"We need to get out of here." Barim eyed the acolyte. "Can you walk?"

Matthias could see the distaste in her eyes despite her covered mouth and offered her a hand up.

"I'll manage." Katrin ignored his hand and grabbed the tabletop, hoisting herself up. She gestured to the back doorway Riez had disappeared through, supporting herself as she took a deep breath. Their eyes met for a quiet moment, his heart racing. After what felt like an eternity, she grasped the lantern.

"Let's go, then." Barim stepped closer to the prince, nodding his chin at the exit.

Katrin slid Matthias's cloak off the table and handed it back to him before she staggered to the door. She paused in the doorway to brace herself, but then turned to descend another set of stairs with uneven steps.

Stubborn, too.

Matthias and his guard followed, exchanging a sideways glance.

Chapter 5

Flecks of snow touched Dani's cheeks, melting on her face. She stared off into the brightness of winter, barely able to make out the shape of the horizon.

A ball of light emerged from the land, rising with the dawn.

She blinked, but her vision would never clear.

"You need to be merciless, my kitten. Revel in the taste of their blood, but remember your training. Remember, we are the ones who will provide what Feyor deserves. The Isalicans will fall to your claws."

Dani sucked in a slow, icy breath, focusing on the feel of supple leather against her skin. She touched the feline tooth pendant around her neck, tucking it under her shirt.

Tallos kept talking. "When the attack begins, they won't see us coming. This is our duty. Our fate. Our privilege."

It is my privilege to serve Feyor.

The first line of her oath swam in her mind, and she still stared at the ball of light. The sweet scent of the surrounding pines mixed in the breeze.

What if I fail?

The snow crunched under her boot as she shifted her weight.

A shape moved into her vision, blocking her blurred view of the sun. "Your blindness won't hold you back. You already see so much more than other humans. Believe in your other senses, and they will not let you down."

The dark mass moved, and she focused again on the bright spot. "I will not fail," she whispered, and his hand touched her shoulder.

"Go. This is your last day scouting. We won't need to after tonight."

Dani tilted her head back and clenched her fists, letting her Art overtake her. It pulsed against her skin, consuming her flesh and the hides she wore until her clawed paws met the snow. Her white fur, invisible against the frozen land, protected her from the winter air.

She took off over the terrain, keeping her claws retracted and letting her tail balance her as she ran. Scents danced across her vision in an array of colors, guiding her east through the shapes of trees and snow-covered brush.

A badger's den.

A hibernating snake.

Dani raced past them and ran until her lungs heaved. She reached a high ledge halfway to the border.

Grey, acrid scent touched her nostrils.

Smoke.

Lifting her maw, she breathed it deeper before aiming her rounded ears in the direction from which it carried over the breeze.

Not from a campfire.

It was too faint to be nearby and, coming from the east, it had to be somewhere in Isalica.

But the siege against the border hasn't started yet. Must be something else.

The fuzzy light in her vision shifted to a deep orange as a cloud of black drifted across the rising sun. The gloom hushed the birds within the trees only briefly before their song resumed.

Should I investigate?

Her scouting route would never cross so far into enemy territory, only taking her close enough to the encampments to verify the information from their informants. Numbers of battalions. Patrol routes. Supply locations.

Venturing deep into Isalica wasn't in her instructions.

Something within her urged her to go, anyway, but she pushed it aside and followed her orders.

Chapter 6

Grass tickled Katrin's ankles as she crossed the lush field with bare feet.

In the distance, the great Yandarin Mountains reached towards the clouds, twisted into the shape of a man blowing snow from the craggy peaks.

Spring shoots budded around her feet, petals uncurling into multicolored wildflowers. They expanded in front of her, creating a trail into the trees.

Katrin followed, watching as each blossom bloomed in expedited time. She stepped around them, careful not to disturb the dreamy depiction of spring. Their scent reminded Katrin oddly of home, the farm where her parents still lived. Her brief vision of her mother, embraced from behind by her father, brought warm tears to her eyes.

The path of flowers entered an oak grove, and Katrin ducked beneath a branch to keep up.

The buds rose from the ground, circling around the stump of an oak. They sprouted vines, snaking up the tree to form a facade at the front. Bunching together, they moved like a face might, but emitted no sound.

Katrin narrowed her eyes, perplexed at the complex vision of her dream. As she approached the tree, the vines melded together and expanded from the bark, forming green skin and white eyes.

"Acolyte."

Katrin gasped, taking a step back from the ethereal face, trying to remember she was dreaming. Her bare foot caught on a twig, and the pain of a splinter in her heel felt real. Hissing, she lifted her foot behind her, a little bubble of red blood oozing from the wound.

Then it disappeared.

Looking up, Katrin focused on the face as the figure moved forward, the bark crackling to release a twist of vine forming a slender arm and hand. An emerald finger pointed, torso and shoulder emerging from the tree to lean out.

"Go."

Katrin narrowed her eyes but followed the gesture to look. Ten feet away, the lush spring of the forest ended in a stark line. Beyond, snow clung to barren branches, coating the forest floor in a peaceful, undisturbed blanket. She squinted at the horizon, but couldn't make out details beyond the trees.

She turned back to the tree as the being settled, as if collapsing into a comfortable chair.

The being smiled, her teeth white like daisy petals. "You know you must."

Katrin's breath caught, her chest suddenly heavy. A cool breeze from the winter-coated forest brushed through her hair, throwing it behind her as she stepped.

Innate knowing... trust... encouraged her into the snowy forest despite her lack of warm clothing. The sheer teal dress, only slightly loose on her small frame, allowed the cold to touch her skin. But it didn't feel uncomfortable. Her bare feet felt the crunch of the snow between her toes, but it didn't freeze.

The trees surrounded her, hiding her path as she turned to look back. The spring forest no longer stood behind her, replaced by endless snow.

Her throat seized when she faced forward and someone stood ahead of her, back turned to her. They stood perfectly still, shrouded in a dark cloak and hood. Broad shoulders and far taller than her.

She stepped towards him, ice crackling with each step. Before she saw his face, she caught the woodsy scent of him, mingled with distant ash and soot. A knot took hold in her gut, the feeling from the courtyard reigniting within her as she suddenly felt warm.

"Matthias?" She reached out, touching his shoulder.

The man turned his head, his blue-green eyes delving into her. "Katrin."

A branch cracked in the forest behind her, snow falling as she spun. She gasped as she met the steady milky gaze of a snow panther, its white fur blurring against the terrain. The edges of its coat wisped like smoke, and it lowered its head with a deep growl.

Reaching for Matthias, her hand closed on nothing, and she dared a look away from the creature. A blast of winter wind filled her vision with a blanket of white, and she fell into the snow.

Her surroundings swirled before she blinked. Her waking eyes stared at the pale linen of the tent above her.

Sunlight pierced through it, creating a constant dim light within. She blinked again, trying to remember where she was.

I was so tired.

Footsteps sounded beside her, and her heart pounded before she tilted her head to see Matthias.

He approached her and sat on a nearby stool. "How are you feeling?"

Katrin touched the distant headache deep in her forehead, noticing how clean her hands looked. Her hair still smelled of the fire, but someone had changed her clothes, and she wasn't covered in soot. The thought of Matthias being the one to have done so sent a rush of heat into her face.

She furrowed her brow and rubbed at the wrinkles it caused. "Tired." She turned her head, looking at him, the entire morning's events crashing back into place. Her head swam, but she forced a hand behind her, anyway, struggling to sit up. "Are you all right? Your back..."

The guard waved off her concern in the same fashion as before. "I'm fine. Thanks to you. Our healers took care of the rest, but they said you did a fantastic job. Merissa found you some clean clothes. I hope that's all right."

Katrin hid her relief that someone else had dressed her. The satin felt odd against her skin, but she focused on Matthias's face. She pushed a loose strand of her hair behind her ear. "I was afraid I'd made it worse, somehow." Her chest ached, and she rubbed it, though the pain resounded in her lungs. She wavered, grip tightening on the wood frame of the cot. "Your fellow elites are awfully protective of you."

"We're a tight bunch." Matthias retrieved a tin cup from the ground beside her cot and approached to offer it to her. "You should drink."

Until she saw the water, she hadn't realized how parched her throat was. She took the cup with a small smile, lifting it to her lips. The cool liquid allowed her mind to sort through everything she remembered.

Lowering the cup, she nestled it in her lap. Studying the surrounding tent, she realized it was quite small, probably intended to be a private place for the prince's guards to have to themselves. The narrow cot dominated one side of it, several locked trunks and chests scattered around the edges. Dirty cloths hung over the edge of a washbasin on top of one of them, along with a pitcher.

She turned back to Matthias, meeting his gaze. "You saved my life. Thank you."

Matthias's face hardly changed. "It's part of my job."

"Your job is to protect the prince. Not an acolyte in a temple you hated being in to begin with."

The corner of his mouth twitched. "All right. It's not exactly my job, but what kind of man would I be if I let an acolyte die at the hands of the books she sought to save?" He glanced at the tent's closed flap. "Your friend is eager to see you. Jelisa, I believe her name is, and another. Shall I tell them you're awake?"

Katrin smiled, but shook her head. "Not yet. I think I need a little more time before I'm ready for Jelisa and Serna's energy." She lifted the cup back to her lips, reflecting on the events of the night before.

She hadn't given it a second thought when Matthias needed her.

They'd been remarkably lucky not to be crushed, but even in that threat, he'd tried to protect her. Even after she'd dismissed him in the kitchens. Looking at her own hand in her lap, it flexed at the memory of his touch. And the emotions it had elicited.

Matthias strode away from her, but didn't take his seat on the stool again. "Can I get you anything? Are you hungry?"

Her stomach writhed. "I'm sorry."

The guard stilled near the tent flap, his expression still unreadable as he looked back at her. "You don't owe me anything."

"It seems hardly appropriate for me to demand an apology from you, then refuse to give one myself." Katrin turned to put her feet on the ground, despite the whirling of her head. "I... shouldn't have told you to go last night."

His brow furrowed for a second before relaxing, and he shook his head. "I clearly made you uncomfortable, which wasn't my goal. I misinterpreted the situation. No apology is necessary."

"No." Katrin's heart sped as her fingers twitched again. "I don't think you did. I'm just..." She chewed the edge of her lower lip. "Not accustomed."

Matthias studied her, opening his mouth to speak, but a shadow appeared outside the tent.

"Am I supposed to announce myself before entering my guards' tent?" The prince's voice came from the shadow. "I don't know how this works. Matthias, you in there?"

Katrin's spine went rigid, her eyes wide as she stared at the shadow. Grabbing the blanket she'd let fall aside in Matthias's presence, she held it up against her chest where the satin dress hung lower than she typically preferred. "Why is the prince here?" She kept her voice hushed, hoping the royal wouldn't hear. But he could probably hear her heart beat with how loudly it thundered.

The guard rubbed his temples. "He needs to speak to you."

"Me?" Katrin gasped in a whisper. "Why?"

"Relax. He's just a man." Matthias's shoulders lost their tension. "I'll bring you something to eat."

"A royal man." Katrin brushed her hands down the blanket, ensuring it fully covered her as she tried to determine how to bow from a sitting position. Matthias's movement towards the tent flap caught her eyes. "Bring something back for yourself, too? I hate eating alone."

Matthias smirked and nodded, pulling the flap aside and staring at the prince. He blocked the way, a silent conversation taking place between them before the guard shook his head and exited.

What was that all about?

Katrin's throat tightened, despite how casual Matthias was with their prince. She'd noticed at the feasts that none of the crown elites saluted their prince like she'd expected. Instead, they seemed more like friends than subordinates.

Prince Alarik entered the tent, and the flap drifted closed behind him. Before she could move, he held a palm out to her. "Please excuse the informality of this."

She swallowed, and bowed her head, anyway.

The man retrieved Matthias's stool and brought it closer to her cot before sitting. "May I speak with you a moment?"

"Of course, your majesty." Her tongue felt swollen as she looked at the prince's face. So close, she marveled at how similar he and Matthias looked. The beard was the defining similarity, which had led to her almost thinking it was Matthias sitting beside the high priest during the feasts rather than the prince. But the prince before her had brown eyes, so very different from the tides of Matthias's.

"You have my utmost gratitude for your healing during the fire." The prince laced his hands together.

"I did what any other member of the temple would do."

His eyes shone. "Regardless. He is my closest friend, and I am deeply in your debt. I wish I didn't need to ask more of you, but I must know. While you were healing him, did you... notice anything else?"

The question sent an odd tremble through her. She'd noticed the way his energy had reacted to hers and tried not to linger on it.

Fortunately, Matthias himself had proven a distraction since she'd woken.

But now that the prince asked so directly...

They had exposed her to many forms of the Art through her years of training. Perhaps more so than other acolytes because of the 'natural gift' the temples deemed her to have. Of all she'd experienced, none felt quite like what she'd sensed while healing Matthias's spine.

The memory of its ebbing power sent a shiver down her body, the tangle in her gut tightening. She couldn't lie, especially not with the prince's eyes on her. She only prayed it was a secret he already knew. If Matthias could access the Art and had remained outside of the temples... Prince Alarik had to know.

Looking at the canvas covered floor, she nodded slowly.

The prince dipped his head to catch her gaze. "I must ask you not to mention it to anyone. Anyone at all, do you understand?"

Katrin gripped the blanket tighter against her chest at the implication. "So you're aware?"

Alarik nodded. "Since we were children. The king is also aware. Can I trust you to keep this secret?" His eyes moved between hers. "If you'd like, I can offer compensation..."

She shook her head, sucking in a breath. "No, that's unnecessary. I will keep the secret. I would do the same if he had asked it of me, rather than you." She lowered her eyes, heat rising in her cheeks as she realized what she'd said. "I mean, I wouldn't keep the secret from *you*, your majesty. I..."

The prince smiled and lifted a hand. "I understand. No need to explain. Is there anything I can offer you as a token of my gratitude?"

Trying not to look directly at the prince's face, she thought for a moment he was Matthias again. The white canvas rippled behind like the snow in her dream. It dried her mouth to consider the message it'd sent.

"Matthias... I don't know if he spoke to you about the offer he made me the other day."

"About joining us on our trek to the border where your brother is stationed?"

I can't believe he actually mentioned me to the prince.

Katrin encouraged her gaze up to meet the prince's. "Is that offer actually possible? If I... wanted to come?"

Alarik straightened. "Of course. We have a fine healer who could continue your lessons during our travels."

The high priest of the temple wouldn't deny a request from the prince.

Her stomach fluttered. "I would like that. I..." She saw Matthias in the snow again, the snow panther prowling in the trees. "Would like to see my brother."

The prince nodded. "I will make the arrangements with your superiors here." He rose from his seat, pausing when the tent flap opened and a blond woman walked inside.

The woman froze, looking with wide eyes from the prince to Katrin and back again. "I apologize. I didn't realize..."

"Perfect timing." Alarik smiled and motioned to the blond while speaking to Katrin. "This is Merissa. She is our priestess and my personal healer." Facing the woman, he lifted an eyebrow, and she bowed her head. "Katrin will join us on our journey to the border. She will be your student. It was a pleasure to meet you, Katrin. Excuse me."

Katrin bowed her head again as the prince exited, her grip on the blanket relaxing into her lap. The chill air of the tent brushed along her exposed skin, and she shivered in the draft pushed towards her by Merissa's white cloak.

"I'm sorry I interrupted. Just getting more linen for the wounded." She crossed the tent to a trunk, placing a bundle of dirty cloths on the ground next to it before digging for new ones.

"You didn't really interrupt. We'd finished our conversation, I think." Katrin rubbed a bit of the satin fabric between her fingers, remembering it was Merissa that Matthias had mentioned helping her. "Thank you for the part you played in cleaning me up. I'm embarrassed I was apparently so tired I don't even remember."

Merissa glanced at her. "Oh, it's nothing." She stood, holding a stack of clean linen.

"Is the fire under control?"

"It's mostly out, now. It didn't claim the entire temple, and everyone is working to establish which areas are still stable."

"And everyone is safe?"

Merissa nodded. "Little beat up in places, some burns. But nothing that those who live here can't handle."

Katrin sighed in relief. "Thank the gods."

"I'm sure the weather helped, too. Everything is damp. Slowed the fire." She paused, studying Katrin. "You did a great job in your healing. I fear what Matthias's fate would have been had you not been there."

If I hadn't been there, he wouldn't have been hurt in the first place.

"Thank you. Everyone cares quite a lot for him, don't they?"

Merissa's mouth flattened into a tight line. "He's family. Excuse me." She ducked from the tent, leaving Katrin alone again.

She stared at the flap tent for a moment, imagining Matthias coming back through it. The unusual draw towards a man seemed hardly fitting of a young acolyte.

I'm just being taken in by a pretty face. There are more important things.

Katrin rubbed her forehead, collapsing back into the pillows. She buried her face among the soft fabric, breathing in the fresh scent to clear the rampant thoughts of the crown elite.

I'm such a love-struck teenager.

She groaned into her pillow.

Someone cleared their throat, and she jumped.

"What are you doing?" Matthias quirked an eyebrow, leaning against the center tent post with a tray in his hands.

Her face flushed red hot, and she patted the pillow. "It's a nice pillow. I'm just... appreciating it."

Matthias approached her, dragging a short table with him that he put the tray on. It carried two steaming bowls emanating with the scents of rosemary and thyme.

"Lucky pillow." He smiled as he retreated to retrieve the stool.

Her stomach flopped.

Why is he so good at doing that to me?

Katrin scooted to the edge of the cot to appreciate the hot meal. Taking a large spoonful, she blew across it before savoring the bite. It tasted like she hadn't had food in days. Expending all her energy healing was likely the culprit for her starvation. She ravenously took another bite.

Matthias sat, picking up the other bowl for himself. "Merissa mentioned you'll probably want seconds."

"She might be right." An odd thought penetrated her mind, causing a tingling hollow. "Is she your wife?"

The guard choked on his stew and coughed, clearing his throat. "My what? No. I'd never marry a..." He stared at her before shaking his head. "No. She's just one of the prince's healers."

Katrin quirked an eyebrow, unable to restrain the smirk even if alternatives soured her growing attraction to him. "You'd never marry what? A woman? I mean, that's all right, too, if you—"

Matthias cleared his throat again, louder this time. "No. I love women. But Merissa is a priestess. And she's celibate, I think."

"Does that mean you'd be with her if she wasn't?" She took another bite, chewing while she eyed him.

Watching him squirm is oddly charming.

"No." Matthias paused, turning his spoon over. "She's a wonderful healer, and a trusted member of this team, but... No. Besides, I think Barim has a thing for her."

"So is it that she's a priestess, then?"

His eyes narrowed on her. "You're enjoying this too much. Eat your stew."

"I am eating." She spoke around a full mouth. "I can ask questions *while* I eat. You're interesting. Far more so than the acolytes in a rural temple."

Matthias scoffed. "The deeper you dig, the more you'll realize my love life is anything but interesting."

"And do you like it that way?"

"It's simpler. Women are complicated." He took a bite of food.

Her heart sank a little, though she didn't know entirely why. She grew quiet and took another bite. Focusing on her stew, she looked down.

"Do you not feel the same way about relationships? Is that not a draw of becoming a priestess?"

She hesitated. "I'm not sure how I feel about them, yet. I still have time to decide." She scooped up her last bite, settling back on the cot. "Relationships are attainable for priestesses, and I just haven't met the right man yet, I suppose. Maybe I won't, and I'll maintain my own celibacy."

Matthias fell silent, still watching her. He circled his spoon in the bowl. "How was your conversation with Alarik?"

She dropped her spoon into her bowl, fixing a glower on Matthias. "You mean *Prince Alarik*? I can't believe you talked to him about me."

The guard chuckled. "You were a difficult subject to avoid after you healed me."

"Did you *try* to avoid it?"

"No."

Katrin imagined the surprise on her brother's face, and it made her smile. She tapped her fingers on the bowl in her lap. Despite already asking the prince, the idea of leaving the temple seemed insane, especially after the fire. But then she saw the goddess in the tree again, realizing for the first time what she believed she'd dreamt.

Aedonai, the goddess of spring, telling her to go to Matthias.

Maybe I'm supposed to save him from that cat?

"Have you thought about my offer to come with us to the border? Maybe see your brother?" Matthias's voice held an air of uncertainty. "If you need more time to think..."

"No." Katrin surprised herself with how determined she sounded.

"I already asked the prince if I could join. He assured me it wouldn't be a problem."

A subtle smile crossed Matthias's lips, and he stood. "Good. Maybe you can lecture me on the temples more." He dipped his chin, his gaze wandering to her empty bowl. "And I'll let Merissa know you'd like seconds." As he exited the tent again, his cloak billowed around his boots.

Chapter 7

Lifting his sword, Liam inhaled into his quivering muscles to hold the block in place. "Good, but too slow."

With a frustrated growl, Neeman pulled back, lunging for Liam's side with his short sword. It clanged against his, deflected once again.

Liam twisted his wrist, wrenching Neeman's at a painful angle, and he dropped his weapon.

"Damn it." Neeman scrambled to pick up his sword as Liam laughed.

"Sorry, Private. Looks like you need more practice."

Several other soldiers jeered from the edges of the practice ring, some cursing louder than others as they exchanged coin.

Chain mail rattled as a hand slammed down on Liam's shoulder. "Won me another ten marks! Now only if we could get away from the border long enough for me to spend it." Xavis dodged Liam's elbow to his ribs with a chuckle.

"I'm not your dog for placing bets on." Liam scowled. "You put Neeman up to this? I thought he was just being arrogant again and needed reminding."

Xavis's full belly laugh made it impossible for Liam not to smile. "It's in my blood. Perk up, Talansiet. I'll split the winnings. Just glad not every private in this camp has figured out they can't beat you."

Liam shook his head, sweat dripping from the ebony locks stuck to his forehead. "Neeman's still good enough to wear me out." He groaned, running his hand through his hair to slick it back out of his face. The cold nipped at his damp face, which he hadn't noticed in the heat of the sparring match. "What I wouldn't give for a hot bath right about now."

Slamming his hand on Liam's shoulder again, Xavis shook his head. "No time. Prince'll be here soon. And you'll be on duty."

"Fucking politics." Liam rolled his shoulders and sheathed his sword. "We shouldn't be wasting our time talking to those damn Yorries. Better to just kill them if they're dumb enough to encroach on the border."

"Ain't exactly your place to decide, Private." Xavis nudged him hard. "And I wouldn't get caught talking like that in front of the *crown prince*." He sing-songed the title, sharing his obvious disdain.

Some spoiled prince in a castle isn't going to know the first thing about what needs to happen here.

Neeman shoved his way out of the crowd of teasing soldiers, snatching his sword from the muddied slush. He met Liam's eyes for a moment and sneered. Extending his hand, the soldier gave Liam a grim smile. "Good match."

Liam studied the hand dubiously. "No hard feelings?" He braced his muscles even as he took the other private's offer.

As expected, Neeman closed his grip around Liam's and yanked.

Liam spread his stance, sliding across the ground with the aggressive pull, and slipped his foot behind Neeman's ankle. With a quick movement and shove with his other hand to the private's chest, he sent Neeman tumbling back with a loud huff, slamming into the ground and spraying mud across the nearby soldiers.

Liam grinned, flicking the stains from his leather breeches.

Neeman sputtered, trying to stand only to slip back down as the other soldiers howled.

Xavis lifted an eyebrow at Liam.

"He started it." Shrugging, he turned away, walking towards the lines of tents coated in a thin layer of snow.

"See, this is why we're friends. No one will mess with lil ol' me with Talansiet at my side." Xavis grinned, tapping the full money bag on his hip.

"You also clearly see me as a business opportunity."

Xavis smirked. "Can't ignore what's dropped in your lap."

Their dark blue linens blended in among the shadows of the trees and icy terrain. Smoke rose from the various fire pits around the encampment, groups of soldiers near them while others marched through the walkways with gear in hand.

Isalica's flag shimmered in the sunlight pressing through the dense pine canopy, positioned on the corners of the stone barracks at the center.

Liam had only been inside the grey walls, peppered with narrow balistraria windows, once to help with a shipment of weapons delivered to the border. The higher ranking military official's dorms and meeting halls were located there.

I'll be much more familiar with the hallways soon, though. At least it'll be warmer inside.

Close to the border with Feyor, the trees grew larger, their trunks as big around as some tents. A constant dimness loomed despite it being midday, and Xavis's eyes darted to the outer edge of camp as they stepped into a patch of sunlight.

His friend shook his head, as if having a silent argument with himself. "I gotta go." He motioned to Liam's pants. "You might want to do something about that."

Liam gazed down at himself. "Shit." Mud spattered his pants and boots, and while he'd removed his armor for the spar, it'd still be visible. He crossed towards the patch of snow he'd stashed his armor on.

"First Private Talansiet." Corporal Brilslow halted in front of him. "Our guests are arriving. Head to your station..." His gaze trailed down Liam's uniform, lips turning into a frown. "Glad to see you're putting your best foot forward, soldier."

Liam's spine straightened. "Sorry, sir. It'll only take a moment for me to clean up."

"Should have thought of that an hour ago. Too late. Take your position and pray that first impressions don't last."

Gritting his jaw, Liam nodded and reached for his armor. He strapped the frigid steel into place on his shins, the wet biting through to his skin.

Liam grimaced, shouldering the partially frozen breastplate into place as Brilslow walked away. "Fucking politics."

Four decadently armored guards marched with the prince at the center, having left their horses at the eastern outskirts of the encampment. Each man wore mottled black furs over the shoulders of their lined cloaks, secured with steel insignia emblems on their shoulders.

Behind them, a troop of soldiers followed.

As they reached the 134th Battalion's welcome line, they halted.

The front two guards stepped aside and Prince Alarik Rayeht walked from the center. Dark chestnut hair fell over his forehead, shorter hair forming a thick beard. A gaudy golden ring indicated his royal status, along with the hilt of the royal sword at his side.

The prince's eyes scanned over Liam's comrades but, when they reached Liam, they stopped. His eyes narrowed before meeting the private's gaze.

Liam controlled his instinct to twitch under the stare, keeping his straight, respectful stance, and averting his eyes from the prince's.

Fuck.

His gaze instead went to the guards who protected the prince, spotting the smirk on one's lips. His stomach roiled, acutely aware he was the source of amusement. He'd tried to brush away some of the mud at a water barrel on the way, but had made it worse. It smeared more prominently down the inside of his right leg, and he'd dirtied the hem of his sleeve.

"Welcome, your majesty!" Corporal Brilslow stepped from the line, stealing the prince's attention. "I'm Corporal Brilslow. I've prepared accommodations for you and your finest in the barracks. I hope your journey was without complications?"

The prince glanced at the barracks. "Complications have their charm." He looked over the soldiers again, gaze lingering again on Liam.

The corporal cleared his throat. "Might I introduce your personal brigade, with divisions led by myself, Corporal Drennich, First Private Redden, First Private Sinka, and First Private Talansiet."

The guard who'd smirked let out a short chuckle.

Liam's skin heated.

What's his problem?

"Very well." The prince nodded at them. "Let's get set up, then, shall we?" He turned to walk with the corporal.

Liam turned with the others and marched alongside the prince's men.

The guard who'd laughed stepped beside him. "You must be Liam."

Surprise soothed his lingering anger, but Liam narrowed his eyes. He glanced ahead to make sure his corporal wasn't watching him too carefully before he looked at the prince's personal guard. "I am, sir. Though not sure if you knowing my first name is a good or a bad thing."

"You can decide later. I have a surprise for you." He smirked and coughed, sidestepping enough to grant Liam a view of the woman between the ranks behind him.

He hadn't even noticed her, having been on the opposite side of the prince's guard, and she'd been hidden behind the tall frame of the man she spoke to now. As they crossed the threshold into the barracks, Liam's feet stopped on their own accord as he took in her features.

Gods, she's all grown up.

"Liam?" Katrin's honey eyes widened in surprise as her fur-rimmed hood fell back from her black hair. She'd knotted it like their mother did, and homesickness tightened his chest.

Before he could remember formality, he laughed. "Kat?"

She lunged in front of the prince's guard, throwing herself at her brother. Her arms wrapped around his neck, and she squeaked into his ear as he spun her in the air like when they were children. Settling her back to her feet, he grabbed her rosy cheeks between his hands.

"Katy girl, what are you doing here?" Liam smiled, despite the confusion.

Katrin tweaked his nose. "I came to see you, stupid."

"Talansiet!" Corporal Brilslow's voice silenced everyone.

Liam straightened out of sheer discipline, spinning to face his commanding officer. "Apologies, sir." He saluted, lowering his chin.

Brilslow's mouth opened again, but Prince Rayeht spoke first. "Formality forsaken for separated siblings. Are these the priorities you teach your soldiers?"

"No, my lord. I don't know what's gotten into him, I—"

"Shame." The prince cut him off. "Family is more important. You should learn from this, Corporal."

Liam's commanding officer stammered. "Y-yes, your majesty."

Katrin giggled, grabbing Liam's arm. She squeezed it hard enough to make him stop gaping.

All right, maybe the prince isn't so bad.

They resumed walking through the barracks as the royal guard looked at Katrin with bright sea-blue eyes. He lowered his voice. "Are you even going to introduce me?"

Katrin's cheeks pinked like they used to when she was a child. She tugged on Liam's arm as she glanced at the guard. "I'm sorry! Matthias, this is my brother Liam. Liam, this is Matthias."

Liam struggled to hold on to whatever formalities should have been in place. "Sir." He nodded to Matthias. "Nice to meet you."

"Likewise." The guard exchanged a glance with a comrade before looking at Liam again. "I've heard a lot about you."

"Matthias is the reason I could come see you." Katrin's gaze lingered on the guard for a moment, and suspicion sprouted in Liam's gut.

"You haven't studied long enough to leave the temples, though. They just let you leave?" Days blurred together at the border, but it would be years before she was a priestess. He'd gotten a letter from his parents about Katrin's transfer to a closer temple, but hadn't had time to consider requesting leave to go visit her. Not with the growing conflict at the border.

"It's a long story, but nothing you need to worry about." Katrin patted his arm. "I'm so glad to see you. I was worried when Ma told me you'd joined the military."

"Needed to do something with the threat to the border. I didn't see another way out of that old farm town." Liam glanced at Matthias, noting his offered hand to support Katrin up a short flight of wide stairs, which she accepted. "Long story though, huh? I hope we get some time for you to tell me."

Matthias released Katrin's hand at the top of the stairs. "There will be plenty of time while she settles in. You aren't required to stay for all the meetings today."

And where exactly is she settling in?

Katrin narrowed her eyes at his pursed lips. Tilting her head, she opened her mouth.

Liam cut her off. "It'll have to wait a little while, I have first shift for guarding the halls around the meetings even if I'm not present." He glanced down the stone corridor, already lost and claustrophobic. "Where will you be staying, Kat?"

Better not be in his chambers...

"She'll be on this floor with us." Matthias glanced at Liam and understanding flickered over his expression. "Not *with* us, of course. Katrin is sharing a room with one of our healers."

Katrin squeezed Liam's elbow. "She's helping me continue my lessons until I return to the temple."

Relief passed through him. While he'd questioned the requirement for Katrin to be taken from her family when she was only thirteen, the idea of all those years spent apart being for nothing made it worse.

If she becomes a priestess, then she'll be able to make a life for herself.

One of the crown elites cleared his throat and drew Matthias's attention.

"Excuse me." He caught up to his comrade and spoke in hushed tones, nodding.

They all rounded a corner and entered a spacious room. A large rectangular table took up the center, with eighteen chairs positioned around it.

Captain Brenna and Lieutenant Verris waited inside, their hands clasped in front of them.

The captain greeted Prince Rayeht first with a dip of her head. "Welcome, your highness."

Corporal Brilslow halted at the entrance once the crown elites and officers had entered the room. Blocking Liam and Katrin's path, he narrowed his beady eyes briefly at his sister. "First Privates. You all have your assigned positions. First shift starts now."

"Yes, sir." The privates responded in unison, and Liam hoped he didn't sound too trite to the corporal. But based on his glance at Katrin, Liam felt like punching him in the jaw more than usual.

Brilslow gave a final nod before stepping into the room and closing the door.

Liam tapped his sister's hand. "Time to get back to work." He smiled, and the lightness in her eyes made it broaden. "I'll come find you when I'm off shift. Then you can tell me that long story?"

A blond woman approached behind Katrin and placed a hand on her shoulder. "Come, we need to unload our things and set up our room."

Katrin nodded and lifted onto her toes to kiss Liam's cheek. "Love you. Talk more soon."

He grinned after her as she disappeared around a corner, and he tried to sort his thoughts. Her presence both uplifted and terrified him.

What if an attack makes it past the border wall? Who will protect her?

The years had flown by after Liam enlisted the year following

Katrin's departure to join the temples. He'd been only sixteen, but without Katrin at home he'd felt directionless. Protecting the country had become his calling.

My duty needs to come first. Katrin is grown now.

Liam nodded to his fellow privates as they shifted off, and he eyed the meeting room's thick pine door. With how turned around he already felt, it was fortunate he didn't need to move to get to his first station. Adjusting his sword belt, Liam checked his armor to ensure it was still in place after Katrin's hug. He glanced up and down the hall, then straightened his shoulders and spread his stance in front of the door.

A moment later, the door opened and Corporal Brilslow emerged with a huff and closed the door behind him. His eyes locked on Liam, emanating disapproval. "Next time you show up covered in mud, you'll be mucking the cattle pens the rest of the day."

"Yes, sir. Sorry, sir." Liam stepped aside, keeping his salute until the corporal stalked down the hall. Lifting an eyebrow, he watched the annoyed corporal vanish around a corner.

Poor bastard got kicked out of the top secret meeting, huh?

Liam stepped in front of the door and resumed his posture. Despite the inappropriateness, he strained to listen through the door behind him.

A bang echoed from within the room, making him jump.

Voices raised, all shouting over each other.

"Enough!" Matthias's bellow broke through the rest and quieted the room, yet he didn't lower his voice. "That's exactly what they want us to do, and we won't fall for their tricks."

"How can you be sure?"

Liam could imagine the captain leaning over the table, her short greying hair sticking out at odd angles. "If they attack our northern border..."

"We will send no troops north. It is not your decision, Captain."

Matthias is the strategist, not the prince?

Liam chuckled to himself.

Just proves my theory. Spoiled castle brat doesn't know a thing about the military.

The voices inside lowered again before an eerie silence settled. A breath later, the door jerked open.

Liam stepped aside, saluting as the captain and lieutenant exited, silent as they strode in the same direction the corporal had gone.

The door shut again, closed by someone inside.

At least an hour passed before it opened again.

Liam dutifully side-stepped, lifting his hand in salute as the prince and three of his crown elites left the room. None of them acknowledged him, but Matthias wasn't in the group. He cast a glance into the room, where Matthias still leaned against the table over maps of the border region. With the door still ajar, Liam stood perpendicular to keep both the room and the length of the corridor in his peripheral vision.

Matthias's finger ran over the maps, tracing some invisible line across them as his eyes darted back and forth.

Clearly the strategist.

Matthias didn't look up. "Enter, Private."

"Sir?" Liam's chest caught as he turned his head more fully. "I'm not to leave my station."

Regardless of how casually Katrin introduced him, Matthias severely outranked Liam as one of the prince's crown elite. Outranked everyone at the border, save for the prince himself.

"You are dismissed from your station. Enter." Matthias met his gaze.

Liam's eyes widened, but he walked into the room.

"Shut the door, Private."

He hesitated, but shut the door as instructed. "Is something wrong, sir?"

Matthias's shoulders relaxed, and he stood straight. "I thought Feyor was posturing, but we have intercepted important letters. We're on the verge of war. Lots is wrong." He studied Liam's stiff stance. "At ease, would you? I wish to speak with you."

Liam pursed his lips and forced his body to relax. It felt completely unnatural as he studied Matthias. No matter how he urged his body, tension lingered throughout, accompanying the roil of his gut. "Me? I highly doubt I have much to contribute." He eyed the maps still in front of Matthias. "Between you and me, sir... I failed my strategy courses at the academy."

A smile spread over the guard's face. "Your courses matter little to me. I'm more interested in your comrades. Take a seat." He pulled out a chair on the other side of the table and sat, propping his feet up on the table.

Liam paused, cautiously approaching as if Matthias was a viper waiting to strike. Chewing the tip of his tongue, he settled into the chair.

Loosen up, Liam. He's just another soldier.

"What about my comrades?" Liam contemplated the conversation he'd overheard and how it might have related.

The encampment had been abuzz for days with news of Feyor's attacks increasing in frequency at the northern crossing, rather than here at the central one. In fact, the skirmishes had taken a steep decline over the past month, just after Feyor requested to open formal peace talks with Isalica.

"I... We believe we may have an information leak within the ranks." Matthias leveled his tone, tilting his head as he studied Liam. "Have you noticed anyone asking an unusual amount of questions pertaining to the prince's arrival here or about anything else?"

Liam's brow furrowed. The trust implied in Matthias asking him made his heart thunder. "Sir. With all due respect, I'm just a first private. I would think that kind of suspicion be kept very need-to-know."

"It is." Matthias tapped a finger on the table. "And I trust you'll keep it to yourself. But do you gossip with Corporal Brilslow?"

"No, sir." Liam swallowed.

"Exactly. No one talks to their commanding officers. I'd like you to pay attention over the next several days for anything that seems abnormal. Anyone... too curious. You understand?"

Anger stirred within his veins, but he did his best to hide it from his face. He rubbed his fingers together, remember how Ollie's blood had warmed his skin as it oozed from the arrow protruding from his neck. He'd done everything he'd been taught. Apply pressure, keep the injured person still.

Just before the Feyorian scout had landed his shot on the unsuspecting youth, Ollie had asked Liam about the likelihood of traitors among their companions. His face had flushed as if embarrassed to be asking, clearly afraid to suggest it in front of a commanding officer.

And Liam had dismissed the idea.

What had he known?

Liam could only watch as life drained from Ollie's eyes. He'd lost more than a soldier that day. More than a friend, and even more than a protege. He'd lost faith that Feyor would see reason. Lost faith in their honor.

They deserve as much mercy as they showed Ollie.

Liam nodded, refocusing on the crown elite. "I understand. I'll do my best, sir."

Matthias grimaced and waved his hand. "You don't need to do that. I know formality dictates it, but please call me Matthias when we're in private."

This goes against so many command rules...

Liam nodded again. "I'll do my best there, too, s... Matthias." He glanced at the closed door, then returned his gaze to meet Matthias's. "Why me?"

Matthias shrugged. "I trust your sister. She saved my life and has assured me I can trust you. I'm not familiar with any of the other soldiers at this encampment as the 134th isn't the one we usually visit, so I will rely on you."

"Because the cap and the lieu don't hear what us grunts are talking about enough?"

"Because *anyone* could be the leak, even them. Anyone but you."

Liam's throat clenched, and he failed to hold in a dry laugh. "No pressure."

Matthias laughed. "None at all."

Liam steadied himself, shaking out the twitch in his fingers as he leaned across the table. "Permission to speak freely?"

The guard nodded. "I'm not your corporal. You may always speak freely without fear of reprimand."

The question erupted before he could further evaluate it. "Why is my sister with you? I don't mean to sound ungrateful, I'm happy to see her... But she's still too inexperienced in the Art to be away from the temples, isn't she?" Removing Katrin from her studies would slow the timeline for her to become a priestess, and as such, limit how soon opportunity might come for her.

Though traveling with the prince and his personal healer could be an excellent opportunity to rise well above her station as a farmer's daughter.

"You should ask your sister her reasons." Matthias paused. "But I invited her along because she isn't like the other acolytes at her temple. She's smart and has more of a mind than the rest of them. That will go to waste at a temple. The prince has ensured her advancement will not be delayed."

"And she earned the favor of the prince by saving you?" Liam watched him carefully as he spoke about Katrin, trying to assess the minute changes in his features.

Matthias ran a hand over his thick beard. "There was a fire at her temple. I think the ordeal contributed to her decision as well as the prince's gratitude."

He tried to digest the information. "This just happened? I suppose we wouldn't have realized there was a fire at the temple because of the campfires and canopy blocking the view. I should be thanking the gods then that she wasn't hurt."

Matthias's jaw flexed. "It was only days ago. Luckily, there were no casualties."

Liam rolled his lips, leaning back in his chair and crossing his arms. There was something he wasn't saying, and Liam had already noticed the familiarity between his sister and the royal guard. Yet, he didn't dare question him about it.

Not yet.

"Anything else you wanted to chat about? Otherwise I should probably get back to my station before the corp tears me a new asshole."

Matthias laughed and stood. "I need to find our chambers, anyway, and prepare for supper. And you should clean up." He motioned to Liam's dirty uniform. "How did that happen?"

Liam looked down at himself. "Fuck." He ran his hand back through his hair, sighing. "Just a little sparring. Boys like to pit me against other privates to extort a little money out of the bets."

"You're that good with a sword?"

Liam shrugged. "Good enough."

Matthias smiled his approval. "I outrank your corporal, I'm pretty sure. Your post is no longer needed, as this room will be empty, so go take care of your uniform."

Liam nodded as he stood. "Thank you, sir." He winced with a smirk. "Matthias. I'll return to my post within the half hour."

Chapter 8

Steel clashed with distant shouts, shattering any semblance of tranquility. Troops marched, bootfalls heavy in the snow as they advanced in full force towards the Isalican border.

Wind carved through the tall pines, guiding Dani to join them. It whipped her hair forward, hair as white as the snow.

We're starting a war.

Her heart raced, pounding in her ears and disrupting the sense she relied on the most. Her hands shook. "I cannot go with you." The words echoed from her lips but lacked conviction.

Tallos moved closer, his breath touching her neck. "Yes. You can. And you will. This is your destiny. You're one of the few who can help us win this war."

"How am I supposed to kill people?"

"With your teeth."

Not what I meant.

The thought of someone's blood spilling over her tongue made her stomach lurch. It wouldn't be the same as killing a deer. "What if I find civilians?"

"No mercy, Varadani."

Dani flinched at his use of her full name. "Children?"

Tallos barked a laugh. "Any fool who has their child at the border deserves to watch Nymaera take them."

She swallowed. "I cannot."

Please understand. Please still love me.

Blacking out her vision, Tallos took her upper arms with a gentle grip. "There's no room for your doubts," he hissed. "Lives depend on you. Feyor depends on you. Pull yourself together and remember the war machine you are. You move faster than any soldier." His breath touched her lips before he kissed her, and her uncertainty faded. "Banish your weakness. Earn the place you deserve."

Dani squeezed her eyes shut, taking a deep breath of his earthy scent as he pulled away and let go. "I shall not fail you."

But I will not kill innocent people.

"Good." Tallos's voice softened with his approval. "I love you."

Goosebumps rose along her arms, hidden by wraps of leather.

She opened her eyes, once again taking in the hazy afternoon light. "Tell me where to go."

"I will take the northern gate, you take the south. Make sure that gate gets opened before you attack the encampment. You can find your way through this forest better than I, but if you get lost—"

"I don't get lost." Dani lifted her chin. "Where do we meet after?"

"Come back to this clearing at dawn."

"Dawn?" Dani faced him, aiming her gaze at the blurry shape of his head. "It's not even dusk yet."

"Fighting through the night gives us the advantage. They'll be tired and ready to sleep. Wine sedating them. They will spare no luxury tonight with the prince's arrival."

As the sounds of the army faded, Dani breathed the winter air to steady her hands.

Tallos whispered in her ear. "Go."

Tilting her head back, she closed her eyes, letting her Art roll through her. Her leather and furs melded with her skin, spreading over her body as four white paws met the snow.

Tallos shifted beside her, falling to all fours as the muskier scent of his bear form struck her nose. He huffed and bounded through the snow, leaving her alone on the ridge.

Dani's ears twitched, and she leapt to follow the army. She kept south, skirting the edge of the advancing soldiers as she raced to join the front line.

She'd scaled the stone wall dividing the countries many times before, though never in a guarded area.

It took the remaining daylight to reach the wall and with the sun's descent, her vision darkened to an array of scent colors.

As they neared the Isalican wall, everyone slowed to skulk between the trees, taking cover in the shadows as they crept towards the structure. The closer Feyorian soldiers threw grappling hooks over the top, the gentle taps against the stone lost in the rising night sounds of the border. In dead silence, they climbed, Isalican sentries pacing unaware.

Listening for any sign they'd been spotted, Dani maneuvered closer to the wall, watching for any shift of light as she neared its base. Crouching, she lifted a paw against the uneven brickwork and pushed all her power into her hind legs. She jumped as high as she could, latching onto the side with powerful claws and hauling herself onto the walkway above.

"What the..." Someone near her drew a sword, but then his voice muffled as her ally silenced him.

The tangy scent of copper stung Dani's nose. Her heart sped, anxiety knotting her insides.

She and her ally hurried along the length of the wall before darkness enveloped her in a tower's stairwell. The scents of stone and dirt created a vague visage of her surroundings. The sound of her comrades' steps echoed back to her, and she descended the steps with at least two Feyorians behind her.

As she reached the bottom, she shifted back to her human form. Air cut above her head, and she ducked, rolling beneath the attacking blade. An ally behind her took care of the Isalican while she raced for the barred gate. Something hot and wet splattered on her face, doubling the scent from before. She fought to keep her stomach calm, gasping.

Torches created spots of light in her vision, beacons framing the gate she needed to open.

Someone grasped the other side of the bar, helping her lift it and quietly place it on the ground. Her muscles burned as she moved a second one, and the gates squeaked open.

Several sets of fast footsteps rushed towards her, and an arrow whistled through the air.

Dani dropped, channeling her Art to retake her panther form.

Swords crashed into each other, and she darted to the side.

The dire wolves' scent hit her nose as Feyor's war beasts barreled through the gate, paws nearly silent in the snow as they tackled Isalican soldiers.

I need to guide them.

It was part of her job. To keep the wolves focused throughout the chaos of battle. They listened to her better than any of the human trainers.

A huff of breath behind Dani made her whirl around, and she jumped to the side to avoid a blade.

Cries of men and women filled the air, stifled when each of their lives ended.

Dani backed up until her tail touched a brick wall, crouching as her heart collided with her ribcage.

What am I doing?

Wet hot blood splattered across her, tainting what little vision she had red. Panic rose in her chest as she looked for a way out of the battle. To the south, the scent of trees lingered on the air, and she made a dash for the forest.

Agony erupted from her front leg, and she collapsed into the snow. Slush sprayed around her as she tumbled, and her shoulder struck a rock hidden beneath.

Panting, she scrambled to find her power, shifting to her human form and cradling her injured arm. She whimpered, lost in her haze of darkness as she struggled to gain her bearings.

Sucking in a deep, shaky breath, she caught the scent of the forest again and lunged for it.

Arrows whizzed past her as she ran, and Dani listened to the wind and rustle of needles to weave through the woods.

Chapter 9

"What do you mean Varadani *ran?*" Tallos glared at the incompetent soldier stuttering in front of him.

"She opened the gate, but an arrow struck her, and she ran for the woods."

A feral snarl vibrated in his chest, and Tallos fought the urge to claw the man's throat open. "You saw this with your own eyes?"

"I did."

"Have you told anyone else?"

"No, Dtrüa."

Tallos nodded once, his veins running hot. "Good. Don't. You're dismissed."

I trained her better than this.

Shrugging the heavy bear pelt over his shoulders, Tallos stared at the tree line between the border wall and Isalica's encampment.

Dire wolves whined, pulling on the chains securing them to the battle wagons and their trainers. The rumble of their growls sent a thrill through Tallos's blood, marrying with his growing anger.

The soldier who'd brought the news hovered, watching the Dtrüa as snow fell in big white flakes.

Insolence.

Jerking his head, Tallos snapped his human teeth at the man.

The soldier jumped with a high-pitched squeak, spraying snow up from his boots as he fled. Even their own people feared them, yet Varadani had run like a startled rabbit.

She better have a good reason for this.

Chapter 10

After the evening meal, soldiers sat around the tables talking. The dining tent dominated much of the east side of the camp, large enough to seat one hundred of the 134th Battalion's command core and the privates tasked with guarding the prince during his visit. The prince's staff had been invited to join as well, spread throughout the various tables. They'd provided an ostentatious high-backed chair for the prince, which Micah lounged in like a house cat.

He's way too comfortable being me.

Matthias watched Katrin, who sat with her brother. She glowed, laughing at something Liam said, and it made the prince's heart lighten.

"Are you even listening to me?" Micah waved a hand in front of Matthias's face. "Gods, just talk to her."

The prince frowned. "I can't do that. She doesn't know. It wouldn't be fair."

Micah shrugged and lowered his voice. "Women sleep with me thinking I'm you, so I'm not really sure what the difference..." His voice trailed off at Matthias's scowl.

"You're shameless, you know that?"

"There's no shame in love, my friend."

Matthias rolled his eyes. "I don't get that luxury, unfortunately. And besides, she's an acolyte."

"Who may or may not be celibate. Have you figured out which, yet?"

"She hasn't decided. And it's not my place to rush her." The prince sipped a goblet of wine, smiling as Katrin laughed again.

I'll never get sick of that sound.

Micah took up his steel goblet and stood, clearing his throat and waiting for silence to give the toast Matthias had written. As he opened his mouth, his body jerked forward with the sound of tearing canvas.

A crossbow bolt protruded from his chest as his eyes widened, a second and third bolt finding marks in his neck and shoulder.

Micah fell forward, blood spewing from his mouth as Matthias shot to his feet.

Chaos erupted around them.

Barim and Riez grabbed Matthias's arms.

Stefan threw the table onto its side, creating a barrier from the area of the tent ripped by crossbow bolts.

Matthias narrowed his eyes at the small opening, his pulse racing with adrenaline.

They shot through the canvas. Too fast to reload. Feyorians. Three, at least.

They'd known exactly where to aim, further confirming his suspicions of a traitor among them.

He looked behind him, trying to find Katrin and Liam, but in the scramble to find the assailants, he recognized no one.

I have to jump before I get hit.

Matthias shut his eyes, flexing the Art in his veins. Heat overwhelmed his skin, and he gasped.

"There's no shame in love, my friend."

Matthias breathed hard, his body still in shock.

Micah's expression fell into seriousness. "What? What happens? You just jumped."

"You don't want to know." Matthias looked behind them at the canvas. "At least three Yorries are outside with crossbows. Aimed for you, when you stand to give the toast."

Micah's jaw flexed. "I die? Again? Gods, why does everyone want to kill you?"

Matthias scowled. "You won't die again tonight." He motioned to his three other guards. When Barim moved to stand, he held his hand out. "No. Don't. Stay seated. There are threats outside."

Micah slunk down in the solid oak chair. "Suddenly I'm glad they had me sit in this thing."

Wracking his brain for a solution, Matthias's gaze landed on Liam and Katrin again. On cue, she laughed, pinching her brother's nose, and he poked her side.

He hardened his gaze on Liam and slammed his goblet onto the table with more force than necessary.

Can't risk standing.

The private turned towards the sound, as did others in the tent. Most settled back to their meal immediately, but Liam caught Matthias's gaze and furrowed his brow.

The prince motioned with his head and mouthed the words, "Come here."

Katrin followed Liam's gaze, a warm smile crossing her lips as she looked at Matthias. Her cheeks flushed as she turned back to her meal, and Liam stood. He stooped to kiss his sister's head before crossing to the front of the prince's table. "Sir?"

Matthias kept his voice low. "Don't draw your sword, yet. There are at least three Feyorians outside the tent behind us with crossbows."

Liam straightened, but only slightly. To his credit, he didn't even reach for his sword. "Shall I investigate, sir?"

"Just take a look. They're waiting for the prince to stand. If there are more enemies than you can handle, come back to the front and give me a signal."

Liam nodded once and turned.

"And Private." Matthias glanced at Katrin. "Get your sister out of here. Tell her to find Merissa and make sure the healers are ready. If we can get one of these assholes alive, that would be ideal."

Nodding again, Liam crossed to his sister. He leaned over to whisper in her ear, and she frowned as he hooked his arm under hers. She didn't fight as he pulled her to her feet, but looked back at Matthias with worry in her eyes. They left the tent together at a relaxed pace despite the tension in both of them.

"You want us to sit here and wait?" Micah eyed Matthias. "With crossbows aimed at our backs?"

Matthias sighed. "If we do anything else, it'll look suspicious."

"How many times have you bounced back so far?"

"Just once."

Micah let out a breath. "I'm a lucky bastard having you."

The prince chuckled. "Yes, you are."

Liam reappeared at the entrance to the tent, pausing in the doorway to act like he spoke to the guard there. But he turned his gaze to Matthias and swiped his hand across his throat.

"Shit. There's too many." Matthias frowned.

Micah shrugged. "So much for just sitting here."

Barim downed the rest of his wine in a single swig. "What's the plan, boss?"

"I'm taking your shield." Matthias reached behind their seats, taking the large round shield Barim had leaned against the back of Micah's chair. He strapped it to his back.

Barim quirked an eyebrow. "Always looking at protecting your own hide first." His tone held a teasing air, but Micah glared.

"You know why, you big lug." Riez looked the most relaxed of all of them. "He dies, no more jumps."

Matthias cleared his throat, keeping his voice low. "Stand with me, Barim."

Barim's eyes widened, but he stood with the prince. "You'd jump to save me, too, right?"

He ignored the question, gesturing instead for Barim to move closer, and they met behind the tall-backed chair. The prince put his hands on his crown elite's shoulders, as if greeting him, and leaned close. "You're going to use that bulky frame of yours to block Micah and get him out of here. You two and Riez first, then Stefan and I will follow in a minute."

The big man nodded, letting out a booming laugh as he nudged Micah to stand.

Matthias held his breath as they walked away, Riez falling into place close to Barim. Their large frames shrouded Micah, creating a melded shadow on the tent wall.

Exhaling a steadying breath, the prince leaned against Micah's empty chair, like he spoke to the person no longer seated there. He waited a full minute before straightening and gesturing for Stefan to follow.

Matthias stopped at the captain's table and whispered in her ear. "Have four men take the crown elite's seats, but keep the prince's empty. I trust you have soldiers of similar statures at your disposal?"

"Of course, sir." The captain started to rise from her seat, but Matthias stopped her with a subtle gesture. She frowned, but obeyed. "Anything else?"

"Not yet. Wait a few minutes and then follow me once it's done." Matthias motioned for his men to walk, and they all joined Liam at the tent entrance. "How many?"

Liam shook his head. "I couldn't get a clear count. Three crossbows, and at least another ten soldiers with them. More in the trees behind. But I didn't stick around for them to notice me."

"Riez, stay here. Someone inside that tent told the Yorries where we were sitting. They're going to leave and either follow us or warn Feyor that the prince is gone." The prince looked at Liam. "We need somewhere away from prying eyes to talk. Know somewhere we can use?"

Liam rolled his lips, hesitating. "The eastern armory supply tent. It's not far from here, and no one goes there for their weapons. They have all the shit ones."

Matthias returned his gaze to Riez. "When the captain follows, tell her to meet us there."

Riez nodded, turning his back to the tent.

"Lead the way, Private."

Liam guided them through a narrow passage between tents, forcing them to walk through an untouched snowbank to avoid being seen through the gaps on either side of the dining tent. They continued between another row of tents in the same way before Liam turned them down one of the main cleared walkways.

"That many shouldn't have made it this close to our encampment." Matthias touched the hilt at his side, the three elites walking with Micah at the center. "Feyor breached the gate."

"We have received no report of that." Barim looked sideways at Matthias.

Stefan shook his head when the prince looked at him for confirmation.

"The shifts at the wall are long this time of night. If they knew what patrols to target, they could delay word several hours." Liam stopped and gestured to a sagging tent with a single guard positioned outside.

"Fantastic." Matthias scowled as he approached the lone guard. "You're dismissed."

The guard glanced at the insignia on Matthias's shoulder, straightening from his previous lethargy. "Sir." He saluted and walked away with wide eyes while Liam pulled the flap of the tent aside for Micah and the others.

Liam stopped Matthias with a quick hand to his chest. "Sir. Did you want me to go back and try to suss out the numbers more? I hardly seem needed here."

And risk Katrin losing her brother?

"No. You're the only one here who knows this camp. We need you with us."

Liam saluted, withdrawing his hand. "Sir." He nodded, and they entered the armory tent together.

Racks of weapons lined the outside of the small tent, large sealed chests of various wear circled at the center. It was dark inside, only the flickers of orange from the torches outside piercing through the pale canvas. The racks would provide protection if the Feyor troops followed and kept Micah targeted.

The captain entered a moment later, glancing at Liam before locking her gaze on Micah. "What are we dealing with, here?"

"A group of at least thirteen Feyorians are behind the dining tent, armed with crossbows and other weapons." Micah crossed his arms. "We suspect Feyor has breached the gate and silenced your warning systems. Investigate immediately, but don't underestimate your opponent. They've planned for this. And there's a traitor among you, so be careful who you trust."

"And evacuate the civilians." Matthias dipped his chin to the captain. "Get them somewhere safe. Tonight will get bloody."

The captain glanced at Liam again, then turned back to Matthias. "With all due respect, we should evacuate *the prince* from the encampment, too. His safety—"

"Is taken care of," Matthias growled. "He's perfectly capable of managing his own safety. Go do your job."

"Yes, sir." The captain saluted Micah and the prince before exiting the tent.

Barim cleared his throat, accepting his shield back from Matthias. "So what's the plan from here?" His eyes drifted to where Liam stood perfectly still in a formal position.

The private's dark brown eyes darted between Matthias and his guards, confusion coloring his expression.

Silence settled between them, and Matthias ground his jaw.

We need to bring Liam into the loop.

Sighing, Matthias unpinned his steel crown elite insignia. "Raise your right hand."

Chapter 11

"Are we doing this?" The red-haired royal guard glanced between them. He focused on Matthias again before redirecting his gaze to the prince. "Boss?"

Doing what?

Matthias huffed. "We are. Raise your right hand, First Private."

Liam's chest tightened, and he swallowed, lifting his right hand. "Uh, what's going on?"

Matthias ignored his question. "State your full rank and name."

Liam's mouth went dry. "First Private Liam Denethir Talansiet of the 134th Battalion."

"Where were you born?"

"The farm region east of the Yandarin Mountains, Isalica, sir."

What in the hells is going on? This isn't how military promotions go.

Liam glanced at the prince, who stood there smirking like nothing odd was going on at all.

"State your loyalties." Matthias's demand drew Liam's attention back.

One guard leaned back, whispering something to the prince, who gave a minute shake of his head with his smile.

The answer flowed easily from Liam, even with how surreal the situation seemed. "I am loyal to the rightfully crowned Rayeht family of Isalica. And to the throne they honorably hold."

"Repeat after me." Matthias pulled the military badge off Liam's shoulder and tossed it across the tent. "I swear to guard the throne and its secrets with my life. My word is my bond."

Liam breathed hard, but repeated as he was told.

"Congratulations, Crown Elite Talansiet. You are now a member of the royal guard." Matthias pinned his insignia to Liam's uniform. "Any questions?"

Liam's eyes darted to the prince again. "Isn't... *he* supposed to do that?"

"*He* is Crown Elite Micah Kathira." Matthias glanced at his friend before meeting Liam's gaze again. "My full name is Alarik Matthias Rayeht. Welcome to the inner circle."

His mouth fell open, but he promptly closed it.

Are you fucking kidding me?

His entire body tensed, as he thought back to earlier that day when he'd sat in the meeting hall with Matthias and spoken frankly.

I said all the shit in front of the fucking crown prince?

His breathing felt ragged, but he forced the frosty air to calm him before he started hyperventilating. He bowed his head to hide how pale he was certain his face grew, saluting. "Your majesty." The hand against his chest felt the cold metal of his new insignia, toying with the etching.

First private to crown elite. How is this happening?

"Should go without saying, Liam, but my identity is something I expect you to keep secret. Even from your sister."

Lifting his chin in surprise, he met the real prince's eyes. "She doesn't know?"

Fuck.

Matthias shook his head. "And, for now, it must stay that way." He gestured to the other two men. "These are two more of my crown elites, Barim and Stefan."

Liam sucked on his tongue to ease how dry his mouth had become. "Pleasure." He nodded curtly, trying to keep his head from spinning.

Barim grunted. "What now, boss?" He turned to Matthias instead of Micah now.

The prince paused, tilting his head.

In the distance, swords clashed and soldiers shouted.

"Now we kill some Yorries." Matthias looked up as the tent flap opened, and Riez stood at the entrance.

The man hesitated before spotting the insignia on Liam's shoulder. "No one exited after you to follow or to warn the assassins. Our traitor either wasn't there anymore, or they're smart. Captain's wrangling troops to the edges of the encampment as fast as she can, but we *are* surrounded."

Liam shook his head, grateful that something was coming he understood.

Fighting.

Maybe the prince isn't such a spoiled brat after all, since he's ready for a battle.

"You don't seem interested in leaving, your highness, so am I to assume we're trying to protect the camp and push the Yorries back to the border?" Liam withdrew his sword, looking to Matthias for direction.

"Finally." Matthias breathed out the word and drew his sword, too. "One of you isn't trying to shelter me. Take notes, you." He pointed the tip of his blade at the other four before exiting the tent past Riez.

A howl shook the air, sending a shiver down Liam's spine.

Barim followed them outside. "Shit. Of course they brought dire wolves."

Tightening his grip on his sword, Liam picked up another from the rack behind him. He tested it, but the loose handle prompted him to go for a different one while he wracked his brain for a plan. "Most important will be to protect the guard towers. Wolves can't get up there to take out the archers who can pick them off."

Matthias nodded. "Take us to the closest tower."

Liam led the way out of the tent just as a pair of soldiers came to acquire more weapons. They stood at attention, spotting Liam's insignia, and gave him a salute.

That'll take some getting used to.

The soldiers held their position until Stefan brought up the back of the line, then disappeared into the tent as Liam took the walkway towards the southwest.

The clash of metal and shouts had spread from the eastern border of the camp near the dining tent, to new ones rising in the west. To the north, one watchtower blazed, arrows peppering the wooden panels where fire caught and spread. A soldier still hung over the edge, bow in hand, loosing arrows at something near the base even as the flames devoured the structure.

The southwest tower remained dark, but Liam could make out the dark shadows of the archers within.

A snarl made his heart thunder, and he spun to look down the main walkway that connected to the center of the military encampment. The stone walls of the barracks stood behind the three massive wolves as they tore around the corner. Their dusky grey pelts shone in the firelight, maws gleaming with blood. They stood as tall as the doorway to the barracks, their paws the size of a man's head pounding on the ground as they charged.

Stefan jumped in front of Liam, crossbow raised and aimed at the center wolf.

"Where'd he get a crossbow?" Riez drew his sword.

Micah chuckled. "The same place he gets everything."

The wolves plowed over the slushy mud, barreling for Stefan, but the elite focused on his aim.

Matthias and Barim flanked him, swords ready.

Liam sucked in a gasp as the wolves neared, and Stefan's crossbow twanged.

The bolt lodged into the middle wolf's head, penetrating deep between his eyes. The beast fell, skidding through the muck to come to a stop at the guard's feet while the other two split to the sides. They dove behind the rows of tents, disappearing.

Micah hooted a victory cry. "Did he land it the first time for real?"

"Sure did." Matthias smirked at his stand-in.

Stefan gripped the bolt sticking out from the wolf's skull and jerked it free, wiping the blood on the animal's fur.

A growl drew Liam's attention to the row of tents to their right.

The dire wolf jumped onto a tent, smashing it into the snow.

Despite the cold, Liam's palms sweated as he braced himself for a fighting position.

The wolf dashed into another tent, tearing through the canvas and posts like it was a child's play fort.

Stefan stepped to the front of the group, lifting his crossbow again, but the wolf had vanished among the tents. A scream rose with a vicious snarl, and the creature reappeared between tents, dragging the body of an Isalican soldier between his jaws.

The damn thing is taunting us.

Matthias, heaving for breath, grabbed Liam by the shoulder. "To the tower. Now! The other is circling behind us."

Liam dared a glance at the tents behind them, but couldn't see anything of the other wolf. The two wolves being separated were going to be their best chance.

How does he know the other is behind us?

Something crunched, pulling Liam's attention back to the wolf as its jaws tore into the soldier he held, crushing his skull despite a helmet.

"Asshole beast," Micah muttered as they rushed for the tower.

"Hurry!" Matthias pushed Stefan to the base of the dark tower where wooden scaffolding supported a ladder.

The missing wolf snarled on the other side of the tents, yellow eyes locked on them.

Both animals surged forward, but they'd already moved out of the way, and the beasts collided with each other, snapping and growling.

Liam slid in the mud, sheathing his main sword as he spun to throw the other at the pair of tangled beasts. His aim imperfect, the blade slashed across the one of the wolf's snouts.

It snapped viciously at its comrade, buying them precious time.

Matthias couldn't have known, but he was right. Just like he was right about the crossbow soldiers behind the dining tent.

Riez and Barim had already started up the ladder, while Stefan gracefully climbed the scaffolding.

Micah looked at Matthias. "Go."

The prince growled and jumped to grasp the scaffolding.

Micah pulled on Liam's coat. "Let's not become dog food." He climbed the ladder as Liam followed Matthias up the scaffolding.

A wolf jumped and snapped at Micah's feet, but the guard kicked at the animal's wounded snout, making it whimper and circle the tower.

The other let out a sharp yelp as a pair of arrows struck it in the flank. It dove into the tents beside the tower, snapping the center posts as it vanished among the canvas.

Once all six of them made it to the top, Micah looked at Matthias. "How many times?"

Catching his breath, the prince shook his head. "Twice now."

"Not bad."

Liam breathed hard, his body aching as he leaned over the edge of the tower looking down at the wolves.

Two Isalican archers stood in the watchtower, staring at them. Liam recognized them both in the dim light.

"Liam! What the fuck, man?" Quill looked from him to Micah with wild eyes, bow in hand.

Matthias hurled himself at the archer, grabbing his bow and wrenching it from his grip. It clattered to the wooden decking. With handfuls of the man's uniform, the prince shook him. "Who else serves Feyor?"

Gregor lunged, but Liam caught him by the shoulder, hauling him back.

What the hells has gotten into Matthias?

Quill snatched a knife from his belt, swinging it wildly at Matthias's throat. The prince leaned back, avoiding the attack before he heaved him over the railing to fall to the ground below.

Liam's gut sank.

Quill's a traitor, and Matthias is right again.

The prince panted, facing Micah. "Three times."

"Shit."

Liam furrowed his brow but didn't have a chance to ask what they were talking about before the tower shook.

Everyone gripped the railing, and Liam looked down.

The dire wolves took turns slamming into the scaffolding, and the structure creaked.

Chapter 12

Katrin dodged the prince's soldiers, scouring through the encampment for civilians still present.

When Liam had told her to head for the barracks, she'd seen the worry in his face. Something was wrong, and he refused to tell her what. Everything in Katrin's instincts told her violence was coming. She could feel a tension in the air even before the shouting and swords clashed.

Swallowing the fear, she'd hurried to the medical tents within the central ring, pulling on an apron and knotting her hair behind her head before anyone could question her presence.

When a member of the prince's brigade paused at the tent doorway to look inside, Katrin leaned over to pick up a basin full of rags soaking in alcohol. She glanced over her shoulder to ensure they were gone.

One of the camp's healers snatched a handful of the soaked cloth, making Katrin jump.

"Hope you aren't like that when the actual battle starts." The matronly looking redhead seemed unimpressed as she cleaned her hands. "It gets loud."

Katrin shook her head. "I'll be fine."

"Since you're here, I take it you want to help. Good healer?"

"Good enough."

"Abrasions or fractures?"

"Abrasions." Katrin sidestepped as another healer came forward, taking the basin from her and hurrying it to the west side of the tent.

The redhead pointed after her. "That side, then. Only heal the ones that you know you can save without draining yourself. Just patch the minor ones with bandages. Give the fatally wounded some Varanithe Danilisca oil."

Poison?

Katrin stared at her for a moment, hiding the shock at how bluntly she suggested she help soldiers die. She swallowed. "Yes, ma'am." She hurried off to the other side of the tent, full of empty cots.

Howls, rising in a hellish chorus, rattled Katrin's eardrums. She ducked behind a cot as the ground shook.

The medical tent exploded with screams and the sound of shattering wood as a blur of grey fur tore through the west edge. The healer ahead of her vanished within the flurry of motion, a crunching far worse than wood echoing through Katrin's hands covering her ears.

She thought she should scream, but nothing came out. A splash of crimson smeared across her apron as everything but her heartbeat sounded horribly far away.

The redhead hauled Katrin to her feet, grabbing her face and speaking. She couldn't make out the words.

"... together... time... need..."

Katrin shook her head, lifting her hand to wipe the tears from her face, but her fingers came away covered in red. She stared at it for a moment, trying to understand where it'd come from.

The healer standing in front of her jerked sideways, crashing to the ground in a flurry of snarls. She screamed, but the sound cut off as the wolf latched onto her throat.

Katrin stumbled back, falling over a cot and rolling to the ground. Her skirts snagged on the bed as she tried to pull away, and the dire wolf's maw turned towards her, coated in blood.

It snarled, teeth gleaming as she kicked. The fabric of her dress tore as the cot slammed into the wolf's nose. She clawed at the one next to her, launching to her feet and leaping over it. Something whizzed through the air beside her ear, and she spun towards the soldier standing at the tent entrance, a crossbow positioned at his shoulder.

The wolf yelped but barreled forward, throwing cots in every direction. One collided with the back of Katrin's ankles, throwing her to the ground as the wolf lunged over her, focused on the soldier as he loaded another bolt.

Katrin rolled, seizing a blanket from the corner of the medical tent, and dove through the tear made by the wolf in the tent's west wall. Her boots sank into the freezing snow, but she didn't feel it against the exposed skin of her calves. Clutching the blanket, she hoped its sterile smell would keep the wolves from her trail.

She ran.

Men and women screamed, bones crunching as the dire wolves' assault spread through the camp. She dodged between tents, keeping her eyes on the line of trees where she would hide until it was all over.

If I can just get up one of those trees.

She gulped frozen air, trying to keep her legs moving. Her run slowed as she reached the edge of the camp, sinking into the deep snow as she wove through the tall pines. She paused, only for a moment, with her back against the bark to listen.

Closing her eyes tight, white spots flecked through the black and she prayed her chest would stop burning. She glanced at the camp, amazed at how far away it already was. She didn't remember running so deep into the woods. She could just make out the dark blue canvas of the outer line of tents, the glow of distant fires.

Facing the black woods, Katrin pressed her hand to her chest, feeling her heart and urging it to slow. As it did, the chill settled into her bones. She hissed, unraveling the blanket in her hands and sliding it around her shoulders. Her breath misted into the air in front of her, steam rising from the hot spots of blood on her apron.

Nothing followed me.

She glanced back again, ensuring no giant paws in the snow pursued her. There was only the single thin trail that she'd left. She fought to sort the crazy thoughts of her mind, trying to find the Art buried somewhere within her.

"Aedonai," she whispered, opening her eyes to stare up at the canopy and stars beyond. "Please help me focus."

Sucking in a deep breath, Katrin's body shook, but she found a sense of calm that she clung to. Using it, she allowed herself to slip into the well of her power, and twist it with the fabric of the air behind her. A gust brushed over her cheeks, warmer than the winter winds. The snow behind her swirled, gently filling her footprints to smooth her passage into the woods.

Katrin sighed as she let the Art go. Closing her eyes again, she nearly collapsed as images of the dire wolves struck her mind, their teeth tearing apart those healers.

She winced, grabbing at her face and rubbing desperately at the dried blood there. She could only smell the coppery tang and picked up a handful of snow to clean her face. The snow came away slushy and streaked with blood. She threw the lump back into the snowbank.

Dark smatterings of blood ran along the bank, and she realized that someone else's passage had left what she'd thought was the natural swell caused by the trees. She traced the trail, trying to see where it came from. It seemed to circle the camp, possibly someone who escaped the chaos.

Someone else is hurt.

Katrin wrapped the blanket tighter around her. She'd gotten herself into this mess because she wanted to help, but had run before she even could. Shaking her head at herself in disappointment, she pursed her lips.

"Get yourself together, Kat," she muttered. She stared in the direction she could see the small footsteps leading. Glancing back at the camp, she wondered about Liam and Matthias.

Gods, I hope they're all right.

She imagined the injured soldier in the woods being the crown elite she'd already grown attached to, and it made her shudder.

But the footprints are too small.

Taking a determined step, Katrin followed them, anyway. If she could help someone, she needed to find them.

The trail wove through the trees in an almost drunken way, splotches of blood leaving little melted divots in the snow.

A bloody handprint marred one tree, no bigger than her own hand.

Deeper in the woods, something scuffled, panting.

Katrin paused when her eyes landed on a young woman clad in white leathers and furs, sitting with her back against a tree. An arrow shaft lay in the snow next to her, surrounded with crimson.

"Who's there?" The woman's eyes darted back and forth, a milky white covering the grey tones beneath.

She's blind. What is she doing here?

"It's all right, I'm not a threat." Katrin lifted her hands to show they were empty before she remembered the woman couldn't see. She took a careful step forward, the snow crunching under her boot as she wrapped the blanket tighter. "You're hurt."

The woman shook her head, shoulder-length locks of stark white hair sticking to her bloodied face. "Leave me. It is not safe."

Katrin paused, studying her. A vague accent colored the woman's words, but she didn't recognize it. The furs clothing her were stained with blood, but it seemed too much for it to all be hers with her still living. The arrow shaft had sunk into the snow, impossible to see. "I'm a healer, and you're bleeding. Let me help you."

The woman's breathing leveled out, but she didn't release the grip over her wounded arm. "What's your name?"

"Katrin." She pushed all the comforting tones they had taught her in the temples. "What's yours?"

The woman swallowed. "Dani." She let go of her arm, revealing where she'd dug at the flesh to remove the arrowhead. "It's still in there."

Katrin moved, but then paused, watching Dani's milky eyes. "May I come look?" At her nod, she approached and knelt. As she parted the leathers on Dani's bicep, blood welled against Katrin's fingers. "Shit." She pinched the wound closed, applying pressure to feel the arrowhead within.

Dani tilted her head back, lifting her chin as she shut her eyes. "Is the battle over?"

"I don't know." The blanket fell from Katrin's shoulders as she brought both hands to Dani's injury. Biting her lip, she tried to remember all her lessons. "I don't have any tools, so this might hurt a little more than usual."

"Please, just get it out."

Nodding, Katrin stilled her quivering stomach as she dug her fingers into the injury. Blood seeped over her fingers as she found the back end of the arrowhead.

Dani yelled, body shaking under Katrin's touch as the acolyte ripped the metal from her arm.

Katrin knew she'd caused more damage by pulling it out the way she had, but she pressed hard to stem the bleeding. She turned the arrowhead over in her other hand. The steel glimmered in the starlight, and Katrin sucked in a breath.

This is an Isalican arrowhead.

"What's wrong?" Dani turned her sightless gaze on Katrin, staring at an invisible spot just above her head.

Katrin glanced at the blood-covered metal in her palm.

She's my enemy.

It'd be easy to take the sharp tool in her hand and thrust it under the defenseless woman's chin, slice the artery there and end it.

Bile rose in her throat, and she swallowed, shaking away the images of the death she'd already seen that night.

That doesn't mean she deserves to die alone and scared.

"Nothing." She choked, throwing the arrowhead into the snow behind her.

Pushing both hands to the wound, Katrin centered herself with a deep breath, and sought the connection deep within her.

Flesh wounds like this were easier to heal than broken bones, and she'd practiced it far more. Closing her eyes, her hands warmed, the wet from the snow evaporating into little puffs of steam. She channeled the energies from within herself to Dani, feeling her soul respond.

And she's an Art user, too.

Katrin buried the panic, forcing herself to remain focused on the task. Determination steeled her power as she opened her eyes in time to see the skin stitching together, pulled by glowing golden strands. The Art-riddled stitches hummed in the frosty night air before they seeped back into Katrin's fingertips, leaving behind a jagged scar.

Dani let out a breath, touching her arm as her eyes flickered back and forth. "You healed me." Surprise etched her tone. "But you know..."

"I told you I wasn't a threat." Katrin picked up a handful of snow, cleaning her hands then picking up another to press to Dani's arm. "And that I would help you. I don't lie. But I hope my kindness won't lead to my death."

"I don't want to kill anyone." Dani's chin quivered. "I never wanted to. The fighting started, and I couldn't..." She grimaced, shutting her eyes tight.

Katrin closed a hand around Dani's. "It's my first battle, too."

"I cannot go back."

Katrin shook her head, looking at Dani's blank eyes. "Me neither. I don't think I'd be much help. Rather, just a distraction."

"Will you stay with me?" Dani rolled her lips together.

Katrin's heart pounded as she considered what it meant. Treason, at the very least, but that seemed so ridiculous. All she did was heal someone who needed it. And Dani seemed hardly a threat.

Besides, if I stay with her, I can make sure she doesn't hurt anyone if she's lying.

"I'll stay." Katrin gathered up the blanket and pressed it to the ground next to Dani before dropping to sit beside her. A shiver passed through her as she pulled up the edge around her shoulders again. "As long as no more wolves come running by."

Dani sighed, leaning sideways onto Katrin's shoulder. "You needn't fear the wolves when you're with me."

Fear rose again, but Katrin breathed it out, another cloud of icy breath rising in front of them. "Some good news, then." She huddled close to Dani, wondering how this had all happened when she'd been comfortably studying in the temple only a few days before.

Chapter 13

With another slam from a dire wolf below, the scaffolding cracked.

"Hold on!"

Matthias rushed to the far end of the tower as the floor tilted. Taking hold of the railing, he heaved himself up beside Barim and braced for the impact with the tents below.

Screams burst from the surrounding soldiers, the cry of the dire wolves responding as Isalica broke waves of Feyorian battle beasts. The tower split and thundered as it crashed. Everything around the prince blurred for a mind-numbing moment before Micah pulled him to his feet.

"Everyone alive?" Riez lifted a beam off of Liam, who winced but stood.

Barim pounded his shield with his sword in response as he shifted to take position between them and the wolves who'd knocked over the tower.

Matthias grumbled under his breath, locking gazes with a wolf's yellow eyes. "For now."

The wolf snarled, froth dripping from its fangs as it advanced. It stumbled, letting out a yelp as a crossbow bolt struck its left side. Another followed it, striking the thing in the temple, and the furry mass collapsed as a troop of Isalican soldiers rushed from between the tents.

Captain Brenna jogged from the back, looking Matthias up and down. Her hard gaze moved to Liam, passing over the insignia on his shoulder. "We've secured the inner ring, sir." She looked back at Matthias, giving him a brief salute. "You and your men should return to the barracks. We'll have these Feyorian dogs retreating with their tails between their legs soon."

The soldiers that'd arrived with her fanned out, lieutenants shouting concise commands as another dire wolf fell to the crossbows.

Matthias nodded. "Are all the civilians inside the barracks?"

She gave a curt nod. "Only the healers who volunteered are out in the medical tents."

"Damn it." Liam stepped forward, holding his hand against a cut on his left arm. "Knowing my sister... She'd volunteer."

The prince scowled. "Are you joking? She's never seen battle. Are you sure she'd put herself in the middle of it?" His stomach dropped, and he scanned the area.

"To help save others, yes." Liam flinched as he checked the gouge under his hand.

Matthias sighed. "You need to get that tended."

"I'll be fine."

"Don't make me order you. Go to the barracks and get your wound cleaned. Check for your sister while you're there." Matthias crossed his arms, fatigue eking through his muscles. "In the meantime, we'll check the medical tents."

Captain Brenna frowned. "Sir, with respect, I don't think one girl, who might not even be missing, is worth—"

Matthias shot her a look that stilled her tongue. "I believe you have duties to attend to yourself, Captain?"

"Sir." Captain Brenna saluted, spinning on her heels to follow her troops still sweeping through the camps.

"Riez, accompany Crown Elite Talansiet to the barracks."

Despite his frown, Liam turned with Riez to jog towards the interior of the camp.

Micah eyed Matthias. "Getting a little attached, aren't you?"

The prince scoffed. "Is that a bad thing?"

"Just never known you to focus so much on one woman."

"I think you're confusing the two of us." Matthias smirked.

"I mean, as opposed to no women. You aren't really the relationship type." Micah looked behind him at the calming battle. "She doesn't even know who you are."

"That's the part I like the most." Matthias motioned with his head. "Let's find some horses. I'd like a chance to come clean to her."

Barim cleared his throat. "About who you are, or all of it?"

Matthias groaned. "Don't get me started on the rest of it."

Of all the people who could make me rethink my future... who would've guessed it'd be a damn priestess.

Checking each medical tent, they found no sign of Katrin or anyone who had seen her. As they rode to the last healer post, hope surfaced in Matthias's mind that she'd followed instructions and gone to the barracks.

Liam is probably with her now.

The prince and his men rode into an area trampled by wolves, and his heart sank.

The southeastern tents lay in tattered piles, canvas stained with crimson. The sprawling length of the medical tent had collapsed on one side, splinters of the beams and cots scattered amid smears of blood, oil-like in the torchlight. Several soldiers gathered the bodies, laying them in a neat row near the half collapsed doorway.

Liam stood at the end of the shrouded row, rubbing his jaw, a bandage wrapped around his upper arm. He held a lantern at his side, flame flickering as he lifted it.

Snow sizzled around the torches lining the walkway as it fell in massive flakes from the dark sky above.

Matthias slid off his horse next to Liam. "She wasn't in the barracks?"

Liam stiffened, still staring at the row of bodies. "No. She was sent here." He crouched, lifting the edge of the first shroud to look beneath it. The healer's red hair shone with copper in Liam's lantern.

Dread gurgled in Matthias's gut as he surveyed the carnage. "This specific tent?"

Riez approached from the other side of the bodies. "She's not here."

Liam dropped the shroud over the mangled corpse, his shoulders sagging. "Shit."

"Barim, Stefan, check the nearby tents. She could be hiding." Matthias mounted his horse again. His gaze landed on the woods surrounding the encampment and he swallowed. "Is she comfortable in the forest alone?"

Liam followed his gaze, pausing. "Maybe? It's been years." He looked up and shivered as a flake stuck to his face. "But the weather..."

Matthias clenched the reins, his breath creating clouds of mist in the air.

Micah nudged his horse closer to the prince and lowered his voice. "Can you go back again?"

Matthias shook his head, turning his horse around to put his back to Liam. "I keep asking myself the same thing, but I can't go back far enough. It's been too long and I probably only have one long jump left. I wouldn't know where to look."

I never should have brought her here.

If he went back now, he'd put them all in the tower again and he'd still be no closer to finding Katrin.

The prince circled his horse, eyeing the tree line.

Liam lifted his lantern as he approached Matthias. "If she's out there, we need to find her soon. If she's hurt..."

Matthias nodded and looked at Riez. "Ride along the southern edge of camp with Micah. Look for tracks in the snow, for anyone who might have fled the camp."

A trumpet sounded from the barracks, shrill and clear.

Liam looked up. "Feyor is retreating. The next call will be to secure the wall."

"Good. Hopefully Katrin is close enough to hear it, too." Matthias watched Micah and Riez ride towards the trees. "You coming?"

Her brother nodded, handing off his lantern to one of the soldiers dealing with the dead and pulled himself up onto the horse he must have taken from the barracks. Snow stuck in his messy onyx hair. "I hope whatever god she prays to has kept her alive."

Chapter 14

Dani adjusted her shoulder pelt so it covered Katrin more. She'd removed it when the healer started shivering, sharing its warmth between them. "You should go back."

Katrin shook her head, nuzzling in against Dani's side. "Not yet. It might not be safe, yet."

"We can check. I can take you most of the way there. You'll freeze out here."

Far enough from the encampment, the scent of blood had diminished, only lingering from the clothing around the wound Katrin had healed. While her eyes saw hardly anything but black in the night, her nose could guide her. Each scent tinged her vision, but the colors were brighter as a cat.

"You don't know what that trumpet meant?" Katrin rubbed her cold nose against a patch of fur sticking out from Dani's shoulder.

Dani wrapped an arm around Katrin. "No. It wasn't Feyor."

She hummed. "It's snowing again. At least I think it is. Hard to tell with how dark it is."

Tilting her chin up, Dani relished in each icy flake's path towards the ground, swooping through the air with the quietest sound. "It's snowing. I can hear it... and the air smells different when it snows."

"You can hear it?" Her tone sounded amazed rather than doubtful.

Dani nodded. "Not every flake, but the way the forest reacts. It gathers on branches, weighing the boughs. And it's actually a little warmer when the snow falls."

Katrin pulled tighter on her blanket. "Could have fooled me. I feel colder." She shifted a little closer. "I wonder if your Art somehow helps your other senses to offset your blindness."

Shoulders drooping, Dani sighed. "My blindness isn't a weakness."

"Sorry," Katrin whispered. "I didn't mean it like that."

"It's all right." Dani tugged her hood further over her head. "I used to wish for sight. Not anymore."

"Trust me, there are certain things I wish I'd never seen." A smile shone through her voice. She grew quiet for a moment before pulling away ever so slightly. "Where will you go from here? You can't go back to Feyor..."

Dani's eyebrows knitted together. "I know not. I've been nowhere else."

Katrin's heart beat harder. "Stay with me. I'll protect you."

"Impossible. Isalica will kill me."

"Not if I ask them to spare you. Especially if you might help. We're not meant for the war Feyor is trying to force us all into."

Dani swallowed. "It's a bad idea. I've been trained for the war as long as I can remember. I know nothing else."

A voice carried over the wind, and she tilted her head, moving her hair away from her ear.

"Katrin!"

Distant.

Male.

"Someone is searching for you," Dani whispered. "You should go."

Katrin's hand closed around Dani's, entangling their fingers. "I have to believe we found each other for a reason. Please, trust me?"

Dani paused, listening to the man call. "You know not who it is. I'll come with you, but I'll stay back."

"Just... don't look threatening?" Katrin stood, wrapping her damp blanket tighter. The edges of it crackled with bits of ice that had frozen while they sat.

Rising to her feet, Dani secured her pelt over her shoulders and patted herself. "Do I look threatening?"

Katrin paused but then laughed. "I suppose not. Come on." The snow crunched beneath her boots as she started towards the camp. She stopped after a few paces. "Which way is the shouting coming from? I can't hear it."

"This way." Dani stepped and clicked her tongue, listening to the sound bounce off the nearby trees.

"How would you describe the voice calling? Is it... more tenor and commanding, or deep and..."

"Sexy?" Dani smirked. "Definitely the latter. Who is it?" She continued through the snow, snowflakes touching her face each time they crossed between trees.

"Matthias." She sighed his name, relief touching her tone. "He'll be able to protect you. I hope Liam's all right, too."

Dani clicked her tongue again. "Just because he can, doesn't mean he will. Not after what my people have done tonight."

"But you weren't part of it. You left. No Isalican blood is on your hands."

I opened the gate.

Dani cringed, not daring to test her new friendship with the information.

"Katrin!" Matthias's voice came louder this time, accompanied by horses' hooves.

Dani sucked in a breath and hopped to the side, throwing her back against a tree. The instinct to shift and run overtook her, but something encouraged her to stay.

"I'm here!" Katrin stepped faster through the snow.

"Kat!" Another voice, also male. Excited and relieved.

Closing her eyes, Dani again debated making a run for it.

Boots hit the snow as riders dismounted, and breath muffled as one of them embraced her.

Katrin sighed happily against him, and the blanket thumped against the snow as it fell.

"You're an icicle." Wool rustled as the man pulled his cloak from his shoulders and wrapped it around her. "Are you all right?"

"I'm fine, Liam. I'm just relieved you're both alive. The wolves..."

Dani opened her eyes, the blackness of her vision disrupted by faint light coming from a torch that smelled of oil and linen.

"Katrin..." Matthias's voice dropped a register, and Dani imagined the tension in his shoulders. "Are you alone?"

Shit. He sees my tracks.

"No." Katrin sounded confident and stern. "Please, don't overreact. I would have frozen without her."

"Why would we overreact?"

Dani took a deep breath and straightened, emerging from behind the tree with slow steps. She lifted her palms, focusing her eyes in their direction, but couldn't see anything but a blurry orb of glowing orange.

The men held their breath, snow crackling as they straightened.

"Who..." Liam moved forward, but Katrin blocked him.

"Don't hurt her. Please. Dani is seeking asylum."

"She's Feyorian?"

They're going to kill me.

Dani backed up a step, and metal sounded against a scabbard. "You needn't fear me. I pose no threat."

"Your comrades killed hundreds of us tonight." The soldier's voice shook with anger and he pushed past Katrin, a blade glinting with orange light at his side.

Dani lifted her chin, cool air wafting off the sword near her throat. She blinked, but forced her feet to stay still. "I'm unarmed."

"Talansiet." Matthias's voice held authority. "Look at her. Lower your weapon."

"Liam, stop." Katrin grabbed at Liam, but he shook her off.

His blade remained at Dani's throat. "Sir, she might have—"

"Stand down!" Matthias stalked towards her. "Get some rope, Liam."

The blade dropped, the soldier obediently taking a step back despite the tension in the air. He backed away, headed towards the horses, who huffed behind them.

Matthias took each of Dani's wrists, gently guiding them together in front of her. "You'll come with us to the barracks."

A hand touched her shoulder, and Katrin stepped close to her. "I'm sorry. But Matthias won't let anything happen to you." Dani sensed the pointed look passing between them as the healer spoke. "Please. You'll speak to the prince yourself, won't you?" The leather of Matthias's tunic creaked as she squeezed his shoulder.

The man holding Dani let out a slow breath. "No one will touch her. You have my word."

Dani blinked the heat from her eyes as she let the men bind her wrists. Her heart sped, and she strained against the rope for a moment to test the knot. It held strong.

I can't even shift now.

A shape passed back and forth in front of her face, making the faint light blip in and out of existence.

Dani frowned. "I'm blind, but I can still tell what you're doing."

Katrin slapped Liam's hand down.

"Ow."

"Don't be a jackass." Katrin laced an arm through Dani's. "I'll walk with her. Back to the barracks, right? It'll be good to get somewhere warm."

"You're freezing. You're not walking. Ride with Liam, and I'll take Dani." Matthias guided Dani to a horse, lifting her hands to the saddle horn.

"Sir, that's not—"

"Don't make me order you again, Liam."

Dani silently thanked Matthias for not making her ride with the angry soldier. She gripped the saddle horn, and Matthias helped guide her foot into the stirrup so she could mount. Letting her feet hang free, the man mounted behind her.

As they rode towards the encampment, Dani kept her eyes closed, hoping it would somehow block out the scents and sounds.

The wounded crying.

The smell of blood and burned flesh.

Her heart pounded, and she focused on the rhythm of hooves.

I made this happen.

Dani rolled her lips together, fighting back her guilt. When two other horses joined them, she stiffened.

"Are you hurt?" Another man.

Dani opened her eyes, but only muddled spots of orange dappled her vision.

"I'm uninjured, your majesty." Katrin sounded embarrassed. "I didn't mean to cause an ordeal. I'm perfectly fine."

Your majesty?

Dani breathed faster, tilting her head towards the male speaker. She kept her voice too quiet to carry over the air. "He's alive."

"He is." Matthias matched her volume. "But they tried to kill him."

"That was the primary purpose for the attack. They failed."

The man behind her paused as they rode. "You sound relieved."

"I am." Dani smiled, her shoulders relaxing. "I wish no one had died tonight."

Chapter 15

Master Dtrüa Nysir,

Varadani has found an opening in the Isalican forces she means to exploit. Her proximity could lead to unprecedented knowledge of their prince's location and their army's potential weaknesses. Perhaps another assassination opportunity will arise, though I know General Teff's patience wears thin.

As she infiltrates their ranks, I will follow to ensure her safety and keep you updated on her progress. She is acting as a prisoner, but I suspect that will be short-lived.

In the meantime, I must alert you to another potential complication among the prince's escort that Varadani may assist with as well. I received word from Xavis that one of the prince's personal guards used suspicious tactics in our attack. Apparently, he appeared to know what would happen before it did. And he suspects is the very reason the assassination attempt failed before Isalica realized our attack. Visions, perhaps? I will investigate this further while I support Varadani.

Faithfully, Tallos

Chapter 16

Chaos around the camp had settled into organization as fortification began. No one slept, despite the late hour, all working to secure the inner ring of the encampment. Debris from the broken towers and tents cluttered the outer ring, creating a barricade against Feyor should they attack again.

Liam squeezed Katrin where she sat in the saddle in front of him, resting his chin on her shoulder. "Don't do that again."

"What?" Katrin patted his hand. "I'm fine."

"But you might not have been. What were you thinking?"

"I was thinking I could help. What good is the ability in the Art if I don't put it to use? I'm no better than those healers who'd already volunteered." She leaned back against him, the knot in her hair digging into his shoulder.

He sighed, roughly kissing the top of her head. "Katy girl, I can't lose you after finally seeing you again."

"Well, seeing as you're a crown elite now, I suspect seeing each other will become more difficult."

The weight the title brought made Liam slouch slightly, even though he should have been proud.

But now I'm keeping a secret from my sister.

He'd almost forgotten until Katrin addressed Micah with the formal royal title. She hadn't known she was asking the prince himself to protect a Feyorian.

I still can't believe we're protecting that Yorrie.

"I didn't have much of a choice in the matter." Liam steered the horse in front of the barracks' gate, looking at the fur and leather-clad prisoner riding with the prince. "Right place, right time, I guess."

"Well, congratulations." Katrin grasped his hand. "You deserve it. Long as you keep that temper in check."

"I don't have a temper," he growled, stiffening at his own tone. Sucking in a breath, he tried to calm himself as Katrin slipped from the saddle.

In front, Matthias dismounted, talking to the Feyorian. "Once we get you somewhere warm, I'm going to ask you more, if that's all right."

Liam's brow furrowed. "What?" He spoke to himself, but dismounted to approach Matthias. "With all due respect, sir... Why are you asking permission? She's a prisoner, not a guest." He glanced at Katrin, who spoke with Micah off to the side.

Matthias turned his gaze on Liam. "And, so far, she's a very cooperative prisoner. I'd like to keep it that way and have found that human decency is a good way to start."

"Where was the Yorries' human decency when they sent dire wolves to tear us apart?" Despite trying to swallow it, fire rose in his veins. "Those healers at the southeast tent were in *pieces*. That could have been my sister."

Dani stared at the ground, jaw locked.

Matthias sidestepped, blocking his view of her. "Yes, it could have been." His voice took on a soft tone, barely more than a whisper. "But nothing can undo the horror that happened tonight. She isn't to blame."

"Sir. They tried to assassinate the prince during a meal—"

"And if I can let that go, you can, too." Matthias motioned to Katrin with his eyes. "Go spend some time with your sister. The *prince* and I will handle this."

Every muscle in Liam's body tightened, and he bit the inside of his cheek to distract from the rage. "Is that an order, sir?"

Matthias's jaw clenched. "Are you only going to listen to me when

I make something an official order?"

Liam glanced around Matthias at Dani, who hadn't dismounted and stared blankly forward. "No." He sighed. "No, sir. I'll see to Katrin and make sure she doesn't wander out again."

Icy blasts through the carved passes towards Undertown prompted Liam to wrap his scarf even tighter. The high winds pushed the storm clouds to the west, revealing a crystal blue sky outlining the craggy peaks of the Yandarin Mountains. Recent snow coated the slopes, hiding any trees that might have grown there.

They'd lingered only a day at the border. The prince needed to reach the northern city to liaise with the officials there, and his elites applauded the choice to leave the turbulent border.

The covered carriage behind Liam thunked over a ridge of ice in the roadway, a girlish yelp of surprise escaping the window before being covered by laughter.

I can't believe Matthias is letting Katrin ride with the prisoner.

He rode nearby, his sword always ready at his side should the Feyorian attempt to make any kind of escape. Frowning beneath his scarf, he eyed the slowing of the lead horses, and Matthias turned his horse to trot back down the line of the prince's caravan.

"We'll stop here for the day. Road gets rougher from here on through the pass, and we'll need all day tomorrow to clear it before nightfall." The prince paused as more laughter echoed from inside Katrin's carriage, and his gaze drifted to where Liam's hand lingered near his sword. "Stay on guard, Talansiet, sounds like she might make a break for it at any moment."

Relieved the scarf hid most of his scowl, Liam bit back his retort. He glanced at the carriage, imagining the smile on Katrin's face. She insisted she join the caravan to Undertown rather than return to the temple, likely to stay near the Feyorian and protect her from Liam.

But being near Katrin reminded him constantly of the secret he held.

Liam pulled down his scarf and met Matthias's sea-colored gaze. "When are you going to tell her?"

Matthias's expression deadpanned. "You know I can't do that."

"Then you expect me to keep lying to her? I mean, I guess you are, too."

People began dismounting and clearing areas for tents.

The prince sighed and angled his horse closer to Liam's. "Look, if I told everyone the truth, whenever I wanted, it wouldn't be an effective secret to keep. I'm sorry you're in this position and, trust me, I don't like it any more than you do. I wish I could tell her, but that isn't an option yet."

"When does it become an option?" His jaw tightened. He'd watched how Matthias looked in Katrin's direction and the color that rose in her cheeks when she noticed.

"When necessity demands it." Matthias dismounted and patted his horse's neck. "A time will come for it, I'm almost certain. And when it does, she will understand you were following orders."

"You better hope you get the chance to tell her before she figures it out. She's never caught you in a lie before. As her older brother, let me assure you it isn't pretty."

Matthias smirked and gestured to him. "Well, since you're still on her good side, I'll take that as an indicator that she also forgives."

Liam grinned despite himself. "Guess it's good the temples preach that kind of thing." He looked ahead to where the other crown elites assisted in assembling the tents meant for the prince.

Even though he never actually sleeps in them. Micah's got the best deal in all of this.

"Do you ever tire of not being you? You miss out on a lot of perks."

Matthias laughed. "On the contrary, it's a pleasant break when I'm away from Nema's Throne."

The door to the carriage popped open, and Katrin's head emerged. "We're stopping?"

Matthias jerked his head towards the tents for Liam. "Go help the others. I'll watch our *prisoner*, or do you not trust me to do that?"

Liam rolled his eyes as he slid from his saddle. "I'm not *that* obsessive."

"You haven't let her out of your sight since we left the border."

Loxith, the prince's farrier, took their horses and led them away.

Katrin hopped out of the carriage, holding the door open for Dani, who followed. A pair of iron shackles bound her wrists, a length of chain following her out from where it was secured inside the carriage.

The Feyorian's shoulder-length white hair blended in with her surroundings like her clothing did. The white leathers and furs hugged her body, her cloudy eyes aimed skyward as a peaceful expression washed over her. Dani's chest rose in a deep inhale, and Liam looked away.

Why does she have to be attractive?

Liam hated the rumble she caused in his gut he assumed to be loathing. The constant reminder of her presence with his sister only made it worse.

"Does the prince really need that big of a tent?" Katrin lifted her hand to shield her eyes from the glaring sun as it reflected off the mountains. "It seems a little... over compensating."

Dani kept staring at the sky. "Maybe he has lots of women. Is he handsome?"

Katrin laughed. "All the rumors say yes to both things. Though, seeing him myself..." She made a contemplative hum. "I suppose he's attractive."

Matthias raised an eyebrow.

Liam cringed. "Trust me, you'll be the one paying for the secret far worse than me," he whispered, slapping his hand on the prince's shoulder. "Good luck."

The Feyorian made a clicking noise with her mouth, eyes aimlessly tracking through the cloudy sky.

Why is she always making that sound?

It grated against Liam's composure, fueling his annoyance with the foreign woman. His shoulders tensed, and an interested look from Matthias implied he'd noticed.

The prince leaned to Liam's ear. "Why do you hate her so much?"

"She's our enemy. I've been trained to despise Feyorians." Liam tugged his scarf back into place across his face to hide any further expression that might give him away. "Course, they encouraged my education by killing our people. How do you *not* hate her?"

Katrin helped guide Dani towards the carriage driver, who unlocked the length of chain restraining her to the compartment. The cuffs remained in place, but she could still escape plenty easily by running into the snowfields on either side of the road.

"She's just a person." Matthias watched the women. "And she has done nothing but cooperate."

"She's hiding something. I can feel it."

"Aren't we all?"

"I'm not. Perhaps I'm the only one that's really being honest here." He winced, looking away from the prince.

This is why I never made it past First Private. My gods' damned mouth.

Matthias shrugged. "Maybe you should be prince, then."

Suddenly grateful for the scarf disguising his astonishment, Liam shook his head. "My temper gets me in enough trouble as a private in the military. Gods know what I'd do to a country. Better the level-headed keep it." He pursed his lips. "I'm... sorry, my lord. That was... out of line."

"Definitely out of line, but proves my point that no one is perfect. And don't call me lord." Matthias smirked, still watching Dani and Katrin as they walked through the snow towards the others setting up camp, arm in arm. "We all have our faults, and if Dani is hiding something, her cooperation is making up for it. Cut her some slack."

The Feyorian moved with grace in each step, despite her blindness, and Liam caught himself staring.

If anything, I should give her credit for her bravery.

"Has her cooperation led to anything actually helpful for the coming war?" Liam met the prince's gaze. "That's what this is all turning into, isn't it? Feyor can't launch an attack on our border and expect anything less than formal declaration."

Matthias frowned. "I wish it wasn't. The assault was an elaborate assassination attempt on the prince, designed to force Isalica to declare war. And Dani told us why they want it."

"Why would Feyor actively hope to make it official? There's always been tension at the border, but never anything this direct."

"Because the only way to contest a border's location is during a state of war. They want the Yandarin Mountains." Matthias's shoulders slumped. "And it looks better if Isalica formally declares war first."

Liam looked at the craggy slopes surrounding them, the wind whipping up little clouds of snow along the peaks. "Why the hells would they want these mountains? Whole lot of nothing up here. They're too dangerous to even build cities."

The prince hummed. "Feyor believes they're home to dragons."

"Dragons?" Liam gaped, his imagination filling with the tales his father used to tell him as a child. "Like, real full-fledged dragons? That kind of draconi hasn't been seen in hundreds of years. They're all dead."

Matthias shook his head. "Feyor disagrees, and Dani has some pretty compelling stories. She might be lying, but we need to take her seriously. It's too much of a risk if she's telling us the truth."

He huffed, looking to spot the women again, but they'd vanished among the tents. Anxiety spiked with her being out of his sight. "Can you imagine if Feyor got their hands on dragons? Their wyverns are bad enough from what I hear. We're fortunate those things can't stomach the cold up here, or we might have lost that fight at the border." He shifted, but every position felt uncomfortable. "I better go help with the setup before Barim gives me shit again." He gave Matthias a brief, respectful nod.

"Mhmm. Give Katrin and Dani my best. I'll be with Micah and Riez if you need me."

Despite the claustrophobic layers of his clothing, Liam jogged towards the tents. He wove between the two he'd seen the woman near.

Far outside the camp, Dani stood in the knee-deep snowfield, blending in with her surroundings. Her wavy hair ruffled in the breeze as she stared out at the wilderness with no one near her.

Why is she standing out there alone?

Fear for his sister mounted, then turned to frustration as he realized she'd likely been the one to leave the Feyorian unguarded.

I didn't think the temples made her that naive.

Liam stalked through the snow, growling beneath his breath.

"And where are you going?"

Liam spun to face his sister, who stood where she'd been just out of his sight behind one of the caravan's carts.

She crossed her arms, her cheeks rosy in the cold beneath the grey fur-lined hood of her cloak. The line of her lips looked just like their mother's when she caught Liam sneaking cookies from the kitchen.

He jerked his scarf down so she could see his frown. "Kat, you can't just walk away from her like that. She's a *prisoner*."

"She's harmless and deserves as much right to privacy from time to time as you or I." Katrin's cloak dragged on the ground with her approach, and she prodded Liam in the chest. "You just can't accept that she isn't our enemy."

"She's a Feyorian! For all we know, she's spying on us and plans to escape and take all the information back to her commanders."

"And do you think the snow out there is telling her all our secrets?"

"No, I think you're giving her plenty by acting like a child who has a new plaything."

"How dare you..."

Liam ignored her as he turned away, trudging through the snow towards Dani.

"You're an asshole!" Katrin shouted after him, and he turned to see her face flushed with more pink. She waved her hand up and down as if gesturing to his whole body. "And this false sense of superiority the military has given you isn't doing you any favors."

"At least I'm thinking clearly in all of this." He continued stomping through the snowfield.

As Liam neared Dani, the Feyorian tilted her head towards him. "Come to join me?"

"Come to take you back to camp."

The chill of the chain bit through his gloves as he grabbed the narrow length between her wrists, and he suddenly wondered how cold the cuffs themselves felt.

Dani resisted his pull. "You needn't fear me just because I'm Feyorian."

"I'm not afraid of you. I'm cautious and realistic." He gave her another gentle jerk. "I thought you were cooperating?"

"Have you ever just listened, Liam?" Her voice stirred something in his gut, her accent making it worse. "Have you?"

"Listened to what, exactly?" He tried to see through the milky sheen on her eyes, studying the grey beneath.

"Nature. The woods. The snow. Have you ever just listened?"

He paused, straightening in confusion.

She's trying to distract me.

"Look, I don't know what bullshit you're playing at, but it's time to come back to camp. You might have my sister fooled, but not me." He motioned before he remembered she couldn't see and sighed. "Move."

Dani let out a breath and dropped her cloudy gaze to the snow. Stepping towards camp, she tried to scratch her arm. "You're exactly how I imagined Isalican soldiers."

"Well, I'd certainly hate to disappoint you." He reminded himself to move slower so she could find her footing.

Even though it'd be easier to just drag her back.

A powerful gust threw a fine spray of snow into the air, the droplets like pin pricks against his exposed skin. He turned to shield his eyes, blinking to clear his vision of Dani.

She closed her eyes as it dusted over her face, turning into the breeze. She clicked her tongue, tilted her head the other way, and clicked it again.

"What the fuck is with that clicking?" Liam grumbled. "It's annoying as all hells."

To his surprise, she smiled at him, her full pink lips framing white teeth. "Because you're so easy to be around." She rolled her shoulders. "It helps guide me, like how a bat flies at night."

"My bestiary classes weren't my best subjects." He started forward again, scanning for Katrin, but she was nowhere to be seen.

Great, so now I'm stuck with her.

Dani stopped, halfway back to camp, and pulled on her shackles to make him face her. Her gaze hovered in the space above his head, a thoughtful expression twitching her lips. "Why are you so angry?" Her tone softened. "Did you lose someone in that battle?"

For a moment, Liam returned to the silent watch atop the battlements of the border wall. Ollie's feet shuffling as he struggled to confide in Liam despite how close they'd grown through training. Then the thunk of the arrow as it sank into his flesh, and his eyes going blank in a flutter of feathers.

Liam swallowed before he could choke. "I don't owe you an explanation." He jerked her forward, and she stumbled, barely catching herself.

Dani pursed her lips, her breath coming quicker as he forced her to keep walking. "You're blinder than I am," she muttered, her tone missing its previous spark.

"Just keep walking."

Chapter 17

Matthias strode away from the largest tent, leaving Micah, Riez and Stefan to their game of cards. He spotted Liam leading Dani back towards their camp, but Katrin wasn't with them.

Damn. Was hoping to talk to her.

Leaving the border in a rush, he'd hardly had time to spend with her. After the fear of seeing the devastated medical tent and thinking her gone, he wondered at the depth of his growing attachment to her.

Someone will end up hurt if I'm not careful.

He waited for Liam at the edge of camp, noting the discontent on Dani's face.

Wonder if she told Liam anything else.

He didn't blame Liam for being untrusting and angry. The brutality of that night haunted his dreams, too. Yet, part of him wondered if Dani felt the same distaste for bloodshed.

She could have lost close ones in that fight, too.

"Hey, where's your sister?" Matthias eyed the Feyorian before focusing on the soldier.

"No clue." Liam's shoulders were tight, and he slowed only a little before he walked past Matthias, keeping Dani in tow.

"What do you mean, no clue?" The prince followed them. "Did she leave the camp?"

"I'm not her babysitter, Matthias. She can go wherever she wants. But she probably wanted to get away from me." He paused, making a face. "I think I pissed her off."

Matthias gritted his jaw. "Fantastic. You're all about making friends today, aren't you?" He glanced at Dani, who looked up.

"I never said I was perfect." Liam sighed, and his shoulders relaxed minutely. "I'm sure she'll be back soon. I'm just going to secure the prisoner in her tent."

"Have you made up your cot? There's a space for yours in the tent with Stefan." Matthias narrowed his eyes at Dani, even though he directed his question to Liam.

What does she see? I can't imagine it's all black.

"Long as it isn't with the brigade soldiers again." Liam grinned. "I don't think they like me."

"Can't imagine why." Dani's airy voice made Matthias smirk.

The prince chuckled at Liam's glare. "Make sure our *guest* has furs tonight, it's going to be even colder than the last few nights."

"I'm not a monster. Even though she isn't our *guest*." The slight tug he gave on Dani's chains seemed more gentle than his movements before. "Come on."

"Wait." Dani stood her ground.

Liam frowned. "For what?"

"Shh."

"Seriously?" He shook her chains, but Matthias gave him a steady look.

Dani closed her eyes and tilted her head, her white hair falling back behind her ear. With a slow breath, she quirked just a little further.

"What is it?" Matthias lowered his voice. "Do you hear something?"

Her cloudy eyes blinked open. "An avalanche. We're not in its path, but it's close."

Matthias stiffened. "There's a chute just east of here, looked like a common location for them."

A low rumble, like distant thunder, rippled through the camp. The whinny of the horses rose with the concerned voices of the prince's escort.

Stefan and Barim emerged from the nearby tent, Barim with

sword in hand as if he'd fight off the snow with his blade. They both relaxed when they saw Matthias, turning together towards the cloud forming to the east as snow tore down the distant terrain.

"Well, guess we're lucky today." Barim sheathed his sword and clapped Stefan on the shoulder. He gestured to the tent, pausing when he spied Liam. A mischievous smile spread beneath his beard. "Wanna join? I'm sure Stefan would love winning your coin and not just mine, for a change. Your girl will be fine without you for a few hours."

Liam scoffed, releasing Dani's chain for the first time. "Not my girl."

Dani rolled her eyes. "I can do better."

Barim let out a low laugh. "Of course you can. Ass like yours, all in leather—"

Stefan smacked Barim in the chest, pushing him into the tent as he coughed on his laughter.

"Join us later!" Barim's voice echoed from inside, still laced with humor.

Liam looked like he might be sick. He put a hand on Dani's shoulder, encouraging her forward without another word. His eyes flickered back to the tent at the sound of cards shuffling.

"Matthias!" Merissa's shout drew the prince's attention to the east. The healer raced over the open snowfield, clutching her skirts. The avalanche behind her still settled, more vapor settling across the barely visible tops of trees.

He jogged to meet her partway, searching her face. "What is it?"

"Katrin." Merissa leaned forward. "We went for a walk, but she wanted to be alone. I'm sorry. I shouldn't have left her."

Liam's face hardened. "Katrin was out there?"

Matthias's heart sped. "Show me where."

The healer took off east, and the prince followed her, ignoring Liam. Merissa stopped partway into the snowfield, a set of tracks leading farther east. "That way." She pointed. "You need to go back. Maybe you can catch her before it happens."

"No, no, no." Liam walked past Matthias, his hands against his head as they stared at the debris of the mountain, the dirty snow piled higher than either of them stood.

"Matthias, go!"

The prince shut his eyes, channeling his power into his veins. His surroundings blurred, skin heating as he pulled on the threads of time to twist them back onto themselves.

The avalanche.

Talking to Liam and Dani.

Emerging from the tent.

I can't go back far enough. This will have to do.

Matthias gasped, holding four cards as Barim groaned at Stefan's third win in a row. His mind raced to catch up, and he listened.

No rumble, yet.

He jumped up from his seat and bolted from the tent, ignoring the surprised shouts of his men. He sprinted through the snow in the direction Merissa had led him before. Pulse pounding in his ears, he found the trail from the women and followed it as fast as he could.

Merissa's tan cloak came into focus within the snowfield, and he ran towards her. She frowned, looking up at Matthias at the sound of his approach. "What's wrong?"

Matthias barreled past her. "Can't explain. Get back to camp, now!" He breathed hard, snow soaking his breeches to his knees as he ran. He wove through the collection of doomed pines along the edge of the avalanche chute. They would be gone in minutes.

Gods, how far did she go? At least she's easy to track.

The prince stepped out of the trees, searching the clear dip in the mountain terrain. It looked no more ominous than the fields, half a foot of fresh powder sloping with the rocks below.

In the distance, Katrin walked towards him. She paused, tilting her head when she noticed him. Her grey-blue cloak blended into the terrain, the fur around her hood rustling in the wind.

Matthias debated shouting, but she'd never hear so far away. He spurred his feet forward, using the path she'd made through the snow to speed his pace.

To his relief, she started moving faster towards him, calling out once she was in earshot. "What is it?"

"Come with me. The snow is unstable." Matthias reached for her hand. "We need to get back to camp."

Katrin cast a hurried glance around them. They stood in the mountain peak's shadow, and she shivered. "I just needed to get away from Liam for a bit." She pressed her pink lips into a line as she crossed her arms, but didn't move to walk with him. "He's so insufferable. I don't understand what he—"

"Katrin." Matthias tightened his grip, pulling her. "We have to go."

Thunder crackled down the mountainside. Sharp, then silent.

Too late.

"Run!" He clutched her hand, and they raced back the way he'd come, eyes locked on the trees.

We're not going to make it.

His eyes flickered at the mountain peak, and his stomach dropped out at the vision of snow and ice crashing towards them. Halting his feet, he wrapped his arms around her and knelt.

Images flashed through his mind of sheltering her in the library at the temple.

The avalanche struck them with impressive force, something rough scraping over his forehead.

Snow muffled Katrin's scream, and he lost his grip of her as they tumbled over the slope.

Matthias focused, yanking on the fabric of time.

The prince coughed, buckling forward as Katrin spoke.

"I just needed to get away from Liam for a..." Her eyes narrowed on him. "Matthias, your forehead, you're bleeding!"

He sucked in a deep breath, regaining his bearings, and looked at the mountain peak. Scanning behind her, his eyes landed on an outcropping of dark stone, a small covered area beneath it.

Worth a shot.

"I don't have time to explain. I need you to run." Matthias tugged her hand, urging his tired legs into motion again.

Katrin shook her head, but followed. "I don't—"

Thunder.

Matthias pulled on her hand, not daring to look up the slope. As the ground vibrated and the rumble grew close, they reached the high ground of the rock. He crouched, helping her hop below before following. Wrapping his arms around her, he spun them under the stone in a crouch, clenching his jaw as the avalanche hit.

Ice and debris launched over the overhang, deafening cracks encouraging him to hold Katrin tighter.

The sky became nothing but snow before darkness engulfed their hollow.

The roar subsided, leaving their frozen cave silent except for their quivering breaths.

Katrin pressed hard against his chest, gripping handfuls of his tunic beneath his cloak. She shook, but he couldn't tell if it was cold or fear. "What..." Her voice squeaked, and she swallowed. "How..." Her grip tightened, the linen pinching his skin beneath. "How did you know?"

Matthias squinted, finding her face with his hands. "Are you hurt?"

She trembled but shook her head. "If you hadn't..." Her breath gradually steadied. She pulled away from him, her cloak rustling as snow crunched beneath her movement. With her exhale, a glimmer of pale white light pulsed to life. Katrin's almond-shaped eyes were the first thing he saw as she blew gently into hands cupped in front of her. A marble-sized ball of light brightened, illuminating their snow cave.

Blue ice mixed with branches and stone surrounded them, the stone outcropping the only thing above to protect them. The space was cramped, and being able to see it sent anxious waves through Matthias's gut. He could stand, but just barely, and reach the snowy walls on either side of him.

"This isn't ideal." Matthias let out a sigh, wishing he'd had more time to come up with a better solution.

Still better than the previous outcomes.

He could try jumping back again, but without being able to go further back than the moment he found her, he saw no point. They had no other options, and saving his strength was more important.

Katrin dug a small hole into one wall, gasping when it collapsed over her hands. She attempted something smaller and nestled her little ball of light into it. Her hair had come unknotted, black locks tumbling from her hood.

Pulling off her gloves, she tucked them into her belt as she stepped to him. Her icy fingers brushed his cheek as she encouraged him to tilt his chin down, and she studied the scrape on his forehead. "It's not that bad. But I swear you didn't have it when you first started talking to me." She brushed her finger along the edge, and he winced.

The rest of his body ached, reminding him that the scrape wasn't the only damage from their previous attempt to outrun the avalanche. "That's because I didn't." His admission made him swallow, and he touched his forehead, looking at his hand as it came away with a smudge of red. Sighing, he ran his gloved fingertips over the snow trapping them.

If we dig and it collapses...

"How did you cut your forehead in the middle of talking to me? And how did you know an avalanche was coming?" Katrin sighed. "Not that I'm not grateful, but..."

Matthias shook his head and lowered his voice. "It's how my Art works." He faced her. "I can... bend time. Go backwards."

Her brow furrowed, her body stiffening for a moment. She

paused, her hands lowering from his face. "I've never heard of the Art working in that way before. Time? As in you can... see an event and then go back and undo it?"

The prince bit the inside of his lip. "Yes." The word felt heavy as it left his lips. "But it's not endless. I can only go back about a quarter of an hour, and only so many times. I went back as far as I could to get to you in time, but last time... We tried to run out of the danger and didn't make it." He motioned to his head. "Hence the blood."

Katrin stopped breathing, her eyes narrowing as she studied him.

Matthias smiled, admiring how cute she looked while focusing.

It made her frown. "What's so funny?"

"Funny? No, not funny. Nothing's funny. You just... look adorable when you're thinking."

She scowled, and it only further added to her attractiveness. "Prove it." She crossed her arms. "If your Art really works like that... Can't you get us out of here?"

Matthias's shoulders drooped. "I can't go far enough back now to change where we are. But I can still prove it." He tilted his head. "Think of something, Priestess. Anything. Hold the thought in your head for a minute before telling me."

"All right..." She chewed her bottom lip. "I've got something I've been wanting to say to you, anyway."

"Intriguing." The prince eyed her. "What is it?"

She looked down, shuffling her boot in the snow. "I've been... questioning the necessity of returning to the temples to finish my training."

Matthias watched her for another moment before shutting his eyes and channeling his power backward only a few breaths.

Katrin chewed her bottom lip. "I've got something I've been wanting to say to you, anyway."

Matthias smirked. "You're wondering if you want to return to the temples to finish your training."

Her eyes widened. "Yes. I..." She studied him again, taking a step closer. "So you really can leap through time. I mean, it makes some things make far more sense. Like how you knew about the attack on the dining tent before it happened. Why didn't you use it during the fire, though? That shelf almost paralyzed you."

The prince rolled his shoulders. "I didn't think it would actually land on me, and by the time I'd been injured, it no longer mattered. My body stays the same when I jump, so I can save others but not myself."

Her hand brushed up over his forehead again. "Like this." She tilted her head, and he nodded. "I can only imagine how useful such a skill is to the throne. No wonder you're in the position you are." Her fingers trailed to his neck. "And today you used it to save me?" She gestured with her chin towards the ice wall. "Even though now you're trapped with me, and we might die from lack of air. Or freeze to death."

"There is some irony in my choice, but I stand by it. I couldn't do nothing."

"Why? I'm just an acolyte." She shook her head, laughing at herself as she brought her arms back to herself. "One who's thinking about abandoning her duty to the gods."

Matthias lifted her chin with his index finger. "I wouldn't call taking a different path *abandoning*. You still serve, yes? You're learning from Merissa."

She pursed her lips, giving a slight nod. "I suppose. I just don't know what's right anymore." Tilting her head back, she met his eyes. "But you're still far more important than me. Why risk yourself?"

"It may have been a rash decision, but isn't it obvious?"

"Obvious?" Her brow furrowed. "No. No, it isn't."

"I'd obviously rather be buried in an avalanche with you than sitting at camp worried you could be dead." Matthias huffed. "I *care* about you."

Her body trembled, and she closed her eyes. "Matthias." She

whispered his name, and it sent a shiver down his spine. "I don't... I'm not sure what to say. I..."

Conflicting emotions warred in his gut. On one hand, her lack of knowledge of his identity made his interactions with her more genuine, yet it meant the opposite for her. "Even if we die here, I won't regret it." He cupped her face and lifted her gaze again. "Tell me you feel something, too."

Her dark eyes shimmered with a glassiness in the dim light. "I... feel it, too," she whispered. "I just don't understand it all yet."

"Neither do I. The last thing I want is to make your life more complicated, but if it's all right with you, I'd like to kiss you."

She tensed, but her lips parted ever so slightly. Reaching for him again, she ran her hand beneath his cloak, touching the bare skin of his neck. Her eyes flickered to his lips as she stepped closer and lifted her chin in a faint nod.

Matthias's heart skipped a beat, and he met her mouth with his. With his eyes closed, he could have been standing anywhere in Pantracia. His hands slid around her, one tangling in the back of her hair as he pulled her against him.

She whimpered against his lips, sending a hum through him. The kiss renewed with additional pressure she encouraged, lifting to her tiptoes to seek better access.

The prince's world blurred, and he tilted his head to kiss her again before slowly drawing away. "I've never kissed a priestess before." He brushed his nose against her heated cheek, trailing his mouth down near her neck as he enjoyed her flowery scent.

She sucked in a breath, a soft moan rumbling near his ear. "I'm not a priestess." Her breathy voice only further encouraged him to trace a circle with his tongue. She gasped, her grip tightening around his waist. "I've never..." She tilted her head and brushed back her hood. "That feels so good."

Matthias hummed against her skin and kissed beneath her earlobe. His touch ventured down her side, finding her lower back. "You've never what, Priestess?"

Her breath hitched as she pressed against him. Her nails bit through his tunic, trailing lines down his back. "Kissed." It came out with a needy breath, and her lips closed in a distracted kiss beneath his jaw.

His chest rumbled, desire threatening to distract him from her confession. Pulling back, he met her eyes. "I don't want to confuse you." He chewed his lip. "Well... Maybe I do, a little, but—"

Katrin twisted her fingers in his hair and pulled his mouth back to hers. The movement of her lips encouraged more from him, their tongues meeting in a flurry.

Could have fooled me with the inexperience.

Matthias tightened his hold in her hair, his heart thudding against his ribs with new vigor.

She pulled her mouth away, as if coming to her senses, and inhaled sharply. Her grip around him remained, her warm breath mingling with his as she pressed her forehead to his. "We'll run out of air faster if you keep raising my heart rate like this."

Matthias chuckled. "My apologies. Though, it would be a worthy cause."

She poked his chest with a smile. "A pleasant distraction from imminent doom." She looked over his shoulder at the snow again, letting her head collapse against his shoulder as she embraced him. "Thank you for coming for me."

He rested his chin on top of her head. "I will every time."

Her lips stretched into a smile against his skin. "Digging our way out is unlikely, right? I hope you might forgive me for selfishly hoping for another day with you."

Matthias swallowed and nodded. "Digging from below can cause a cave in. But someone will find us. We'll have another day, don't worry."

A chill soaked through his cloak, and she shivered against him again, teeth rattling.

Assuming we don't freeze.

Chapter 18

"They will die because of your foolish pride!" Dani jerked on her chains, now secured to a center post in a tent.

He needs to let me find her.

"A search team is already out looking for them. It's possible they weren't even in the avalanche's path." Liam ground his teeth, radiating nervous energy.

"Your other healer said they were. If they're buried, you won't find them in time."

"And what exactly are you proposing to do to help?"

"Unchain me." Dani strained on the cuffs and the metal bit into her wrists. "I can find them better than anyone else here."

The soldier moved closer to her in the dim tent, and his presence hovered in the air directly in front of her. "How?"

"With my nose, genius. Just let me try. Don't you want your sister to live?" She raised onto her knees, inching closer to Liam. The blur of his form shifted minutely at her advance. "Let me save them."

"How do I know you won't run the second I uncuff you?"

"You don't." Dani huffed. "It's called trust. Maybe not your trust in me, but your trust in your sister's opinion of me. Trust that I give a damn what happens to her, which I do."

"A Feyorian caring about an Isalican." He scoffed. "Hard to believe."

"How about a woman caring for her friend? She saved me first."

He stiffened. "Saved you?"

Dani yanked on her sleeve where the arrow had already torn the leather and revealed the smooth scar left behind from the arrow. "I was hit that night at the border. Your sister healed me, even after she saw the *Isalican* arrowhead in my flesh."

"That little idiot." Liam groaned, pacing to the back of the tent. "What was she thinking? Healing the enemy..."

"Gods, you're so closed minded you can't even see that I'm not your enemy. I'm trying to help you save your sister's life and all you can focus on is where I was born!"

"Damn it." His scent drifted to the other side of the tent as he moved to the entrance. He hesitated there, before the canvas billowed into place behind his exit.

Dani growled and threw herself backward, kicking the tent post. She pressed her boots on it as hard as she could, yelling as the metal cut into her hands.

A breeze rushed into the tent as the flap opened again, followed by Liam's familiar footfalls.

"I'm going to have a crossbow on you the whole time, you understand?" The mechanics of the device clicked as he dropped it to the canvased floor. More metal jingled as he grabbed her wrists and inserted the key. "So don't do anything stupid."

Dani stiffened as he unlocked the cuffs, shutting her eyes and cringing at the sound. The weight fell from her wrists for the first time in days, and she rubbed her raw skin, rising to her feet. Shuddering, she motioned with one hand. "Take me to where they were last."

Leading her by the elbow, the soldier retrieved his weapon and took her outside.

The chill blast of the mountain winds carried the scent of destruction with it. Exposed dirt and broken pines. Upturned roots and crushed ice.

Light shone between hazy clouds, dappling her vision with bright spots.

"Move a little faster, would you?" Dani shoved him with her elbow. "I can keep up to your clumsy ass."

He ground his teeth again, a slight growl rising in his chest as he quickened his pace. Other members of the prince's escort had already gathered, and she recognized the voice as one of the prince's elite gave orders to the crowd.

"Liam, what the hells is she doing out here?" Riez.

Katrin had told her the voice belonged to the soldier, but she'd never formally met him.

"She claims she can help." He let go of her, and the mechanism of the crossbow clicked as he loaded it.

"Under threat of death." Dani threw her hands up in the air.

"Under threat of precaution," Liam grumbled. "Don't try to escape, and I won't have anything to shoot at."

"Where are their tracks?" Dani ignored the anger heating her veins.

Liam nudged her forward, and the voices of the other search parties faded. "It's a little more trampled, but Merissa said they were straight..." He grabbed her wrist, lifting her hand to point east toward the mountains. "That way."

"We should get away from other people." Dani trudged east ahead of Liam, feeling the breaks in the snow where others must have stepped.

"Why? So they won't see you take off and help me catch you again?"

"More so that they don't see you freak out in a moment." She glanced back in his direction. "Wouldn't want to ruin your reputation."

He snorted. "Woman, you're freaky enough on your own."

Dani huffed. "And you said you weren't afraid of me."

The leather of his tunic creaked as he lifted the crossbow. "Well, get to it. Whatever you can do to help find them."

She stiffened, halting and facing him. "Look, this will not be what you expect. Just don't shoot me, all right?"

"All right..." He elongated the word and shuffled back as if stabilizing his stance.

"Promise?"

"No."

Dani frowned. "You're an ass."

He chuckled. "My sister makes sure I remember that every day. Now, I'd like to hear her say it again tomorrow, if you don't mind."

Closing her eyes, she tilted her head back. Warmth cascaded through her veins and she let it fuel her change. Leathers melded into skin, fur reshaping over her body until her paws met the snow. Her white tail flicked behind her, the scents of the forest springing to heightened life.

"What the fuck..." Liam's teal scent danced bright around him, lingering on what he touched and where he walked. Wafts of fear mingled with it, now.

The surrounding snowfield solidified in her mind, each scent and sound crafting the image in her head, forming the vision she maintained while a panther.

Liam still held the crossbow, but it'd lowered slightly in his surprise, the aim too low to catch her if he pulled the trigger.

Dani waited. She lifted her head and let out a purring sound before taking a tentative step towards him.

He didn't retreat, but the crossbow shifted in his grip, and she halted. "Adds a little more to the freak factor." He shook his head, blurring his scent in the air. "Go. Find them."

Turning from him, she breathed deeply, picking up Katrin's scent still clinging to the snow and another she assumed was Matthias. Ahead, the avalanche had left a steep hill of ice and debris, consuming the trail. Leaping along the ridge, she carefully navigated up the slope, her claws digging into the soft wood of a partially fallen tree.

Liam scrambled behind her, abandoning his grip on the crossbow to climb to the top of the condensed snow.

At least he hasn't shot me, yet.

Other people searching spoke in the distance, too far away to see her.

Dani bounded over the terrain, her tail balancing her as she pranced over a shattered log. Sniffing the snow, her whiskers tickled on the ice, and she caught the remnants of Katrin's scent.

They were near here.

Glancing back at Liam to ensure he still followed, she carried on at a slower pace. Every time she found her friend's scent, she dug a foot into the snow to see if the scent grew stronger. Each time, it vanished, and she moved on.

Liam heaved for breath, loudly stumbling up behind her. "Any luck?"

She swung her maw towards him and tilted her head, letting out a quiet chuff.

And I answer you, how?

"Right." Liam rolled his shoulders. "You... probably can't talk." He looked around, scanning the uneven terrain. "Well, don't let me distract you." He bobbed his chin to encourage her to keep going.

Dani eyed where the wooden crossbow hung at his back.

Ah, progress.

She leapt away, but the snow beneath her disappeared as she landed. Her paws scrambled for the edge, but she missed and fell, yeowling before landing on her feet ten feet beneath the surface. The narrow opening didn't give her adequate space to jump, and snow crumbled around her feet.

If I jump, the bottom might collapse again.

Dani growled and breathed in her power, returning to her human form. She looked up, but could only see brightness. "Liam?"

A slight shadow blocked the sky, his head peeking over. "That was rather clumsy of you." His voice sounded lighter than she'd heard before. "I thought snow panthers were graceful."

"I'd like to see you fall this far and land on your feet." Dani turned to the side of the hole closest to him. "Help me up." She reached, touching the snow.

"I've heard rumors about your kind, but hoped they weren't real." A bit of snow fell from the edge of the hole as he crouched.

Dani's heart sank.

He wouldn't leave me here, would he?

"What I *am* is the only one who can find your sister." Her boot slid sideways as snow compacted beneath her. It made her heart jump, and she wondered if another air pocket hid under her.

"You're a *deruta* or whatever." He waved his hand in the air over the hole, casting shadows over her face. "A Feyorian shape-shifter."

"Dtrüa." Dani rolled the 't' into the 'r'. "At least say it right."

"Derua."

Closer.

His hand closed around her wrist, and she let out a breath of relief as he lifted her.

Once out of the hole, she crawled away from him. "Can't shoot me if you're not holding your crossbow, you know."

"I know." He sounded annoyed again as he pushed to his feet, brushing snow off his tunic and breeches. "You also probably can't find Katrin while you're a human... so..."

Dani sighed, frowning. She closed her eyes and sparked her Art again, retaking her panther shape.

Insufferable asshat...

Without waiting for him, she maneuvered around the pit and ventured down the slope, looking for more traces of Katrin. A swirl of sunny yellow scent hovered near the snow further down the chute, and Dani leapt towards it. Extending her claws, she dug down before pausing. Katrin's scent grew stronger, and her heart jumped.

She's here.

Dani hurried, sending clumps of snow, ice, and dirt flying behind her.

Beside her, Liam dropped to his knees and helped, rolling larger stones out of the way as they worked together.

Chapter 19

Questions flooded Katrin's mind, despite how good Matthias's arms felt around her. She'd crawled into his lap, burying her face against the warmth of his chest. The memory of his lips on hers still tingled, an odd sensation she'd never expected. Lifting her fingers to touch her mouth, she wondered how they'd known what to do. How kissing him had come so naturally, despite everything she'd sworn to within the temple.

My pledge to the gods should come before a man.

Matthias stroked her hair, his chin on top of her head. His beard tickled her scalp, and he shivered.

Please let them find us.

The light she'd conjured had faded at her decision to conserve energy, though the dim glow still revealed the claustrophobic walls. She'd never had a problem with small spaces before, but this one felt impossibly tight. The only comfort remained in the steadiness of him and the beat of his heart in her ear.

She focused on it, listening to each thrum. The silence of the pocket in the avalanche lulled her eyes closed. Squeezing him again, she nuzzled closer, listening to the rustle of their cloaks brushing against each other.

When she settled, the sound continued.

That's odd.

Matthias's head lifted from hers. "Do you hear that?"

She held her breath, moving her head from the sound of his heart. More rustling, crackling. It filled the space, but she looked up, squinting at the dark ceiling. "Someone's digging." Her stomach jumped in hope, forcing herself away from Matthias to stand.

He rose to his feet, pulling Katrin away from the sound as snow fell in clumps from the spot. A breath later, sunlight burst into the cave.

Katrin opened her mouth to speak, but a giant white paw reached through the hole, claws scraping at the snow to make a bigger opening.

Matthias tugged her back again, stepping in front of her as she squeaked in surprise. "What the..."

The snow beneath the big cat gave way and a pure white panther landed on the ground in front of them.

Katrin's back hit the wall of snow as Matthias backed her up, pulling a knife from his belt.

"Matthias? Kat?" Liam's voice drew her gaze back up to the hole, and her brother leaned to peer through the opening, his tunic and cloak soaked through. When his eyes met hers, his shoulders slumped with a sigh.

Why is he...

Matthias lowered his knife, his brow furrowing.

The snow cat's form shifted, blurring in a haze of fur as shoulders rose higher and a face emerged over fur-laden shoulders.

Dani smiled, and Matthias gaped.

"So... Dani's a derua." Liam grinned at Matthias before he held out a hand to him, crouched in the long snow tunnel they'd dug.

The Feyorian scowled. "Stop saying it if you can't put the effort in to say it right."

Matthias glanced at Katrin. "Look, they're getting along." He pushed Katrin towards her brother's hand.

She frowned at her brother as he hoisted her up. She glanced back to make sure Matthias was directly behind her as she scrambled through the tunnel and over the edge of the snow. Looking up, she blinked at the bright blue sky and let out a breath.

Someone shouted from down the slope, and she wrapped her arms around herself despite the soaked clothes as she shivered.

Matthias helped Dani out of the cavern. "Thank you. I'd rather not imagine how that would've ended without your aid."

Katrin stepped into her new friend, pulling her into a tight hug before she could react. She opened her eyes over Dani's shoulder and met Matthias's. It sent a rumble through her, but she buried it as she rubbed her cheek against Dani's dry furs.

Liam clapped a hand on Matthias's shoulder. "Looks like you took a bit of a bump there." He gestured to his own forehead. "But I'm glad you're both safe. We should get back to camp to get you both warmed up."

Matthias nodded. "A fire sounds pretty good right about now."

When Katrin released Dani, the Feyorian faced Liam and held her wrists out. "The end of my freedom, I assume."

Her brother frowned, giving a curt nod. He reached back into a pocket of his cloak and produced a pair of cuffs.

"What do you see when you're a panther?" Katrin sat next to Dani by the fire, a woolen blanket over her shoulders.

Dani stared at the flames, wind brushing her hair to the side and ruffling the fur on her pelt. "Scents, mostly. I see light... a bit more than as a human. Cats' eyes are more efficient, so it's almost like being able to see. Everything has a smell, though, and they appear in different colors in my vision."

"Do you miss that when you're a human?"

Dani paused, rolling her lips together. "Yes, though if I focus, I still see the scents in this form. But I'm comfortable with this, too." She twisted her wrist, shuffling the cuffs away from her hands. Cuts marred her skin, dried blood on the metal. "Most of this, anyway."

"Did Liam do that to you?" Katrin touched the superficial wound and Dani twitched.

"No. That was my fault."

"Want me to..."

"No." Dani's eyes glistened, and she closed them.

Katrin nodded, turning back to the fire. She stared through the top of the flames, watching Liam as he took a whetstone to his sword. Matthias sat beside him, talking quietly with the prince.

He's a personal guard and friend of the prince... and I kissed him.

She shrugged beneath the heavy wool and winced at how foolish she'd been. Looking at Dani and the shimmer of tears in her eyes, she suddenly felt even more so for focusing on herself.

"I'm sorry," she whispered, reaching out from beneath the blanket to take Dani's hand. She tightened her grip, making Dani look at her. "I'm so sorry for everything you're going through."

Stars reflected in the Feyorian's glassy eyes. "I did this to myself. Tallos warned me what would happen if I..." She gulped. "I can never go home."

"Then this will be your new home. I know it doesn't seem like it right now, but..." Katrin shifted to meet her blank gaze. "I won't let anything happen to you. Liam will come around and realize you're really no different from any of us."

"I don't need your brother's approval." Dani shook her head. "I know he matters to you, but I hope you don't expect him to ever matter to me."

"Of course not. That's not what I meant. Just... he'll stop making you feel so unwelcome. Eventually..."

Dani huffed what sounded like a laugh meant to cover a sob. "I'm not welcome here. This isn't my home. These aren't my people. I will never belong here."

"You belong with me." Katrin lifted the blanket, plopping it around her friend's shoulder to pull her closer. She pressed her forehead against Dani's temple, hugging her tight. "I hope I'm not the only one, but I know you're supposed to be here with me. I can feel it."

She'd dreamt of Dani several times since they'd met, and every nerve within her pointed her back to the Dtrüa over and over again. And with the new truth about Dani's animal form, the dream of the goddess, the panther, and Matthias made more sense. As did the panther tooth necklace she'd observed around Dani's neck.

I was meant to find her.

The bond had formed so rapidly, and she'd had so little time to process it. She felt as if she couldn't exist without speaking to Dani every day. Without confiding in her.

Dani leaned her head on Katrin's shoulder. "I'm here for you. I would've run today, otherwise."

Katrin rubbed her hand along Dani's back, feeling the ridges of her leather tunic against her palm. "Who's Tallos? Unless talking about him is too much."

"Tallos is my betrothed." Dani's tone lacked emotion.

Sorrow for Dani's additional loss filled Katrin, and she squeezed Dani harder.

The Dtrüa remained rigid, a thoughtful look on her face. She played with the thin braided leather band around her thumb.

Maybe she thought she knew exactly where her life was going before, and now with all this...

"Do you regret running from the battle?"

Dani's gaze darted towards her, hovering near her face. "No. I cannot be the person I was supposed to be, even if it changes the way Tallos sees me."

Katrin toyed with a strand of Dani's hair. "Do you love him?"

"Of course." Dani paused. "I depended on him for everything. He taught me everything. I had no friends, just him."

Katrin frowned. "But that's not what I meant. Love is a choice." She tucked the white lock behind Dani's ear. "But betrothed... Whose choice was that?"

"His. He chose me." Dani looked at the fire. "He could've had anyone. I was lucky."

Katrin glanced, too, as Liam slid his sword into its sheath.

He looked up, as if able to tell he was being watched, and saw Dani first. A frown deepened on his face, but then he caught Katrin's scowl. Rolling his eyes, he stuck his tongue out at his sister.

Katrin huffed, returning the expression.

"What's happening?" The corner of Dani's mouth twitched as if she already suspected.

"Just my stupid brother. Being a child again..." Katrin waved her hand in his direction, and he laughed, drawing Matthias's attention. Catching his eye, everything within her stiffened, and the flutter in her stomach returned.

Why does just a look from him do that?

Katrin averted her gaze to the ground, trying to get her emotions under control. "With Tallos..." She chewed her lip, searching for the right words. "Did he make you feel vulnerable, yet safe at the same time? Like... a whirlwind in your stomach?"

Dani's chains clinked as she adjusted her hands and lifted her head off Katrin's shoulder. "I'm only safe with him, and, until I ran away, I didn't think I could exist without him. Without him, I'm nothing. Is that what you mean?"

"No, not like that." Katrin brought her leg up beneath her so she could turn to look at Dani, removing the distraction of Matthias from her vision. Taking her friend's hands, she held them between them. "That's different, that's a feeling from not having a choice. Someone else never defines your worth." She pursed her lips, trying to think of the proper question. "Do you miss him? What do you think it would be like if you saw him again?"

Dani straightened, her breaths coming quicker. "Do you think he's here? He'd be so angry with me." The muscles in her jaw flexed, and her eyelashes fluttered. "Gods, if he found out I've been helping Isalicans..."

Katrin poked Dani in the side. "That doesn't sound like love to me. That sounds like possession." She stroked Dani's white hair behind her ear again, loving the way the firelight reflected off it. So much more interesting than her plain black hair. "You don't belong to anyone but yourself, Dani. And you running away from that fight and walking into that border camp with me... that was *your* choice. And you have a choice now, even if it doesn't feel like it." She leaned in close, whispering. "You know I can get the keys to your shackles if you really wanted..."

Dani bowed her head. "Then I'd have to run. You're the only person here who understands me. I don't want to leave you... but thank you." The woman smiled, and it touched her eyes. "Does someone give you a whirlwind in your stomach? A certain guard seems pretty protective of you..."

Her cheeks heated, her eyes darting to Matthias as he laughed at something the prince said. A flutter returned in her stomach, but she cleared her throat and looked at Dani. "We kissed." It blurted out before she could control the instinct to say it.

The Dtrüa's eyebrows rose. "In the cave?"

"Yes, he asked, and I just... I kissed him back, and gods..." She shook her head, resisting the temptation to touch her own lips. "But... We both thought we might die, so how do I know if it was real?"

Dani smirked. "You'd have to be blind *and* deaf to miss how that man sees you. This isn't the first time he's protected you. You tell me, was it real for you?"

She hesitated, glancing up to look at him again through the dancing fire.

All I can think about now is kissing him. Feeling... that again.

Her chest tightened, and her lips buzzed with the desire. "I'm afraid I'm making a mistake."

Dani stared at the fire. "By loving Matthias?"

Katrin twitched. "Loving Matthias? I don't know yet if that's what this is..." She refused to let her head turn towards him at the inclination.

He threatens every possibility of logical thought just with his stupid... handsome... face.

Huffing, Dani tilted her head. "Whirlwinds in your stomach... and I can hear your heart racing. Does he make you feel vulnerable and safe at the same time? Do you miss him when he isn't close?"

She winced, but couldn't help the smile. "That's not fair..." Her amusement shone through, but the doubt in her doubled. "But yes, I suppose that's what I'm afraid of. If I end up loving him, or any man, won't it cheapen the love I've already dedicated to my service of the temples?"

Running her finger over the chain connecting her wrists, Dani hummed. "When you love your mother, does it cheapen your love for your father? What about your children? Is it impossible to love them the same? Do we only have a finite amount of love to give away, or is it boundless? I know little about love, but I don't think it's measurable like that. If anything, the more you love... maybe it increases the more you *can* love."

A smile crept across Katrin's lips, despite trying to hold it in. "It sounds to me like you understand love pretty well." She nuzzled against Dani's shoulder, the fur tickling her cheek. "Priests aren't required to remain pledged only to the gods, but it's certainly what they encourage." She sucked in a breath, pitching her voice to impersonate Mistress Felhort, the priestess who'd first trained her. "*Boys are distractions. And to fall to one's baser desires is an affront to the gods.*"

Dani made a face. "Somehow I think the gods have bigger problems with this world than two people falling in love." Her smile vanished after she spoke, and she looked away.

"Maybe." Katrin studied the shift in her friend's features. "Do you want to talk about whatever you're thinking about?"

"Another time, maybe."

Katrin frowned, placing her chin on Dani's shoulder and pushing down. "Do you want to go back to the tent? I can sneak the key away and at least undo those for a bit?"

Dani's shoulders drooped. "Liam would be upset with you. He really hates me, not that I blame him."

Katrin blew a breath between her teeth, waving her hand. "You don't deserve the suspicion he has, but it'll get better." Poking Dani in the side again, she smirked. "I had hoped he was getting his head out of his ass when I saw you without cuffs today. That's a step in the right direction, isn't it?"

Turning her hand over, Dani flexed her fingers. "I got trapped in an air pocket under the snow while looking for you. He helped me out of the hole, but I wasn't wearing gloves."

"See, more progress! But why does it matter that you weren't wearing gloves?"

"Other men aren't allowed to touch my skin. Tallos would hurt him. Liam might be an ass, but he doesn't deserve *that*. Tallos could rip him apart in his animal form."

"Well, I haven't met Tallos, but so far I don't like him. Threats to my brother notwithstanding." She rubbed her chin against Dani's shoulder again. "He's a Dtrüa, too, then? Is he a panther like you?"

Dani shook her head. "He's a bear. But it's not his fault. He's just protective."

"Seems a little extreme to me. Not allowing other men to even just touch your *skin?*"

"I'm *his*," Dani hissed under her breath.

"You're *yours*. Only you get to decide who can touch you."

She's been so controlled until now, she doesn't even know how to be her own person.

Katrin jumped to her feet, pulling the blanket back into place as it almost fell onto the stones around the fire. With a smile, she held her hand out to Dani. "Come with me." She looked from Dani's clenched hand to her own, then laughed at herself as she remembered Dani couldn't see. "I'm holding my hand out to you right now. You should take it."

Dani paused, a hint of a smile on her lips. She lifted her hand, reaching, but missed Katrin's. "You might need to be more specific where your hand is."

Stepping forward, Katrin seized her hand and entangled their fingers as she pulled Dani from where they'd sat together. "I'm getting too warm here, anyway. Besides, I want you to tell me more about the Dtrüa."

"Where are we going?" Dani stepped closer to Katrin, gripping her hand tight.

"I think I saw the cook stowing some cookies in the supply tent earlier."

"Cookies?" Dani tilted her head.

"Oh, don't tell me you don't know what cookies are!" Katrin bumped Dani with her hip. "Sweet little round things, made with dough and ginger spice? At least sometimes."

The Dtrüa shrugged, clicking her tongue. "Like bread?"

Katrin shook her head, taking Dani's hands in hers as she skipped ahead. Walking backward, she led them towards the supply tent. "I am about to completely change your world."

Chapter 20

Shadows loomed through the streets despite it being midday. Liam had expected Undertown to be dark, but not so beautiful.

Deep within a mountainside cave, the dark stone and wooden structures clung to the rocky slope and walls like lichen. Their windows glowed from within, but each wall glittered with a kaleidoscope of pale gold, reflecting the flowing aqueducts and channels zigzagging along the streets.

The enchanted water originated from the temple at the city center where practitioners infused light into the liquid. It glimmered off the horses as people parted to make way for the prince and his entourage.

Micah, Matthias, and Riez rode in front, with Liam, Barim, and Stefan behind.

Katrin tugged on a strand of Liam's hair from her spot behind him, and he pulled back on his horse's reins.

"Ow. Watch it."

"You're going the wrong way. The temple is down that street!" Katrin pointed away from the main road, towards the market district. "Merissa said to take a left past the clothiers, and then a right at the floral shop."

Liam batted her hand. "When I volunteered to take you to the temple to check in, I didn't think you'd be so abusive."

"It's important, Liam. I'm an acolyte, I have to..."

"Yes, yes, I understand." He gave a quick nod to Barim, who'd glanced back at the commotion, and steered their shared mount away from the royal escort. They gained the interested glances of the crowd, the glow of the partially frozen channels at their feet creating sinister lighting on their faces.

But these are our people, it's just a trick of the light.

A jubilant child tugged on his mother's skirts, shouting and pointing at Micah as he posed as the prince.

His sister actively avoided Matthias, while also watching him intently any time it was unavoidable. Since finding them together in the avalanche, Liam couldn't deny the sense that something far greater had occurred between her and the prince. Though both remained tight-lipped about it.

Instead of dwelling, Liam focused on Dani with more interest. The discovery of her ability in the Art only made him more cautious, more suspicious.

She could transform at any moment and take my head off my shoulders. Or the prince's...

Yet, she hadn't, and the cuffs likely played a role in it. Just another reason for him to make sure they remained firmly in place at all hours.

"Stop!" Katrin pinched his sides, and he cried out in irritation, batting her hand again. She didn't wait for the horse to stop fully before slipping from the saddle behind him. "I need to get some flowers. For the altars."

He'd been so lost in his thoughts, he hadn't realized they'd made it so far already.

The glittering shape of the gold and white temple stood at the end of the roadway. Stalagmites around its base framed the curved steps leading to the front doors. Depictions of the gods and their stories rimmed with gold seemed to move in the caustics of the moat that flowed along the pathway and the structure.

He whistled, the low sound of appreciation dissipating among the growing commotion of the main avenue echoing back from the cave ceiling far above.

His horse bucked its head, and Liam patted its neck. "I know, she annoys me too. But... little sisters..." Dismounting, he tried to spot the knot of Katrin's black hair as she vanished among rows of flowers.

The sweet scent didn't match his expectation of Undertown.

Sighing, he moved to shower his horse with affection rather than bother chasing her.

How much trouble could she get into in a flower shop?

Even as he thought it, his stomach twisted, knowing with certainty now there would be trouble.

"Do you think Aedonai would like pink or yellow roses better?" Katrin called from somewhere invisible.

"She's a goddess. I doubt she cares much about roses."

"You're right, I should go with daffodils."

He snorted, glancing up at the sound of steel-plated boots approaching. A pair of city guards had rounded the corner opposite of the temple, and the horse blocking the middle of the street caused them both to pause.

"Son, you can't just..." The guard's grey mustache twitched as his eyes fell to the insignia on Liam's shoulder. He quickly adjusted, bringing his fist to his chest in salute, his companion doing the same. "Apologies, sir. No disrespect."

Still not used to that.

Liam shook his head, tugging his horse's reins to move out of the way, closer to the floral stall. "No apologies necessary..." He eyed the guard's insignia. "Corporal."

A week ago, he would have been higher ranking than me.

"So rumor's right then, the prince is back for a visit. Been a while, but I don't remember you, and I thought I knew all the crown elite."

"I'm new." Liam controlled the discomfort in his voice. "But pretty sure the others are probably the same."

"Micah still his spitting image?" The corporal gave an apologetic glance to his companion, but then focused on Liam.

"Not sure what you..."

"Don't worry, sir, I know the truth of it already from his last visit. Besides, it's not exactly uncommon for a royal to have a double for public occasions, especially this close to the border. The king used to do the same."

Liam stiffened, glancing behind him, but couldn't see Katrin. "All the same, probably best if I don't say. I'm sure you understand..." He gave a conspiratorial smirk.

The guard winked and nodded. "Certainly, sir. Hope to see you tonight at the festivities then. Apologies for disturbing you."

Liam shook his head again and watched as the guards walked away, his stomach calming.

Maybe she didn't...

"Who's Micah? The prince uses a stand in? Why wasn't he with us?" Katrin pulled on Liam's arm to make her brother face her.

"Uhh..." Liam swallowed. "Micah?"

Katrin narrowed her eyes. "Liam..."

Fuck.

"Look, Katy girl. I don't know what that guy was talking about."

"But you know the prince uses a double?"

"I mean, sure? Don't most royals do that in situations like this? But I—"

Katrin held up a hand, her face paling. "Are you saying the prince I know *is* the double?"

Liam tensed, unable to control every instinct in his body. "No, I'm—"

"Don't lie to me, Liam Denethir Talansiet." The rage of his mother echoed in Katrin's bright eyes.

"I wouldn't! I'm not! Micah isn't—"

"So you know Micah."

"I—"

"And he's the spitting image of the prince, which means that whichever member of the prince's escort looks like Micah is..." The rest of her color left her face, and she touched her bottom lip. "No..."

"Katrin." Liam grabbed her shoulders. "Listen. I wanted... He wanted..."

She shook her head, wielding the collection of daffodils and lashed at him with them. "You've known the entire time?" She beat him again, the petals exploding with the sweet scent over his head.

"Whoa, hey, I—"

"I can't believe you kept this from me. That he kept this..." Her cheeks turned bright pink as she froze and touched her mouth. "Oh gods. Matthias is the..."

"Katy girl, take a deep breath." Liam grabbed her shoulders again, but she'd gone rigid, still clutching the broken stems of the flowers. "He's just a man."

Her gaze wandered somewhere behind him, and she shook her head wildly. "He's more than just that to me, don't you see?" She sucked in a shaky breath, turning to the temple. "I need... time alone."

Liam squeezed her upper arms. "I'm not leaving you right now."

"Go away, Liam." Her voice took on a harder edge as she thrust the broken flowers into his chest. "Your lying face isn't what I need to see right now."

He winced. "Kat... Try to understand..."

She shoved him again. "Just go." Twisting from his grasp, she spun towards the temple and stormed off. The pale yellow light flickered on the daffodil petals as they fell from her cloak along the path like gold leaves.

"Damn it." Liam threw the flowers down, stomping on them. "Matthias is going to kill me... Katrin is going to..." He tugged his hair, starting as the flower merchant loudly cleared his throat.

The man's grey eyebrows furrowed as he looked down at the mess of his flowers and held out his hand without a word.

Shaking his head, Liam dug a few iron marks from his money pouch and dropped them into the waiting palm. "Sorry about the mess," he muttered, turning to take his horse's reins.

The temple loomed, his sister gone somewhere within. Chasing her into the temple seemed like a worse idea than lying to her in the first place.

Right now, I need to focus on remaining in Matthias's good graces.

She's family, she'll forgive me... eventually.

As he mounted, Liam racked his brain to find something, anything, that could help him in his plight. In his frustration, one face continued to appear in his mind.

The Feyorian. Maybe if I...

Tapping his heels against his horse, he clicked his tongue to encourage it forward. Another image of Dani and her clicking habit popped into his head. The way her mouth and lips moved with the action. It stoked the growing fire within him.

He cantered back through the market and hurried down the main avenue to the city's barracks. The wagons were gone, likely continued to wherever the prince actually stayed in the city, but Dani's carriage had stopped in front of the barracks' portcullis.

A pair of the prince's brigade guided her to the entrance, her white hair standing out in the dim city.

As he approached, dodging the curious citizens as they gathered in the road, he planned what would come next.

She's keeping a secret, and I'm gonna make her talk.

Chapter 21

Matthias reread the note from his father. "I should have seen this coming." He sighed, lowering it and tossing it onto the table that stood between him and his elite guards.

Micah lounged across the entirety of an elaborately embroidered couch he'd pulled up to the table, while Barim and Riez sat in high-backed armchairs near the low burning hearth. They'd stopped only briefly at the barracks before proceeding to the royal mansion closer to the temple.

The only ones missing were Stefan, who'd gone to liaise with a representative of the barracks regarding their chambers elsewhere in the mansion, and Liam, who had escorted Katrin to the temple. The multi-roomed chambers reserved for the prince ended up being their meeting room in the meantime.

"You made the mistake of telling him about the attempt on your life, didn't you?" Micah smirked, pouring whisky into a glass. "Your adventurous days are over, my friend."

The prince scowled. "I don't know why you think that's funny, considering it means yours are, too."

Micah paused, making a face before righting the bottle. "You're right. We need to fix this."

Barim laughed, smoothing a hand over his beard. "Where is the wedding?"

"Lyon." Matthias sank into his seat, catching a glass Micah slid across the table. "My father and brother will meet us there."

How am I supposed to wed a stranger now?

When he'd agreed to the arranged marriage between himself and Ziona's princess, he'd been putting the country's needs first. With no relationship in sight, the choice had been easy.

There still isn't one in sight, either. Katrin's been avoiding me since I kissed her.

The door to their meeting room opened, and Stefan poked his head in. "Our rooms are ready, and dinner is being served in the mess hall." The man hardly spoke, so each time he did, the raspy tenor tone surprised Matthias.

Riez's chair ground out from under the table. "Don't gotta tell me twice." He and Barim glanced at Matthias and Micah. "You ready to go?"

Matthias shook his head, eyeing his closest friend. "I'd like to talk with you, first."

"You got it." Micah waved the others off. "We'll join you later."

Barim cast a confused glance at Micah, but then followed Riez's shove to the door. It clicked shut behind them, and Matthias eyed the glass of whisky in his hand.

"More business, I assume?" Micah lounged back into the sofa he'd claimed for himself. He smiled broadly beneath his beard, downing the last drops of his drink.

"Actually..."

"This is about Katrin." He rocked the empty glass on his knee.

The prince cringed. "I don't think I'll be using you as a stand in for our time here. I'd like to tell her."

Micah hesitated, growing still. "You sure that's a good idea? You just got a summons to your own wedding. The poor girl is confused enough as it is. This..." He gestured around the lavishly decorated room, sporting cerulean wall hangings and his family's crest. "This is going to just make it worse, isn't it?"

"It might." The prince groaned and rubbed his temple. "But I can't go get married to someone I don't know unless I know with certainty it wouldn't have happened with anyone else."

"You're talking about an acolyte, Matthias." Micah leaned

forward. "You're the crown prince of Isalica. It wouldn't happen. Not like this..."

Matthias sipped from his glass before putting it down. "I may have kissed her."

Micah groaned, throwing his head back onto the couch. He touched his brow as he shook his head. "That explains why you've both been so weird since the avalanche. Assuming that's when it was..." He sighed as he sat forward, putting his glass aside and leaning over his knees. "Matthias, you know I'm not one for telling you what to do... but if you call off this wedding with Ziona, there's going to be a lot more damage than one confused acolyte. The war..."

"I know, I know." Matthias sucked in a deep breath. "But... Ziona may settle for a different prince."

"That's a hell of an ask."

"Believe me, I know. And it might not even matter. I think Katrin regrets it, anyway. It will probably all be over the next time we're alone, so I may as well tell her the whole truth. She already knows about my power, and this way... she can reject me for me at least."

Micah buried his face in his hands, raking at his beard. "She knows the details now?" He stretched his jaw while he shook his head.

Motioning to the scabbed-over scrape on his forehead, the prince shrugged. "This appeared out of thin air, I couldn't keep lying."

"You've known her, what? A few weeks? Where is this all coming from? You've never been like this before. Promoting Liam the way you did. He's a good soldier, but gods..."

"I did what I needed to in the middle of an unprecedented situation. And I've never met someone like *her* before!" Matthias downed the rest of his drink and slid the glass back to Micah.

"I've never known you to be so reckless." Micah met his gaze. "Are you sure a woman who makes you like that is a *good* thing?"

A grin spread over Matthias's face before it faded. "If I don't pursue this, at least until she turns me down, I'll always wonder what could've happened."

Micah sighed. "Gods know I can't change your mind if this is really what you want..." He settled back into the couch again. "Though, I am a little disappointed at losing these comfy accommodations. I might have had my own plans..."

Matthias smirked, crossing his boots on the table. "A handmaid catch your eye already?" Before Micah could answer, someone rapped on the door with enough force that the prince raised an eyebrow. "That was pretty fast, even for you."

Micah shrugged. "Not me this time."

Chuckling, Matthias leaned back. "Enter!"

The door swung open, and the lantern light highlighted Katrin's face. Cheeks slightly rosy with the winter chill, she'd shed the layers of cloak and tunic to don attire more similar to when they'd first met. The pale blue of the simple cut dress perfectly complimented her, following each curve of her body.

She looks more than a little annoyed.

"Katrin." Matthias's boots hit the floor, and he glanced at Micah. "What is it?"

The priestess's fiery gaze flickered to Micah, but quickly returned to him. A little more color rose. "I need to speak with you."

Micah stood, crossing his arms. "We're in the middle of—"

"No." Katrin held up a hand to Micah, her tone steady. "No. I don't need you to speak right now, only him." She met the prince's eyes again, something unreadable in her expression.

Matthias's spine straightened, and Micah lifted an eyebrow. Katrin had always been proper, if not overly so, when addressing Micah as the prince.

Shit. She knows. I'm gonna kill Liam.

Matthias stood and gestured with his chin to Micah. "I'll meet up with you later."

His friend nodded and walked to the door, waiting for Katrin to step out of the way before dipping his head. "Always a pleasure." He disappeared into the hallway, leaving them alone.

Katrin stood in the open doorway for a moment, just staring. Her shoulders lifted slightly with a breath as she turned and closed the door. She froze there, with her back still to Matthias and a hand on the handle.

"I wanted to tell you." Matthias cringed at how trite it sounded. "Please try to understand."

"I was really hoping you'd snap at me for speaking to the prince in that way just now." Katrin bowed her head, her voice softening. "But I guess this means it's true. That he's just been pretending to be you."

Matthias swallowed, rubbing the back of his neck. "It started when we were kids, after I needed a stand in for the first time..."

This isn't how this was supposed to happen.

"Will you please look at me?" He stepped towards her but stopped. "Can we talk?"

Her arm shook as she dropped it from the door. "All those things I said to you *about* the prince. About *you*..." She leaned closer to the door, muffling her voice. "Gods, I'm so embarrassed."

The prince winced. "I didn't mean to embarrass you. If it helps, I agreed with a lot of your observations."

She shook her head, the knot of hair at the base of her neck wobbling. "Not really." Her body shuddered with another deep breath as she slowly faced him. She remained against the door, trapping her hands behind her lower back. "I'm sorry. I almost turned around so many times on my way up here. I'm just..." She chewed her lower lip. "I don't know what I'm supposed to feel right now."

Matthias resisted the urge to move closer. "Well, you can hate me for lying, if you want. You'd be justified to never speak to me again, but I'd hope for something less permanent. It's still me. I'm still the same man."

Her eyes brightened for a flash. "Oh, I'm angry," she whispered. "I want to just scream at you for being so selfish, but now I know you're my prince and I shouldn't." Her shoulders shook again. "And then I think about the avalanche and..." Her cheeks reddened. "It's very conflicting feelings..."

"Don't worry about what you should and shouldn't do."

"I'm always worried about those things." She took a step away from the door. Her eyes lingered on his chest for a moment before she heaved a breath and walked past him further into the living room. "You might still be you, but now there's a whole extra layer, a new complication." She turned to him, her voice rising. "You're the damn prince! And you lied about it. And you *kissed* me. Me!"

Matthias huffed. "Is that such a bad thing?"

"Yes!" Katrin spun. "No." She groaned, running a hand over her hair. "I don't know! And that's the problem. You make me question everything."

Doubt churned in his stomach. "Well, now you know. So if you'd rather go back to your life at the temples, just say so. I may have lied about my blood, but everything else has been honest. Everything else is real for me, and if you don't know what you want, maybe you should go figure it out."

"What do you think I'm doing here right now? Going to the temple didn't help a thing. It just brought more questions."

"Then tell me what would." Matthias stepped towards her. "What would help you figure it out, because I'm just as confused as you are. One moment you want me to kiss you, the next you can't even be in the same space as me. I know you've been avoiding me..."

"It's because of what you make me feel!" Katrin's hand ran down her body, rubbing at her stomach.

Matthias let out a sharp laugh. "Gods, that's ironic."

She frowned. "Forgive me for not exactly having the best grapple of my own emotions. I may or may not have been taken into a place when I was thirteen and told all those things are a weakness."

He groaned. "No, Priestess, you misunderstand me. Micah was *just* giving me hell for wanting to tell you the truth. Says you make me reckless."

"Do I?"

"Yes!" Matthias threw his hands up at his sides. "I ran into a fucking avalanche to save you. That's not very princely of me, is it?"

Katrin froze, her gaze falling to his chest. "I'm just an acolyte."

Chapter 22

Dani's hands shook as the guards locked her in the cell. She held her breath while listening to the footsteps walk away, vanishing behind another heavy door. Without the sky above her, her sense of direction suffered. The lack of light only made it worse.

The whole city worked against her. Loud, dark, and mercilessly overwhelming. And Katrin hadn't even been with her. She'd trembled the entire way there, alone in the carriage with her imagination adding to her torment. At least with the door closed now, the chorus of footsteps in the barracks dimmed to a manageable whisper.

Swallowing, she tentatively reached out, touching the cold stone wall. She followed it around the small cell, the chain between her cuffs clinking. At the fourth wall, she found the iron bars. Her heart quickened, and she reached as high as she could, but couldn't touch the top.

Will I ever be free?

Dani shut her eyes tight, willing her shaking to stop.

A door squeaked open somewhere in the barracks prison, and she jumped.

"Katrin?" The Dtrüa opened her eyes, but the oil lamps provided no more light to her than tiny specks amid the darkness.

When the acolyte didn't call back, Dani drew a shaky breath and backed up until her back hit the stone.

She won't let anything happen to me.

An uneasy feeling washed over her. "Tallos?"

Footsteps echoed in the chamber as a familiar gait approached.

"Liam," she whispered, feeling a vague sense of relief.

He paused, his new leather tunic creaking as he straightened. It still hadn't broken in since he'd received it with his promotion to the prince's personal guard.

His fingers tapped against the hilt of his sword. "Who's Tallos?"

Dani clenched her jaw, grasping the chain between her cuffs. "It matters not."

"It matters. Especially if this Tallos would come for you." He stepped to the bars. His voice turned harder. "Who's Tallos? Another shape-shifter?"

Cooperate. Just appease him.

"Yes." Dani dipped her chin. "He's my partner."

"And he'd come for you? Even here in the middle of an Isalican city?" Liam scoffed. "He'd have to be a cocky bastard or come with one hell of an army."

Memory of Tallos drifted his scent over her nose, and dread gurgled in her gut. "I hope not."

Liam's breath stopped, and she imagined his frown. "So you don't want him to come for you?"

Dani shook her head.

Suffocating silence filled the room as they both remained perfectly still.

She couldn't bear it. "Why are you here?"

"I still don't trust you. You're hiding something."

If I tell him I opened the gate, he'll kill me.

"Nothing I say will make you trust me." Dani blinked through the darkness to no avail.

He laughed, but it sounded harsh. "Maybe. Sure is a lot harder after learning you were keeping your Art secret, too. Would you have even told us if the avalanche hadn't—"

"If the avalanche hadn't what?" Heat rose in Dani's veins. "Threatened *your* sister's life? Are you angry because *I* saved her, or because *you* couldn't?"

He growled, boots scraping as he spun and paced away. "You're just trying to gain favor. Get us all off guard so you can accomplish whatever your agenda really is." He didn't stop moving, walking dizzying circles she tried to track. "You've got Katrin fooled, and even the prince, but not me."

"Well, why don't you give yourself a pat on the back? You see right through me. Me and my plans to free myself and sink my fangs into your throat while you sleep." Dani stalked towards the bars. "I'm right where I'm supposed to be, only confined because I let you."

"Exactly." Liam faced her again, his heart rate rising to a tempo she could hear. "You're guilty, I can tell."

Dani gritted her teeth. "You won't be first, you know. When I'm loose, running rabid. It'll be the prince first, then your sister. I won't even touch you until you think I'm gone." She leapt and grabbed the barred door so it sent an echo of metal through the prison corridor.

The whisper of his sword sliding from its sheath reached her ears, but it paused half way.

"Come on, Liam. I'm telling you all the things you want to hear. If you want to kill me, now's your chance." Dani shook the door. "Kill the unarmed blind woman and feel fucking better about yourself!"

His teeth ground and his hilt clanked against the sheath as he dropped it back in. "That's all this is, isn't it? Just telling me what I *want* to hear."

Dani let go of the bars. "You want the truth? You want to know what I'm hiding? So you can turn Katrin against me and leave me to rot in this cell for the rest of my life?"

He stomped forward, and she felt the air shift as he stepped right in front of her. "I still find it hard to believe that someone like you, a shape-shifter crafted for battle by Feyor, just doesn't have what it takes to be a soldier. That one arrow to the arm scared you away from what you'd been training your whole life for."

"I never wanted this." She lowered her voice. "But you're right. It was all my fault. I opened the gate. I opened the south gate and let

Feyor into Isalica. Tallos opened the north gate." Putting her hands through the bars, she rested her forearms on the horizontal iron beams as far as the chain would allow. Closing her eyes, she braced herself for Liam's rage.

His stillness somehow seemed worse. The soldier's heart pounded, but his breathing remained perfectly steady. "You are the reason Feyor made it across the border." It came in a low whisper, anger seething through each syllable. "The reason crossbows nearly killed our prince."

Dani's chin quivered, and she nodded, her chest lightening with the confession. "If I could take it back, I would."

He shook his head with a gruff snort. "We lost one hundred and six lives at the border. Twenty of them civilians. Their blood is on your hands. You can't take that back."

Her eyes burned, tears welling on her lower lids. "I made a mistake. I never wanted to hurt anyone."

Liam's knuckles popped. "Then why become a soldier?"

Dani leaned her forehead against the bars, her tears cooling as they rolled down her cheeks. "I had no choice."

"What?" His breath caught with genuine surprise.

Anger built in her throat, and she cringed. "I never asked for this. I never wanted to be a Dtrüa. They took me when I was a child. I can't even remember my family... if I had a family. They experimented on me, over years, trying to make me the war machine they wanted." She lifted her sightless gaze, aiming it where she thought his face might be. "They got what they wanted, but they didn't account for my weakness. My fear. I don't want to hurt anyone, and yet... I did. It's my fault all those people died." Her voice rose. "You can berate me and yell at me all you want, but your hate can't possibly compare to my own."

"So this is all about making amends, then? Saving Katrin. Saving Matthias... What made you follow Katrin into the camp that night?"

"She told me I'd be safe." Dani closed her eyes. "She was kind to me. And now you're going to tell her what I've done, and she'll hate me, too." Tears dripped from her face. "Why are you still here? You got what you wanted."

The soldier didn't move, his heart rate slowing. "But what were you hoping for when you followed her? There had to be a hope..."

Dani choked on a sob. "I just wanted a life. My own life. Whatever it looked like... But I guess this is it. And you know what?" She shook her head with another sob. "It's still better than being in Feyor."

The warmth of his hand closed around hers, making her flinch. His grip tightened ever so slightly, but it felt oddly comforting instead of entrapping.

"So you didn't choose to be a soldier? To fight for Feyor?"

"No," she whispered. "And I'm so sorry."

His other hand moved to cover her other, his calloused hands scraping gently against her skin. A strange chill passed through her.

Why is he tormenting me with kindness? He hates me.

She clenched her jaw, rubbing her thumb over his hand.

"Thank you," he whispered. "I don't think I said that before. But thank you for saving my sister."

Emotion tightened her throat, and fresh tears sprang from her eyes. She sank against the bars, sobbing as she bowed her head.

I don't know if I can handle it if this is temporary.

Liam's grip tightened briefly, then his right hand slipped away. The familiar jangle of her cuff keys came from his pocket before he gently turned over her wrist and inserted them into the lock.

Dani cringed and turned her face away.

When the cuffs fell from her wrists into his waiting hand, she sucked in a deeper breath, rubbing her skin. "Thank you." Her skin cooled without his touch, and she almost reached for him.

"I..." The cuffs clanked against his sword as he secured them to his belt, the key slipping back into his pocket. "You're welcome. I hope this might help you be a little more comfortable."

Dani retreated from the bars, wiping her face with her arm. For the first time in days, she ran her hands through her hair, nodding. Exhaustion eked through her muscles, and she turned away, her bottom lip still trembling. "I appreciate the gesture, but there's nothing *comfortable* about this place."

His feet shuffled minutely against the dirty stone floor, a stark contrast from his usually confident strides. "They rarely design these places with the inhabitant's comfort in mind." A gentleness remained in his tone, though his dryness had returned.

The Dtrüa scoffed. "Not the prison. I mean, yes, the prison, but... The city. The people, the... smells." She angled her face to aim one ear in his direction.

"But you'd still rather be here than back in Feyor?" He snorted, his leather tunic creaking as he crossed his arms. "You are a strange one."

"Is it so wrong to long for the sky? For fresh air? For quiet, instead of all the footsteps?" Dani faced him, her breathing quickening. "I can hear everyone through that open door. It's like being surrounded but alone at the same time. Are you all going to leave me here?" Disgust radiated through her at the tinge of fear in her voice.

Tallos would be so disappointed in me.

Liam stiffened, speaking quietly. "I don't know, yet. There are certain considerations..." He paused before his footsteps sounded, moving towards the door. "I shouldn't have bothered you."

Dani's chest tightened at the notion she might never see the sky again, and she squeezed her eyes shut. A tear escaped anyway, betraying her as it rolled to her chin.

He stopped again, hovering near the stone doorway so many sounds echoed through.

Bars and chains.

Laughter.

Someone coughing.

"Would you like me to leave?"

Does that mean he'd stay?

Dani wiped the fallen tear off her face and wondered if his presence was worse than being alone. Or if he'd learn her preference to do the opposite.

He hates me.

"No," she whispered, the truth escaping her. "And how pathetic is that? I'd rather be around someone who despises me than be... alone, here." Swallowing with the admission, she retreated to the side of her cell until her back hit the wall. She slid down, hugging her knees to her chest.

The iron hinges creaking preceded the latch clicking into place. Muffled quiet descended, but the smells and darkness remained.

Dani winced but then held her breath, finding a second rhythm still by the door. "Are you still here?"

Liam's footsteps answered before his voice. He walked to the distant wall, his form shifting in front of the single amber ball of light in the room. Iron clinked before he turned, the lantern in his hand. "Still here."

His shape and the spot in her vision moved closer before he settled the lantern on the ground beside the bars of her cell door. It created a halo of orange light in her vision, flickering against the blurry shapes, including his as he turned and walked back to the distant wall again. A soft breath escaped him as he sat, the wooden bench creaking beneath his weight. Metal clanked as he removed the cuffs from his belt and placed them on the bench beside him. "I'm not much of a talker, and doubtful I'm good company."

A smile tugged at the corner of her mouth, and she shook her head, chin on her knees. "You needn't talk."

Chapter 23

"I'm just a man." Matthias's shoulders relaxed. "You know me better than most, because you didn't have each interaction tainted with the knowledge of my future." He walked away from her, facing one of the tall windows overlooking the center of the city where the temple stood. "But you have regrets, don't you?"

Katrin stared at the temple over his shoulder, the glittering light from the moat around it making it shine like a jewel. The faces of the gods, carved within the facade, stared at her. All the questions came rising within her again.

She wrapped her arms tightly around her twisting stomach. "Regrets." The word tasted sour, and she wished she had a glass of water, her tongue swollen as she met the prince's gaze in the window reflection.

Those eyes made her weak in the knees, and she wavered.

She stumbled back against the arm of a couch, her head spinning as she tried to shake the feelings away to allow her the thoughts.

They were so clear in the temple...

"I regret nothing," she whispered. "But I'm afraid I might. And I don't know what I'll regret more."

Matthias faced her with a somber expression. "I know what I want, but I can't play that game. I don't want to be a regret for you." He approached, taking slow steps. "But for clarity... I'd like to explore the connection we have. I want to spend time with you, know you, and be a part of your life as more than a friend."

Her entire body buzzed, and she tried desperately to swallow as she looked at his face. "I do, too..." Even as she said it, the doubt clouded back in.

The prince shook his head, leaning back against the table. "But you're not sure. And that's all right."

"I... feel like I'm trying to make a half-informed decision, though. I know what life in the temples is like. I've been there for five years." She caught herself studying him, looking from his feet all the way up his muscular body to his handsome face beneath his beard. "But I don't know what I'm missing with you. I haven't experienced..." Her fingers brushed her lips, a heat rising in her chest. "I want to kiss you again. That's why I've been trying to stay away." She laughed at herself. "I want to feel your arms around me again. But knowing now that you're the prince..."

Matthias tilted his head with a subtle smirk. "I'm less appealing?"

"No, your appeal is still very much the same." Her eyes betrayed her with a flick to his mouth, then arms. "Nothing's changed that, but now I'm concerned about the appropriateness. I'm an acolyte."

"You said that already." His gaze drifted down before returning to her eyes. "If you're hoping I'll convince you one way or the other, I won't. This isn't my choice."

"But what future is there? I knew exactly what it was going to be in the temples, but with you..."

He shrugged. "I can't stand here and make you promises of what the future holds. There would never be certainty. You didn't seem concerned about the future when you left the temple with me... so why did you do that?"

She shook her head. "I thought it was what I was meant to do. Everything in me was telling me to stay near you. I thought it was a message from the gods."

The corners of his mouth twitched in the hint of a smile. "Then what's changed, Priestess?"

Her breath caught, and she looked at him. Even from across the room, she could imagine his woodsy scent. Stomach clenching, she pushed away from the couch arm and stood.

I need to trust in what I'm feeling.

The short walk across the rug towards him felt as if an eternity passed in a blink. Touching his cheek, she ran her hand over his soft beard and back into his hair. She watched him as he stiffened, but then relaxed beneath her touch, his lips parting. It made her blood run faster.

Before she could further question the need, she brought her mouth to his, sinking into the passion so rapidly that the room blurred.

Matthias's arms wrapped around her, and his mouth responded. The kiss renewed with escalating energy before he broke away from her. "What are you doing?"

Her lips tingled, craving more of him. She ran her tongue over her top lip, and the taste sent a shiver down her spine. "Making a choice." She ran her hands down his chest, slipping them around his waist to pull closer to him. "I want to know what this feeling is. What it can be."

Cupping her face, the prince ran his thumb over her bottom lip. "Are you sure?"

The question felt like it held so many implications, and she rapidly tried to evaluate everything she'd considered while still angry with him. She looked back and forth between his eyes as her lips formed a kiss on the pad of his thumb. Taking his hand, she turned it and kissed his knuckles then palm, teasing his fingers with her tongue and watching the way his face changed, a low rumble in his chest.

It made her squirm, craving so much more. "I'm sure," she whispered between kisses. "I want to know."

Matthias leaned forward and kissed her again.

Katrin's lips parted, and she tasted his tongue, vaguely aware of him turning her so she was against the edge of the table. Her hands moved to the buttons of his coat, but her elbow hit the whisky decanter.

It teetered and fell over with a clatter, rolling to the side. She smelled it first, then cold soaked through her dress, and she yelped.

The prince pulled away and caught the bottle before it could roll off the table, setting it upright and inspecting her clothing with a chuckle.

She buried her face against his neck, seeking the bit of skin she'd exposed and giggled. "My clumsiness is already messing this up."

"I can draw you a bath." Matthias kissed her head. "Perks of having a temple nearby with so much interest in water."

The mere mention of a bath made Katrin's body ache for it. But it still screamed for more of him, too. She ran her hands over his shoulders, kissing beneath his jaw. "I haven't had a proper bath in years. All sponges and showers in the temple." But even as she spoke about it, the feel of his skin against her lips threatened any composure. Her heart raced at the next thought to enter her mind. "Will you join me?"

Matthias stared at her. "In the bath?"

Katrin playfully frowned, hiding the smile his surprise inspired. "Would you rather not?" She kissed up his jaw to his earlobe like he'd done to her in the snow cave. She hoped it felt as good to him as it had to her. "I don't think I want to stop doing this to you."

He hummed, squeezing her waist. "I don't think I could ever resist bathing with you."

"Then lead the way, Prince," she whispered in his ear.

His eyes narrowed at her before he took her hand. Leading her out of the lounge, they passed through the lavish bedroom before entering the bathing chamber and approaching the large porcelain bathtub at the far side. A copper pipe extended from the wall, forming a wide, flat spout into the bathtub. An Art-laden aura surrounded it.

Katrin slipped her shoes off and tiptoed across the cold tile floor. She leaned close to him as she twisted the tap.

The gurgle of water preceded the eruption from the spout. The warm water splashed up at them, and she flinched away in surprise with a smile. She watched Matthias as she backed away from him, her heart racing.

The prince studied her before turning around. "I'll give you some privacy."

"No." Katrin's throat tightened. She shook her head as she turned, exposing the buttons on the back of her dress. While she could unfasten them herself, she'd prefer the excuse to have him close again. "Could you...?" She pulled her hair from its knot, guiding it over her shoulder as she looked back at him.

The muscles in the corner of Matthias's jaw flexed. He let out a long exhale and walked to her, fingers finding buttons. Lowering his mouth near her ear, he whispered, "What exactly is it you want, Priestess? I'm happy to oblige."

Every time his deep voice echoed in her ear, she craved more. Especially the way he said the title she hoped for one day. She tilted her head, pulling her hair over her shoulder to expose her neck for him even more. "I want to know what your touch feels like. What our skin together feels like."

His chest rumbled again, and he kissed her neck, unfastening the last button at the back of her dress. The chill air of the room would have made her shiver, if not for how close Matthias stood behind her. His fingers brushed her spine as she shrugged off the shoulders of her dress, pulling down the sleeves and letting it drop to the floor.

Exposed, she expected to feel awkward, but Matthias's hands sliding around her bare waist calmed her nerves.

The prince's rough touch ventured down her sides, toying at the top of her underwear. His breath cascaded over her neck as he kissed her again, pushing down the last bit of clothing on her body.

She closed her eyes and leaned her head back against him, placing her hand on top of his as it explored her abdomen and hip. A hum escaped while she savored the scent of him, despite the roughness of his clothes at her back.

The dainty piece of cotton hit the floor and his hands left her as she stepped out away from the pile of her clothes and faced him.

Matthias's gaze trailed down her body while he removed his tunic and undershirt, revealing thick, curved muscles. Dark hair dusted his chest, and he dropped the collection of clothes onto the floor with his cloak.

Katrin's heart pounded, and she caught his glance down at her exposed breasts before he met her eyes again. She ran her hands over his chest, entranced by the way his skin felt. Her mouth found his skin, tongue playing along his muscles as she unfastened his belt.

His breeches fell to the floor with her encouragement, leaving him naked before her.

She marveled at his body, not hiding her curiosity.

With a smirk, she turned away, crossing to the tub and shutting off the water. She peered over her shoulder, her stomach quaking at the intensity of his gaze.

In a subtle gesture, he motioned with his chin for her to get in the bath.

She smiled, looking over to the shelf beside the tub filled with salts and soaps. "Do you want bubbles?"

"If you don't get in the bath right now..." His deep voice sent a quiver through her muscles. "I'm going to take you to bed instead, whisky smelling and all."

She laughed, and it felt amazing.

Bed.

Katrin contemplated it briefly before stepping into the tub. The warm water sent a lovely shock through her body as she lowered herself in. She cupped water over her arms. "Coming, then?" She leaned forward, leaving space for him in the tub sized for one.

Matthias huffed, climbing into the water behind her. As he sat, it rose to cover her breasts. His hands found her waist again and encouraged her back against him. "You spilled the whisky on purpose, didn't you?"

"I did not." She shook her head, her hair soaking into the water as she leaned back. "But it was rather genius." The feel of his skin against her back threatened all control, especially with the embrace of the warm water. She sighed, turning her mouth towards his neck. "This would have been a better way to recover from that avalanche."

He kissed her temple, sliding his left hand up her body until it cupped her breast. "I couldn't agree more."

His touch sent jolts through her, so strange for it not to be her own. A soft moan escaped her lips as he took her nipple between his finger and thumb and gently rolled it.

Matthias whispered near her ear. "You're beautiful." He kissed her neck, running his other hand over her thigh. "You want pleasure?"

Anxiousness rose in her, but she didn't know exactly what it was for. Her heart pounded as she accepted his kisses. Everything burned for more. "Yes. Please."

As his hand ventured back up her leg, he guided it to the side. "You want bubbles first?"

She laughed, turning her head, and nipped at his earlobe. "Stop teasing me."

"As you wish, Priestess." Matthias's hand slid between her legs, finding her sex, and a thunderstorm shocked through her. He hummed against her skin when she gasped and stroked her again.

Her body went through conflicting states, straightening and relaxing so rapidly her breathing escalated.

"Relax," he whispered near her ear, keeping the movement of his hand slow. His other twisted her nipple again, moving in tandem with the building heat between her legs.

Desperately, she touched his hip beneath the water, nails trailing along his skin as she urged her body to do as he suggested. Each wave passed through her and built into the next as his touch evoked completely new sensations.

Matthias circled the bundle of nerves, adding more pressure as she moaned. He grew harder behind her, his own body tensing at each rise within her.

The sensations blurred, and she closed her eyes as his fingers slipped inside her.

Back arching, she pushed her heels into the porcelain, tilting her head back. Her hips rocked with his touch until the heat overtook her. She cried out, unable to restrain the sound as her body exploded with euphoria. His caress carried her through the climax, slowing and easing her down the other side.

More.

Her nails bit into Matthias's skin as she shifted against him, turning in the tub. Her lips found his in a flurry, and she moaned into his mouth. Breathing heavily, she touched his body and closed her hand around his girth, eager to feel more of him. She bit his lower lip as she pulled away enough to speak. "I want to pleasure you, too."

Matthias touched her shoulders, his eyelids fluttering. He leaned his forehead against hers, hot breath on her lips. "I'm all yours."

Her heart pounded as she gripped him, teasing his tip with her thumb.

The prince sucked in a breath through clenched teeth, lowering his face to kiss her neck.

She pressed her body against him, her wet breasts tracing over his chest. She lifted herself, placing her knees on either side of his hips. She felt the pulse of him against her palm as she stroked, maintaining a steady rhythm. "I want to try," she whispered. "I want to feel you inside. Can we...?"

Matthias groaned against her skin. "Absolutely."

Her eyes darted down into the water, admiring the look of him within her hand before she lifted her hips. Nerves erupted through her as she hovered, watching his hungry eyes as water trailed down his neck from her fingers.

She expected the pain as she lowered onto him, slipping his length inside her already sensitive sex. The tightness and vague snap. She winced. But then the motion came naturally, as she rocked against him and the pain subsided into something far better.

"Are you all right?"

"Yes."

His grip on her tightened, and he took her mouth again.

She returned the passionate kisses as she moved, his hips tilting with hers as his hands traced her body.

Pressure built in her core again as they moved in tandem, and she cried out when it peaked. Her mouth left his, finding his shoulder as waves rocked through her.

Matthias's body stiffened, and he grunted, stilling as she collapsed on him. His arms wrapped around her, holding her close. Each rise of his chest took her with him, the subtle movements of their skin brushing together beneath the water.

She ached as she slowly rose off of him, water running from her hair over her breasts.

The prince met her gaze, his eyes boring into her. He stroked her hair, tucking it behind her ear. "How are you feeling?"

Turning her head, she kissed the inside of his wrist with a smile. "Happy."

A smile spread over his face, and he sat straighter, kissing her softly before rising to his knees with an arm around her. As he lifted her from the tub, she wrapped her legs around his waist.

She broke the kiss, resting her head on his shoulder as he carried her to his bed.

Setting her down, Matthias gazed into the sitting room, and his brow furrowed. "Wait here." He kissed her forehead, collecting his breeches before crossing from the bedroom to the lounge, still naked.

Katrin rolled onto her stomach and watched him, enjoying the view from behind with her feet in the air. The sheets beneath her soaked with the water from their bath, but she didn't care. Her stomach still fluttered and seeing his bare body again as he walked without shame allowed her mind to finally catch up.

How many can say they had their first time with a prince?

Matthias retrieved a piece of parchment from the floor, flipping it open to read. He chuckled, tossing it onto the table before pulling on his pants. "You hungry?" His eyes lingered on her before he opened the door to the hallway.

She held up her chin with her hands, frowning before she realized why.

I like him better without the pants...

Kicking her feet a little, Katrin wondered if she actually had an answer as Matthias rolled a cart in from the hallway, shining silver domes on top of it. "Mmm," she hummed as she considered. "Not yet."

Matthias shut and latched the door, dragging the cart closer before abandoning it to crawl onto the bed. "Compliments of Prince Micah." He rolled over to face her, playing with a lock of her wet hair.

"A full service prince, indeed." She traced a finger down his side.

"He's quite thoughtful." His tone held play, but something deeper shadowed his expression.

Katrin hesitated as she ran her touch along the line of his pants. She rolled onto her side, touching his cheek. "What's wrong?"

Matthias propped an elbow on the bed. "My father needs me in Lyon."

"Lyon?" The lingering joy twisted into sudden concern. "That's... very far away." Suddenly considering the reality of his responsibility, along with her place in the country, filled her body with an odd numbness.

"I'd like you to come with me." Matthias touched her cheek. "Assuming you haven't now decided to return to your temple."

She swallowed, touching the back of his hand to entwine their fingers. "Come with you to Lyon?"

The prince nodded, an edge of vulnerability in his face. "Will you consider it?"

Could I really go back to what my life was like before all this?

She chewed her lip, quickly evaluating the last few weeks. As crazy as it all had been, she felt only gratitude for it. For getting to know him... and the friendship with Dani.

She brought his hand to her mouth, kissing his knuckles. "I would like to come, but there are some things we need to discuss first." She hated how logical she could be, even lying naked beside him. "First, are you to be Matthias or Prince Alarik while we travel?" Her brow furrowed. "Wait, should I call you Alarik?"

He rolled onto his back, sighing. "Please don't. It's my

grandfather's name, and other than during formal introductions, no one uses it. I will probably be Matthias. At least until we get further from the border. By the time we reach Omensea, I think I can go back to my own identity."

"And in all that, what about this?" She crawled partially onto him, leaning on her elbows as she gazed at his face. "You must realize now that you've spoiled me, I'm going to want more."

Matthias grinned. "None of this needs to stop."

"But do we need to keep it secret?"

He shook his head. "Not unless you want to. The guys aren't stupid, they know I care about you. Micah more than the others."

Her cheeks heated at the realization that Micah's choice to leave the food at the door likely meant he knew what might be happening. "But what about the rest of your entourage? Won't they talk?" She touched his chest, tracing his muscles. "I don't want to be an embarrassment for you."

Matthias tilted his head. "You could never embarrass me, but they aren't coming. It would just be my elites."

"What about Merissa?" Katrin relied on the priestess's miniature lessons to keep her somewhat focused on her continued growth.

"She'll come, too, but only until the temple near the border. She's expressed interest in staying there for a while and has faith you can serve as the prince's personal healer in the meantime."

Katrin quirked her brow. "It sounds like you were already planning on me saying yes."

Matthias chuckled. "A man can hope, can't he?"

Her heart lightened, a new eruption of butterflies in her stomach. Watching her own hand, she ran it down his body. "I do have a favor to ask, then." She drew a circle on his abdomen. "Dani. Can she please come with us?"

"I'm not oblivious. I can see the bond forming between you two. I figured you and her would be a package deal, assuming she keeps cooperating." He stroked her cheek. "Anything else?"

She smiled, leaning into his touch. "One last thing." She touched the buttons of his breeches, flicking to release them. "I want these off again."

The prince chuckled, grasping her hand and rolling her onto her back, hovering over her. "Is that so?"

Chapter 24

One week later...

Liam flinched and covered his ears as a girlish squeal exploded behind him. It continued into a trill as an acolyte skipped behind Katrin and wrapped her arms around her, despite her sitting on a bench in the large dining hall, her food half eaten.

His sister laughed as she grabbed the woman hovering over her, rocking back and forth with her. "Jelisa!" She tapped on her friend's arm, her face flushing. "I can't breathe."

The blond's wavy hair shone in the temple's candlelight chandeliers, laughing as she released Katrin. "I'm sorry. I'm just so excited to see you again."

Katrin wriggled free of the bench, pulling her emerald skirt after her as she took the other acolyte into a tight embrace. "I missed you, too."

"Jelisa, won't you join us?" Micah lifted his goblet of wine, dressed in his formal princely attire.

Matthias elbowed him, and they exchanged a glance.

The acolyte's eyes widened over Katrin's shoulder, and she quickly released her to enter a polite curtsy to the prince. "Your highness, I'm so sorry for interrupting your meal."

Liam chuckled, taking another bite of potato as his sister scowled at him.

"Not at all. You're a friend of Miss Talansiet, and there's an open seat here." Micah motioned across from him at the space next to Liam.

Katrin jumped, batting at Jelisa as Liam realized the girl must have pinched his sister. She rolled her eyes and nudged her friend with her hip. "He won't bite."

Matthias chuckled. "Unless you ask him nicely."

Both Katrin and Jelisa's cheeks flushed, but the girl seemed undeterred as she shuffled around the table to sit where Micah had invited.

Katrin climbed back into her seat beside Matthias, poking him hard in the side. She twitched again, and Matthias grinned as she smacked him in the chest.

My sister... and the prince. Totally normal now.

The two had been inseparable since Undertown. And he'd caught several stray kisses between them when they thought no one was watching.

Liam downed the rest of his wine, reaching for the bottle to pour more.

The surrounding hall filled with the chatter of the temple's residents, though the formal table at the front remained empty. This visit of the prince was less formal, and Micah had assured the high priest there was no need for extra measures.

Micah poured a goblet of wine for Katrin's friend. "Are you a priestess, Jelisa?"

She tittered. "Oh, no. Not yet. Only an acolyte, your majesty." She took the glass delicately between her fingers, back straightened in formality. "Just like Katrin."

"Though you are a year ahead of me." Katrin's right hand disappeared beneath the table, along with Matthias's left. "And my training may very well be more gradual now."

Jelisa sipped her drink, but it turned into a frown. "What?" She leaned on the table towards Katrin, forcing Liam to lean back to avoid her pressing right into him. "Kat, aren't you back now?"

A fruity fragrance assaulted Liam's senses from the acolyte's hair, and he tried not to wrinkle his nose.

Matthias met Liam's gaze, and the prince's cheeks tightened as he tried not to laugh at the soldier's discomfort.

Katrin shook her head. "No. I'm going to be continuing on to Lyon with the prince and his elites. Assuming the high priest accepts my request. I'd like to continue to spend time with my brother." She gestured across to Liam.

The prince quirked an eyebrow at Katrin.

Jelisa's attention redirected to Liam, and he tried not to look like a mouse being hunted by a hawk, but her gaze locked on him. "You're Kat's brother?"

Liam pursed his lips, but nodded. He slowly leaned forward again when she seemed ready to stay in her seat and offered a hand. "Nice to meet you."

Jelisa grinned and threw herself against Liam, squeezing him as if they'd been lost lovers. "I've heard so much about you!"

He struggled to keep his hand steady, and just caught his glass of wine before it toppled. He glared at his sister as she laughed.

Matthias gestured to the girl with his eyes at Liam and shrugged.

Liam opened his eyes wide and rapidly shook his head, mouthing the word 'no.'

Katrin gave a playful frown.

Sighing, Liam gently patted Jelisa on the back as she rubbed her cheek against his tunic. He lifted his goblet over the girl's head and downed half the glass before she finally let him go.

"I, uh." Liam looked to the plate beside his, which he'd slowly collected food onto as the dishes were passed. He'd nearly forgotten about it, but his purpose returned as he guided Jelisa away by her shoulder. "I hate to be rude, but I need to... go make sure someone else gets dinner, too."

Katrin's brow furrowed as Liam climbed out of his seat. "Leaving already? You didn't even finish your meal."

"I'll finish it in my room. I..." He eyed Jelisa, who batted her eyelashes at him. "Don't feel comfortable leaving her alone. I didn't have time to check the window properly."

"Her?" Jelisa's pretty face grew suspicious.

"You need to go easy on her." Matthias leaned on the table. "I know you made some progress with information from her in Undertown, but try to be civil, would you?"

"Take this." Micah corked the bottle of wine and slid it across the table at Liam hard enough that the soldier had to catch it to stop it from flying onto the floor.

Liam ground his jaw. "I'm perfectly civil." He shoved the bottle under his arm as he picked up the full plate of food and an unused goblet. Balancing the two in one hand, he struggled to pick up his own plate.

"I'll help you carry it all." Matthias stood, touching Katrin's shoulder before reaching across the table to pick up the other plate of food and Liam's goblet. "I'll be back shortly."

Katrin smiled at him with a nod as she scooted closer to Micah to converse more with her friend.

The acting prince nudged her with his shoulder. "Bread was better when you made it."

Her cheeks pinked. "Well, thank you." She reached behind her to subtly touch Matthias's hip as he stepped away from the table.

Liam eyed her and the prince, trying to read the tension in the air. He pursed his lips, then turned towards the hall with Matthias behind him. The chatter of the dining hall faded as they crossed into the wood-paneled hallways, Art illuminated sconces lighting the way back to their chambers.

No evidence of a fire marred the residential hallways, but Liam had seen the charred remains of the north wings when they arrived. Yet, life at the temple seemed to have resumed to what he suspected was normal.

"So..." Liam eyed the true prince, sucking briefly on his teeth. "When are we going to talk about how you're sleeping with my sister?" A smile twitched at the side of his mouth.

Matthias coughed and looked behind them. "Gods, Liam, crass much?"

"You don't deny it, then?" He slowed so they could walk side by side in the wide hall.

"I'd rather not lie to you." The prince gave him a sidelong look. "But I'm also not one to kiss and tell, so you can come to your own conclusions."

Liam snorted and shook his head. "Honestly, I don't want to know those details about my sister, anyway. But do I need to give you the whole *you-break-her-heart-I-break-you* speech?" He eyed Matthias. "Though I'm not entirely confident I could beat you."

The prince halted and faced Liam, all humor disappearing from his expression. "Are you threatening the throne?"

Liam choked, nearly tripping as he gaped at Matthias. "You're not serious? Of course not! I'm threatening my sister's lover."

Matthias's stern look vanished as he laughed. "Don't worry, I won't break her heart." He kept walking. "Though I think you broke Jelisa's."

Frowning, he shook his head. "Girl like that isn't for me. Besides, she's all over the *prince*."

Chuckling, Matthias jutted a thumb back the way they'd come. "That's where my reputation comes from. That guy and his ever-flowing charm."

"Seems some of the charm belongs to you, all things considered." Liam glanced down the hall, even though his sister was long out of sight. "I didn't think she'd choose to leave the temples. But she's ready to drop it all for you."

"She'll still become a priestess. Merissa has agreed to mentor her and continue her education once we return from Lyon. One might argue a practical education is worth more than one from books." Matthias quirked a brow and stopped next to the door they had locked Dani within.

"Long as that education happens away from the war, I'm all right with it." Liam slipped the base of the goblet he carried between his fingers, holding the plate while he pulled out the key.

"Something we agree on." The prince glanced at the closed door and lowered his voice. "I don't know what happened in Undertown, but your *prisoner* has been withdrawn lately. Katrin mentioned it. If you still think she needs to remain cuffed, I trust your judgment, but at least try to be kind. I don't blame her for holding back that bit about opening the gate."

Pursing his lips, Liam paused with the key in the lock.

Withdrawn?

"I'm not as forgiving as my sister, but I'll keep it in mind." He twisted the key, and Matthias handed him the second plate and goblet once he pocketed it.

The prince nodded and started back down the hallway towards the dining hall.

A crisp breeze almost blew the door closed again, and he shoved his foot into the doorway just in time. The half-full wine goblet jostled, sloshing crimson over the lip and onto his tunic.

"Damn it." He elbowed the door open, and it closed behind him with another gust as he slid Dani's plate onto the desk near the door. Freeing his hands, he rubbed at the soaked spot on his chest, but the stain was already setting into the grey fabric.

He reached for a cloth by the washbasin as he inspected the darkening room. Finding her on the far side, his heart jumped.

Dani had opened the window as far as it would go, and she sat sideways on it with both feet on the sill. She faced the western sky, where the sun would have set hours ago. Her hands lay draped over her bent knees, the chain between her cuffs over her shins.

I knew I should have checked the window.

Liam grumbled as he rubbed at the wine stain, stomping across the room to her. "I thought I asked you not to open that."

Dani didn't even flinch. "I wanted fresh air."

"You always want fresh air. What, the ride through the mountains and camping along the way wasn't enough?" He went to reach for her, but stopped when she looked at him.

Her wavy white hair whipped past her face, contrasted by her dark eyebrows and red lips. "No." She clicked her tongue, and her cloudy eyes centered on his face. "I'm still here, aren't I? I could have left."

He heaved a loud sigh. "Do you want dinner? I brought you some.

Or are you just going to stay there tonight?"

"Will you let me?"

"Is that a trick question?"

"Because you doubt your ability to force me to move?" Dani tilted her head.

"Do you really want to test that?" Liam gritted his teeth.

Infuriating woman.

The Feyorian crossed her arms. "I think I do."

Liam shook his head as he stepped closer to her. "Get down."

To his surprise, she turned and hopped onto the carpet, approaching him. She sniffed, furrowing her brow. "Did you spill wine on yourself?"

He grumbled, stepping out of her way as she moved to the desk. "Only because you opened the bloody window."

"Yes, all your problems are my fault." Dani clicked her tongue again.

"Lately, I would describe that as pretty accurate." He followed her, and in a now familiar way, he took her wrist and guided it to her plate. He took her other hand and helped her find the fork. "Want me to tell you what's where, or just be surprised?"

A smile touched Dani's lips. "I'm all right with the surprise." She passed the fork to hold it with the plate and picked up the goblet. "There's nothing in this."

"No, and if there had been, I'd be covered in it." He took up the bottle Micah had encouraged and uncorked it, pouring it for her.

"You're giving me wine?"

"Are you complaining?"

"No. Just surprised." Dani took her things to her bed, crawling onto it and nestling the goblet in her lap and the plate in front of her. "Almost as surprised as I was when I heard *you'd* volunteered to share quarters with me."

"Not like Katrin can do it. Gods know she doesn't stay in her room at night anymore." Liam poured a bit more into his own goblet and lifted it to sip. As he did, his mind reminded him of the forgotten key. He turned, quickly opening the door to pluck it from the lock.

How am I forgetting these things now?

"Matthias has other elite guards." Dani sipped her wine.

Liam pursed his lips and hummed around a mouthful of wine. He shook his finger at her. "I see what you're doing. And while *the prince* has other guards, I'm the most invested in ensuring you remain a *prisoner*."

Dani rolled her eyes. "Katrin already told me the truth."

Tannin stuck to the back of Liam's throat, and he coughed. "Damn it, Kat."

A glimmer surfaced in the Feyorian's eyes. "Gotcha."

Liam growled and crossed to the window. He eyed Dani as he closed it, sliding the lock into place. "You probably overheard it, anyway."

"Riez called him Micah when he thought I couldn't hear. I'm not dumb." Dani ate a bite of food, humming and taking another.

Liam smirked at her obvious enjoyment. "Priests know how to cook, I'll give them that." He returned to his own plate, picking up a Brussels sprout that he popped into his mouth.

Dani felt around her plate with her fork, and the tines bumped one of the round green vegetables. She stabbed it, putting it in her mouth, and then recoiled. Spitting it out into her hand, she dropped her fork. "Blech! What is this?"

Liam laughed, unable to control it no matter how restrained he remained around her. Her scowl only led to another chuckle. "Have you never had Brussels sprouts before?"

"No, and I'd rather not repeat the experience."

"They're good!"

"Then you eat them." Dani pushed her plate a few inches towards him across the bed. Holding her hand out awkwardly, she looked ready to throw the bitten vegetable, and Liam wondered if he'd have to dodge. When she moved her arm back, he started to move, but she threw it straight at the window.

It splatted against the closed pane before falling to the floor, and Liam groaned. "Really?"

Dani shrugged. "Shouldn't have closed it without saying anything."

"You heard me close it, and there's no way you didn't notice."

"Then you just shouldn't have closed it."

Liam downed the rest of his wine, pleased with the slight haze it left his mind in.

Though being drunk while watching a prisoner seems like a bad idea.

He shook his finger at Dani. "You're cleaning that."

"You want the blind woman to clean the window?"

"I have faith in your ability to adapt without your sight."

Dani scowled at her plate.

Liam poured more wine, emptying the bottle despite his better judgment. "What? Now you're turned off to the rest of your food? There are perfectly good potatoes and roast there."

"I can't trust my plate until I know they're all gone." Dani felt around on the blankets for her lost fork.

"You are the most high maintenance..." He grumbled as he plucked up her plate. He popped one of her sprouts into his mouth as he crossed to his own plate to transfer them. Holding her plate back out to her, he waited. "Removed for you, princess."

Why don't I just let her starve?

Dani clicked her tongue before taking it from him, once again holding her lost fork. "Vile little things," she muttered. "The roast is good, though. Make sure you eat that last so I don't have to smell your sprout breath all night."

"Just for that, I'm saving all the Brussels sprouts for last." Liam smirked, happy she couldn't see it. He leaned against the edge of the desk, picking at the piece of bread on the edge of his plate.

He eyed the muck on the window and the sprout on the floor. "And you're still cleaning that."

"That's what you think." Dani put a potato into her mouth, her chains clinking against the plate every time she reached for another bite.

Each tap made Liam flinch, and he groaned around his mouthful of bread. "Can you stop?" he whined.

Dani shook her head and sipped her wine. "Is there anything I do that *doesn't* offend you?"

He sighed, putting his goblet down. "Very rarely." The lull in his mind allowed him to see the easiest solution, and he withdrew the key for her cuffs from his pocket.

Her eyes darted up, locking on his hand. "What are you doing?"

"Taking them off. So you can stop making that awful sound."

Dani stiffened, closing her eyes as he approached.

She always does that, like she's expecting a strike instead.

Liam took the plate from her hands, putting it beside her as he lifted her hands up. The cuffs clicked as he unlocked the first, and her eyes opened. He met her strangely entrancing gaze for a moment before he focused on the second cuff. "There."

Rubbing her wrists, she retracted her hands to herself. "Thank you."

Pursing his lips, he handed her back her food, and returned to the desk. The cuffs clanked together as he dropped them on the wooden surface.

Why am I being so soft?

Liam picked up his goblet and a napkin, making his way to the window. With a quick scrub, he did away with the smears on the glass, and crouched to pick up the pieces on the floor in the cloth.

Moonlight shone in the drifts of snow that remained in the shadows of the trees. He leaned against the sill, considering the view towards the border. His position as a first private seemed so long ago, and oddly, he missed it.

He drank again from his goblet as he considered the state of the camp he'd called home for nearly two years. There hadn't been word of more fights, but they were certainly coming. Feyor would declare war whether or not Isalica did it first.

With a sigh, he turned back to the room, and stiffened when Dani's blank stare was clearly in his direction. Frowning, he leaned against the wall beside the window. "What?"

Dani slid off her bed, taking her plate back to the desk. She clicked her tongue on the way before setting it and her empty goblet down. Facing him, she held out her wrists. "If it's all right with you, I'd like to get some sleep."

Liam eyed the red marks on her exposed skin, irritation from the metal along with old cuts that had never fully healed. He frowned, considering her face for a moment. Other than her shockingly white hair, she didn't look any different from most Isalicans. The only thing that gave her away as Feyorian was her accent, which he'd grown accustomed to and even enjoyed noticing the subtle differences.

He touched her wrist, avoiding the wounds as he gently pushed her hands down.

Those could use some proper time to heal.

"You move around a lot in your sleep. I'd rather not hear you clanking all night." He stepped around her, finishing his goblet as he put the napkin onto the desk next to the cuffs.

Dani paused before nodding, clicking her tongue as she started for the bed. Running her hand along the blankets, she chewed her bottom lip. "I could take the floor as a cat."

Liam shook his head, unfastening the buttons at the front of his tunic. "We'll share the bed. It's plenty big and I'll notice if you get up."

"Not worried about sleeping next to me? I mean, I threatened your life. Fangs in the throat and all." She climbed onto the bed.

Liam chuckled. "If you wanted to kill me, you'd have managed it a hundred times by now. I know how open I've left my sword." He shrugged off the tunic, frowning at the red spot on his white undershirt where the wine had soaked through.

"I don't know how to use a sword." Dani sat cross-legged.

"I have faith in your ability to adapt without your sight," he repeated, tugging his shirt free of his pants and slipping it over his head. He shivered at the slight chill in the room as the draft ran across his bare skin.

Dani still wore her white leathers and furs, but she removed the pelt over her shoulders. It exposed her collar, where tiny scars dotted along her skin above the bone. "I could probably wield the knife you keep in your boot."

He rolled his eyes as he lifted his foot onto the chair beside the desk, pulling the knife from his right ankle. "How do you know I keep one there?"

"Your right foot steps a little heavier than your left and the hilt taps occasionally. Educated guess."

He plopped it on the desk before untying his laces and slipping off his boots.

Dani laid on top of the blankets after kicking off her own boots, her back to his side of the bed.

Lifting the lantern from the desk, he moved it to the small table beside the bed and removed his belt to prop his sword beside him. His eyes danced to the back of Dani's neck, the tiny round scars more visible with the closer light and her hair strewn to the side. Different from other scars he'd seen, they couldn't have been caused by a blade. Settling onto the edge of the bed, he turned to inspect them, reaching out to touch them before he remembered himself and recoiled.

"What are you doing?" Dani's voice came as barely a whisper, but she didn't move.

Liam hesitated, folding one leg beneath him. "What are those scars from?"

The Feyorian brushed her shoulder-length hair down to cover them. "You don't want to know."

"I'm asking, aren't I?"

Dani rolled over, facing him. Her gaze stared blankly ahead, fingers playing with a thread from the blanket. "Maybe it's more that I don't want to think about it. Please don't make me."

He chewed his lip as he studied her face. He could see the pain and wished he could do something about it. Craving to touch her cheek, he swallowed and banished the thought.

She's still a threat. And I'm compromised by wine.

Gritting his jaw, Liam turned back to the table and lifted the lantern hood to blow it out. It clicked back into place as he settled beneath the blankets, wrestling briefly with the pillow behind his head. "Sleep sounds good, then."

Dani rolled over again, keeping her back to him. Her breathing gradually slowed, and in focusing on it, Liam found sleep.

A chill breeze brushed over Liam's face, rousing him, but darkness still enveloped the room. He shivered, pulling on the blanket and expecting to wrestle against Dani's weight for it, but it came easily. Throwing his hand out to her side of the bed, he found an empty mattress and shot up off the bed.

His foot hit the bottom of his sword, and it clattered to the ground as he blinked to get his eyes to adjust to the moonlight streaming through the wide-open window.

"You've got to be fucking kidding me." He ran his hands up through his hair, pulling on the front of it as he growled. "You're such an idiot, Talansiet. Fell right for it."

He snatched up his boots, thrusting them on and pulling his laces tight without tying them. Grabbing his stained tunic, not bothering with the undershirt, he threw it on as he grasped his cloak from beside the door.

He checked the room quickly, confirming that she wasn't just playing a trick on him again as he stomped to the window. Peering out at the paw prints the size of his hand in the snow beneath the window, he tracked them as they faded into the mud beyond. "Nymaera's breath." Buckling his sword belt, he thrust his leg over the sill and jumped out the ground-level window.

The chilly night air pinched his cheeks, and he pulled his hood up before finishing the buttons on his tunic. Scanning the night shadows, he followed the tracks across the wet ground, hoping he was following the right ones.

What was I thinking, letting her sleep without the cuffs?

The darkness hindered his vision, but he felt certain he moved west towards the country border.

And she knows about Matthias using a double now. Fuck.

An animal growled somewhere off to his right, a rumbling sound that reminded him of a cat's purr.

Abandoning the tracks, he sprinted towards it, dodging beneath low branches to catch up to Dani before she disappeared forever.

Something shuffled against the forest floor, nose snuffling through the undergrowth.

The dark shapes of the trees rushed around him as his boots slid in the mud. Reprimanding himself, he ignored the branches that snapped and struck him as he pushed ahead.

She's been manipulating me the whole time. Using Katrin...

"Dani! Stop!" Liam drew his sword as he emerged from the thicket. His stance wavered as he halted, nearly slipping as the animal in front of him came into focus.

That's not Dani.

Dark brown fur framed the bear's face, amber eyes locking on Liam. Its massive maw whipped towards him, bits of forest floor falling from its snout where it'd rummaged. The creature's bulk hung loose, confirming it'd only just emerged from hibernation, and hunger glazed its gaze. Lumbering forward, it bared its yellowed teeth and huffed as it rose onto its hind legs. Razor black claws glistening in the moonlight, it let out a bellowing roar.

Regardless of his years of training, Liam froze, wide-eyed. He stepped back, positioning his feet in his customary fighting stance.

The bear dropped to all fours and charged, saliva dripping over its jowls.

A white blur streaked from the underbrush as Liam lifted his sword. Chunks of slush cascaded through the air behind the snow panther's muscular form.

Vulnerable to her attack, Liam braced himself for the pain she would inflict

The large cat dodged around him, claws digging into the forest floor in front of him as she stopped. She emitted no sound as she shifted, and the Feyorian appeared between him and the angry beast.

Dani held up her palms, and the bear refocused on her.

It huffed as it rose onto its hind legs again, watching Dani as she approached.

Liam lunged for her, his hand closing on her shoulder. "What are you doing?" He tried to pull her back, but she slapped his hand away.

"Let me handle this," she hissed, shirking from his second attempt to grab her and continuing her approach of the bear. She held a hand out, walking within swatting distance of the bear.

It groaned and dropped again, shaking the nearby trees as it landed before her.

If she dies, Katrin will kill me.

After a moment, Dani tilted her head and touched the bear's ruff, stroking its fur. "We won't hurt you." She patted its nose, and it pushed its forehead into her stomach.

What in Nymaera's name... I'm dreaming.

Liam rubbed his eyes, blinking as the bear chuffed again, pushing harder against Dani, causing her to stumble back with a little laugh.

She gazed in Liam's direction. "Come here."

"You're joking."

"I'm not." Dani held out her hand. "Come here."

Liam eyed the bear again, then his sword, calculating where best to strike if necessary.

This is insane.

He took a wary step forward, anyway.

"You needn't be afraid," Dani whispered, meeting him partway and taking his hand. "He just woke from hibernating... and you startled him." She guided his hand towards the giant beast, pushing it into the bear's coarse fur.

Liam held his breath, fingers rigid as she guided him through the first stroke.

The bear pushed its head up against Liam's hand, and he started to draw back before Dani encouraged his hand beneath the creature's chin. Chuffing again, the bear shook its neck and lumbered away from them, disappearing into the shadows between trees.

The soldier watched, not moving from where Dani still partially held him from behind, his sword limp at his side. "What... just happened?"

"You got lucky."

"I'll say. If you..." When he turned to look at her, she was holding his knife out at him. He stiffened, eyeing the weapon before he gingerly took it from her. "Thank you. For... whatever you did there."

"I spoke to him." Dani stuffed her hands into her pockets.

"I see..." He looked her up and down before he slid his knife into his boot. "And you ran out here because...?"

Dani took a step back from him, playing with the braided leather around her thumb. "I heard a bear, and I thought it was Tallos. I didn't want him to see you and get the wrong idea."

"The wrong idea..." He repeated slowly, looking in the direction the bear had disappeared. "I take it Tallos can transform into a bear?"

Dani nodded. "If it was him, he would've killed you."

He pursed his lips. "And why's that? Other than that I'm Isalican and he's a Feyorian derua."

Cringing, she ran a hand through her hair. "Because we were sleeping in the same bed. He's protective of what's his."

"And... you're his?" Liam examined her as she nodded again, sliding his sword back into its sheath. "What would you have done if it was him?"

"I don't know. Tried to convince him to leave, maybe. But it wouldn't have worked. He would've wanted me to return to Feyor, but..." She swallowed. "I'm just grateful it wasn't him."

He furrowed his brow as his heart finally slowed. "You could have woken me."

Dani shook her head and stepped closer to him. "I needn't be responsible for more death. I'm sorry I snuck away... You... you probably thought..."

Liam nodded. "I did think." He reached for her, grabbing her upper arm, but tried to remind himself to be gentle. "I shouldn't have left the cuffs off tonight."

Her shoulders slumped, but her jaw worked. "Then I shall enjoy my last moments of freedom."

Chapter 25

Tallos pulled his gaze off Varadani and the Isalican soldier, side-eyeing the approaching black mastiff. "You didn't have faith I could handle this alone." He returned his sights to the Dtrüa who'd saved an Isalican, an enemy, from a bear.

Why didn't she let him die?

He'd made enough noise to lure her from her room, but before Varadani found him in the forest, the guard had chased her and interrupted their attempt to communicate.

He stared at her hand, trying to determine if the leather band he'd given her still rested there. The dark line at the base of her thumb became clear as she waved her hand in the bear's direction and said something to the soldier.

She's still mine. She will find another way to get a message to me.

The dog chuffed before its fur slipped from its skin, drifting like ash into the air. The shadows rippled differently than other Dtrüa transformations Tallos had seen, but not all of them were identical. The canine's spine arched upward as the limbs straightened to those of a man. A thick black pelt shrouded his shoulders, blending into his dark skin.

"This has nothing to do with my faith in you." Nysir's raspy voice rumbled like his animal form's growl. He stepped beside Tallos, peering through the shadows between them and Varadani.

She and the Isalican walked side-by-side, his hand gripping her arm.

Tallos's inferior human hearing while out of his form didn't allow him to catch the words spoken in the stillness of the frozen night, but he could see the way the other male looked at her.

He's getting into her head, trying to turn her against me.

Rage stoked the fire in Tallos's chest. "Come. Let's kill the Isalican and debrief our Dtrüa before she becomes inaccessible again." He stepped forward, feet silent in the snow.

"No." The command in Nysir's voice set every muscle in Tallos's body rigid. "You will leave this as it is."

Anger tangled with frustration, but Tallos swallowed both. "Of course, Master Dtrüa."

"Varadani may continue as she will, and you won't interfere. I am interested in this royal guard you mentioned in your previous letters." Nysir turned, his dominating stance forcing Tallos to take a step back from his superior. "Have you learned more of him?"

Tallos cleared his throat. "I have seen his ability myself, now. Though I'm not sure what to make of it. Uncanny timing, foresight like none other. His predictions are always correct, but without speaking to him, I cannot be certain how it works."

Nysir hummed, running a hand through his shaggy onyx hair. "Disappointing. But intriguing. I'd like to learn more."

"Why?" Tallos tilted his head. "How does this affect the Dtrüa?"

The master Dtrüa snarled, striking fast.

Tallos's cheek burned, the cold snap of the air sending the pain ricochetting through his jaw and neck.

"Dare to question me again, and my next strike will be with claws." Nysir's eyes flashed with flecks of pale gold. A predator in the night. "This is far larger than merely our order. Especially if it relates to the prince." He rubbed his knuckles as he stretched his hands. A flicker of shadow danced in his palm, but disappeared in a blink.

"Apologies, Master."

Nysir's pearly smile shone in the darkness. "I will seek more knowledge here. The prince stays at the temple, I presume?"

"He does. I believe the stop will be brief. I plan to follow him and Varadani when they depart. It appears she's charmed his healer."

"Impressive that your Dtrüa has managed to so thoroughly infiltrate the prince's escort. And remain there even now when that guard clearly understands her true nature."

"They underestimate her." Tallos crossed his arms.

Nysir pursed his lips. "Or you overestimate her. Keep me informed."

Chapter 26

Morning sunlight shone through the tall windows, highlighting Katrin's face while she slept.

Matthias laid next to her and stroked a shiny lock of black hair behind her ear. He admired her low, curved nose and high cheekbones.

She's gorgeous.

His heart thudded harder as he imagined what the future could hold for them, but the shadow of Lyon lurked in the back of his mind.

This can't be another thing she finds out by accident.

Her dark eyelashes fluttered as the sun brightened in its ascent, and she moaned, rolling onto her back.

"Priestess," Matthias whispered, running a fingertip from her chin down her throat to her collar. "Wake up."

She moaned again, a smile twitching her lips even as she refused to open her eyes. "What's my motivation?" She peeked through a half-open eye.

He kissed her bare shoulder. "I need to talk to you before we leave today."

"There's time before that, isn't there?" She turned back to him, running her fingers over his arm. "You can kiss me for a bit, first?"

Matthias chuckled and kissed her, giving into the warmth of her mouth before drawing back. "I think I'd find greater joy in kissing you after."

Her brow knitted as she blinked her warm honey eyes open. She touched his jaw, running her nails through his beard. Examining his face, her eyes flitted between his brow, his mouth and his eyes. "You look worried."

The prince forced a smile. "I need to tell you why we're going to Lyon."

"I thought you're meeting your father there."

"Yes, I am." He sighed. "But it's for an event."

She shifted, propping her head up with her hand. The delicate sheets draped over her body, hiding the perfection of her nakedness beneath. "What event?"

"A couple years ago, Isalica and Ziona agreed for a treaty in our mutual defense against Feyor."

"That sounds important, especially considering the recent aggressions."

Matthias nodded. "But part of that agreement was the marriage between the crown prince of Isalica and Ziona's second-to-the-throne princess."

Katrin straightened, the line between her brows hardening as she gripped the top of the sheet against her collar. "Marriage? You mean you're..." Her gaze fell to the bed, shifting wildly back and forth.

"Hold on, Kat. Hear the rest of what I have to say, please." Matthias took her hand, dipping his head to catch her gaze. "When I agreed to those terms, I had no idea... I had *no idea* this would happen. I can fix it."

"Fix it?" Her cheeks flushed. "How? You don't imagine I'd agree to be your mistress, do you?"

"Of course not." Matthias tightened his grip on her hand. "The only reason we chose *me* for the marriage was it would be a stronger bond than my brother, but he volunteered, too. I can convince the royal councils to sway towards Seiler, instead."

She bit her lower lip, meeting his gaze. "I don't want to be responsible for breaking this treaty. Isalica needs this right now, doesn't it?"

The prince nodded. "It does. But Ziona needs it, too. They'll see reason, trust me. I don't want to marry her."

She squeezed his hand, worry still clouding her eyes. "Is it really that simple, though? Matthias, I..." She looked at him, brushing her fingers over his beard again. "It feels so selfish to keep you for myself when there's so much more hinging on this. Are you sure?"

"I am. I've never been more sure of something, but on the off chance you disagreed..." He looked down. "I wanted to make it easy for you, since we're still at the temple."

Katrin tensed, glancing over his shoulder at the doorway of their room. She slowly sat up, holding the sheets still to her chest. The fabric cascaded down her side, exposing her back to him as she ran a hand through her hair.

Don't hold back now.

"I'm in love with you, Priestess." Matthias flattened his palm on the bed. "I want to figure this out with you."

She looked back at him, head tilted and a glassiness in her eyes as she sucked in a breath. "You what?"

Matthias sat up, touching her jaw. "I love you."

She closed her eyes, dark eyelashes feathered against her cheeks. A shiver passed through her as she touched his hand, lowering it from her face as she tangled their fingers. Slowly, she opened her eyes and met his gaze. "I love you, too," she whispered.

He let out a breath, happiness jolting through his veins. "Does that mean you'll still come with me?"

A small smile twitched at the edge of her lips. "I don't think I could honestly stay here again. Everything... feels different, looks different, somehow." She turned to him, the covers slipping down to her waist as she touched his chest. "I think you're crazy, but I want this, too, and I'm not ready to let it go." She leaned into him, placing a slow kiss on his mouth.

Matthias grinned into the kiss, wrapping an arm around her and pulling her down beneath him onto the bed.

Chapter 27

Nysir has served his purpose.
A shame I can't keep two.
But this Isalican royal guard...
Too interesting to pass up the opportunity.
Pity. I liked this one's ability.
Lasseth will keep me apprised of the Dtrüa.
Poor Nysir. He broke so easily.
Tallos is no threat with his distraction. He's gone after her already.
And they've left their healer at the temple.
Merissa.
All alone.
Fools. I will take her.
Her and her prized position next to the prince.
She knows his secrets.
She'll tell them all to me.

Chapter 28

Spring, 2597 R.T.

Spring banished the snow, but a chill breeze still rushed down the mountains as they entered Omensea. The ocean reflected the brightness of the sunset down the coast, creating glittering hot spots in Dani's vision.

The Dtrüa leaned against Katrin's back as their horse walked over the cobblestone road. "What does it look like?" Her cuffs prevented her from putting her hands around the acolyte's waist, but she balanced fine without it.

Liam won't trust me again after the last time he took them off.

Katrin's hair trailed against Dani's face as she turned slightly. "It's quite the view. I can see the cliffs beyond the city streets, and it looks like the water is at least a hundred feet down. Omensea's on the cliffs over the Trytonia Strait." She leaned back against Dani. "I can see the lights in Hammerdale across the way, glittering like little jewels in the black silhouette of the land on the other side. But we won't get a ship until the morning."

She heard the familiar trot of the other horses around, recognizing that Stefan rode the closest.

Of course, it hasn't been Liam guarding me anymore.

Dani wondered what made the soldier finally pass the duty of watching her off to the other crown elite. Stefan was kind enough to her, in his quiet, stoic way, but she missed teasing reactions from Katrin's brother.

Even if he is an asshole to me most of the time.

Placing her chin on Katrin's shoulder, Dani huffed. "I can tell

Stefan is riding beside us, but what about the rest of them? Is Mister Prince leading the way?"

Katrin stiffened, but nodded. "Matthias is playing himself now. There's less of a threat here. It'll be odd, considering now I need to be even more careful about how much affection I show in public." She reached behind, touching Dani's thigh. "I'm sorry I didn't tell you."

Dani scoffed. "It's all right. I know they already give you extra privileges with me as it is. You're allowed to keep your lover's secret. Where is everyone else?"

"Micah is up with Matthias at the front. Liam and Barim are behind us. I think Riez rode ahead to secure us a place to stay. There's no royal estate in Omensea, and the barracks is a mile west of here, but Matthias wanted to stay in the city."

The Dtrüa hummed. "What does that mean for me?"

"Pretty sure it means a bed. They were talking about inns at breakfast, but I've never been here before, so I don't know the names."

"Why do I get the feeling it won't be a bed to myself?" Dani turned her head to the side, listening behind her to Liam and Barim's horse's hooves.

Katrin patted her thigh again. "I'm sorry they're still so overbearing. Hopefully, when we get to the southern part of the country, they'll all loosen up. Further from Feyor."

Dani sighed but held her breath when something else made a sound behind the men's horses. Closing her eyes, she breathed deeper, picking up a faint scent that made her heart leap.

He's not here.

Even as she thought it, doubt crept into her mind and she breathed in Tallos's scent again. Her fingers rubbed against the spot on her thumb where his ring still sat. It felt tighter than usual, irritating the skin beneath.

Paranoia seared through her veins, and she suddenly wished she could see. Vague shapes moved in her vision, blurred and incomprehensible.

"Dani? Did you hear me?"

The Dtrüa turned to Katrin again, trying to slow her breathing. "No, sorry. I was distracted. What did you say?"

"I asked if you're all right not having dinner together tonight. Matthias said there was some place he wanted to take me." Katrin turned over her shoulder, shifting in the saddle. "What's wrong?"

"I'm fine. And that's fine. I can eat with the others." Dani sniffed the air, trying to catch his scent again, but found nothing.

It's my imagination.

Pots clanked from somewhere to their left, making Dani flinch. Taking a deep breath, she focused on the sound of clip-clopping hooves beneath them.

The horses came to a stop and Dani braced herself on the saddle before swinging down to the ground. Her boot caught on an uneven stone, but a strong hand steadied her by the elbow. "Thanks, Stefan."

The quiet guard patted her forearm and let go, his boots tapping over the road.

"I'm perfectly capable of carrying my pack, Barim." Katrin's voice.

The big man huffed, throwing her satchel over his shoulder. "But carrying everyone's packs makes me look strong. I enjoy showing off for the city ladies."

A conversation continued between Micah and Matthias. "That place? Really? A little formal, don't you think?"

"What's wrong with formal? Will be a pleasant change from campfire food."

"How much is it to stable the horses?"

Shutters snapped shut, and a dog barked.

"I'll take them."

Dani's heart picked up speed as the sun disappeared, taking most of her blurry vision with it.

"Let me at least carry that!"

A cart rumbled past, wooden wheels crunching over loose stones on the road.

"Do you want to hit up O'Conivers tonight like the ol' days?"

"We can introduce our newbie to their amber whisky."

A bell tolled, and keys jangled somewhere close.

Dani covered her ears, closing her eyes.

Make it stop. Make it stop.

She backed up but tripped on something. A pair of warm arms wrapped around her from behind.

"Whoa." Liam helped her back to her feet, grabbing her shoulders. "Where are you going?"

Her breathing came quick, the sounds and smells of the city still overwhelming her senses. She covered her ears again, keeping her eyes shut, and ignored his question.

Something smacked hard against the leather of Liam's chest.

"Ow."

"What are you doing, you brute?" Katrin smacked him again. "Leave her alone."

Liam's hands disappeared from her shoulders, and he stepped back. "I didn't do anything."

Katrin touched Dani's arm and leaned close. "Come on, let's get inside. It'll be quieter there."

Dani nodded furiously, clutching Katrin. "Quieter would be good. I need quieter."

A fur pelt brushed over Dani's wrists, hiding the cuffs.

"No need to alarm the poor innkeeper." Katrin's voice was gentle and understanding.

Tiny bells on the door chimed as they crossed the threshold into a building. The door settled shut behind them, and the roar of the outside dimmed. The smell of freshly baked bread filled Dani's nostrils.

Her heart slowed, and she opened her eyes, swallowing. "I don't like this town."

The door swung open again, bringing with it the noise and Barim's footsteps, made louder by the plethora of bags he carried.

He froze. "Sorry, sorry." He spoke to them, and Dani could imagine the glare Katrin gave. The door swung open again, and

Matthias and Micah's voices entered.

Katrin sighed, pulling Dani along a plush carpet. "Is your dining area through here?"

A cheery female voice responded. "Yes, miss."

Taking Dani's elbow again, Katrin guided her on and the sweet scent of the bread doubled, mixing with the now familiar smell of ginger cookies.

The acolyte hummed as she guided her friend into a dimly lit room and pulled out a chair for her. "I wish you could see the view from here." She squeezed Dani's hand as she sat across from her, the polished surface of the table smooth under her fingertips. "Hammerdale looks like a bunch of diamonds sparkling in a coal mine, and the moon is lighting up the whole strait like it's a river of silver. I don't want to know how much Matthias is paying for rooms in this fancy inn."

Dani focused on calming her emotions. "And to think, maybe one day you'll live in a palace with him. You might want to get used to the fancier things."

Katrin's grip doubled. "I've caught myself thinking about that, but it still seems so foolish. With Matthias talking about calling off the marriage to the Zionan princess, I don't rightly know what to think of it all."

Furrowing her brow, Dani leaned closer. "Try to enjoy it. I know that's hard when our countries are on the brink of war, but... you're in love with a prince, and he feels the same. Isn't that at least a little exciting?"

"And terrifying!" Katrin's hair brushed over Dani's hands as she leaned in, too. "Acolyte to princess? That's like a children's story."

What do prisoners turn into in children's stories?

Dani chewed her bottom lip. "I hope you have a good time tonight. You two haven't been alone in days."

She groaned. "I know, it's been awful. I've got so many things I want to talk about with him. And I still don't know how to say half of it."

A glass smashed on the floor, and Dani jumped, stiffening. "What was that?"

The shards shuffled as someone began sweeping, and Katrin squeezed her hands.

"Just a clumsy barmaid. You're safe."

"Clumsy? Or swooning over royalty?" The Dtrüa took a deeper breath, trying to focus.

"Or the crown elites with him. They're honestly not bad looking for soldiers." A smile hung in Katrin's tone.

Dani chuckled. "You said they were handsome before."

"I mean, they are. I just... don't care anymore?" She laughed. "Gods, listen to me. I'm completely smitten."

"There are worse things." Dani smirked. "I wish I could be of more help... But I like him. He seems like a good man."

"You do plenty, all things considered. I'm just grateful to have you. Can you imagine if it was just me traveling with all these men?"

Dani scoffed. "They all like you."

They hate me.

Katrin ran her thumb over Dani's skin. "Do you want anything to drink?"

Nodding, Dani swallowed. "I've never been in a city this loud before. A glass of wine might help take the edge off."

Katrin squeezed again before she scooted her chair back and stood. "I'll be right back."

The Dtrüa touched the chain under the fur, wishing she'd not broken Liam's trust at the temple.

"She's leaving you alone already, huh?" Liam spoke from the doorway, taking quiet steps towards her.

Can't he give me a break?

"Just getting us some wine," Dani whispered, pulling her hands to herself and tucking them under the table.

The chair Katrin had sat in across from her ground against the floor as Liam settled into it, his elbow thunking on the table. "Spoiling you, too."

"Are you just here to harass me?" Dani tried to keep her voice even. "I have done nothing wrong."

He sat quietly for a moment, the heel of his boot tapping on the floor. "You looked like you were having a hard time outside. I came to check on you."

"I'm fine." Dani faced the window, resisting the urge to push it open. "I'm not used to so many sounds and... smells. This place is worse than Undertown."

Boots stomped into the room as Barim's baritone laugh echoed, Riez slapping him on the back.

"Liam!" Micah paused at their table. "We have a bit of a tradition every time we're in Omensea. Involves drinking and cards at a place down the street. Join us."

A bottle clinked against a glass as Katrin placed it on the table's edge. "Can't you four keep it to a reasonable volume?"

"Not tonight." Riez laughed. "But we'll be out of your hair as soon as your brother gets off his ass."

"It's in my seat, anyway." Katrin kicked Liam's tapping foot.

"Aren't you leaving for dinner with Matthias soon?" Micah at least tried to lower his boisterous voice. "You should probably freshen up. It's a fancy place."

"So who's staying here with Dani?" Liam shuffled his legs under the table, his knee bumping Dani's.

"I don't need a babysitter," Dani mumbled.

"She's no danger. Take those cuffs off and she'll be fine." Micah sounded far from worried.

Liam never told them I ran off.

"She's still a prisoner."

"Lay off that will you?" Katrin sounded terse. "But I should go bathe before Matthias comes to find me." Her hand closed on Dani's shoulder.

"You know what, guys, I'll pass for tonight." Liam tilted his chair back, and it creaked on two legs. "I'll stay here to keep an eye on her."

Lucky me.

Micah sighed. "Suit yourself."

The four of them resumed their conversation, exiting the room and taking their noise with them.

The cork popped off the wine bottle. "Thanks for the drink, Katy girl. But you go have fun." The wine sloshed as he poured it. The sound paused while he slid the glass across the table to Dani, then filled another.

Katrin hesitated. "Dani?"

"I'll be all right. Go enjoy yourself." Dani kept her face angled at the window, not reaching for the wine.

"You tell me if he's an ass when I get back, all right? I'll make sure he regrets every vile thing he does."

Liam gave a low chuckle. "I'm not a villain."

"Prove it." Katrin walked away, her footfalls fading from Dani's hearing.

The dining room was suddenly quiet, except for the gentle swoosh of the barkeep's towel as he cleaned a distant counter.

Are there any other guests in this place?

Liam's chair creaked again as he leaned back, sipping his wine. He hummed. "Oh, that's actually good."

Dani ignored him, staring at where the window would have provided her a beautiful view if she could see it.

His chair thunked against the floor, the table shifting as he leaned against it. "I'd offer to open it, but the sounds outside would probably make it a lot worse in here for you. I know my company is enough to tolerate."

"You should have gone with the others." Dani lifted her hands from beneath the table, resting them on top again with the fur still hiding her cuffs. "You would've had fun."

"Doubtful." He tilted the wine bottle on the table as if studying the label. "I don't play cards."

"No. I'm sure you prefer interrogating prisoners and keeping an eye on your enemy."

"I'm no fool."

Dani laughed, but it held no mirth. "Agree to disagree."

Liam snorted. "I guess so." He leaned back again. "So, what'd this Tallos guy do to you?"

Her skin tingled. "Why do you care?"

"Because I can tell how much just hearing his name affects you." His glass clicked on the tabletop as he set it down. "And ever since you thought he was outside the temple, you keep checking over your shoulder."

"He did nothing to me." Dani reached for her wine. Finding it, she sampled the sweet alcohol.

"Then why are you afraid of him? I'd think a fellow shape-shifter coming after you would be a relief. Get you back home again."

Frustration heated her face. "I don't want to go back to Feyor. Tallos... Tallos loves me, he just..."

How am I still telling myself that?

"Can I get you two something to eat?"

The same cheery voice from the front room made Dani jump and tuck her hands under the table again. She hadn't even realized the girl approached, too angry with Liam to have heard her footsteps.

"Chef's smoked pork is best in the northern isle."

"Sounds good, thank you." Dani rolled her shoulders.

"Sir?"

"Me, too." Liam sounded distracted.

The girl's footsteps carried her away from the table, moving to the bar.

"Give me your hands." Liam's voice was stern, but held an edge she didn't recognize.

Gulping, Dani slid her hands across the table towards him.

The key jangled from his pocket, reminding her yet again of the time before her training started in Feyor. She grimaced and squeezed her eyes closed, willing away the memories.

The muffled lock clicked beneath the fur, and he moved to her other wrist.

"You flinch every time I pull out the keys," he whispered, taking the fur and the cuffs together as he pulled them across the table.

Dani drew her hands back to herself, rubbing her wrists. "This isn't the first time I've been chained."

"Feyor chained you?"

Anger spiked in her chest, and she aimed her gaze at him. "Wouldn't you put up a fight if someone tried to inject *you* with another's blood?"

Liam's breath slowed. "I suppose I would." He slid his glass to the side, abandoning his drink. "They did that to you to make you... " He hesitated, trying to say it right but still failing. "Drua."

Dani picked up her wine and downed the rest of it. "For years." She put the glass down, exhaling slowly. "You can't even *imagine* the agony."

The bottle slid along the table before he lifted it, pouring more into her glass. "No... I'm sure I can't."

"Tallos supervised the end of my... transition. He helped me adapt to what they'd done, cared for me after each session. He told me it would be worth it, and that without this, I would live a meaningless, blind life."

"I'm sorry. That you had to endure that."

Liam's words hit her like a bucket of water on a fire, and she blinked, falling silent as the innkeeper brought their food.

Chapter 29

The plates thunked down in front of them, and no one said a word as the innkeep walked away.

Dani's brow knitted together, and she whispered, "Going back to Feyor terrifies me, do you understand?"

Liam stared at the fork beside his plate, wondering how he could eat after hearing what she'd suffered. Her own people had tortured her to make her into what they wanted.

I'm such a fucking asshole.

The realization of her innocence had come gradually over the days after leaving the temple. He noticed her cautious glances more frequently as they got closer to Omensea. The constant fiddling with the ring on her thumb that clearly held some significance. He'd avoided her to allow himself the time to contemplate what he really believed. What Dani's true motivations were.

She hadn't run. Even when she could have while the bear killed him. Instead, she'd intervened and saved him. He'd been cruel and didn't deserve the kindness.

He picked up his wine, taking a gulp of the fruity white. "I've been completely unfair to you, Dani." He slid the glass onto the table, twisting its stem between his fingers. "And I'm sorry for that, too."

She sipped her fresh glass of wine. "So if you'd known I wasn't secretly a spy, you wouldn't have snuck those vile vegetables onto my plate at the temple?"

He laughed, a wave of relief washing through him at knowing she forgave him enough to joke. "I had no idea you wouldn't like them."

He picked up his fork, the sweet tang of the bourbon sauce on the pork enticing him. "None on this plate, though."

"Thank Nymaera." Dani patted the table to find her fork, picking it up. "So does this mean I'm free of the cuffs for the rest of the night?"

"Don't push your luck." Liam took a slow bite, watching her.

Her shoulders slumped, and she gaped at him, her stark white hair framing her clouded grey eyes.

A knot formed in his stomach as she lifted her glass to her lips again.

"Really? I tell you my darkest secrets and I'm *still* your prisoner?" Dani sipped before putting it down.

He shrugged. "Until there's a formal royal pardon, that's just the way it goes." Liam took another bite, moaning at the flavorful taste.

Dani narrowed her eyes and sighed. She delicately checked the plate with her empty hand before spearing a potato with her fork. "What if I promise not to run away tonight? Then can I sleep without cuffs?"

"I'll take it under consideration. You are rather cute when you're asleep."

His fork paused as it pierced another bite.

Did I just say that out loud?

Her jaw flexed, and she stilled. "Can I ask you something?"

He hesitated, narrowing his eyes as he chewed. "Sure?"

"What... do I look like?"

"Really?"

Color rose to her cheeks, and she averted her gaze. "Well, how would I know?"

His chest tightened unexpectedly as he looked at her. Really looked. He swallowed, setting his fork down. "You... have a good face."

She frowned.

He chewed his lip before he continued. "Your chin is a little rounded, small, and it meets your cheeks in a gentle curve. Your eyes are a little bigger than some girls, but they look perfect on your face. I admit I've been a little confused by your white hair compared to the dark eyebrows, but haven't thought too much about it. The white works really well with your skin." He passed his eyes over again, as he tried to consider what else he hadn't described. "Your nose is cute, I'm not really sure how to explain beyond that. And your lips..." His stomach clenched. "They're..." He licked his own, a sudden fire in him making it difficult to speak.

"They're what?" Dani touched her full, pink lips and rolled them together. "Are they hideous?"

"No!" He blurted the word, wincing. "They're... very nice."

She relaxed, dipping her chin before putting her fork down. "Maybe... someday, you'll let me touch your face. So I may see it the only way I know how."

His body ached, and he wanted to drag his chair beside her. "Are you curious?"

Dani nodded, her chest rising faster.

Everything inside him screamed. Before he knew what was happening, he pushed his chair back. "You could right now, if you'd like? Maybe not here, though..." He stood, his fingers brushing hers on the tabletop. "If... you want?"

She took his hand and rose to her feet, nodding again.

Her hand fit perfectly in his as he led her away from the table, abandoning their food, drinks, and the cuffs, still shrouded in the fur. He needed to get away from the prying eyes of the innkeep, and took Dani to the narrow hallway leading to the stairs. He paused, turning to her as his heart thundered.

What is wrong with me?

Taking both her hands, he lifted them to his cheeks, watching her mouth part ever so slightly.

Dani's eyes danced around where she touched, blinking. Her fingertips trailed over his cheeks, moving around his clean-shaven jaw before venturing to his eyebrows and forehead. Her touch softened over his nose, ending with her thumb caressing his lips.

Her chest heaved, matching his own quickening breath. Touching her hair, he followed the strand down her jaw as he stepped into her.

Their mouths met in a flurry, and Liam lost all sense of the space around him as her lips pressed against his.

Her hands met his chest, shocking him from the moment as she shoved him away.

Horror rocked through him as he realized what had happened, and he pressed himself against the wall opposite her. He panted as he braced his hands against the wall to keep from reaching for her again. "Dani." He felt like he could hardly breathe. "I'm—"

"Don't." She swallowed, still breathing fast as she crossed the hallway to him. Her hands found his chest again, sliding up to his face and pulling his lips to hers.

He tried to restrain himself, but the allure of her encouraged his hands forward again. They brushed her hips as he hungrily returned the kiss she gave before he broke away. "Dani, I—" He slid his hands to the small of her back.

"Shut up and kiss me." Dani ran her hands through his hair, nails dragging over his scalp.

He smiled and obeyed, leaning down and claiming her mouth again. He guided her back until she hit the opposite wall, caressing her body. Their tongues danced against each other, each kiss growing deeper and more desperate.

Dani pulled his hips close, but stopped the kiss. "Aren't we in a hallway?"

Liam tried to understand her question as he sought another kiss, resolving to taste the skin on her neck. "Hallway? Yes."

She gasped in his ear as he sucked beneath her earlobe. "Let's *not* be in a hallway."

He nipped her, his hands finding her backside as he lifted her from her feet so he could gain better access to her skin. "There's stairs." He kissed down her neck. "Those sound hard right now." He savored the feel of her against him as his hips pressed against her.

Dani whimpered, clutching his shoulders. "Liam."

He growled as he released her, and she landed on her feet as he steadied her. He kissed her again before taking her hand and tugging her gently down the hallway.

She clicked her tongue and then cringed. "Sorry."

"For what?"

"You hate that noise."

"Does it help you?"

Dani nodded.

"Then I don't hate it." He wrapped an arm around her, nuzzling close to her ear, whispering. "Now get up these stairs before I carry you."

Her boot hit the first step, and she took the rest as if she could see them, slowing near the top and tentatively walking down the upper hallway. She turned towards him, licking her lower lip.

The fire in him lit again, and he hurried up the final stairs. He couldn't contain the need to feel her again as he wrapped his arms around her, pulling her close with a fevered kiss.

Her back thumped against the wall, her arms circling around him.

She tasted of the wine, the sweet tannins further seducing his tongue against hers. She moaned into his mouth as he lifted her again, unable to control the needy rock of his hips against her despite their clothing.

A latch turned close to them.

Too close.

Liam opened his eyes, seeing the door he'd pressed Dani to. He dropped her as the knob twisted, and she hurried away from him, running her hands over her hair.

"Shit." He spun, looking down to the front of his breeches and seeing the effect Dani had on him.

There's no hiding that.

The door swung open as Dani retreated further down the hall.

Liam followed her a few steps, keeping his back to whoever came to check what the noise was. His eyes drifted down Dani's body, admiring the curves he'd previously denied himself from observing. His mouth felt dry.

Damn.

"Liam!" Katrin's voice made him cringe. "What the hells is going on?"

Dani lifted her hand to her mouth while facing away, looking almost upset, but Liam knew she was catching her breath.

"Hey, Kat." He failed horribly at disguising the awkwardness of his voice. "You haven't left for dinner yet?" Keeping his body facing away from his sister to hide his arousal, he looked over his shoulder at her.

Katrin held a towel up to her wet hair, rubbing it. "Not yet." She glanced past him. "You all right, Dani?"

Dani nodded, finally turning. "Yes. I just want to be in my room." She reached for the closest door.

"Other one. Across the hall." Liam looked at the ceiling as Dani found the right door and shoved it open, disappearing inside.

Katrin sighed. "Thank you for at least taking her cuffs off. She's having a hard time here."

Shit, I left those downstairs.

"Like I said, sis. Not heartless." Liam started after Dani, waving over his shoulder. "Have a little faith?"

Katrin narrowed her eyes. "What's wrong with you?"

"Nothing!" He reached the door Dani had closed behind her, checking the knob. "I'm... going to make sure she's comfortable." He pushed the door open before Katrin could ask another question, hurrying into the darkness and shutting it behind him. Sighing, he leaned against it.

Dani stood a few feet away, facing him. "I thought you hated me."

"I..." He eyed her, her entire being entrancing him in the moonlight of the window behind her. "I'm an idiot, and I made a mistake. I shouldn't have."

She took one step towards him. "Shouldn't have...?"

"Hated you. Doubted you." He remained still, watching her approach more slowly. It made his heart thunder at her subtle grace. "I've... denied the little tugs I've been feeling towards you, but after hearing what you've survived... I see you. And Dani." Her name still felt odd, yet it made his heart beat faster. "You're beautiful."

Dani pulled at the tie attaching the pelt to her shoulders and let it drop to the floor. "I wanted to touch you again after Undertown and then..." She swallowed, slipping out of her boots. "At the temple. I..."

His chest heaved as she grew closer, pulling her thick leather tunic over her head.

The thin undershirt glowed around her where the moon cut through the sheer material, allowing him the view of her hourglass shape. It made his breath hitch.

Dani stopped in front of him, touching his chest again before sliding her hands up his neck. "You should take your boots off."

He licked his lips and obeyed, loosening his laces so he could slip out of the boots. His knife's hilt thunked against the ground. He grinned. "How do I know this isn't all part of your evil master plan?" He allowed himself to look down at her cleavage, visible beneath the neckline of her shirt.

A smile twitched at her lips. "How long are you going to wonder?" She touched his face again, running her thumb over his cheek to his mouth. "What do I have to do to prove myself to you?"

Liam's mind fell to the baser instincts of his body as he imagined all the ways. "Let's see what I can do to apologize first." He touched her hips, sliding his hands up under her shirt to touch her skin.

Her eyes closed, and she leaned into the touch, seeking his mouth again.

Gently, he guided her back across the room, lowering her onto the bed while he unbuttoned the front of his tunic. Her hands found the part, helping him shrug it off, and she pulled his undershirt from his breeches.

Each kiss led into the next until he kissed down her body,

kneeling between her legs as he slid her pants from her.

Dani arched her back, lifting her shirt over her head and letting it cascade to the floor.

He lavished at the sight of her, running his hand along the outside of her leg and to her hip as he teased a gasp from her with a flick of his fingers between her legs.

She tugged on his arm to bring his torso back to hers. "I want to feel your skin. All of you."

He savored her lower lip with a low hum, teasing a circle with his hands. "I wasn't done here, though."

Dani pressed against him, wrapping her legs around his as she moaned. "I don't care. Take off your pants."

He gave a low chuckle, teasing it against the skin of her neck as he bit her. "Yes, ma'am." He reached for his belt, unbuckling it and slipping out of the rest of his clothes in one movement.

Her breathing sped, legs returning around him. She pulled him against her, and he teased her warmth with his tip.

Liam's mouth fell open as he sank into her, a loud growl mingling with her gasp.

Dani held him close, nails digging into his back as her hips rocked with his. She pressed her heel into his leg and twisted against him, rolling them over until she straddled him.

Moonlight glimmered off her smooth skin, her upper body leaning over him with her hands on the bed. Her necklace swayed with her movement, the white tooth hovering between them.

He took in the sight of her as their bodies rocked in tandem, her warmth creating a spiral of pleasure he wasn't yet ready for. Pulling her closer, he claimed her mouth again, and her pendant grazed over his chest. Gripping the curve of her backside, he lifted her, despite his body's protest.

Dani's head sank into the pillows as he shifted over her, his hand trailing over the curves of her side as he plunged his tongue against hers. Their lips moved in a dizzying rhythm as his hips surged against her. He paused within her, straining his muscles to remain in control.

She breathed deeper as he pulled his mouth from hers, his lips finding her neck as he kissed his way down her. His body throbbed, but he withdrew from her, his mouth leaving a wet trail down her body. He encouraged her legs apart as he kissed her abdomen and ran his fingers along the inside of her thigh. She twitched, and it only made him smile as he moved his mouth lower.

Dani gasped as his mouth closed on her, tasting her sweetness with a press of his tongue. He explored, marveling at her whimpers at each reverent stroke. Each twist and pulse of his mouth made her legs quiver, her breathing uneven.

A thrill filled him when her hips rose off the bed. She cried out, gripping handfuls of the blanket at her sides. He encouraged more from her with a low hum against her sex, and her hand found his shoulder.

She pulled, and he obliged, allowing his kisses to trail back up her body until they met her dry mouth.

Her legs wrapped around him again, guiding his stiffness back to her. The warmth of her greeted him as he dove inside her, unable to hold in a ragged gasp of ecstasy. Everything in him crashed like a storm.

Dani pushed back with her hips, one of her hands exploring up to grip his hair. She broke away from his mouth to kiss and bite his shoulder, whimpering as she tightened around him.

Another growl rumbled from his chest, breath rising as he watched her body shift with his, every inch of him growing more taut.

His skin muffled her cry, and she gripped him tighter.

He slowed, forcing himself to hold to his own control at the sound of her, riding the slow wave of her pleasure before he began again, more urgently than before.

Dani gasped, finding his mouth as another shudder of pleasure shook her body, propelling him over the edge with her.

His body shook against hers as he broke the kiss, pushing as deep as he could a final time as the euphoria roared through him. The room brightened, and he stroked her cheek, twisting a strand of her hair, silver in the moonlight, around a finger.

As she opened her eyes, they glistened, and tears slid down her temples.

Sudden guilt and fear filled him as his thumb traced the trail. "What's wrong?" He shifted his hips to draw from her, but she held him tight.

She smiled, touching his face, and kissed him. "Nothing. Absolutely nothing."

He brushed his thumb over her eyelash, swiping a tear as he leaned down and kissed her again. He took his time with it, drawing out the sensation as he lifted from her, settling onto the bed beside her.

Dani turned with him, running a hand down his chest. Her fingertips traced each muscle, exploring his skin and studying each little scar she found.

Touching her hair again, he played with a strand while studying the lingering wetness in her eyes. "Did I hurt you?" he whispered.

Her gaze found his face, but didn't focus on a particular spot. "No." She grinned and laughed, shaking her head. "No, not at all."

"Then why the tears?"

Her eyebrows upturned in the center and she swallowed, fingers moving to his face. "I don't know. I just finally feel like my life is mine. That was..." Color pinked her cheeks. "Incredible."

He smiled, sliding his hand into her hair and leaning to kiss her forehead before encouraging her against his chest. The way she fit and the warmth of her made him want to never let go. His fingers played along the leather band at the back of her neck, which held the feline tooth necklace he'd admired before.

She nestled in close, her nose at his neck as she took a deep breath. "You smell good."

"Not like Brussels sprouts then?" He traced lines along her back.

Dani laughed and nipped him. "Not even a little. Your scent is very... teal."

"That's an interesting way to describe it." He heaved his own breath of her hair, picking up the smell of the pines and fresh snow. "Do you often smell colors?"

"Well... It's more the other way. Scents have colors, but I see them brighter as a cat."

He hummed, his eyelids suddenly remarkably heavy, yet he didn't want to sleep and wake to find this a dream. He held her tighter, wrapped his leg around hers.

Dani reached behind her, patting her hand over the bed until she found the edge of a blanket. Pulling it over them, she returned her face to his skin. "Trust me without cuffs yet?"

He laughed, kissing the top of her head. "Hardly. In fact, now that I know you wield this power over me, I'm inclined to be more cautious."

She nipped him again. "I promise not to misuse it."

He narrowed his eyes, catching her gently beneath the chin and lifting it. "Please do. As often as you want."

Dani's hips rocked against him and she brushed her lips over his. "I'm going to hold you to that." Her tongue flicked over his bottom lip, and she teased him with the hint of a kiss.

His chest rumbled, the heat she elicited rising again as she rolled on top of him, and he pulled her to him for another kiss.

Morning light washed through the room, but Liam resisted the inclination to open his eyes. As his senses cleared, the lingering worry that Dani had vanished in the night faded with the gentle pressure of her breath. It tickled his chest where she still lay curled in sleep. His chest tightened as he inhaled her familiar scent, hand brushing her bare back, tingling with numbness beneath her.

I'd willingly lose the arm to keep this position. But the others will wonder where I am if I miss morning routine.

He winced, chewing his bottom lip as he tried to conceive how he could escape without waking her.

Admit defeat, Talansiet.

Liam chuckled at himself as he placed a soft kiss on Dani's hair.

She stirred, her hand sliding over his chest as her eyes fluttered open.

"Good morning." His voice came out surprisingly low, memories of their night lingering. Brushing his fingers beneath her chin, he encouraged her lips up to his, desperate to savor them again.

Dani's mouth responded to his, but she hesitated and pulled away. "Liam." Her hand moved over the side of his neck, and she shook her head. "This was a bad idea. If Tallos finds out..."

The words caused his gut to clench at first, but then that name came up again. He stroked her hair, kissing her forehead. "Don't think about him. I won't let anything happen to you."

She shifted closer, pressing her bare skin to his chest and nestling her nose into the crook of his neck. "What are we doing?"

"Acting on mutual attractions?" He held her tight, tangling their legs together. "I don't regret last night." His stomach churned. "Do you?"

Dani shook her head again, touching his lips with her thumb as her hand caressed his face. "No. I just... I guess I'm surprised. Not exactly how I thought the evening would go."

He laughed, shaking her with it. "Neither did I. But I'll say it was a pleasant surprise." He stroked her hair, looking into her foggy eyes. "And I don't know about you, but I certainly wouldn't mind waking up like this more often."

A smile twitched Dani's lips. "Me, too."

He brushed her mouth with another warm kiss, mind fluttering back to his usual morning routine with the other guards. He nipped her lower lip before pulling away with a slight flinch. "I need to get moving, though."

Dani nodded, drawing from him and sitting up. "I know. You boys have to go spar and compare muscles." She smirked at him before feeling around the bed. Finding her undershirt, she pulled it on. "They're going to wonder where you are."

Liam crawled behind Dani and slipped his hands around her waist beneath her shirt as he nuzzled into her neck. His fingertips played along her abdomen. "Maybe we should let them wonder."

She touched his face with hers. "It might be better if they don't know."

His brow furrowed, but realization began to settle in his mind. Drawing his hands slowly from her, he kissed her temple. "You might be right." It pained him to say it, suddenly thrilled with what he had discovered about Dani and him. He buried the instinct to tell the world. "This... could look really bad."

The Dtrüa turned around, lacing her arms over his shoulders. "But we know it's not." Kissing him, she sighed. "We can keep it as our secret."

"But then it feels like something we should be ashamed of." Liam touched her jaw. "And I'm not."

Dani smiled. "Neither am I. But let's at least figure out what this is for us before we start telling other people."

He nodded. "You're right." He brushed her lips again as a knock came at the door.

"Liam! What's the holdup? I'm hungover and still out the door before you." Barim's groggy voice trailed down the hall as he walked away.

"Shit." Liam slid from around her, yanking on his pants and tunic.

"Bring breakfast back with you after?" Dani leaned back on the bed, crossing her bare legs.

His eyes betrayed him, following the smooth line of her body up, and his mouth went dry as he imagined pulling her shirt off. Groaning, he buttoned his breeches. "Will you still be dressed like that when I get back?" He cinched his sword belt into place while slipping on his boots.

Dani laughed. "Unlikely."

"Damn." Liam smirked as he crossed back to the bed, teasingly running his hand up the inside of her thigh. "I guess I'll just have to fix that when I get back, then."

She quirked an eyebrow. "Better get going before I change my mind and make you stay."

He groaned as he leaned to kiss her again, walking his fingers up beneath the hem of her shirt. "See you soon."

Chapter 30

Matthias narrowed his eyes at the white owl on Stefan's forearm. "Why does Snow always go to you? He's bonded to *me*."

"He's got the touch." Riez smirked, sliding a whetstone down his blade. "Maybe it's because he never tries to talk to him."

Stefan glanced sideways at his comrade, his lips twitching.

"Or that he didn't give him a silly name like *Snow*." Micah, leaning nearby on a fence post, smirked.

Matthias scowled. "I was *eight*. You wanted to name him Hooty, remember?"

Riez snorted. "Hooty?"

Micah frowned, crossing his arms. "It sounded good at the time."

Barim howled as Liam struck his backside with the flat of his blade again.

"Too slow, big guy." Liam grinned, running his hand through his sweaty hair.

He's in a good mood this morning.

With a bellow, Barim surged forward, and the young soldier caught his blade above his head, bracing his block with his other palm. He loosened his block, letting it fall towards his shoulder as he juked sideways, catching Barim's ankle with his boot and sending the big man stumbling. Barely catching himself, Barim swung again, but Liam parried it, continuing the defensive movement with each attempt the other made.

Micah chuckled under his breath as his attention returned to the spar. "You're giving him a run for his money, Talansiet."

"I got him on the run!" Barim growled, lashing at Liam as his back neared the fence of the inn's back patio they'd claimed for their morning practice.

The new crown elite ducked, swinging his sword around until the flat of it smacked Barim's lower back. "Not so much. You left your right side completely open." Liam huffed, pushing his sleeves up as a bead of sweat ran down his brow. "Next time, keep your guard lower." He tapped his sword on Barim's, forcing it down as the big man sputtered.

Matthias took the owl's parchment Stefan handed him and unrolled it.

> *Son,*
>
> *I write this with a heavy hand. Feyor has declared war. In light of this, Ziona retracted their offer of a treaty. I am departing Hammerdale, and I need you to remain in Omensea until I can come to an agreement with our allies. Seiler is with me, and he seems confident we can convince them to carry on with the arranged marriage.*
>
> *Stay safe.*
>
> *Geroth Rayeht*

"Fuck." Matthias paced away from the group, rereading the note.

"Bad news?" Micah crossed his arms, eyeing the letter in Matthias's hands.

The prince grunted. "We're officially at war. The wedding is off."

"Your dad actually declared war?"

Matthias shook his head. "Feyor did."

"Shit." Riez stowed his blade, despite preparing to face Liam.

"So what does that mean?" Liam straightened, his sword dangling at his side in a relaxed grip. "Where do we go?"

"We stay here." Matthias folded the letter. "My father is on his way to Lyon and will update us on any progress. Until then, we wait. I need to write him back." He motioned to Stefan with his head. "Come with me, owl whisperer."

Chapter 31

Tallos leaned against a stone wall, watching the crown elites laugh as they finished their sparring. Their voices didn't carry over the breeze enough to hear their words, but he couldn't risk getting closer.

As they walked back to the road, Tallos averted his gaze, listening.

"Next time I think I'll let you keep sleeping. Where did you learn to sword fight like that?"

"Nowhere special. Went to the military academy in Nema's Throne. Then practice. Just picked it up."

"Well, it's impressive." The auburn bearded man snorted.

Tallos waited for them to walk past before he stood straight and sauntered after them, keeping his distance. A waft of Varadani's scent hit his nose, and he frowned.

"Where can I get a decent breakfast here?" The man who smelled like Tallos's Dtrüa looked at the other.

"Ameliana's bakery has a few carts around town. One by the fountain in the square. They sell the best pastries." The burly guard patted his belly. "Just be careful, Liam, or you might lose that youthful figure."

The soldier laughed. "I'll keep that in mind."

Liam split from his companions, Varadani's lilac scent still drifting from him.

Tallos's throat clenched, and he followed.

Has she forgotten she belongs to me?

The guard approached the cart vendor, and Tallos fell in line behind him.

Anger seethed in his gut at how strong his lover's scent became, and his breath quickened.

Control yourself. This isn't the place.

Dousing his rage, he stretched his jaw. "If you haven't tried the chocolate danish, you should. It's to die for." He relaxed his speech into the timbres more common in Isalica.

Liam turned only partially towards Tallos, but maintained a relaxed position. The hilt of his sword sat easily within reach of the Dtrüa. "Chocolate, huh?" He rubbed his chin, peering into the baskets of pastries. He chuckled, muttering to himself. "I don't even know if she likes chocolate..."

She. He's fetching breakfast for her, now.

Tallos willed his breathing to remain even, his upper lip twitching.

The soldier pointed at several baskets, and the girl managing the cart plucked up the various confectionaries.

"Thanks for the suggestion, friend." Liam nodded to Tallos as he produced several iron marks and dropped them into the seller's waiting palm.

"Anytime." Tallos turned as Liam started away. "Say, do any of your comrades want to make a few coin?"

The plan rapidly assembled itself in his head. He'd passed an abandoned structure while approaching the city from the south to stay downwind of Varadani.

The soldier paused. "My comrades?"

Tallos lifted an apologetic hand. "I assumed." He gestured at his own shoulder, and Liam eyed the insignia on his, then relaxed. "News of your party's presence in the city is the gossip of the morning."

The man's stance relaxed further. "Oh. That makes sense, I suppose."

Use his empathy against him.

"See, I need some help this afternoon at the mill, and I have had no luck finding someone strong enough to help me. If I don't get the grinder working again, we're going to have a flour shortage here. I was going to post a notice this morning, but the sooner I find someone, the better."

I want him alone.

Liam paused, eyeing Tallos as he tucked the paper package of pastries under his arm. "Must be a big job if you can't handle it on your own." He glanced over his shoulder towards the ostentatious inn Tallos had spied them exercising behind. "Probably not the best time for a food shortage. What kind of help are you looking for?"

"I need someone who can lift the barrel of the mill so I can fix the gears underneath." Tallos forced a charming grin. "And, ideally, someone who can hold it long enough without crushing my head. My wife can't manage it."

"And I'm guessing I look strong enough?"

Take a shot at his ego...

Tallos laughed. "Well, I saw you with that burly guy a moment ago, but if you think *you* could do it, I'd be ever grateful." His pulse echoed in his ears, and he resisted the instinct to wrinkle his nose at the lingering smell of his woman on another man.

Varadani has taken this too far. Toying with the boy would be one thing, but allowing him to touch her... They both need a lesson.

The guard frowned. "I'm just as strong as Barim, even if it doesn't show as obviously." He switched the pastries under his other arm, chewing his lip. "But I can come help. Which road should I take? I didn't see a mill on the way into town."

Gotcha.

Tallos jerked a thumb south over his shoulder. "Follow the road behind the butcher, it'll take you southeast along the strait. Bit of a walk, so bring a horse. There's a river next to it that runs off the cliff side. You can't miss it. Big ol' building."

"This afternoon, then. I'll come a little after lunch."

"Thank you." Tallos dipped his chin. "Maybe you'll even learn something."

Chapter 32

Stefan leaned against the wall while stroking the snowy owl under its beak.

I don't think I've ever heard him speak.

Katrin's stomach did a somersault as she considered who the beautiful creature came from. "What are you telling him?"

The prince dipped his quill in ink before writing again. "That I'd rather not follow through with this wedding, anyway. My brother has waited for his chance for years, and I bet he'd jump at this one. So I'm recommending him, which works, since he's already with Dad."

Hearing Matthias refer to the king of their country as Dad made Katrin swallow.

Why is the familial term even more intimidating than the formal one?

Katrin hugged herself, eyeing Stefan again as she considered all the questions she wanted to ask. But it didn't seem appropriate with an audience.

Matthias looked up, following her gaze to his elite. "You don't need to censor yourself."

She pursed her lips. "I don't know if that's the right phrase for what I'm doing..." She tugged on a loose strand of her hair, fidgeting with it before tucking it behind her ear.

Get yourself together, Kat.

"Would you like to speak alone?" The prince straightened and caught her gaze.

She shook her head with a sigh. "No. Just... thinking." She gave a dry smile. "You know, the thing that gets me into trouble."

A smile spread over Matthias's face. "You do think quite a lot." He returned to writing. "But Stefan knows all this already, so there's no need to be shy."

She forced her arms to relax, crossing the lush carpet to the table Matthias sat at. Running a hand through his hair, she studied the gold signet ring on his left hand. Micah had worn it previously, and now it seemed odd to see it on Matthias. But it only further enforced the truth. She bent to kiss him on the cheek. "I know. But I still worry, especially what your father would think if he knew the truth."

Matthias's pen paused, and he met her eyes. "My father is a good man. You should be more worried about how many whiskys he's going to make you try or how many times he'll ask you for decorating advice."

She smiled, a short laugh escaping despite the tightness in her stomach. "You're really sure? You know I wouldn't blame you if you felt you needed to marry that Zionan princess. Our country is at war now..."

Rolling his eyes, the prince shook his head. "I think Dad will be happy when he learns I've met someone on my own. Ever since my mother... the home has lacked a feminine presence."

"You're talking about the castle." Katrin stroked his hair again.

Matthias huffed. "Yes, the royal palace in Nema's Throne. My home." He took her hand. "*Our* home, assuming you want it."

Her breath stilled. "*Our?*"

A latch clicked, drawing her attention to the door.

Stefan had slipped out of the room without her even noticing.

The prince stood, squeezing her hand. "You're not obligated, of course. This won't change my response to my father. And there's no rush, but I know what I want."

"This is a dream." His beard tickled her palm as she stepped into him. "How did this even happen? It feels like yesterday I was still in the temple, more worried about having time to study instead of attending a stupid royal feast."

"It *was* a stupid royal feast, but I'm glad you found the time to attend." He kissed her forehead. "Even if you ended up arguing with a bullheaded guard in the snow."

She tugged on his collar. "A very handsome bullheaded guard. And I like the snow." She encouraged his lips to hers, and the rest of the room disappeared. The rest of the country and all its problems faded as she felt his lips against hers.

Trying to imagine herself in the halls of the palace, she considered what Matthias said to her. Her hand traced a line down his jaw, and she slowly pulled from the kiss. "When do you think I'll meet your father?"

Matthias hummed. "Probably at my brother's wedding." His eyebrow quirked. "Or the next time we return to Nema's Throne."

"I suppose the war will mess up some of that timing, won't it?" She leaned her head against his collar, snuggling into his soft scent.

"It will. But please try not to be concerned. He'll love you, too." Matthias wrapped his arms around her, enveloping her in a feeling of safety.

Katrin nodded against him. "I wish I could have met your mother. Everything I ever heard about the queen..." She pulled back to meet his eyes, brushing a lock of his chestnut hair from his brow. "You don't talk about her much..."

"She would've loved you, too." Sadness clouded his gaze. "Talking about her always seemed to cause my father pain, so I just..." He shrugged.

"You can talk to me about her, if you want." Katrin rested her chin on his sternum, looking up at him.

Queen Rehtaeh Rayeht had been a matriarch of charity, spending copious amounts of time with the people to ensure their wellbeing. Katrin had always admired her as a child and had cried when she'd passed.

And to think I'd end up with her son.

Matthias kissed the tip of her nose. "I'll keep that in mind."

"Are you going to tell your father about me?"

"Once you let me finish writing this letter."

She groaned and nuzzled her face against his chest. "Does that require you to let me go? Because I like this."

His chuckle echoed through his chest. "We have time."

Chapter 33

Dani set down her fork and leaned sideways on Katrin's shoulder.

Silverware and porcelain plates clinked all around her, but the noise didn't speed her pulse as it had the day before. The men talked, discussing politics and war. Dread built in her stomach at the knowledge her country had made the formal declaration, but butterflies distracted her.

How has my opinion of Liam changed so drastically so fast?

Wood squeaked as Liam tilted his chair back onto two legs across the table from her, drinking from a heavy ale tankard. "How long do you think we'll stay here in Omensea?"

"A week, maybe." Matthias's deep voice prompted Dani to chuckle.

"At least the walls are thick," she whispered to Katrin.

Katrin poked Dani in the ribs. "Hush. I'm allowed to enjoy myself, aren't I?"

Afternoon sunlight shone through the tall windows, keeping the Dtrüa's vision bright. No other guests filled the tables.

"Of course. Especially since your prince rented the whole inn." Dani sat straight, clicking her tongue and reaching for her wine. Finding the glass, she brought it to her lips. "An expensive one at that." Setting the glass down, she clicked her tongue again.

"Do you have to keep doing that?" Liam grumbled from across the table, rocking his chair so it squeaked again.

"Do *you* have to keep doing *that?*" Dani clicked her tongue again for effect. "You know I could make you fall."

"You should, might teach him a lesson," Katrin whispered.

"Needn't tell me twice." Dani kicked under the table, her boot meeting Liam's raised chair leg.

Liam grabbed for the edge of the table, but his hands slipped as his chair teetered away. He let out a yelp as he toppled backward, thumping onto the ground.

Barim's boisterous laugh overshadowed the others', and Liam clambered to his feet.

"That's it, back to the room with you." Liam huffed, righting his chair and sliding it under the table.

Katrin giggled. "Oh, come on, Liam. It was funny. And you deserved it."

Dani followed his shape as he rounded the table towards her, her heart picking up speed. "Maybe I don't want to go back to my room."

"Talansiet." Matthias's warning quieted the laughter.

Liam growled, returning to his chair and crossing his arms. He leaned against the table. "I'm watching you, Feyorian."

"Now you're rubbing in that I can't see?" Dani scoffed and stood, her chair grinding on the floor.

"No, I'm telling you so that you know, *since* you can't see..."

"Fuck you." Dani spun, clicking her tongue again as she strode into the hallway.

"Liam!" Katrin's tone sounded like a disapproving mother as she smacked something. "Why do you insist on being such an ass all the time?"

"I'm sorry if I'm the only one who can see who she really is."

Their voices faded as Dani crossed to the stairs, her heart echoing in her ears as she made her way to the second level of the inn.

Chairs scrapped across the floor below, rumbling up the stairwell before someone hurried up behind her. They slowed near the top of the platform, as if looking back, and the gentle teal scent of Liam returned.

"Not even going to let me be alone, huh?" Dani jerked the door to her room open.

"I've been ordered to apologize." He caught the door before she could playfully swing it into his face. He slipped in, closing it behind him.

Before Dani could take a step away, his powerful arms encircled her waist, pulling her backward into him.

His lips found her neck, his tongue playing towards her ear. "And I intend to. Quite thoroughly."

Heat rushed through her veins, and she ran her hand through his hair, finding it damp. His skin smelled fresh with the hint of soap. "Think they bought it?"

"I have bruises to back up the act." He nipped her earlobe.

Dani laughed. "Sorry about that." She twisted in his grip, facing him. Lacing her arms over his shoulders, she lifted herself to wrap her legs around his midsection. "I..." Hesitating, she kissed him.

Love? What am I thinking? I can't say that to him.

He returned it, a hand playing up her side before he pulled away. "What's wrong? Do you not want this?"

Dani grinned, kissing him again before letting her lips linger against his. "I do. I've never... felt this way."

He sauntered to the bed before laying her down on it. He crawled over her, fingers playing with her hair against her cheek. "Me neither. Not anything close to this." He lowered his hard body against hers, kissing her collarbone.

"Does that not scare you?" Dani closed her eyes, tracing a line down his jaw.

His heart pounded against her chest. "It's terrifying." He pulled back, pressing his forehead to hers so she could feel his breath on her lips. "But that doesn't make me want you any less." His hand trailed down her side. "You're special, Dani. And I want to remind you of that every day, now."

Wanting to see his face, she touched his cheeks, following their curve to his straight nose and chin. "I can hardly think around you." She smirked. "But I think you've forgotten something."

He hummed, his touch cascading along the neckline of her shirt, teasing near her breasts. "And what's that?"

"You're supposed to help that farmer this afternoon."

Liam groaned, shifting himself against her as he kissed her chin. "It can wait. This is more important. I need to apologize, remember?" The next kiss moved under her jaw, forcing her chin up. His tongue sent a warm pulse through her body.

"I'll still be here after." Dani opened her eyes to the dim room, licking her bottom lip.

He sighed, pulling back and pushing himself up. "Fine," he whined. He took her hand, kissing her knuckles while sliding off the bed. He paused as he rotated her hand in his, placing another kiss. "You took off your ring?"

Dani brushed her fingers over the soft skin where Tallos's band had rested for years. "I am not his anymore."

His mouth brushed over her knuckles again. "Tallos, you mean." He rubbed his thumb against hers. "Whose are you now?"

A smile tugged at her lips. "Mine." She squeezed his hand, teasing him with the promise of a kiss. "I belong to me."

He hummed near her mouth. "Good." With a subtle shift, he caught the edge of her chin with his mouth and led the kisses back towards her ear, sending a shiver down her spine.

Smiling, she pushed on his chest. "Don't start that again. You know I can't resist, and you need to go."

Liam groaned, stepping away quickly as if he'd lose control, too, if he remained. "You're clearly the more responsible between us. If I work up enough of a sweat, I might need a bath when I get back."

"I'll scrub your back." Dani quirked an eyebrow. "Will you be back before dinner?"

Liam's sword clanked as he secured his belt, which had been left in the room for lunch time. "I should be. I don't think it'll take long. Just lifting one thing. Do you need anything before I go?"

Dani shook her head, unease touching her stomach. "Who is the man who asked you for help again?"

"He didn't say his name, but he must be one of the local millers.

He told me to meet him at his mill to the southeast." The bed flexed as Liam leaned across it to kiss her forehead. "Just a local who needs some help, and I can spare the time. Even if I wish I could stay here with you."

"Be safe." Dani swallowed, listening to the door latch behind him.

He didn't lock it, and his footsteps disappeared down the hallway.

Rising from the bed, Dani strode to the window and let the brightness wash over her vision. Distant, blurry shapes formed the forest and mountains. Streaks of color danced across her sight as her eyes moved, unable to focus on anything. Letting out a sigh, she opened the window and waited.

Her eyelids grew heavy nearly an hour into Liam's absence, and Dani resigned herself to nap. They had slept little the night before, and the memory left a smile on her lips as she drifted off.

Rousing, Dani blinked her eyes open. "Liam?" She could smell his scent left behind on the bed and her clothing, but he hadn't returned. Groaning, she rolled off the bed to her feet and stretched as she walked to the window.

The sky darkened with the colors of twilight, shadows stretched long behind the inn.

Where is he?

The unease from before doubled in her gut, and she debated seeking Katrin's help.

But then she'll find out, and it could jeopardize his position as a crown elite.

Dani pulled her gloves and thick tunic on, followed by the pelt over her shoulders, tying it in place. "Southeast. At least I can avoid the city." Climbing onto the windowsill, she swallowed.

The loud sounds of the city touched her senses from the other side of the inn.

Merchants bartering.

A cart full of chickens bouncing down the road.

Coins clinking in the palms of vendors.

She stared towards the horizon that would take her away from all of it. "This better not be a joke, Liam."

She slipped off the sill, falling into open air. The Art flooded her veins, her skin tingling as it shifted. As she landed in her panther form, her eyesight brightened with light and colored scents, guiding her as she took off towards the darkening horizon.

Slowing once she entered the woods, she sniffed the air and altered her course north to find the road. Her paws hit packed dirt, and she stopped.

He passed by here.

Dani focused on the teal wisps lingering behind from when he'd ridden through the area, and she raced to follow it.

Scents lit her surroundings with varied shades of green and yellow. Vibrant plumes drifted from night jasmine and a nearby rabbit hole. Flower buds dotted the tree limbs with sparks of pink and orange.

The forest thinned, but Dani kept up her pace. Her paws touched grass as she ran beside the road, careful to stay quiet in her approach.

By the time Liam's scent intensified, night had fallen.

Dani slowed, catching her breath as she stalked closer to the mill. A familiar, heart wrenching scent struck her nostrils, and she balked.

Tallos.

She sniffed again, seeking confirmation of the scent she'd imagined so many times.

Unless it's been real this entire time.

Anxiety gripped her chest as she prowled closer, listening to the murmured voices in the distance.

No other people had been in this area for weeks, at least. The structure ahead of her rotted in places, tainting the woodsy scent grey. No animals remained nearby, only the horse Liam must have arrived on and the hint of blood.

Tallos lured him here.

Guilt flailed her insides, and she paused near the large door at the front of the mill. A gap let lantern light flood the grass in front of her, and her ears swiveled to listen.

"Tell me!" Tallos's voice sent a shudder through Dani's feline body.

"You'll just kill me, anyway." Liam spat, coughing.

The fleshy sound of something colliding with Liam's body shocked through her ears, and he groaned.

I have to make it stop.

Dani darted through the opening in the door, snarling through her fear as the smell of blood tripled. She charged towards them, claws extended.

Tallos stepped in front of Liam, facing her. "Shift!"

The order rippled through her, and she skidded to a stop, returning to her human form on her knees with her head bowed. Her vision darkened, barely able to discern the men's shapes in the lantern light.

Liam sat in a chair, but the twine scent of rope mixed with his.

Moldy old wheat grains slid beneath her feet, a light powder coating the ground. The air hung heavy with mildew, with a tall black structure behind the men adding rust to the mix.

"Good. You've finally joined us." Her ex-lover circled Liam again.

She smelled the familiar tawny bear pelt around his shoulders and the worn leather tunic. It all mingled with the coppery scent of Liam's blood, making her nauseous.

"Dani." Liam wheezed. "My sword is near the wall to your left, grab—" He hissed as Tallos struck him again.

She flinched and dipped her chin, staring at the black ground.

Tallos chuckled. "She isn't yours to command, foolish grunt. Varadani. Look at me."

Her gaze shot up, centering on where he stood. "Don't hurt him, please."

"But he has hurt you. Taken you away from what you were made for. From me." Tallos's shape crossed behind, moving towards the dim stone pillar. The mill's grindstone sat dormant with the broken waterwheel outside.

Liam's shape jerked, the chair beneath him groaning as he tried to move away from Tallos's grip.

Dani's breath quickened. "No. He didn't hurt me, he didn't—"

"He chained you!" Tallos's bellow vibrated through the room. "Your wrists are still cut, and you're so ignorant of his influence you believe him to be genuine!"

Dani cringed, lowering her voice. "You chained me, too."

"I made you what you are! I gave your life meaning. Purpose. For the poor little blind girl who would've rotted in a sewer. You owe me everything."

"Don't listen to him, Dani. You owe Feyor nothing. They—" Liam's voice cut off as his breath choked, and she whimpered.

"Traitor! You pledged yourself to Feyor. To me. Say it."

"I cannot," Dani whispered, pushing herself backward in the dirt.

Liam choked again, kicking against the ground as Tallos prevented air from reaching his lungs.

Panic danced through Dani's body, and she cried out. "Stop!"

Tallos's voice lowered, turning sickly gentle. "Say it, kitten."

Heat built in Dani's eyes, and tears trickled down her cheeks. "It is my privilege to serve Feyor." She almost choked on the first line of her oath. "I'm yours. Please, don't kill him."

Liam gasped, wheezing in a breath.

"Good girl." Tallos strode towards her and grasped her upper arm. "Get up."

Chapter 34

Dani shirked sideways as Tallos hauled her to her feet, but it wasn't enough to free her of his grip.

Liam's throat burned, the chill air stinging as he sucked in grateful breaths. He swallowed, trying to relieve the pressure that felt like Tallos's arm was still wrapped around him. As he pulled at the rope binding his wrists to the chair, slivers bit into his skin.

Tallos leaned into her, placing his mouth near her cheek. "What did you tell these iceheads about us?" He let go of her, stepped back towards Liam.

"I told them nothing." Dani closed her eyes.

"You must have said something. Your soldier toy wasn't even surprised to see you as a cat." The back of Tallos's hand struck Liam's face, and the mill spun around him.

Blood pooled on his tongue, and he spat it out before righting himself again. Looking at Dani, his chest tightened.

Her hair had fallen in front of her down-turned face, making her look so much weaker than he knew her to be. So unlike the powerful Dtrüa he'd fallen for.

He eyed Tallos's fist hovering near him.

I'm an idiot for not being more suspicious.

Now he understood the necessity behind all of Dani's leather clothing, and Tallos's attire was no different. His long, shaggy honey blond hair made him look feral.

"I made a mistake." Dani's shaking voice broke the silence. "I was confused."

She doesn't mean that.

Tallos chuckled. "And you were doing so well, sending me information about the prince's location. The mountain pass. Undertown. Then the temple. But my love, don't you remember that I can always find you? Your messages only confirmed what I already knew."

Dani's chin lifted, her cheeks wet. "What?"

Doubt, raw and ugly, reared in Liam's chest. He met Dani's eyes, but could read nothing in them.

"We're bonded, *my* kitten. Not just you and I, but all of us. A family. And family looks out for each other." Tallos stroked a hand over Liam's hair before gripping a handful at his roots. "And this icehead is not one of us. He hates us. Wants us dead. Don't you, grunt?"

Liam grimaced, breathing into the pain. "Right now, just you."

Tallos laughed and threw the soldier's head forward. "Not your prisoner, too? She betrayed you. Played you this whole time, and your weak little mind fell for it."

He chewed his lower lip, but winced as he bit into where it'd split. Running his tongue over the cut, he tasted his own blood. "She's not yours anymore."

"She will always be mine." Tallos eyed Dani. "One step back."

Dani obeyed.

Tallos's sinister gaze returned to Liam. "Shall I continue to demonstrate?"

Liam growled, tugging at his bonds again, his skin tearing. "Then let's stop playing, shall we? Aren't you going to kill me?"

"I considered it." Tallos stooped to whisper in Liam's ear. "But it would be more fun to watch Varadani do it, don't you think?"

Liam straightened, his body screaming. "What?"

Chuckling, the male Dtrüa straightened. "You chained her! You treated her like an animal, even when she didn't fight back." He gazed at Dani. "Do you like chains, Varadani?"

Dani's cheeks had dried, and no new tears fell. "No."

"Did this man chain you?"

She hesitated, but nodded. "Yes."

"Did he abuse his power over you?" Tallos frowned, pacing away.

A knot formed in Liam's throat as he considered the truth of the statement. The moment his attraction had overcome him and he'd kissed her in the hall. She'd pushed him away at first.

Perhaps that was her true response, but she saw something to gain in the rest.

When she didn't answer, Tallos stomped a foot. "Speak!"

Dani jumped. "He misused the power he held over me."

Liam winced. "Dani, I—"

"Shut up!" Tallos's fist hit him in the jaw again, cracking his head to the side.

The Dtrüas' voices garbled in his ears, and he blinked to make his eyes focus. His sword became clear first, where it leaned in its scabbard on the wall opposite the millstone.

But what chance do I really have against a Dtrüa?

"Reclaim your power, Varadani." Tallos paced behind Liam, standing several feet back. "Kill the one who chained you."

Dani's eyes flickered down to Liam, her chest rising with fast breaths.

"That's an order, my love. Kill him," Tallos snarled. "Shift!"

Gasping, she leaned forward, and her furs spread over her body. She landed on the ground on all fours, white coat shimmering gold in the lantern light. Her claws flexed, scraping the ground as she stalked towards him.

"Shit." Liam kicked out, awkwardly skidding his chair back across the dust-covered floor. "Dani, wait." His heart pounded in his ears, deafening the low growl of her panther form.

Dani lunged, charging at him with her teeth bared. Six feet away, she leapt. Her giant paws impacted his chest, sending him and the chair crashing backward.

All air left his lungs as the wood shattered beneath him. The rope slackened against the fractures, and he tore his wrists free as her weight landed on him. Instinctively, he threw his arms over his head, but his gaze met her cloudy cat eyes for a breath before she launched off him.

"Varadani! No!" Tallos lifted his arm as the white panther collided with him, tackling him to the ground.

Brown fur erupted beneath her, throwing her off him.

Dani landed on her feet, claws tearing at the dirt floor, and charged at the bear.

The monstrous grizzly threw his head to the side, opening his maw in an ursine roar as Dani struck low, slamming into his front legs and sinking her teeth into his flesh.

Nymaera's breath.

Fur tumbled together, and Liam scrambled to the far wall to retrieve his sword, blinking through the blood pouring from his forehead. Wood cracked and splintered as Tallos rammed into one of the mill's half-collapsed walls, narrowly missing crushing Dani. She clawed her way up the bear's flank, burying her teeth into the back of his neck.

Tallos flung her off, slamming her body into the ground before pressing his weight onto her chest and neck.

Dani's paws lashed, but didn't connect, scraping the floor as she struggled to breathe.

Drawing his sword, Liam threw the scabbard aside as he charged, trying to remember all his father's instructions on bear hunting.

Gods, I wish I had a spear.

Blood oozed down Tallos's leg and neck, dripping onto Dani's white coat as she yeowled.

Running at full speed, Liam threw himself onto the floor in a slide behind Tallos, slashing his sword along the back of the bear's rear ankles.

The bear roared and spun faster than Liam thought possible, swatting the soldier to a stop with an enormous paw.

Covering his head, Liam rolled to the side, but the bear stayed over him. Fabric tore, along with flesh as a horrible burning pain spread across his chest before abruptly feeling numb.

Growls echoed in his ears before the bear's shadow disappeared from over him.

Liam gasped, rolling onto his side to watch Dani bite the bear's throat and hang on. He swatted at her, again and again, coating her in blood, but she didn't let go. Crimson flowed over her face and down her neck as he bled out.

The bear stumbled and fell, sprawling limp over the musty ground, the panther still latched to his throat.

Blood seeped over the floor, spreading like tar as the last twitches vibrated through the bear's body. Once the bear's breath ceased, Dani released her hold.

She groaned, trying and failing to stand. Using a clawed paw, she dragged herself a few feet from the fallen bear, then stilled. Her chest heaved, clouds of dust pluming around her face.

Agony radiated through every muscle, but Liam shuffled on his stomach across the ground, holding the torn flesh on his chest. "Dani." Panic flooded through him as he got closer, realizing how much blood covered her fur, the bright red of exposed muscle at her abdomen still bleeding from the gash.

"Shit, shit." Liam forgot his own wounds as he stripped out of his tunic, ignoring the cold on his bare skin as he balled his undershirt and slid close to Dani, pressing the fabric against her. Warmth seeped with the red through the white fabric.

She chuffed, her breathing labored as her claws flexed against the dirt. Her tail twitched before she closed her eyes.

"Don't you dare." Liam pressed harder against the wound, brushing his free hand up over her ears. "Stay with me."

Chapter 35

"Liam's usually a bottomless pit, it's not like him to miss a meal." Katrin led the way down the hallway of the inn, glancing back at Matthias.

Matthias huffed. "I've noticed. Dani isn't the lightest eater, either." He took her hand, ascending the stairs to their rooms. "They better not have murdered each other."

She chuckled, and it lightened the weight on his chest. "I'd like to think Liam knows his limits and that he wouldn't win against Dani."

The prince thought back to when the panther dug through the snow, freeing them from the avalanche cave.

That cat could destroy any of us if she wanted to.

"He's not *that* cocky, is he?" Matthias made a face and let go of Katrin's hand to knock on their door.

Silence.

Furrowing his brow, he tried the knob. It clicked open, and as the door widened, cool air wafted into the hallway.

"The window is wide open." Matthias strode into the room, looking for any sign of a struggle, but found none. He stuck his head outside the second-story window, and his eyes focused on the yellowed, tall grass below.

The foliage parted in a trail away from the ground, like something hip-height passed through.

"Dani went this way as a cat." Matthias faced Katrin. "You see any sign of Liam? His sword isn't here. Maybe he hasn't returned from helping that miller."

Katrin lifted the flap of Liam's satchel, revealing the formal crown elite armor he'd been assigned. Frowning, she dropped it back into place. "Maybe. But it didn't sound like the job would take long, and I thought I saw him leave just after lunch."

"Come on." Matthias took her hand again. "We should follow the tracks. If Dani left, I'm willing to bet she had a good reason. Liam may have gone after her, too."

She squeezed his fingers. "She wouldn't run. I hope Liam knows that."

"All the more reason to hurry. There will be horses at the stable I can borrow."

They slipped back into their room only long enough to grab their warm cloaks, fastening them as they rushed down the stairs.

"Where's the fire?" Riez bellowed after them as they passed the dining hall, where the rest of the crown elites drank and played cards.

"Liam and Dani are missing." Matthias didn't pause, even as chairs ground from the room.

His guards funneled into the hallway behind him, pulling cloaks over their shoulders.

"What do you mean, they're missing? Did Dani make a run for it?" Micah didn't sound convinced.

"Dani wouldn't run." Katrin's voice hardened as she shoved through the front door. "Something must be wrong."

"We need to catch them before anything happens. Learn the truth."

A block down the road, three finely dressed traders exited the stables with tacked mounts.

"I'll take care of the horses." Stefan raced ahead, sprinting through the streets.

Matthias nudged Katrin. "Told you he speaks."

Katrin frowned to hide the smile he knew was there as she poked him in the ribs. "Tease me about that later."

The quiet crown elite stopped the traders from mounting, tossing one a pouch and receiving the reins of the horses in return.

"We'll bring them back." Matthias spoke once they were in earshot, and a blond-haired woman nodded, her gaze darting to the signet ring on his hand.

Her eyes widened with another hurried nod. "Of course."

"We'll tack two more and catch up." Barim patted Matthias's back and disappeared with Stefan inside the stable.

The prince swung himself onto a horse, while Riez and Micah took the other two. He held his hand out to Katrin. "Stuck with me. Liam said the mill was southeast, right?"

She grabbed his hand, hiking up her skirts to reveal the leather breeches beneath as she mounted behind him. Wrapping her arms around his waist, she squeezed to let him know she was ready. "Yes. Do you think he could still be there?"

"That's the same direction Dani ran. It can't be a coincidence." Matthias squeezed his calves, urging the horse into a canter.

Micah and Riez rode behind, keeping pace as they found the road leading away from town.

As they entered the forest, Katrin's hold on his waist tightened.

Matthias tilted his head to see her face, but her eyes glazed, tinted with a white film. His heart sped, and he grabbed her hand. "Kat. Katrin, what's going on?"

Katrin tilted her head to the side, her eyes unfocused. Inhaling sharply, she dug her nails into his hand. "They're at the mill. The blood..." She blinked, the cloudy haze in her irises fading. "Ride faster." Desperation filled her tone.

How does she...?

Matthias kicked his horse into a full gallop, hooves pounding behind them as the others kept pace. "What's wrong?" he shouted over the noise. "How do you know?"

Katrin buried her face against Matthias's back, shaking her head. "I don't know." She choked on a sob before she hardened her voice. "I just know Dani is hurt. And Liam is there."

"Shit." The prince leaned into the gallop, eyes pinned ahead of them in the darkness of night. "There!"

A shambled roof came into view, sheltering a mill that looked like it had seen better days. A yellow glow illuminated the inside, spilling out from the tall open door at the side.

Hooves slid to a stop outside the wooden structure, and Katrin disappeared from behind him before the horse had even stopped. Wind whipped in her skirts as she dashed ahead, slamming into the ajar doorway.

Matthias leapt to the ground, tossing the reins to Micah before running after Katrin. As he barreled into the mill, the sight stopped him.

Blood coated the ground, the sharp sting of its scent filling his nose. Most of it pooled near a giant dead bear, but then his eyes trailed to where Liam knelt next to a dark mass. The soldier sat shirtless, his body and face covered in cuts and bruises.

What the hells happened here?

Katrin slipped in the blood, but kept herself upright before diving to the ground beside Liam, crimson wicking up the linen of her skirts as she thrust her hands towards the dark heap. She gazed at Liam, her eyes shimmering in the dim lantern light, but her jaw hardened as she looked back down.

The bloody mass of fur twitched, and Liam shifted to support the panther's head in his lap.

Is that...?

"Dani, just hold on." His voice cracked with emotion the prince had never seen from the man. "Please."

Matthias approached, his gaze finding a patch of white fur in the darkness. Panic gripped his insides, and he glanced at the bear. "Katrin, can you save her?"

She didn't respond, holding a bloody bundle of material to Dani's gut. She slipped one hand below it as her back straightened. Locks of black hair fell from the knotted bun at the back of her head as she bowed her chin.

Liam collapsed backward, his face pale as he stared at his sister. He lifted a bloody hand to his face before he stared at the blood and tried to wipe it on his breeches. "Katy girl?" His voice was a mere whisper.

Dani's paws twitched, and Katrin sucked in another sob before she looked up at Matthias. "It's... she's lost too much blood." She brushed a bloody hand over Dani's ears.

Liam choked, his hand running through Dani's bloody fur. "No, you can't go."

Katrin stared at her brother, slowly lifting her hands away from Dani. Her eyes grew glassy as she looked up at Matthias.

"I'll go back. And I'm taking you with me." Matthias hauled Katrin to her feet, gripping around her waist as he flooded his body with energy.

"You can do—"

"—that?" Katrin blinked at her clean hands as she skidded to a stop in front of the inn door.

"Where's the fire?" Riez leaned on the doorframe, his brow furrowing at the pair of them.

"Dani's hurt. She needs us. Bring the medical supplies. Now!" Matthias jerked his chin to Katrin. "We'll get there faster this time."

Chapter 36

A low buzz tingled on Katrin's skin, a tangle of the lingering Art she hadn't even felt Matthias access as he'd pulled her to her feet.

The blood was gone, but she could still feel the bruise forming on her shoulder where she'd slammed into the mill's door.

By the gods...

Matthias squeezed her shoulder, urging her out of the inn, and she stumbled, her body still humming from the panic of trying to heal Dani.

The Art still flowed in her veins, hungrily seeking what remained of Matthias's from the time jump. But with him tugging on her hand, she ran.

The elites charged after them, barreling outside into the night air.

They dashed down the street, reaching the stables while the traders were still inside paying the stable boy for his services.

Matthias plucked the reins of the horse from the blond's hands.

"Whoa, excuse me." She glowered, but her gaze caught the glimmer of gold on Matthias's left hand and her eyes widened as the prince swung onto her horse.

"We'll bring them right back." Katrin hurried to mount the second horse. "Stefan will pay you."

The horses will run faster with one rider.

Matthias didn't wait for the others to catch up and mount before he kicked the horse forward.

They burst outside and rode straight into a gallop towards the mill.

The same trees rushed past them, and the fallen pine she'd seen just before the darkness had penetrated her vision, but it didn't come.

We're moving faster.

She opened her mind to the gods, praying they would make it in time.

The horses' hooves echoed over the old foot bridge before the path opened to the old mill, the orange light of a lantern glowing from inside.

She sucked in a breath as her vision fogged over, fading to shadows and shapes as it had the first time. Blood. So much blood filled her nostrils, the copper of it stronger than she'd ever noticed before. She could tell there were multiple sources. Three, at least, that fueled the wafts of strange grey mists drifting about.

I'm seeing what Dani is seeing.

A haze of teal hovered near her.

Liam's voice. "Stay with me."

And the thunder of horses' hooves somewhere outside.

Katrin shook the vision from her mind, blinking to clear it as she pulled back on her horse's reins, skidding to a stop just beside the door. She slid off the saddle, not bothering to check in with Matthias before she slammed through the door again, her already bruised shoulder smarting.

She didn't have to look to know exactly where Dani was. She altered her steps to avoid slipping like she had before, collapsing to her knees and grabbing Liam's shirt from his hands. The blood hadn't completely soaked it yet, bits of white still visible as she shoved her hand beneath the cloth. She swallowed to control the impulse of her body to revolt at the feeling of Dani's exposed muscles and organs as she pinched the artery closed.

Please, Aedonai, and any god listening. Help me.

Katrin bowed her head, more hair tousled free from her bun from the rougher ride. She forced herself to ignore Liam, even though she knew he bled, too, and tugged desperately at the weaves of her Art within her.

"Please save her," Liam whispered, pulling Dani's head into his lap. "Hold on, Dani."

The warmth passed from Katrin's chest down her arms, flickers of gold pulsing along her veins as she worked to sew the damage done to Dani's body. She knew exactly where the severed artery was, and her power quickly repaired the gash. Moving outward, she funneled all she could into the muscles and flesh, knowing the importance of working within the deeper parts of the wound before worrying about the surface.

Dani whimpered, her paws twitching.

A faint hissing filled the air as heat from the Art worked with the flesh, sealing it together one agonizing layer at a time.

Katrin's strength waned as she lifted the fabric away from Dani, exposing the still angry wound. Her fingers brushed the sticky surface of Dani's fur, twitching to lace together the final Art laden stitches.

Dani's head tilted back, her fur shifting over her body. It formed leathers, skin appearing over her limbs as she retook her human form. She gasped, touching her stomach before lifting her hand to feel through the air.

A sob of relief echoed beside Katrin, and she opened her eyes in surprise as Liam took Dani's hand, bringing it to his cheek despite the blood. "Thank the gods," he whispered, leaning down and placing a kiss on her forehead.

Katrin stiffened, leaning back.

What in the hells...

Dani touched Liam's face before her chin quivered. "I'm so sorry." Her voice caught, tears racing down her temples.

"No, no." Liam kissed her forehead again, brushing his hands through her hair, leaving streaks of red. "This isn't your fault."

Katrin blinked as Dani reached for her hand, and the acolyte took it.

The Dtrüa squeezed. "Thank you." Her weak voice barely carried over the air, exhausted. "Can you heal him, too?"

Katrin looked at Matthias. "Not yet. I need a little time to recover." She entwined her fingers with Dani's. "You were more important."

Matthias crouched next to them as the other elites paced into the mill, and he turned Liam away from Dani.

Riez thrust a piece of gauze at the prince, and he pressed it to Liam's chest.

"What happened here?" Matthias kept his voice low.

Liam hissed, but took the gauze to hold it himself. "Trouble happened."

"That's a fucking huge bear." Micah approached the dead animal, glancing at Dani. "Did you kill it?"

"Him..." Dani cringed. "That's Tallos."

"Tallos?" Katrin's chest tightened as she recalled all Dani had told her about the other Dtrüa. "Dani..."

Dani tried to sit up, but winced and gave up. "He was the man who asked Liam for help. He... He attacked him..." She wiped her mouth, propping herself up with an elbow before spitting red onto the floor.

"He tried to exercise his control over her." Liam accepted Matthias's help to get to his feet, leaning heavily on the prince. "But I don't think it went exactly like he planned."

The Dtrüa gazed at the dead bear as Riez picked her up. "I cannot leave, yet. Please take me to him."

Riez exchanged a look with Matthias, but the prince nodded. The guard carried her over to Tallos's body, setting her down to kneel next to him.

Dani's hand shook as she reached for the bear, fingers sinking into his fur.

After a breath, the bear shrank, body reforming into a man. He lay on his stomach, body shrouded by the thick bear pelt over his back and shoulders. His green eyes remained open, staring at nothing, his throat a tattered mess.

Touching his face, Dani closed his eyes. She tried to stand, but stumbled, and Riez caught her.

The guard lifted her again. "Micah and I can clean up this mess. You all should get back to the inn."

Stefan motioned to his horse. "She can ride with me."

Liam pushed away from Matthias, a slight tremble in his stance before he stood strong. "I'll take her."

Katrin eyed her brother, rolling her eyes. "Too damn stubborn." She stepped towards him, rubbing her bloodied hands on her skirts before she pushed her palm against his chest.

I can at least help a little.

She focused what remained of her power into the jagged claw marks beneath the gauze he held, encouraging the blood to clot and scab quicker. It'd help until she had more energy to heal him properly.

Her stance wavered as she opened her eyes, the mill spinning.

Liam caught her arm, giving her a stoic, grateful smile. He glanced back at Matthias, and they had a silent conversation before Matthias came to support her arm.

"And you'll be riding with me." The prince guided her from the mill, helping her onto a horse before mounting behind her and taking the reins. "You were incredible in there."

Liam and Stefan helped Dani onto another before Katrin's brother hefted himself up behind her.

Something definitely changed between those two.

Katrin looked back at Matthias. "I could say the same about you. You never told me you could take another with you when you jump through time."

Matthias shook his head and nudged the horse into a walk. "I've never tried before, but I didn't want to waste any time explaining the situation."

She leaned back into his chest, tilting her head so she could hear his heart beat. She evened her breath with each steady thud, trying to ignore the scent of blood still on her clothing. "Thank you," she whispered. "You didn't have to save her, but you didn't think twice even though we didn't know what happened. At first I thought

Liam..." She nuzzled into his neck, frowning against his skin. "But now I'm fairly certain I missed something that should have been obvious."

"Pretty sure we all missed something, there." Matthias kissed her head. "It didn't matter what happened. Her life is important, and she matters a lot to you. I'd never let her or anyone else die if I could stop it."

She smiled, kissing near his collar. "That's why you're an amazing man." She closed her eyes, allowing her mind to settle with the steady movement of the horse, Matthias's arms protecting her.

The prince lowered his mouth to her ear. "I love you."

She hummed sleepily, drifting off with the sound of his deep voice echoing in her head.

Chapter 37

Hushed arguing roused Dani, pulling her from her dreams of the bear swiping open her abdomen.

"I can't believe you didn't tell me," Katrin hissed, her tone sharp despite the lowered volume.

"Tell you what, exactly?" Liam's growl reverberated through his whisper. "It's none of your business." Something smacked him, and he grunted. "Watch it, you just healed those."

Sensation flowed into Dani's limbs, bringing the agony of her battle wounds with it. Katrin had healed the gouge, but the rest remained. She sucked in a shaky breath, rolling onto her side and blinking her eyes open to darkness.

"Damn it, Liam, you woke her." The bed flexed as Katrin's soft scent drifted from where she sat, her hand closing around Dani's.

"I woke her?" Liam's voice rose to a more reasonable volume.

Dani cringed, keeping to a whisper. "Please don't fight." Her throat rasped, burning as she tried to swallow. The lingering taste of Tallos's blood made her stomach lurch.

Katrin stroked a piece of Dani's hair from her face, her fingers featherlight. "How are you feeling?"

Liam's shape shifted beside her, rising from the chair he'd positioned beside the bed, and porcelain clinked. His warm hand closed around hers, encouraging it to grasp the cup. "Here. Water. Do you think you can sit up?"

Dani sniffed the cup before reaching with her other hand. Her grip found Liam's arm, and she sat up with his help. Sipping the water, she savored the cool, clean taste as it refreshed her mouth. She let go of Liam and touched her stomach, cringing at the memory of bleeding out on the ground. "Just sore. Tired. Hungry. With a terrible taste in my mouth." Lifting the cup, she sipped again.

"Liam can go grab you something to eat, if you'd like." Katrin squeezed her hand.

"What? No. I'm not leaving her."

Katrin sighed. "You haven't left this room all day. You can go for a few minutes to fetch something from downstairs. I just need a minute with Dani."

Dani resisted the urge to reach for Liam again. "Please?"

Liam hesitated, and she heard him chew on his lip. "All right." He leaned closer, his scent drifting over her as he kissed her forehead. "I'll be right back."

How can he still kiss me?

Swallowing the lump in her throat, Dani nodded, listening to his steps take him from the room and the door close behind him.

Katrin ran her thumb over Dani's, shifting on the bed as she took the empty cup. It forced Dani to scoot so Katrin could bring her feet up, crossing them beneath her skirts. "So... You and my brother..."

The Dtrüa huffed, heat building behind her eyes. "He almost died because of me." She collapsed backward and buried her face in the bed's blankets, sniffling. "I should have said something all those times I caught Tallos's scent, but I thought it was my imagination."

"That isn't necessarily the part I was talking about." Katrin's voice held a light smile.

Dani whimpered a laugh. "Your brother. He's an asshole. I don't even like him." She turned her face away, hiding her smile.

"Oh, horseshit." Katrin laughed, poking her high in the ribs, away from her wound. "He obviously changed your mind somehow, or you changed his."

"I have no idea what happened." Dani sat up again, wrapping her arms around herself. "We had a moment in Undertown, and then another after I ran off at the temple..."

"You ran off at the temple?" Katrin's grip tightened.

Dani bowed her head. "I heard a bear, and I thought it was Tallos... So I went to investigate. Then Liam chased me and almost got eaten by a *real* bear."

"By the looks of it, he almost got mauled last night, too. Though, that was Tallos?"

Nodding, Dani blinked through the darkness to no avail. "Tallos wanted me to kill him. Ordered me. I've never disobeyed before."

"For what it's worth..." Katrin slipped away, her bare feet padding on the floor towards the pitcher Liam had gone to before. Water trickled into the cup. "I'm rather grateful you didn't kill him. Ass or not, he's still my brother." She handed the cup to Dani, settling onto the bed. "But you died. Almost died. Protecting him." Katrin touched her knee. "And Tallos... Are you all right?"

Dani breathed in the scent of the fresh water and nodded. "I think so. I don't understand why Liam isn't upset with me. This is my fault."

"I think he's relieved you're alive. And this wasn't your fault. Tallos is the only one to blame in all of this. I'm just relieved Matthias could help me get to you in time." Katrin encouraged her hand up. "You should drink more. You've been out all day."

Drinking, Dani furrowed her brow. "It's been a whole day?"

"Mhmm. Giving me plenty of time to consider what actually happened last night."

"What do you mean?"

The fabric of Katrin's skirt rustled as she fiddled with it. "When... you were lying there, bleeding... Do you remember anything about what you were thinking?"

Dani gulped. "I remember wishing you were there, to help us. I called to you, in my head."

"I think it worked," Katrin whispered, as if speaking too loud would make it sound more crazy. "In a way. I think I heard you. I... saw through your eyes."

"How is that possible? What did you see?"

"Not a lot, to be honest. Mostly dark shapes, and some strange colors floating about. Grey, and I think that was the blood. And teal?" Katrin shook her head. "It sounds insane."

Dani's lips twitched. "Liam's scent is teal."

Katrin huffed, taking the cup. It clanked onto the bedside table, then the acolyte took Dani's hands. "Matthias said my eyes clouded, like yours, at the moment it happened. I've... heard of connections like this before. Read about them... Two people connected by the Art."

"Clouded? So you think what you saw was what I was seeing?"

"You just said yourself that the teal was Liam. You never told me that before."

"That sounds impossible. We weren't even born in the same country."

"Dragons sounded impossible a month ago, but here we are with a war started over them." Katrin shifted closer, shaking the bed. "Where we were born doesn't make a difference. There are hundreds of theories to what causes it, but I definitely remember reading about a connection like this. It was called élanvital or something. And I can't deny what I saw."

Dani rolled her shoulders, wincing. "So you can see through my eyes when it happens? Doesn't seem very useful, considering." She motioned to her face.

"But it happened when I wasn't near you. I was still in the middle of the forest at least a quarter mile away the first time."

"The first time?" Dani tilted her head. "I don't understand."

"It doesn't matter, listen." Katrin's grip doubled. "Maybe we could talk through this bond. It could be very useful. And if I can see through you, it should work the other way, too."

Dani's stomach flopped. "Wait. Are you saying that I could... possibly see? Through you?"

Katrin stilled, her grip tightening. "We can try? But you'd have to open yourself up to me. I think I did it accidentally when I was praying to the gods to save you." She scooted closer, their knees touching. "You want to? Right now?" Her tone took on a playful tone, excited.

A shiver passed through Dani as she nodded. "I do."

It'd been years since she'd last wished away her blindness, but the possibility of gaining glimpses of the world gave her unexpected hope.

Katrin turned Dani's hands upward, sliding her arm along hers until they gripped each other's wrists. "It should be easier if we're touching, according to the laws of the Art. And... I guess just... clear your mind? And I'll try to project myself into you."

Dani drew a shaky breath and closed her eyes, doing as Katrin suggested.

A flurry of her friend's power brushed against her own, her pulse impossibly strong against Dani's palm. She heard Katrin inhale, centering on that as the darkness behind her eyelids shifted.

The next breath was different. A faint taste lingered on her tongue.

Blueberries?

Her hearing dimmed, along with her sense of smell, but her vision of the room cleared as Katrin's eyes fluttered open. For the first time, she saw herself through Katrin's eyes, and her breath quickened.

Is that what I look like?

Bruises marred Dani's face, but they had cleansed the blood from her skin. Instead of her leathers, she wore a sleeping gown. As Katrin's gaze moved through the room, tears flowed from Dani's eyes. She took in the simple sights. The sky outside the window and the water in the glass pitcher.

"You're crying?" Katrin's voice sounded different, shifted because she heard herself. "Is it working?"

Dani choked, keeping her own eyes closed to focus on what Katrin saw. She saw herself nod, unable to find her voice.

The latch on the door clicked, and the door swung open.

"Good news, no Brussels sprouts." Liam didn't fully look in the room as he smiled, carefully closing the door with his foot behind him.

A sob escaped Dani's throat as Katrin focused on her brother. His dark eyes and handsome face. The slight shadow of a beard on his chin and his onyx hair. A purple bruise marred the underside of his jaw, a few cuts near his thick eyebrows.

He pursed his lips as he turned with the food tray, sporting vibrant sprigs of grapes and a crusty round of bread. She marveled at the variations of tan and brown on the crust, and the tiny holes in the soft inner white. Little flowers, at least she believed they were flowers, ran in a painted ring around the teapot, their delicate petals shades of yellow and pink.

She heard herself sob again as Katrin glanced back at her. More tears slid down her cheeks, and Liam shifted in his sister's peripheral vision.

"What's wrong?" Liam slid the tray onto the bedside table, and Dani briefly saw him move to the bed, his dark eyes filled with worry for her.

Dani's energy waned, and her vision dimmed as the connection broke. She let go of Katrin and used the back of her hand to wipe the tears from her face. "I could see," she whispered.

Liam's hand brushed her cheek, damp from her tears. "I don't understand."

The bed shifted as Katrin stood, smoothing her skirt with her hands. "I'll give you two a little time." She touched Dani's shoulder. "We'll play more with that later, when you've had some proper rest."

"Thank you." Dani smiled at her friend, and the room stilled once the door shut again, leaving them alone.

"Was that some funny priestess business?" Liam caressed her cheek again.

"No. She saw through my eyes when they were rushing to help us, and we just tried to see if it would work the other way around." Her voice caught, but she kept going. "I saw the sky, the room. Myself. You…"

"Ugh, I don't exactly look my best right now." She heard the smile she could properly imagine now.

"You look perfect." Dani reached for his face but hesitated.

He gently took her hand, and finished the movement for her, placing her palm against his stubbled chin. "Don't do that to me again." He kissed her wrist.

Worry rose in her chest. "Do what?"

"Almost die." He scooted closer. "Though that also could apply to making me think you were going to kill me... And then risking yourself to save me." He smiled against her palm. "How about all of it? Don't do any of it again."

Dani laughed. "So I shouldn't search for you if you go missing?"

"No! I had Tallos right where I wanted him."

She snorted. "Right."

Liam chuckled, leaning into her and pressing his forehead to hers. He breathed, tone growing serious. "I'm sorry it came to all that. I'm sorry I ever doubted you."

Dani bit her bottom lip. "He was lying when he said I'd sent him messages. I never did, I swear. And I didn't mean what I said. About you misusing your power. I just wanted him to stop."

The most disturbing thing he'd said to her still rattled in her mind. That he could always find her. That the Dtrüa were bonded.

I need to find a way to change that.

"I didn't think you'd sent the messages, I certainly never gave you much opportunity when I was still busy being an ass. But I *was* afraid for my misuse of power." He sat back from her, pulling away slightly. "I don't want that to be true."

"It's not." Dani shook her head and crawled after him. She touched his neck before sliding her hand into his short hair. "All I want is you, if you still want me, too."

His breath tickled her lips. "Well, everyone knows, now." He brushed his thumb up over her lower lip. "And it has changed nothing about how I feel."

The Dtrüa crawled into his lap, lacing her arms around his shoulders and ignoring the protests from her bruises. "How *do* you feel?"

Liam's arms wrapped around her, somehow avoiding all the most sensitive muscles. His calloused hands touched her bare shoulders, tracing the thin strap of the silky sleeping gown. "I can show you if you'd like," he whispered. Tenderly tilting her chin up, he brought his lips to hers, starting a slow, sensual kiss.

It sent a wave of tingles through her body, happy to return each subtle movement of his mouth. But his lack of an answer made her wonder.

Maybe he doesn't know how he feels.

Dani drew from the kiss and nuzzled into his neck, burying her nose in his scent as she held him close. "It's all right if you don't know. This is so new, and it started rather..."

Her mind whirled back to how it began, and she mentally connected it to Tallos.

I need to go back to where it started.

Dani's heart sank as the truth settled in.

Liam stroked a lock of her hair, twisting the strands between his thumb and finger. "Rather suddenly?" He paused as she pulled away, and he touched the furrow of her brow. "What's wrong?"

"Tallos said we're all bonded. All the Dtrüa. And that he could always find me." Dani swallowed. "That means others can, too. I need to return to Feyor, Liam."

Chapter 38

Liam sat up, his body rigid. "What? No, that's crazy." He grabbed her hand, interlacing their fingers, his heart racing. "Dani. No. You can't go back there. If they figure out what you've been doing here... the information you've given us?"

"They'll kill me, I know." She sat straighter in his lap, facing him and running her free hand through his hair. "But they won't find out. And I can't spend the rest of my life looking over my shoulder. I need to remove the bond."

"What if you can't?" Liam's tone softened. He sighed, stroking her jaw and memorizing every gentle curve of her. "Will you still come back?"

Dani tilted her face into his touch, closing her eyes. "Would you want me to?"

His chest tightened. "Yes." It came out in a breathy exhale. "Yes, I'd want you to come back. I don't even want you to go in the first place. I—"

His stomach fluttered at the thought, at the next words he wanted to say.

That's crazy, she's...

Just looking at her sent his mind whirling, questioning... everything. He thought back to the moment he first saw her in the forest outside the border encampment. He'd hated her immediately, dictated by how different she was. Because she was Feyorian. They'd killed his countrymen, his comrades. Ollie.

Her actions had directly led to more bloodshed, but the more he learned, the less he realized her choice in it all. She was a victim, too. A victim of Feyor and the war machine they sought to continue building.

And all I want to do now is protect her from all that.

Squeezing her hand, he felt pressure building behind his eyes as he kissed her knuckles. He shook his head, unable to form the words. He pressed another hard kiss to her skin, remembering the heat of her blood pooling from the wounds inflicted by Tallos. The fear that raged through him.

She ran from the battle at the border to avoid killing, but she killed Tallos. For me.

"I will come back." Dani's voice quieted. "No matter what, I will find you." Her hand moved from his hair to his face, tracing over his skin in the way she did to see him. "I'm so happy I had the chance to see your face. I'll never forget that."

He shook his head. "I don't like this, Dani. I... can't come with you."

"I know." She leaned into him again and wrapped her arms around him. Her heart thudded against his chest. "But what happened yesterday can never happen again. This is the only way." Her lips hovered near his ear before kissing his neck. "Do you trust me to do this?"

"Yes." It came too suddenly to be anything but the truth. He tilted his head, their temples touching before he leaned back to catch her mouth. He tried to memorize the taste. The feel of her. Breaking away, Liam met her eyes in the dimness of their room.

The only candle flickered on the bedside table beside the tray of untouched food.

He stroked her hair, tucking it behind her ear. It still felt partially damp from when he and Katrin had cleaned the blood off her.

"It can wait until morning, though, right? And do you have any idea what this will do to Katrin?"

"It can all wait until morning." Dani's brow upturned in the center. "You'll think of me, won't you?"

He smiled, but it only hid the growing sorrow. "Every day."

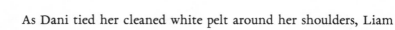

As Dani tied her cleaned white pelt around her shoulders, Liam wished he could reverse time. Go back to an hour earlier, when he'd woken with her in his arms.

When will I be able to do that again?

Once, he would have questioned her ability to fend for herself, but after seeing her take down a grizzly, he no longer worried how she'd fare in the wild. What concerned him more was what she would encounter on returning to her home country. If Feyor suspected her a traitor, they'd take her life.

But what if they're kind to her?

The fear she may choose to stay in Feyor, now that Tallos wouldn't be there to harass her, lingered in his mind.

We've made no pledges. No promises to each other. I don't even have something to give her. How will she find me? We won't be staying in Omensea for long.

"I wish you'd speak." Dani's voice pulled him from his worries, and she approached him. "Are you angry with my choice?"

Liam swallowed, shaking his head before catching himself again. "No, I'm not angry." He wanted to wrap his arms around her, but somehow it felt like that'd make the whole thing worse. "Worried." He stuffed his hands into his pockets. "Trying not to make this harder."

Her shoulders slumped. "I think nothing you could do would make this harder."

"I could ask you not to go again?" The words tumbled out. He winced, staring at the floor. "Don't go? With the declaration of war..."

Dani clicked her tongue and crossed the room to him, touching his cheeks with both hands. "I have to. With the declaration of war, things will only get worse. This is my only chance, but it won't be forever."

"How long?"

"I don't know." Dani sighed, retracting her touch to pull the thin leather strap from beneath her shirt that held her feline tooth pendant. She draped it over Liam's head, her hands lingering on his neck. "But it's temporary."

He pursed his lips, wishing he believed her. "I've never felt like this before, Dani." He traced a strand of her hair over her cheek. "About anyone. I hope you know that."

She stepped closer and kissed him. Pulling away enough to speak, she let her lips graze his chin. "Neither have I. I wish I could reassure you somehow. Tell me what to say."

Sliding his hand behind her head, he met her mouth again, pushing all he could into the movement of their lips together. His eyes burned when he pulled from it, running his hand down her spine. "Please, just stay alive."

"I will if you do, too." Dani pressed her hand over the tooth pendant at the top of his sternum.

"Did you already say goodbye to Katrin and the others?" His chest tightened as he already knew the answer. They couldn't delay any longer.

Dani nodded once. "I did." A breeze from the open window kicked up her white hair, trailing it in front of her face. "I... should go." Her eyes grew glassy, and she stepped backward, her fingertips on his chest the last to part from him.

He nodded, forcing a step back to stop from reaching for her again. "I know." He watched her as she turned slowly to the window, clicking her tongue. He'd miss the sound.

Pausing with her hands on the windowsill and her back to him, Dani tilted her head back. Her body shifted, white pelts spreading over until her hands morphed into large paws on the sill. Glancing back, her rounded white ears swiveled towards him. Her claws flexed, scratching the windowsill before she leapt out into the chill morning air.

Liam stepped forward, watching the white cat race through the grass. He ran his finger over the rough edge of the scratches on the sill, his chest hollow.

A flurry of movement near the corner of the inn's exterior caught his eye as Stefan caught an owl on his outstretched arm.

Leaning his head against the cool frame of the window, Liam sighed.

Word from the king. Guess we'll be leaving sooner than I thought.

Turning to catch the blur of Dani's shape, he couldn't find her.

A subtle tap echoed on his door, and he contemplated ignoring it before the hinges squeaked.

"Guess I should have locked it..." Liam grumbled.

Katrin's soft footsteps fluttered along the floor. Her soft hand closed around his, her cheek pressing up against his shoulder. "You all right?"

"You mean, after watching the woman I..." He shook his head again, squeezing Katrin's hand.

Her chin dug into his shoulder, her dark eyes boring into him even as he avoided her gaze. "She had to go back."

"Doesn't mean I have to like it."

Katrin rubbed her thumb along his, a smile playing on her lips. "I could have sworn a week ago this would have gone very differently."

Liam heaved a breath. "Me, too."

She tugged on him. "She'll be fine. She can take care of herself."

"I hope so."

Footsteps echoed from the hallway where Katrin had left the door open.

Matthias paused in the doorway, eyeing Liam and then the open window. "And here I was worried about cutting your farewell short." He held up a piece of parchment. "Get your things together, there's been a change of plans. We're returning to the border."

Katrin tensed against him.

The prince patted the door frame, looking at Katrin. "I'll be in our room writing a response." He disappeared, another door clicking open down the hall.

"He looks upset," Katrin whispered, patting Liam's shoulder.

"Is that what that face was?" Liam slipped his hand from his sister's, kissing her forehead. "Go check on your man."

Katrin frowned, her lips a thin line. "But you—"

"I'm fine." Liam gripped her shoulders, pushing her away from him. "I'll pack up and see you downstairs."

She narrowed her eyes but stepped away. "I don't know how I feel about going back to the border."

Liam shrugged, reaching for his sword belt and securing it around his waist. "Sounds busy, which I like. I need the distraction right now." His hand idly reached up, his fingers grazing over the tooth pendant.

And it's closer to Dani.

Katrin paused in the doorway. "See you downstairs."

Chapter 39

Four days later...

Matthias blocked Katrin's advance, twisting his quarterstaff to the side and flicking hers five feet away into the fresh snow.

"Damn it!" Katrin spun, diving after it.

Matthias tapped the back of her legs with his practice weapon and smirked. "Down again."

Liam rubbed his eyes with his thumb and index finger. "Stop opening up, even when you've been disarmed." He sounded far more annoyed than he should. "That's the most important time to stay facing the enemy."

Katrin growled, plucking up her quarterstaff and brushing the snow from it with bare hands. Her skin looked slightly blue from the cold, but a bead of sweat ran down her brow.

"We should take a break." Matthias planted the end of his staff on the ground.

"No. I've got this." Katrin spread her feet and readied herself as Liam had instructed, though she held the staff slightly crooked.

"Your fingers are blue, and your form is getting sloppy." Matthias spun the butt of his staff and knocked hers to the side. "Better to recoup and practice more when you've rested."

"I need to know how to defend myself."

The prince strode towards her. "You're getting better. Be patient. We'll do some knife work later."

Liam chuckled. "Depends on your definition of better."

Katrin spun and threw her staff at her brother, but he caught it before it smacked him in the face. "Ass." Snow sprayed up around the side of her skirt that'd fallen from where she tucked it into her belt while she stormed away.

Matthias shot Liam a look. "Can't you be nice?"

The scent of cooking venison emanated from the circle of tents erected around their campsite within the trees, hiding the road and open meadows to the west. Only a thin wisp of smoke drifted into the clear blue sky.

Liam shrugged. "Someone's got to be tough on her. Since you're not."

"I'm going as hard on her as I can without killing her spirit." Matthias used the end of his staff to flick snow at Liam. "She'll get there."

"Before the border?" Liam brushed the snow from his breeches, turning slightly to eye the open meadow.

"How good with a sword were *you* after only a few days?" Matthias tilted his head. "Of course she won't be ready before the border, but we've got to start somewhere. I know you're upset about Dani, but—"

Liam straightened, stamping the end of the staff onto the frozen ground. "Don't bring her into this." He glowered, moving to walk past Matthias back towards camp.

The prince clenched his jaw and caught the soldier's arm with a gentle grip. "Katrin will be safe and so will Dani."

Liam ground his teeth, his chest rising in a breath. He exhaled a cloud into the air. "You sure we can't leave her at the temple?"

"It's an option." Matthias let go of Liam. "If your sister is willing, I'll have Merissa accompany us instead. We can reach the temple before sunset."

"A hot meal will be good, first, though." He sighed, running a hand back through his hair. "I'll start packing up—"

Movement spurred to Matthias's left, deep in the trees. Someone raced away, dressed in white and grey.

A Feyorian scout? This far in Isalica?

Panic jolted the prince's chest. "Stefan! Scout to the northwest!" He dropped the staff and grabbed his sheathed sword from the snow as he sprinted after the spy. Withdrawing the blade as he ran, he tossed the scabbard.

Liam huffed behind him, boots crunching through the snow.

Hooves pounded to their right, then the familiar twang of the crossbow's mechanism echoed through the clearing, the dim figure in front of them collapsing into the snow.

The scout screamed, trying to stand while clutching his leg. He stumbled and fell back into the snow, a patch of crimson spreading beneath him. The man drew his sword, but Stefan's chestnut gelding stomped to a stop next to him.

The elite aimed the crossbow at the Feyorian's head, and the scout dropped his weapon. He snatched something from around his own neck, popping the top off a tiny vial as he lifted it to his lips. His body dropped into spasms after he drank the liquid, froth spewing from his mouth.

Matthias skidded to a halt as Stefan lowered the crossbow. "Damn."

Liam jogged up to the scout's body, kicking the man's sword further away before he crouched, his blade in hand. He picked up the man's arm, tugging his sleeve down to show the tattoo on his wrist Feyor's prized scouts received as a badge of honor. The simple shape of a sika, the stealthy cats the country trained to work with their spies, usually a quarter of the size of Dani's panther form.

Too bad a black cat doesn't blend in so good up here in the snow.

Stefan let out a slow breath, meeting the prince's eyes. "Worth a jump?"

Chewing on his lip, Matthias shook his head. "No. He wouldn't have told us anything, anyway."

Liam looked up at the prince, furrowing his brow as he dropped the scout's arm. "What the hells is he doing this far across the border?"

"Stefan, ride to the ridge." Matthias motioned in the temple's direction. "We must be missing something if he made it this far. Go look."

The elite nodded, wheeling his horse around to go investigate. He skirted their camp, disappearing north.

Liam started picking through the scout's pockets, pulling open his jacket to rifle through the inside. "What'd Stefan mean when he said jump?" He didn't look up as he continued searching. "I thought I heard Micah say something like that back at the border."

He's more than proven that he deserves to know.

Matthias retrieved his scabbard before approaching Liam and the dead scout. "I have the Art. Only my crown elites know... And Katrin. I can..." He circled his hand in front of him. "Jump back in time."

Liam froze, his hand still inside one of the scout's pockets. He remained like that for a moment before he looked up at Matthias as he pulled out a small leather-bound book. "Through... time." The soldier chewed his lower lip, tapping the book in his palm. "I... didn't know the Art worked like that."

"It doesn't. Usually." Matthias narrowed his eyes. "Before you go jumping to conclusions on my mental state, let me prove it to you."

Liam chuckled and shook his head as he stood. "Not necessary. I don't expect you to perform like a carnival show." He unwrapped the length of leather holding the scout's journal shut and started thumbing through the pages. "But you want me to believe that the prince... has the Art? Shouldn't you have gone into the temples like the rest of the country's practitioners?"

Disgust rose in Matthias's chest. "I kept it secret. You know how I feel about the temples."

Liam shook his head, meeting Matthias's eyes. "You want me to speak frankly?"

The prince straightened. "You're always welcome to speak frankly, but I tell you this because I trust you as one of my closest guards, not to seek your approval."

Liam shrugged. "Fair enough. And I appreciate the trust. But you do sound crazy."

"You're not the first to think so. So do me the honor of telling me something completely random, and I'll jump back and tell you first." Matthias leaned sideways on a tree.

"Sounds like a parlor trick. Those fortune tellers in Mecora do that, don't they?" Liam sighed when Matthias only waited. "Fine. This scout being this far past the border only makes sense if Feyor has pushed past the wall. So... tell me that I'm worried about my old comrades or something."

Matthias made a face, but sucked in a breath of the Art.

"Sounds like a parlor trick. Those—"

"Fortune tellers in Mecora do that? They do, but this is different. The scout being this far means Feyor has pushed past the wall, and you're worried about your comrades." Matthias tapped his foot.

"Well, I could have told you that..." Liam paused, straightening. "What am I thinking about right now?"

The prince laughed. "I can't read your mind. You have to tell me once, so I can go back and tell you before you tell me."

Liam licked his lips. "I still think this is crazy. And I'm thinking that this is you just being good at reading body language, or something. I'm giving you hints without knowing it."

"Then tell me something I can't possibly read from your body language." Matthias quirked an eyebrow. "Anything at all."

"Anything?" Liam narrowed his eyes.

"Anything."

"I don't like you and Katrin together."

"Anything?" Liam narrowed his eyes.

Matthias swallowed. "Even that you don't like me and Katrin together."

Liam straightened again, the book in his palm snapping shut. "I didn't say that."

"You did." Matthias frowned.

"Shit." Liam kicked a lump of snow and shook his head. "Well. I don't."

"Why?"

He shook his head, averting his gaze. "Just... doesn't seem right. And I don't want to see her get hurt."

"She won't." Matthias stood straight. "I won't let her. How do you think she survived the avalanche? How we made it to you and Dani in time?"

Liam's eyes widened, but he gritted his jaw. "Doesn't change how I feel about you and Kat."

"I could never hurt your sister."

Liam gave a dry chuckle. "Physical hurt ain't what I'm talking about."

Matthias's chest squeezed. "I won't break her heart, if that's what you mean."

"So you're what, then?" Liam crossed his arms. "Gonna marry her, make her queen? She comes from a family of farmers and is meant to be a priestess. Maybe more because people can actually move up in standing within the temples. But then you come tromping into her life and mess all that up."

The prince stared at Liam, his gaze hardening. "We don't choose who we fall in love with, do we?"

His arms fell loose. "Not fair."

"But true. I didn't want to mess up her life, but she chose to come with me. *She* chose to stay with me." Matthias stepped towards Liam. "What was I supposed to do? Tell the woman I love to pack it up and go back to the temple? Never. Call it selfish if you want, but I will *move mountains* to be with her. And something tells me you might understand that feeling, just a little."

Liam stiffened, but held his ground. "What about the rest?"

"Will I marry her?" Matthias laughed. "One day. And she'll make a damn fine queen."

A horse approached, snorting and sending a cloud of frost from its nostrils as Stefan encouraged it to a stop. "Interrupting?"

Liam glanced at him and shook his head, eyes returning to Matthias's for a moment before he crouched to search the scout again.

"What did you find?" Matthias faced his guard.

Stefan dismounted. "It's not good news. Feyor has pushed the border back. Our soldiers have set up a new encampment around the temple ruins."

"Ruins? They destroyed the temple?" Liam looked up as Stefan gave a slow nod. "Fuck."

Matthias shut his eyes for a breath.

Katrin will be devastated.

The prince looked at Liam. "Let's go. Leave him."

Stefan led the horse back to their small camp while Matthias walked with Katrin's brother.

Liam tucked the scout's journal into his coat pocket. "Did..." He hesitated, looking at the ridge they still needed to ascend. "Did Dani die? The first time you got to the mill?"

Matthias's heart ached for his friend. "We were too late. She'd lost too much blood."

Liam paled. "I'm sorry," he whispered. "I... shouldn't have—"

"You're fine." The prince patted his shoulder. "It worked out, didn't it? And, in time, perhaps you'll trust me with your sister."

Nearing the camp, Katrin looked up from where she stooped, packing. Worry clouded her eyes, the small knife he'd given her latched to her belt. "What's wrong?"

Matthias glanced at Liam, silently asking if he wanted to be the one to tell her.

Liam shook his head discreetly before walking to his tent, already partially collapsed thanks to Barim. He patted Katrin on the shoulder as he went, leaning in to give her a quick kiss on the hair.

"Come with me." Matthias offered her his hand.

Katrin narrowed her eyes, but closed her pack before she stepped towards Matthias. She'd pulled her pale yellow skirt back down over her breeches, the hem stained with mud from their travels. She slipped her icy hand into Matthias's palm. "Did the scout get away?"

"No." The prince led her from the camp, letting the sounds of packing fade behind the trees. Once they'd gained a modicum of privacy, he stopped and faced her. "Feyor pushed the border back. I'm sorry, Katrin. They destroyed the temple."

Katrin's cheeks flushed, a hand lifting to her mouth as she stared at him. "What?" She gasped, shaking her head. "No, no. Why would they attack a temple? They're just priests and..." She looked down, but then quickly back up again. "Is everyone all right? Did anyone..."

Matthias tightened his jaw and put his hands on her shoulders. "We don't know the details, yet, but... I don't expect there were many survivors."

Katrin's eyes glassed over, a boil of tears falling over her lower lids. "But—" Whatever would have come next disappeared beneath a sob. "They're just..." She sagged.

Stepping close, Matthias wrapped his arms around her and held her against him as her legs gave out. "I'm so sorry, Kat." He pressed his mouth to the top of her head, cringing.

Burying her face in his tunic, she cried out, her screams muffled by his shirt.

No smoke rose from the charred remains of the temple, any embers long extinguished by the fresh coating of snow that had also collapsed the east wing. The ashes of the funeral pyres remained, dusting grey across the ground clear of the ice from the fires that'd burned there. The patch stretched towards the base of the mountain, large enough to suggest the burning of several hundred bodies.

Matthias's stomach churned.

Katrin rode beside him, her back stoically straight. Red still rimmed her eyes, but she pursed her lips to keep more tears in.

The troops had erected a makeshift wall in the fields between the temple and the western tree line, stumps of pines showing where they'd cut the wood for the spiked barricade. A wooden gate lay open for them, Riez having gone ahead to announce their arrival. A shallow line of tents rose behind, forming a crescent around the foundation of the temple ruins.

Micah rode in front, wearing the prince's signet ring. Liam and Stefan flanked him, Katrin's brother casting the occasional glance at his sister.

Riding into the encampment, Matthias spotted Riez standing beside a familiar face.

Lieutenant Verris saluted Micah as he dismounted, a soldier hurrying forward to take the reins. She glanced at Matthias with a discreet nod of her head. "Good to see you again, your majesty. Pleased to see you've stayed safe, all things considered."

Micah lowered his fur-lined hood. "And you as well. We have much to discuss."

"Will you be stationed here for a time?"

"We will. Our king has asked that I liaise with him from this encampment, to remove the burden of difficult decisions from your captain's shoulders."

"That's greatly appreciated, seeing as I'm in command. Captain Brenna fell in battle."

Matthias dismounted, the familiar feeling of losses at war washing over him. He approached the lieutenant. "Were there any survivors from the temple?"

Behind him, Katrin's boots hit the ground, and he knew she listened.

"Sadly, only one." Verris motioned to Micah. "Your healer, actually. Merissa was quite shaken up, but she's working with the few healers we have left."

Matthias cringed, unable to bring himself to look at Katrin.

The frosty ground crunched as she walked away from where they stood.

The lieutenant's eyes passed from Micah and Matthias, seeming to watch the acolyte as she started towards the ruins.

The prince turned to follow her gaze.

"Katy girl..." Liam caught her wrist, but she tore her hand away.

"I need to be alone." Her voice sounded hollow. "To pay my respects."

Liam stepped back, letting her go. He turned and met Matthias's eyes.

I wish I could fix this for her.

Matthias faced the lieutenant, sighing.

Micah cleared his throat. "Let's get inside, and you can brief us on everything."

Chapter 40

Everything ached, as if she'd been running for miles. Katrin's mind felt stuffed with cotton, her eyes sore and heavy as she carefully stepped around the charred walls. Hiking her skirt up, she tucked the hem into the sides of her belt like she did when sparring. Her fingers brushed the metal scabbard of her dagger, still so foreign.

Her boots crunched in the thin layer of snow, coupled with the crack of remaining cinders. It felt so far from the home it'd been before.

She eyed the partially collapsed stairwell that led down into the basement kitchens, flashes of Serna and Jelisa dancing in the hearth light corrupting her vision. She flinched, looking away as hot tears threatened her again.

Rolling her lips together, Katrin closed her eyes. "Nymaera, please grant them passage." She touched her chest, the thunder of her heart tickling her fingertips. A chill breeze rushed from the mountains, flapping her cloak back and rustling her hair beneath her hood.

Shivering, Katrin followed the ashes of the walls from the kitchen, counting the steps as she had when bored during her turn to sweep the hallways.

Feyor did this. They destroyed the innocence here.

Memories of the dire wolves tearing through the medical tent made her steps falter, her boot catching on a fallen beam. Striking the ground, her knees roared. Her palms scraped the ground, breaking through the snow to slide within the muddy ash, leaving black stains along her skin.

A shaky breath rocked through her body as she stared at the black smears on her hands.

Why? Why did this happen?

Another icy blast struck her face, skin stinging where new tears trailed. Her hood fell back, the rest of her hair pulling free from the knot at the back of her neck. Blinking at the sun reflecting off the snow still high on the Yandarin peaks, she considered the grey behemoths. Feyor wanted them. They were the reason for the war. For all the death.

Closing her eyes, she bowed her head into her dirty palms. The flap of tent canvas sounded with another shocking breeze. Her mind flooded with images of Feyor's armies on dragons, their leather wings beating in the frosty air, sending a flurry of snow into the air.

Katrin's Art swelled without her bidding, filling her chest with a thrumming heat. The mud on her skin hardened as the power rushed through her, banishing the cold. Rage built in her stomach, creating an inferno within her as she fell onto her palms. The snow at her fingertips steamed, and the ground turned to hard stone. Her limbs weakened as she tried to pull off her cloak, struggling with the clasp before letting it drop.

Dully, she rose to her feet, swallowing the energy in her veins. Rubbing her hands together, the black stains on her palms flecked away, falling like sand to the melting snow as she strode.

I can't allow this to happen to my country.

She stepped over the debris, following the familiar curves of the foundation towards the north wing which had already been ravaged by fire before Feyor's attack. Some of the charred beams looked new, proving that the priests had begun to rebuild around the library.

Katrin stepped to the center of the ruins, funneling more into her power. The Art writhed within her, willing to answer the call she made of it. Crouching, she pushed the heat within her into her hand as she drew a simple circle in the fresh powdered snow. The circle sizzled and steamed, the power passing beyond its boundary to ripple outward like a drip in a pond. The snow shook, then faded, wafts of warm air brushing through her skirts and over her skin.

Pages fluttered and wood cracked as it dried.

Katrin turned in a slow circle, eyeing the tattered library around her. She tried to remember the sections, their catalogs unlikely to have survived. Brushing her hands back through her loose hair, she caught the wild strands and knotted it at the back of her head as she strode to the section she recalled housing histories.

Stooping low, she grunted as she lifted one of the smaller collapsed bookshelves, relieved to see mostly intact books buried beneath it. She picked up the first, rubbing dried dirt from its cracked leather spine.

"I need to find the truth," she whispered, as if saying it aloud would coax the book into helping her.

She knelt, gathering several more books before she conceded to the easier solution and bunched her skirt beneath her to sit right there among them. She read each title, sorting them from left to right on how likely they would discuss the subject she cared about most.

Let's learn all I can about dragons.

Chapter 41

Dani halted in the snow, cat nose twitching in the air.

Dire wolves. I'm close.

The multipurpose facility for the Dtrüa also housed a third of the country's dire wolf population. With her comrades' ability to communicate with the beasts, training became swifter with fewer casualties.

Dani ran on, her muscles aching from the long journey. It'd taken her longer than it should have to get home, slowed by her recovery from blood loss and the other damage Tallos had inflicted.

Her scent-filled vision brightened as the sun emerged from behind a cloud, contrasting the looming dark shape in the distance.

I don't remember the walls being so tall before.

Memories of debriefings of other Dtrüa muddled in her mind, ones they had permitted her to watch and learn from.

I never saw Tallos.

She reminded herself of the lies she would need to tell, but uncertainty ran rampant in her mind.

Give them information, but nothing they can use to gain an advantage. Use the material Matthias offered me.

Dani slowed near the tall gate and channeled her Art back into her veins. She rose onto her human feet, taking a deep breath of icy air.

The wolves beyond the wall howled, shouts from their trainers rising. A pack rushed by the wrought-iron gate at the front of the compound, their fur a mottled blur in her vision. One spotted Dani, sliding to a stop on the flagstone, maw gnashing as he snarled and growled.

She gasped and held out her hand. "Easy, girl." Seeking the wolf's innate connection to Pantracia's fabric, she pushed her thoughts into its mind. *Calm. I am your friend.*

The wolf stopped, pushing its nose between the bars as it let out a long whine.

Dani smiled as she crossed to the gate, lifting her hands to stroke the dire wolf's snout. The animal licked her, tongue completely encompassing her hands as the Dtrüa reached through the gate to scratch its ears.

The wolf's back leg thumped against the stone with another happy whine.

Hooves clattered, a whistle blasting from the trainer's lips, his shape dark against the cloudy sky above the training grounds.

The wolf yanked its head away, spinning towards the trainer before yipping and running after the pack, leaving Dani resting with her arms between the bars of the gate.

The rider circled their horse, moving closer to the gate before dismounting, their boots loud on the stone.

"Varadani." His voice took her a moment to place, and her heart thundered at her ill luck. "Didn't expect to see you back." The locks of the gate clicked, the iron grinding as Lasseth slid the massive bar out of place.

"It's good to be home." Dani kept the smile on her face, entering the compound and waiting as the other Dtrüa locked the gate. "It's been too long. How are things here? I saw the border and our victory over the Isalicans."

Lasseth chuckled, approaching his horse again. "We are at war, so things are busy. The king demands more wolves, so this pack will be sent to the border within the week, despite some free spirits like Nia, there."

Dani's smile grew. "I remember Nia when she first arrived here. Always had a fondness for me. Don't hold it against her." She smirked, striding over the slushy road towards the estate.

Lasseth walked beside her, leading his horse. "Can hardly blame her."

She could feel the man's eyes on her, burning over her skin as he analyzed her.

As Nysir's right hand, he could change the fate of her return with nothing more than his opinion. Dani never fully understood why Nysir kept such close company with the trainer, but assumed it had something to do with the difference of his Art. Lasseth, although a Dtrüa like her, emanated a different energy pattern compared to the others.

"Shall we step inside so you may enlighten me to your whereabouts the last several months?" The reins of his horse jangled as he passed them to someone who approached from the stable side of the grounds.

Dani furrowed her brow. "I assumed Nysir would debrief me."

"Nysir is unavailable. Called away on business." Lasseth touched her lower back, encouraging her to the stairs. "I'll see to your debriefing."

Swallowing, she stepped ahead and clicked her tongue. She tried not to show her relief that the intimidating master Dtrüa wasn't present. "Of course." Her boot hit the first step, and she climbed, the familiar scents of the building sparking memories she longed to forget.

My eyes are open now.

At the top of the stairs, Dani touched the wall and trailed her fingers along it as she walked, pausing at the first door she passed.

"You can enter that room."

Chains clattered to the floor further down the hallway, and Dani flinched, touching her wrists.

Lasseth opened the door for her, waiting as she entered and clicked her tongue again.

Finding her chair, she sat, remembering Matthias's advice.

The anxious can't sit still.

The chair opposite her dragged from under a table before her superior sat in it, still not speaking.

He's trying to make me uncomfortable.

Dani tilted her head, leaning back in her chair and catching the scent of water.

"Tallos reported in nearly three months ago, immediately after the assassination attempt on the prince, and we haven't heard a word since." Lasseth poured water into a goblet and slid it across the table to her before pouring another. "He said you'd intentionally allowed yourself to be captured by Isalica."

Sipping the drink without hesitation, Dani nodded. "I did. The battle at the border wasn't going as well as I hoped, so I thought we could gain a better advantage if I tried to get closer to the prince."

"Because you already knew our assassination attempts had failed?"

"Yes."

"How?" Lasseth's gruff voice sounded almost bored.

"I heard talk during the battle while I was sneaking closer to the barracks."

"After you opened the gate?"

"Yes."

"Why did you believe us to be losing the battle?" Lasseth's cup clinked on the table, chair creaking as he leaned back. "I heard it was dumb luck that the prince even survived the dire wolf assault."

Dani's gaze fell in an attempt to portray regret. "Dire wolf blood smells different from human blood, and there was a lot of it. I don't know how they killed so many of our pups, but I wanted a shot at redeeming the night."

Lasseth hummed. "And what did your infiltration reveal?"

She lifted her blurry eyes, focusing on where the man's voice came from. "That Isalica has no idea why we're attacking. They are oblivious to the weapons hiding in their mountains. There was also discussion of a treaty with Ziona, but when we declared war, Ziona reneged on the deal."

"We're aware of the attempted treaty. And its recent dissolution."

He sighed. "Surely there's more with how close you were to the prince and his crown elites."

Dani drank her water, giving herself time to remember what she was to offer them. "They were planning a wedding to seal their relationship with Ziona."

"Between which royal parties?"

"Isalica's crown prince and Ziona's second princess, Kelsara. The last I knew, the prince and his guards were boarding a ship to Hammerdale. I escaped them in Omensea."

"And how did you accomplish that?"

"I convinced one of the elites I wasn't a threat, and he took my cuffs off. I shifted and ran."

"And what information did you provide to convince the Isalicans you were cooperating?" Lasseth's fingers tapped on the table, the rhythm pounding in Dani's head.

"Nothing." Dani paused. "I earned their trust by not trying to fight them."

"So they remain ignorant of your ability as a Dtrüa?"

"Yes."

Lasseth paused, sucking on his teeth. "The guards left you alone without cuffs?"

"No." Dani shook her head.

"Then how did they not see you shift?"

Her breath caught. "It was night."

The table shifted as Lasseth leaned forward. "You're a truly horrible liar, Varadani."

Dani stiffened, swallowing. "I'm not lying. I—"

"Did you see Tallos in Omensea, before you fled?"

"No. He was there?"

"I find it surprising that your mate would be present and not reveal himself to you."

"So do I." Dani chewed her lower lip.

"Unless he no longer trusted you. Why do you think that might happen?"

"This feels more like an interrogation than a debriefing." Dani tried to steady her breath, reaching for her water again. "I don't know why Tallos came to Omensea, or what he wanted from me."

"I never said he wanted something from you. Why did you say that?"

Dani cringed, blinking. "I didn't mean that. I meant... I meant I don't know why he was there."

"Do you like being a Dtrüa, Varadani?"

"What?"

"Do you resent Feyor for what they did to you, to make you into this?" Lasseth lowered his voice, prodding painful memories.

Dani's eyes burned. "Why are you asking me this?" She touched the back of her neck, where ghost pains still prickled from the needles that had pierced her flesh.

"Did you come back because Tallos told you about the bond?"

Dani fell silent, mouth agape as she breathed.

Lasseth leaned back in his chair again, crossing his arms with a rustle of his cloak. Another difference between him and the other Dtrüa. He didn't have to wear all animal-derived materials to shift.

Why is that?

She shook her head. "Tallos didn't mention a bond."

"In Omensea?"

"Yes. No. No, I didn't see him there."

"But you saw him somewhere else?"

"No. I mean, I thought I smelled him on the way to Omensea, but I assumed it was my imagination."

"Because you missed your mate?"

"Of course." Dani spoke through a clenched jaw.

"Another lie."

Closing her eyes, Dani glanced towards the door and wondered if she could make it through before he caught her.

Lasseth's chair ground over the floor. "Get up."

Her heart sped, but she obeyed.

"Come." Lasseth stepped loudly towards the door, blocking her.

"I wouldn't run. We both know my shape is faster than yours."

Damn mountain eagle.

All the other Dtrüa had land forms, and his flying one only added to the enigma.

What if he isn't like us?

Dani crossed to him. "Where are you taking me?"

His hand closed around her bicep. Without answering, he opened the door and pulled her down the hall deeper into the keep.

The air smelled stale, tainted only by the oil of the lamps on the walls. They passed dark hallways and doors, and she felt certain he was leading her towards the dungeons below. When they reached the hall, she contemplated her chances of breaking his grip and running, but he turned sharply down the opposite way.

Where is he taking me?

Pushing through another doorway, the world brightened.

Dani blinked, fresh air hitting her senses. "Outside?" She stumbled on something, but Lasseth's grip tightened and righted her.

Another gate squealed open, her arm scraping along the stone archway as he took her through, and it snapped shut behind them. Needles crunched beneath their boots as he pulled her into the freshness of the forest. Her nose twinged at the sharp scent of Lasseth mixed among the flourishing undergrowth. It was different from the other Dtrüa and set her stomach uneasy.

"Will you say something, please?" Dani jerked her arm free. "Panthers eat birds, remember?"

I could so easily kill him.

Lasseth laughed. "I'm far more than a bird, girl." He grabbed her arm again. "Come on."

She planted her feet, resisting his tug. "What the hells does that mean? You're not a Dtrüa, are you? You aren't the same as us. Did you even go through the transformation process?"

Lasseth's nails bit into her skin, a cold permeating from him. "I went through my own transformation process." He growled. "We're not far enough from the training grounds, yet. Move."

Dani huffed and gripped his forearm, twisting her body. Her kick contacted his back, and he stumbled forward. Free of him, she focused her power, and her furs melded into her skin. Once her paws hit the snow, she burst into a run away from the compound.

Trees whipped past her, low branches hitting her face as she maneuvered through the forest. The woodsy scent shifted, and the stench of decay struck her nose.

The surrounding shadows wriggled, tainted by the noxious green odor.

Dani leapt to the side, but a black tendril lashed from her left and yanked her to the frozen ground. Her body screamed as she slammed into the forest floor, another onyx shape snapping over her. She shifted, regaining her human form to pry at the vine-like traps, but they nipped at her skin.

As the darkness coalesced over her, Lasseth appeared. He pressed his knee into her chest, holding her hands over her head. "Will you stop? I'm not your enemy."

She struggled, but the remnants of shadow held her still. "What *are* you?"

The stench of death thickened, the grass beneath her dying.

"Not a Dtrüa." Lasseth growled, sitting up as he released her arms. He didn't stand, keeping the pressure on her chest. The folds of his linen cloak fell around her, suffocating. "But that doesn't mean I can't help you."

Dani froze. "Help me?"

"You want the bond gone, don't you?" Lasseth hovered over her.

"Yes." A weight lifted off her chest at admitting the truth, even if his knee still pressed against her sternum.

"Then I can help you. Or at least introduce you to someone who can. But we need something from you."

Dani rolled her lips together. "What do you need from me?"

"Souls are complicated things, and I have a friend who would benefit from studying yours."

That doesn't sound ominous at all.

"I'd like to talk to your friend before I agree to anything."

Lasseth's weight disappeared from her chest, the light shifting as he stood. "Want a hand? I'll take you to her."

Clicking her tongue, Dani accepted his hand to rise and brushed snow off her leathers. "All right. But... you won't turn me over to Feyor or Nysir?"

"There are bigger things at work than the Dtrüa and Feyor."

They resumed walking, leaving behind the stench of decay.

Dani fell silent, listening to the crisp snow beneath their feet. A quarter of an hour passed before she paused again. "How far is this place?"

"Another few hours. Though, we could speed up the journey if you prefer? Assuming I can trust you'll follow me." Lasseth's tone shifted with his smile. "Despite me telling you the truth about not being a Dtrüa."

She smirked. "Let's speed it up. It makes little difference to me what you are if you will help free me of the bond."

The tang of death caught the breeze again as Lasseth's shape dissolved. An eagle cry confirmed his transformation, wings beating as he took to the air. The draft ruffled the fur on her shoulders as she embraced her own power.

Following the eagle as he wove through the trees proved exhilarating, lightening her heart with each bound. She chased the bird, who screeched occasionally to keep her with him. She raced over the terrain, finding freedom in the run.

A dull snap reverberated against her senses, leaving Dani light headed as she slid to a stop in the snow. A dark hole in the mountainside that hadn't been there a moment before gaped in her vision, the musty scent of cave mold and lichen assaulting her.

How did I miss that?

Lasseth's raptor cry echoed against the stone, bouncing back from the opening of the cave as he slowed his descent, wings brushing against the stones. His human scent returned, accompanied by the rot of cave moss.

"There you are!" A feminine voice called from within the cave, soft footsteps echoing up an incline from within. Her scent, tainted with campfire smoke, wrapped around Lasseth's as their shapes merged in Dani's vision. "I was getting worried."

Lasseth's voice took on a gentle tone. "I told you I might have to stay away longer with my master gone."

The woman whined. "Hush, I didn't ask you."

Dani sniffed, but caught no scent of another.

Who is she talking to, if not him?

Pulling her Art, Dani breathed deep and shifted to her human form. The colorful scents in her vision dimmed, only brightening when she focused on them.

Light flared around the woman, like little suns swirled around her. Her ability in the Art was impossible to miss, buzzing against every inch of Dani.

"Who's this?" The woman grew closer. "Her ká is in chaos."

Forcing herself not to recoil, Dani lifted her chin. "My name is Varadani. I am a Dtrüa."

The woman squealed, clapping her hands together. "Oh, the trees are so happy. And the lichen is singing." She skipped forward, but cleared her throat, her coppery hair shining. "Stop being such a pessimist. We'll help her."

"How do you know what I want?" Dani narrowed her eyes.

Her warm hands took Dani's, tugging her forward. "Your ká told me, silly."

The Dtrüa stiffened. "My what?"

"Oh, Lasseth, did you tell her nothing?" The woman scowled in his direction.

He chuckled. "I thought it better for you to explain. I'm still not entirely sure about all of it." He waited as they grew closer to the cave opening. "Just... try not to overwhelm her, Ailiena."

Dani dug her feet into the ground and stopped walking. "I think I'd like to know a little more before I go in there and end up as an experimental panther stew."

Ailiena laughed, and the lights around her twinkled in time with it. "I like Varadani. Though, your ká suggests you don't like your name very much when I say it." She let go of her, taking a few steps back.

"I prefer Dani."

"Dani." Her voice calmed like a clearing storm. "Much better."

"Lasseth said you could sever my bond to the other Dtrüa."

"I can. Probably..." Ailiena's tone grew softer. "Though it'll be harder without Paldeshé. But I'm certain your ká will guide me to the right answers."

"And what do you want in return?" Dani glanced at the sky, still bright with the sun just past its zenith.

"I suspect I will gain it simply through working to grant you the separation from the other Dtrüa." Ailiena paused. "Stop it!"

Dani flinched and backed up. "Stop what?"

Ailiena groaned, and Lasseth stepped towards her.

"They starting up again?" he whispered.

"Mhmm. Damn things won't stop now that the sanctum is gone. Always wanting something or another fixed." Ailiena sucked in a deep breath, hissing in pain.

She's insane.

"I'll make some of that tea you like." Lasseth kissed the top of Ailiena's head. "It'll help with the headache."

The woman hummed, letting out a long exhale. "Thank you. And then... then we can start on Dani."

But she's my only chance.

"What are you?" Dani narrowed her eyes, trying to make out any details beyond the shine of her hair.

Ailiena patted Lasseth's arm, righting herself. "I'm the Rahn'ka."

Chapter 42

One week later...

Liam stared at the tree line, his eyes flickering to every subtle movement of the shadows. But each one disappointed him.

Not her. It's never her.

He sighed, forcing his eyes closed. The chatter of the men in the nearby camp overpowered everything, and he growled as he stomped through the crisp snow. His boots crunched, the sound thundering as he kept his eyes closed, trying to understand what Dani experienced.

I'm going to get myself shot by a scout.

The voices faded as he grew closer to the trees, birdsong and rustling needles replacing the noise. The more ambitious birds had returned from their migration to build their summer nests, despite the early spring snow.

He stopped, listening again, but heard nothing save the wind in the pines.

Dani's voice popped into his memory. *Have you ever just listened, Liam?*

His heart ached, its beat overwhelming everything else.

"Damn it." He opened his eyes and glared at the shadows of the woods towards Feyor. Towards more war, and what stood between him and her.

Turning, he accepted whatever arrow might fly from the trees at his back, and started towards the camp. He paused when he saw a hooded soldier making his way out the same side gate Liam had used.

Matthias's stormy blue eyes found his as they met halfway. "What are you doing out here?"

Liam frowned. "Hells if I know." He studied the prince, trying to determine his purpose as well. "What are we all doing out here?"

"Is that a literal question, or are you having an existential crisis?"

Liam sighed. "I don't fucking know anymore." He threw his hands up at his sides. "Feels like we're just biding our time here. That Feyor is toying with us with these stupid skirmishes. Like they're just trying to distract us from what they're really doing. Which we know... but we're not doing anything about!"

"Not yet, but we will. Once we have more information." Matthias glanced at the tree line.

"What do you mean, more information? What are we waiting on?"

The prince's jaw flexed. "Dani. We're waiting on Dani."

"Dani?" Her name reopened the invisible wound in his chest. "Why are we..." Realization flooded through him, quickly followed by anger. "You... you can't be serious? You asked her to steal intelligence from Feyor?"

"She's perfectly capable of handling herself." Matthias met his gaze. "We can't traipse off into the mountains without a clue where to block Feyor's advances. We need more. She can get it."

"You're a bastard, you know that?" Liam jutted his finger at Matthias's chest. "She was going to be in enough danger just trying to break the bond."

The prince sighed. "I didn't twist her arm into it, and if she can't, she won't. Have a little faith, Liam."

He growled, gripping his fist and willing his anger to subside. Shaking his head, he stomped around Matthias back towards the camp. "Wish faith was all the priests at this temple needed," he muttered.

"Something else you'd like to say, Talansiet?"

Liam paused, glancing over his shoulder. "No, sir. Believe I've said enough." His body tensed, irritation for losing himself in front of the prince again forcing him to remember his place.

He might be with my sister, but that's no excuse.

"Liam." Matthias's softened tone halted his feet. "Dani wanted to help, and I let her. But that's not why you're angry, is it?"

Gritting his teeth, Liam steeled the instinctual response. "Then why am I angry?"

"I can only guess, but if it were me... I'd be pretty pissed that ten seconds after I decided I wanted to be around someone, they left."

He huffed. "I don't blame her for going. I understand her reasons."

"Sure. But I meant more that I'd be pissed it took me so long to see the real person behind all the white fur." Matthias walked around Liam, stopping in front of him. "I'd be angry at myself for not giving her a chance sooner."

He narrowed his eyes. "You trying to make me feel worse, or something?"

"Of course not. I'm—"

"Well, you are."

Matthias's upper lip twitched. "Forget it. Look, I came out here to talk to you because I'm worried about Katrin."

Liam shook his head, sighing. "What about her?" He rubbed the back of his head, trying to push away the painful thoughts of Dani. Though thinking of Katrin wasn't much better, considering the way she'd been behaving since they'd arrived at the destroyed temple. "She still not sleeping?"

"I don't even know anymore, because she never leaves the damned library. I had my men set up a tent around it this morning to help protect her from the elements. I think she's sleeping there, now."

"Gods." Liam rubbed his chin. "Lucky she hasn't gotten sick. But I don't know what to do, she won't listen to me."

"Pretty sure the only one she'd listen to is..." Matthias huffed and looked at the sky. "Unavailable."

"She told you any more about what she's looking for?"

"Information on Feyor. On dragons."

"And she really thinks she's going to find it in a burned out library?" Liam pursed his lips. "She'd be better off if you sent her back to Nema's Throne. Send Merissa with her."

Matthias scoffed. "And lose two more healers? I can't do that, though I thought about it. I doubt I could convince her to go farther from Dani, anyway."

Liam flinched. "Doubt you could convince either of us." He glanced at the trees again, only to see more empty shadows. "But these skirmishes feel pointless."

"Feyor is trying to keep us on our toes. Distract us from their next move."

"Dire wolves howling all night certainly accomplishes that."

The prince cringed. "It's shaking morale, but it's all manipulation tactics. We'll get through them."

"Then what?" Liam had been holding in the question for days, but Matthias had been vague about any of his father's correspondence. *Not that it's any of my business, anyway.*

"Ziona will sign the treaty, I'm confident of that. My brother is to wed their princess. Hasn't been finalized, though, so that's not shareable information."

"And they'll send troops to push the border back?"

Matthias nodded. "We'll have the support of their armies, and our reinforcements are on their way, too."

The looming shape of the Yandarin mountains drew Liam's eye, the sun shining off the snow caps. "And what if Feyor already got troops into the mountains? What if they find what they're looking for?"

The prince quieted for a breath, clouds misting with each exhale. "Then we best hope our friendly Dtrüa returns to aid our cause, lest we learn to fight dragons."

"I hope your speech to the armies is better than that." Liam smirked.

Matthias chuckled. "Micah's speech, remember?"

"He is better at it than you."

The prince barked a laugh. "He's better at a lot of things, even if I'm the one writing them."

Liam gestured to the gate with his chin, and they started walking, the snow crunching beneath them. "What are you going to do about Katrin?"

"I don't know. Keep covering her with blankets in the night and bringing her meals. I think I need to let her go through whatever this is."

"She's just trying to find purpose in all of this madness. But she's lucky to have you."

Raising an eyebrow, Matthias studied Liam. "Excuse me? Not that long ago you said you didn't like us together."

He shrugged. "I can change my mind, can't I?" His expression sobered. "If Katrin hadn't come with us to Omensea, she would have been *here* when..."

Matthias nodded, patting Liam's shoulder. "But she did come with us, and she's fine."

For now.

Chapter 43

Been centuries since I experienced such mediocre ability in the Art.
No wonder Merissa accepted my offer.
Anything to serve her prince.
How lucky to discover the Art lies in the prince and not his guard.
She broke quicker than Nysir, with only a little blood spilled.
Disappointing.
That lovely priest served as excellent motivation with his screams.
This may prove worth ditching the Dtrüa's body.
No word from Lasseth.
I require better from my Shades.
He will be punished.
Patience.
Get closer to Matthias, first.
He'll be mine.

Chapter 44

Matthias strode behind Micah and Lieutenant Verris through the encampment, Stefan next to him with Barim, Riez and Liam behind.

Two soldiers moved the command tent flap aside, and they all entered, waiting for it to fall back into place before eyes shifted from Micah to the prince.

"Your majesty, I apologize for the unexpected meeting, but one of our scouts made an unsettling discovery this morning." Verris rounded the long rectangle table, but didn't sit.

Matthias sighed, bracing himself for whatever new bad news she had for him. "What is it?"

Verris glanced over his shoulder at the tent flap. "The body of a priest, though this one appears to have died before the attack and in rather gruesome conditions."

Matthias exchanged a glance with Liam before meeting Verris's gaze. "Wild animals?"

The lieutenant shook her head. "Too precise. And damn strange from what the scout managed to get out. He's in the medical tent gibbering still." Her hazel eyes darkened. "The sight messed him up."

"Where's the body?" Micah crossed his arms.

"Was in a cave about a half mile northwest. But now..." She sighed. "No one knows where it's gone."

Matthias straightened. "What do you mean... Where it's gone? Did one of our soldiers move it?"

"Fucking Art is at work for sure." Verris leaned on the table. "Near as we can tell, it just vanished. While under guard, no less."

"So the crazy scout is the only one who saw the body?" Liam lifted an eyebrow.

Verris frowned. "I thought the same thing, but apparently one of the guards took a peek inside and saw it, too. Otherwise I would have written it off as Gevis finally losing his mind and we wouldn't be having this conversation."

"Fantastic." Matthias paced away from the table, running a hand over his hair. "So you're telling me it's possible whoever killed the priest is here and covering their tracks."

"They killed the priest before the temple was attacked. None of us were here when that happened." Micah gestured to the room. "Could a Feyorian practitioner sneak into that cave?"

Verris nodded. "That's what we think. It's to the northwest, and likely the work of a Feyorian interrogator. But I felt it my duty to inform you."

Matthias rubbed his temple. "All right. There's nothing we can do about that now, unfortunately, but I appreciate being in the loop."

"It's the body's disappearing trick that's got me interested." Liam crossed his arms.

"Feyor must have returned to hide what they did." Barim poured himself a goblet of water.

"What for? We're already at war?"

"Could be the use of a different form of the Art." Matthias shook his head. "Could be whatever information that specific priest had, if we could identify him. Who knows."

"Without the body, there ain't much we can do." Verris straightened. "Still damn strange. When Gevis calms down, I'll try speaking with him again. But we got another Feyor troop inching their way closer. I'm willing to bet on another skirmish this afternoon."

"Prepare the archers. We can take a lot of them out as they enter the clearing. Order our scouts to return. Keep the encampment gates shut. No one leaves today." Matthias rolled his shoulders, facing the lieutenant. "Have the fourth and fifth regiment ready to fight, but keep an extra scout in the north and south towers. I want to know if they try to skirt around us."

"Yes, sir." Verris brought her fist to her chest in a salute. "I'll see to it." The lieutenant departed, leaving Matthias with his crown elites.

Micah hopped up to sit on the edge of the table. "Tortured bodies now?" He watched Stefan step back and lean on the center post of the tent. "And Art-using Feyorian scouts?"

"Something doesn't seem right." Liam rubbed his jaw, staring at the maps strewn across the table.

"No, it sure doesn't." The prince looked at Stefan. "I want you to try talking to the one who found the body before Verris tries again."

Stefan nodded once and exited the tent.

"Merissa is the only one who might have seen something before the attack. I'll talk to her." Matthias glanced at the others in the room. "We need to set up a stronger defense to hold this location. I want the rest of you to come up with some plans for fortification. Feyor will use more force eventually, and this is the last place to make a stand before they gain access to the pass into the Yandarin mountains. And we all know what's on the other side of the mountains, even if they don't find what they're looking for."

Barim growled. "Damn Yorries ain't getting to Nema's Throne."

"Think strong and silent will get anything out of Gevis?" Liam looked up at Matthias. "If someone's out there torturing priests..."

"I'll double the guard around Katrin." Matthias ground his teeth. "I'm hoping Stefan's quiet demeanor will calm the shaken soldier." He sighed, pulling up his hood. "I'll be back after talking to Merissa." He ducked out of the tent, light blinding him momentarily before his gaze landed on the very healer he sought. "Merissa. What... I needed to talk to you."

Merissa gave him a warm smile. "Oh? What is it?" Her look sobered as she studied his face. "Is something wrong?"

"Not here." Matthias motioned with his head. "Walk with me."

Merissa nodded, falling into step beside him.

The walkways of the encampment were well worn and slick with mud from recent icy rain fall. Bits of snow still clung in the shadows of the military tents, and the constant haze of campfire smoke permeated the air.

Soldiers, their armor dirty and faces haggard, hovered around the open flames to keep warm while not on duty. They'd grown used to the crown elites, and the salutes had gradually become more relaxed. One lifted his chin to Matthias after glancing at his steel insignia, but no more. It allowed him his usual anonymity around the camp while Micah continued to play his part. Regardless of how often Micah requested the soldiers to stand at ease in his presence, they rarely did.

Matthias waited until they'd passed the circle of fires. "We found a murdered priest." He kept his voice low, glancing sideways at her. "From before the temple's fall."

Merissa's hand raised to her mouth before she steeled herself. "Murdered?" She crossed her arms against her abdomen. "Why would someone murder a priest?"

The prince filled her in on the details as they maneuvered through the camp to one of the small unoccupied tents. Picking up a lantern off a crate outside the entrance, Matthias lit it and stepped inside. "You're the only one who saw anything before Feyor destroyed the temple. Do you remember anything suspicious? Any priests acting different or anyone out of place?"

Wrinkles appeared at the corners of Merissa's eyes as she narrowed them in thought. "I..." She walked away, fiddling with the hem of her corset. "I admit there were a lot of priests in the temple, and I didn't get to know all of them. I recall a small bit of concern around a Master Yelisen when he missed dinner. But they found a note the next morning that he'd been transferred urgently to Undertown."

"Do you remember who found that note?"

Merissa shook her head, wrapping her arms around herself. "I'm sorry. Do you think this murdered priest was him?"

"Not sure. But I'll look into that transfer. Thanks. I'll let you know if I have more questions."

Merissa met his gaze. "Who do you think it was?"

"Probably Feyor." Matthias nodded to the exit. "Unless there's something you need from me, I need to think."

She nodded, starting forward. "Do you think it'll happen again?"

"I wish I knew. Hopefully not."

"If it does, do you think you'll be able to stop it?" She paused beside him, her eyes reflecting bits of gold in the lantern light.

The prince hesitated, studying her. "You know the answer to that already. Why are you asking?" He looked closer at her face, noting how much older she looked than the last time he'd seen her. A few grey hairs even streaked her blond. "Are you all right?"

Her brow furrowed, but she looked to the floor. "As well as I can be, all things considered." She touched his wrist. "I'm sorry, you must be exhausted with all you've had to deal with. And Katrin..."

Matthias sighed. "Yes, I should go check on her." He patted her on the shoulder before exiting the tent, holding the flap open for the healer before they parted ways. Venturing towards the library, he shook his head.

Something is off with Merissa, but after what she went through, I suppose I can't blame her.

Katrin's black hair danced in the mountain breeze as she crouched beside a crumbled bookshelf. Ash coated her hands as she dug through the muck beneath it, pulling out one book after another and placing the dirty tomes reverentially beside her. Her eyes flickered up to him as he stepped over the wall of the library, but she immediately refocused on her work.

"I'm sorry I didn't make it to bed last night," she whispered as she picked up another book, brushing dirt from its spine.

"Are you sleeping at all?" Matthias lowered to one knee beside her.

"Here and there." She placed the book on the pile and leaned towards the hole she'd dug, carefully carving into its side where a maroon cover lay partially exposed. "This is just..." She grunted as she pulled it free. "Too important."

He tilted his head, trying to catch her gaze. "Will you please look at me?"

She huffed, brushing the leather with her already dirty skirt. Looking up, she met his eyes, but only for the briefest moment before returning to the book, and she started flipping brittle pages. "Did you need something? It's only midday..."

The prince swallowed, his shoulders slumping. Waiting a few more breaths, he stood. He clenched his jaw and turned, walking away over the rubble.

"Matthias." Katrin's tone softened, and he looked back at her. "I'm... I'm sorry. This is..." She gestured at the piles of books around her.

"Too important?"

She gave a weak smile. "I'll find something soon."

Nodding, Matthias looked at the western horizon. "We've heard reports that suggest a skirmish this afternoon, so be careful."

Katrin stood, scooping the books into her arms. "I will stay inside. You should be careful, too." Navigating over the rubble, she paused, her dark eyes glassy. "I do love you."

She needs time and space to heal. My hovering isn't helping.

The prince nodded again, his heart weighing heavier. "I'll have someone bring you something to eat."

Three months later...
Summer, 2597 RT

Katrin? Are you there?

Startling awake, Katrin winced as her neck smarted. Lifting her head, she rubbed at the muscles as she straightened in the chair, a blanket falling from her shoulders onto the piles of books encircling her seat.

Rubbing her face, she felt the crease that the edge of the book had left after serving as her pillow. The lantern beside her had been turned low, the dim orange flame blurry in her vision.

"Matthias?" She touched the hem of the blanket she knew had been him, even though she hadn't seen him.

When was the last time I even really talked to him...?

She rubbed sleep from her eyes, a yawn forcing itself out of her.

No, it's me. Can you hear me? The voice in her mind wasn't her own, and Katrin's spine straightened, excitement bubbling in her stomach.

"Dani?" She spoke aloud, eyeing the shadowed corners of the library's tent.

Katrin? The Dtrüa's voice echoed in her head again.

Sucking in a breath, Katrin closed her eyes, willing her Art into her veins. Thinking only of Dani, she imagined the familiar feel of the Dtrüa's power, seeking it out. Her head spun, but she steadied herself on the edge of the desk, fingers rustling against the pages and parchments that covered it.

I'm here.

Katrin opened her eyes, but they weren't hers.

A bright spot hovered in the center of her vision before the blurry shapes moved and Dani spoke. "Oh, I've missed your voice." The colorful scents of fresh linen and burning wood filled her vision in an array of red and ivory.

Her surroundings stilled as Dani sat, night's darkness dominating her sight.

I've missed you. Are you all right? Katrin wanted to look around, and the lack of control felt odd while so aware.

Summer frogs chirped in the distance.

An owl hooted.

"I am." Dani kept her voice low, vision flickering over the orange pulsating light of her fire. "I found allies."

Katrin breathed a sigh of relief. *Good. I've been worried. Liam's been a mess. More of an asshole than ever.*

Dani chuckled. "I miss him so much. He hasn't forgotten me?"

No, of course not. I still can't say your name without him looking like a sad puppy. Katrin felt her hand brush over the pages on the desk in front of her, even though she couldn't see them. *Have you had any luck with breaking the bond?*

"I think I'm close to a solution. Where are you all?" Movement shifted to Dani's right, and she glanced that direction, but nothing else moved.

The Yandarin Temple. Or at least where it used to be. Feyor pushed the border back. Her throat seized as she thought about what used to stand here. *They destroyed the temple. Killed everyone. But the armies have set up camp here.*

Dani's vision darkened. "I'm so sorry."

It's not your fault. They're all with Nymaera, now. Feyor's been pushing in on the camp here for months, but Matthias has forced them to retreat every time.

"I'm glad Matthias is with you. I—"

"Varadani." A hushed masculine voice hissed near Dani, and the Dtrüa turned her head towards it. "Who are you talking to?"

"No one." Dani stood, glancing at the bright spot from the moon. "What is it?"

"Come with me, we need to talk about Tallos."

The connection between Katrin and Dani strained before it faded, returning Katrin's gaze to the book in front of her. Her gut knotted.

Who was that? And does he know what Dani did to Tallos?

Leaning over the table, Katrin plucked up the lantern, twisting the knob to lift the wick and brighten the light. Hoisting her skirt up, she maneuvered over the piles of books, hurrying out of the tent.

She shivered, despite the season, wishing she'd brought the blanket. Ignoring the goosebumps on her exposed arms, she crossed the rubble onto the narrow path she'd worn in the grass leading to the military tents.

Bowing her head at a pair of guards patrolling the walkways outside the crown elites' tents, she ducked inside her brother's. "Liam, wake up."

The soldier started, lunging up from his pillow, the glimmer of a knife catching the lantern light.

She'd learned early on to keep her distance when waking him.

He groaned as his eyes focused on Katrin's face where she held the lantern up. "Fuck, Katy girl. It's the middle of the night."

Katrin shuffled across the rug. "Not really. It's maybe one hour before sunrise." She shone the lantern light in his face, and he winced. "Dani contacted me."

Liam jerked upright, dropping his dagger into the blankets of his wide cot positioned near the center of the space. "Why didn't you start with that?"

"I just..." She sighed, placing the lantern on the short table beside his armor rack.

"Well?" Liam's feet landed on the ground as he ran a hand through his messy hair. "Is she all right? Where is she?"

Katrin cringed. "I didn't ask where she was. But she's all right."

"What the hells, Kat. You didn't even ask where she was? Is she alone?"

"No, there was a man with her. He interrupted our conversation. Before that, though, she said she'd found allies."

Liam scowled. "So you're telling me we don't know where she is, she's with another man, and you have no idea what's happening."

Katrin chewed on her lower lip. "The man who interrupted us mentioned Tallos, is that helpful?"

"No!" Liam flopped backward onto his cot, rubbing his forehead. "No, sis, it's not. Can't you try reaching her again?"

Katrin sighed, plopping onto the bottom of Liam's cot and crossing her arms. "I'll try, but it probably won't work."

Liam lifted his head to look at her and didn't have to say anything before Katrin closed her eyes to attempt. She felt the buzz of her power, but it found nothing to grab onto as she sought Dani.

Rolling her shoulders, the acolyte shook her head. "Nothing. But she said she was close to figuring out a way to separate herself from the Dtrüa. And that she misses you."

Blinking at the ceiling of his tent, Liam looked distant, but nodded. "Something, at least." He shifted, wincing before he tugged his knife out from underneath him. "Other than the man and Tallos bit."

Katrin frowned. "She's thinking about you, you dolt. She misses you. She'll be back."

He huffed. "She's been gone longer than we even knew each other, and I was a complete dick to her most of that time." He shirked away from her poke to his ribs.

"Who's fault was that?"

Glowering, he swatted at her hand. "Gods, I can't stop thinking about her. I even dream of her most nights. That she's back. And it's fucking cruel."

Katrin snatched his hand, squeezing it hard. "Do you love her?"

Liam stiffened, blinking at Katrin. "What?"

"Do you *love* her?" Katrin shifted, tucking her leg up underneath her skirt as she met her brother's gaze.

"I..." Liam averted his gaze, shifting to sit up. His bare feet touched the floor, leaning against his knees and burying his face in his hands. "What does it matter if I don't see her again?"

"It matters." Katrin shifted closer and rubbed her cheek on his shoulder. "Did you tell her?"

Liam grumbled beneath his breath. "Nope."

Katrin held him tighter. "Why not?"

"Because it sounded stupid. It'd been two days."

"Technically two months."

Liam groaned. "So much wasted time."

Katrin smiled, digging her chin into his shoulder and making him flinch. She placed a quick kiss on his cheek. "At least you admit you messed up."

He gave a short laugh. "Will you keep trying to reconnect with her?"

"Of course." Katrin stifled a yawn.

Liam rolled his eyes. "You spend too much time in that library. You need rest, too."

"I'll rest when I find out the answers." Katrin pushed away from him, standing before Liam could force her to lie down. She picked up her lantern, and Liam glowered from his cot. "What?"

"Will you just... stop for a minute?" Liam stood, crossing to her. He took the lantern back from her and set it aside. "I know this dragon stuff is important, but there are other things, too."

She frowned. "Like what?"

"Like Matthias." Liam thumbed her nose. "He's been worried about you. Distracted."

"I'm perfectly safe."

"Katy girl." Liam's hands tightened around hers. "Do me a favor and actually learn from my mistakes. Don't you want to be with him anymore?"

"What?" A hole formed in her stomach. "Of course I do. Why would you say that?"

"Could have fooled me." Liam released her hands, picking the lantern back up to hand it to her. "And him."

Katrin stiffened. "I..." She took the lantern, studying its flame for a moment. "I'll fix it, all right?"

"Good." Liam sat on his cot, collapsing back and pulling his blankets up. "I'm gonna get some more sleep, then."

Katrin pursed her lips, walking backward to the tent entrance. "I'll let you know if I hear from Dani again."

Liam didn't answer as she stepped back into the early morning chill. She looked down the walkway towards the library, the books and research already beckoning her back.

I could get an early start since I'm awake already.

The stars twinkled, the black shape of the Yandarin Mountains blotting them out of the sky. The flap of canvas tents thrummed like dragons' wings.

She shook the inclination from her head, turning down the opposite way. She began walking before she could question it. Guilt clenched her stomach as she hurried to Matthias's tent, directly across from the one Micah occupied with a pair of soldiers positioned outside.

They both looked at Katrin, giving her a quick nod of recognition as she lowered the lantern before stepping past the flap of Matthias's tent.

Matthias's sleeping form dominated the right side of the cot, his typical position between them. As if he still waited for her to come take her place beside him. Her heart fluttered at his familiar scent, thick within the tent considering how long they'd been at the encampment. She craved to be beside him.

She crossed quietly to the left side of the bed, placing the lantern on a small crate beside it. Untying her boots, her fingers brushed the dirty hem of her skirt.

Best change, too.

As silently as she could, she unfastened her clothing, draping it over the end of the cot. Her exposed skin prickled with the fresh air, and she left the sheer chemise in place, crawling beneath the blankets to lie beside Matthias.

Rolling onto her side, she shifted closer to his slumbering face, studying his features in the dim light.

I almost forgot how handsome he is.

She smiled to herself, thoughts of the library and dragons fading as she followed the finely trimmed edge of his beard with her eyes, then reached to run her fingertips along his jaw.

Matthias's eyes fluttered open, meeting hers.

"Hi," Katrin whispered, touching his hair.

His brow furrowed. "Am I dreaming?" His voice, even gruffer than usual, sent another shiver through her.

She frowned. "That's a really bad sign if just seeing me is a dream, now." She scooted closer, tangling her legs with his. He was warm beneath the blankets, and she selfishly sought the heat for her chilled limbs. "But no. I'm here."

Matthias touched her cheek, his gaze thoughtful before he leaned closer and kissed her.

Everything suddenly felt as it should be, her lips moving against his. It felt almost new again, the old excitements rekindling within her. She renewed the kiss with a steady movement closer, tracing her hand down his bare chest.

A low growl rumbled from him as he rolled her onto her back, leaving her mouth to kiss down her neck.

Sparks ignited through her, breath hard to find.

Gods, what the hells was I thinking? I've missed this.

Her fingers brushed through his hair, and she tilted her head to give him better access to her skin. She whimpered, wrapping her legs around his hips.

Matthias's touch trailed up her waist and over her chest, finding the button closer at the front of her chemise. With a flick of his fingers, it popped open, and his warm palm found her breast.

Back arching against him, she dipped her chin to find his mouth again. She kissed him hard, her moans vibrating across their tongues. Desperately, her hands ran along his sides, pushing his silk sleep pants down. She did away with them with a careful kick of her feet, eager to feel the warmth of him against her. Her hand found him, encouraging a shift of his hips and his moan into her mouth. It set her body into spirals.

Working in tandem, they removed the last bit of fabric from her body, and her legs wrapped around his again.

The prince twisted her nipple, a gasp escaping her as his hardness teased her sex.

She bit his lower lip, nails trailing over his shoulder as she broke away slowly from the kiss to meet his eyes. Her lips parted in another light whimper, a hand gripping the pillow above her head. "Please." She breathed. "Stop teasing me."

A smile twitched his lips, and he cupped her breast, thumb still stroking the tip. His hips drew away, hands finding hers as he sat back on his heels. "Roll over."

Her heart pounded at his words, toes curling in excitement as she obeyed.

The warmth of his chest lowered on her back, and his hand reached around her waist to touch the sensitive bundle of nerves between her thighs. He kissed her neck, pulling her hair to the side.

Her body howled in pleasure as she pushed her hips back against his, unable to contain the moan echoing from her mouth. Everything within her tightened in anticipation.

Supporting himself with his elbow, he gripped a handful of her hair by the roots, sending a thrilling shock through her, while his other still caressed circles between her legs. His hips rocked, easing his hardness into her.

Katrin gasped, clutching the pillow beneath her head as she turned and muffled the cry.

Fully inside her, he paused, breathing hard near her neck. With a gentle motion, he withdrew before pushing deeper than before and applying more pressure with his fingers.

Another wave of pleasure, demanding and hungry, tore through her. The desire that came surprised even her. "Harder." She nuzzled her cheek against the pillow, glancing back at him.

Matthias hummed near her ear. "Yes, Priestess." Drawing from her again, he slammed into her, rattling the crate next to their cot.

The pillow did little to muffle the cry when she failed to bury her face in time. Her body trembled as he kept stroking her, thrusting deep.

The tension in her steadily rose, hovering at the peak for an excruciatingly wonderful moment before euphoria cascaded through, a high-pitched scream hidden within the pillow.

The prince's touch slowed only for a breath before it picked up speed again, demanding more from her. He didn't let her ecstasy subside, riding it straight into another peak as he growled into her skin.

His body, slick against hers, pressed against her as his rhythm finally slowed, his grip in her hair loosening. Reluctantly withdrawing from her, he lowered himself next to her, meeting her gaze.

Katrin breathed heavily, trying to regain coherent thought as she lay there, unable to move for a moment. Blinking, she watched him and smiled. "Still think I'm a dream?" she whispered.

Matthias hummed, tucking her hair behind her ear. "If you are, then the quality of my dreams is vastly improving."

Her smile broadened as she turned onto her side and scooted closer to him. Pressing her body against his, she placed a gentle kiss on his lips before pulling away to stroke his bearded jaw. "I'm sorry."

The prince shook his head. "I'm glad you're back." He nuzzled into her neck, kissing her skin as his touch found her breast again. "Sunrise is still some time off, and I'm not finished with you."

She hummed. "Making up for lost time, Prince?"

"Every moment I can."

Chapter 46

Several days later...

The sun peeked over the horizon, brightening Dani's vision and warming her face.

Speaking with Katrin had made her hope blossom.

They're so close.

Dani stepped over the grass, soft beneath her leather soles, and followed Lasseth to the campfire.

Two other Dtrüa waited, talking under their breath too quietly for Dani to hear. As she and Lasseth approached, they quieted.

"Varadani. Thank you for meeting with us." Resslin. A Dtrüa Dani had only met twice before, and both times in passing. But she spoke with a similar accent, suggesting she'd grown up around the same compound Dani had. Yet, she was several years older.

Four of us in one spot, if you still count Lasseth. Doesn't happen often.

"Of course." Dani clicked her tongue and took a seat on a log stool. "But I've already told Lasseth everything about my time in Isalica."

"We know. They kept you in cuffs the entire time, keeping their conversations private. Though Tallos's earlier correspondence suggested that you'd purposely gone to infiltrate. Pity you failed and couldn't gain more intelligence." Resslin's voice was terse and held no patience.

"I gained the best information from what they *didn't* ask me. No questions of dragons or the Dtrüa. Isalica is ignorant of our intentions." Dani lifted her chin.

"Foolish of them, then." Jorce sounded smug. Less concerned. His typical overconfident self, which Dani had tried to beat out of him in their early training sessions. Even his repeated losses couldn't damper his arrogance.

"What of Nysir? Did you meet with him during your time there? We believe he acted on intelligence Tallos sent." The woman's auburn scent reminded Dani of crushed cherry blossoms.

Dani frowned. "I never saw him."

Lasseth cleared his throat. "Nysir? So there has been no further word from him?"

"No." The woman grunted.

"Resslin is master of the Dtrüa in his place until we discover his fate. But he also ventured into Isalica. Perhaps the iceheads are smarter than we give them credit for." The man's leathers creaked as he leaned back.

Nysir is missing?

A bellowing screech in the distance to Dani's left made her flinch. Similar to the howls she'd heard near the training grounds in Melnek. She faced the sound. Sniffing, she listened as it came again. "Is that a drake? What about the wyverns?"

A smile colored Resslin's voice. "It is. The wyverns are better behaved than the drakes, and we hardly hear them, but they're there."

Dread built in Dani's stomach, but she hid it from her face by smiling instead. "Let's see those Isalicans hold the border now."

Jorce laughed. "They'll fall faster than icicles in spring."

I need to warn them.

Dani glanced at Lasseth, his shape silhouetted by the rising sun. "Will we advance with them?"

"No. They will attack tonight. We will follow tomorrow. Let them wreak most of the carnage. Their handlers can risk their skins. The Dtrüa are too valuable in the second assault." Jorce leaned forward, poking at the campfire.

A log sizzled as it fell into the flames, collapsing the embers below.

The drake screeched again, setting Dani's nerves alight. "Is there any other information I can provide you?"

"No, though you should know that we've determined that your betrothed, Tallos, is dead." Resslin's tone held no sympathy. "We will choose a new mate for you after the coming battle."

Dani sucked in a breath, clenching her jaw. "Tallos is dead?" She closed her eyes, the memory of his attack on Liam aiding in her act. "How?"

"We haven't recovered his body, but his bond disappeared months ago and hasn't resurfaced. It is the only explanation."

"We hope you understand the necessity of not informing you of the bond until your latest ascension among us." Jorce threw the stick he poked with into the fire.

"I explained the policy." Lasseth put a hand on her shoulder.

"I'd like to be alone, if that's all right." Dani stood, her legs unsteady.

No one stopped her as she ventured away, clicking her tongue. *At least they don't know I killed him.*

Lasseth caught up to her a few moments later, keeping his voice low. "Convincing..." He chuckled. "Almost had me believing you cared for Tallos, if I didn't already know the truth."

Dani huffed. "I've gotten better at lying since returning here."

"Understandably." Lasseth grew quiet as they walked deeper into the woods, his long cloak catching occasionally on the summer undergrowth. "This doesn't change any of our plans."

"You're joking?" Dani halted and faced Lasseth. "It changes everything."

"Don't be impatient. Once Ailiena breaks the bond, everyone will know."

"I realize that. But they're about to attack the border. With drakes and wyverns!"

Lasseth sighed. "You're the only Dtrüa Ailiena has been able to use to learn more about the bond. She can't learn how to reverse the process if you leave."

"She'll find another way." Dani stomped off, heading to where the mysterious woman had made her home in a cave an hour away. "This was the deal. I help her, she helps me. The time has come for me to leave and don't think I've forgotten your end of the deal."

Lasseth's knuckles cracked, a moment of hesitation lasting longer than it should have. "I'll catch up. I need to retrieve it."

The trek to the Rahn'ka's new cave took her southeast, and she ran through the soft grass in her cat form. With summer having melted the snow, her white coat no longer blended in, leaving her a bright spot amid the forest. Discomfort stirred in her stomach at being so visible, even if not to herself.

As she arrived at the cave, the familiar sensation of crossing through the woman's barrier passed over her fur.

Dani shifted, retaking her human form as Ailiena emerged from her makeshift home.

"It's time." The Dtrüa stepped forward. "Break the bond, let them think I'm dead."

Ailiena's energy brushed over Dani in an oddly comforting wave. "Where's Lasseth? I don't know if we're ready to—"

"He will be here soon. Please. I'm ready. My friends are in danger. This must happen now."

Ailiena muttered under her breath in a language Dani didn't understand. "I don't think I can rush this process, Dani."

The Rahn'ka's senses had seemed to return to her the further they grew from Melnek. Ailiena had tried to explain the voices she heard thanks to her unique access to the Art, and Dani could see the similarities to how she communicated with animals. Yet, the Rahn'ka's connection encompassed souls beyond those of animals.

"Look, I'm leaving whether or not you break my bond. You cannot make me stay, and we had a deal." Dani ground her teeth.

"I don't want to make you stay. Just..." Ailiena sighed, stepping forward with inhuman silence. "Come on. I'll need the quiet of the cave. But Dani, you should know... there could be side effects. You will feel different."

Dani followed the woman inside, her heart pounding in her ears. *This is it.*

An eagle screeched outside the cave, and Lasseth's cloak whispered against the dirt floor before his boot steps. "Here."

Dani held out her hand, and Lasseth placed the strap of a satchel into her palm.

"You're just going to have to trust me that it's all there."

She lowered her hand, and the satchel rested on the ground. "How am I supposed to shift with this?"

"I'll secure it around you after you've taken your cat form."

Dani paused, taking a deep breath. "Thank you."

"By the time you get there, the attack could only be hours away, you know that, right?"

"Hush." Ailiena's annoyed tone. "I'm trying to focus."

Worry wracked through Dani, speeding her breath. "I must try."

 Chapter 47

"Gods, lighten up Talansiet. I yield." Barim grunted from behind his shield, which sported new dents with each of Liam's swings.

Heaving a breath, Liam swiped sweat from his brow, muscles aching. "You're going easy on me again."

"Am not," Barim whined. "You're going harder!"

Liam snorted, tossing his sword into the grass as he glanced at the setting sun. Feyor lay beyond the pine trees. And Dani.

Fuck.

Running a hand through his damp hair, Liam lifted the bottom of his shirt to wipe the sweat before pulling it completely off. Deep pink scars ran in four jagged lines across his chest, and the memory of Dani's blood on his fingers urged him to clean the sweat off faster.

"Anyone ever tell you you've got an anger problem?" Riez crossed his thick arms, umber skin darker in the approaching twilight.

Liam snorted. "No shit? I had no idea." He threw his soaked shirt at the other crown elite, who cringed as he batted it away.

"Fuck, Barim's right. Lighten up."

"How about you fight me next?" Liam stooped, picking up his sword again and pointing it at Riez.

The elite scowled. "Your cockiness will land you on your ass, Talansiet."

"Prove it."

"Boys, boys." Micah strode over to the training ring, dressed in his regal attire. "The enemies are over there, remember?" He jutted a thumb towards the border. "Let's save it for them."

Growling, Liam thrust his sword's tip into the ground, and the hilt wobbled back and forth. "Whatever you say, *Prince.*"

"Sounds like he wants a challenge." Matthias's voice carried over the breeze from Liam's right. The real prince tilted his head, hopping over the low fence separating the sparring ring from the camp. Untying his cloak, he draped it over the wood. "Perhaps you'd like a taste of fighting *royalty.*" The prince drew his sword, spinning it in his grip.

A wry smile tugged at the corner of Liam's mouth. "I'll give you a head start." He stepped away from his sword, opening his hands in invitation. "Better stop me before I get that blade back in my hand."

"Save your charity, Talansiet." Matthias drew a circle with the tip of his blade. "Go on. I don't need anyone saying you gave me an advantage, now, do I?"

Liam chuckled as he grasped his sword hilt. Instead of re-centering himself, he lunged from there, swinging low.

The prince had already backed up, a bored look on his face. "You can do better than that."

Drawing back, Liam growled as he shifted his weight and withdrew, only to be parried by Matthias. They exchanged blows, each following the steady rhythm of battle.

Every advance Liam made, Matthias either blocked or sidestepped perfectly to avoid.

Feigning left, Liam swapped sword hands, but Matthias's blade flicked down to once again stop him.

"Ooh, almost got me there." The prince smirked, a shimmer of sweat on his brow.

Chuckles murmured from the other elites, a couple of them whispering to each other.

Liam roared in frustration as he swung high, and again, Matthias ducked. Panting, the soldier stepped back. "You're fucking cheating." He narrowed his eyes, pointing at his opponent. He bit his cheek to hold in the smile as he recalled perfectly what Matthias claimed his Art could do.

The prince laughed, spinning his sword again. "Aren't you using every skill you have to your advantage right now?"

"Yeah, but mine isn't considered *cheating*." Liam couldn't hold in the smile as he huffed for breath, bending over to lean on his knees.

"I don't know if I'd call it cheating, really, just effective. And I only did it once because you landed on your face and I doubted the mud tasted good." Matthias caught his breath, grinning.

"Fuck you." Liam stood, stretching his back. "I'd outlast you if the big brute hadn't already worn me out." He jutted his chin towards Barim.

"Perhaps." Matthias sheathed his sword. "Perhaps not. Maybe another time, we'll find out."

"Sir!" A soldier riding a horse halted next to Micah, looking at the stand-in prince. She saluted, bowing her head. "We've captured a Feyorian scout trying to sneak into our camp."

"Not exactly news, Private. We catch scouts all the time." Micah leaned against the fence.

"This one claims she knows you. The men are roughing her up a bit to make her talk, but she's sticking to her story."

Liam's heart thundered.

She?

He swallowed, controlling whatever hope sprang up within him.

Micah exchanged a look with Matthias before studying the private. "What color is her hair?"

The private huffed. "You'd hardly believe it. She doesn't look a day over twenty, but her hair is as white as snow."

A bolt of lightning ruptured through Liam, making every muscle numb. "Where?" he demanded, the tone of his voice surprising him.

Micah took the private's horse by the bridle. "Gonna need your mount, Private."

The soldier dismounted, looking at Liam. "They're detaining her near the south gate."

The horse sidestepped from Liam as he hurried forward, but Micah held it still as he pulled himself into the saddle. Nodding at

Micah, he squeezed his calves to spur the creature south.

Dani.

Behind him, Matthias's voice echoed. "Go tell Katrin. I'll catch up to Liam."

After that, all he heard were the horse's hooves as he rushed through the camp, forcing soldiers to dodge out of the way.

The south gate could hardly be called that, not even wide enough to allow a horse out of the camp. Several logs, tied together, were propped up over the hole, secured in place with more rope.

Soldiers gathered near the tents to the left, shouting. They formed a haphazard circle, attention all drawn to the center.

"Yorrie filth!" One stepped forward, swinging a kick at his target low to the ground.

The tent blocked his view until Liam grew close enough to peer over the soldiers' heads and spot a flash of white leather marred by splotches of mud. It took everything in him not to barrel the horse straight into the soldiers.

"Hold!" The command rang out over the excited shouts egging each other on against the woman who refused to fight them.

The air stilled with the word, silence blanketing the gathered crowd. They turned together to look at the hardly impressive crown elite in nothing but a plain dirty undershirt and breeches, hair slicked back with sweat.

The horse backed up as he pulled on its reins, dropping from the saddle as a ragged cough echoed from within the bunch.

"Sir, we—" Whatever the private was about to say ended when Liam shoved him out of the way, pressing through the knit of soldiers. When he reached the center, his knees weakened, the exhaustion from his training returning in a great wave.

On her hands and knees at the center, Dani panted, her muddy hair clinging to her face. Her cloudy eyes lifted in his direction. Blood dripped from her cheek, her eyebrows upturned in the center. "Liam?" Her voice barely carried over the air, gaze flickering around his form.

He managed the three steps to her before he collapsed, attempting to swallow a betraying sob, but failing. "I'm here." He took her hands, ignoring the muck before he placed them on his cheeks. "It's me."

Dani whimpered and pulled herself into him, letting go of his face and wrapping her arms around him.

He held her as tightly as his strength would allow and buried his face against her neck.

Another set of hooves came to a stop behind him, but he didn't turn to look.

"Get back to your positions!" Matthias barked the order loud enough that Dani flinched.

The soldiers hurried to disperse, one of them speaking in low tones to the prince before departing.

Liam willed himself to let go of her, so he might look at her face, but his body wouldn't cooperate. He shook as he took in a steadying inhale, kissing the top of her dirty hair. "You did it?"

Dani nodded against his neck. "The bond is broken."

Relief washed over Liam as he rocked her in his hug. He wanted to tell her how afraid he'd been. How horrible the last three months had been. But Matthias's nearby steps interrupted his thoughts.

"I'm sorry." The prince hesitated. "I know this isn't the ideal moment, but Dani... I need to know where these documents are from."

Leaning back, Dani touched Liam's face again, the blood on her cheek smeared. Her gaze flickered towards Matthias.

The prince stood with a satchel in his hands, the leather flap pulled back enough to show the parchment inside.

Dani winced as she straightened, touching her ribs where a soldier must have kicked her. "I know little about those papers. A friend gathered them for me. But it matters not, because they're attacking tonight."

"Another skirmish? We'll push them off again." Liam brushed a hand through her hair.

"No. Not a skirmish." Dani caught Liam's hand and squeezed. "The wyverns and drakes have arrived. It's a full-scale attack, and it's coming tonight. In hours, at most."

Liam's heart seized, and he looked at Matthias. "When are our reinforcements from Lyon supposed to arrive?"

"Tomorrow." Matthias's voice hung in disbelief. "Maybe they'll be ahead of schedule... I'll take care of this." He spun, pulling the satchel over his shoulder as he returned to his horse. Mounting, he galloped back the way they'd come.

Dani breathed an airy sob. "I'm sorry. I tried to get here as fast as I could to warn you, but the process took—"

"Shhh." Liam brushed his hand up into her hair and kissed her forehead. "You have nothing to apologize for. You made it in time. We'll do what we can with the time you've given us." Touching her chin, he lifted her mouth to his. The kiss felt odd at first, foreign, but then settled quickly as they moved into rhythm. He broke away, pressing his forehead to hers. "Let's go get you cleaned up?"

She nodded, clutching the back of his neck. "You'll stay with me?"

"I won't be leaving your side." He checked the abrasion on her cheek, careful not to smear mud into it. Looking down at the pair of them, he couldn't help but chuckle. "We both need to clean up."

Rising to his feet, Liam ignored the curious glances of the lingering soldiers. Considering the state of the camp and the bodies they buried after each skirmish, he didn't blame them for being suspicious. He was only glad that Dani couldn't see them.

Lifting Dani to her feet, Liam cast a glare at any onlookers, who quickly busied themselves. He had to repeat the process several times during their walk through the camp.

"Everyone's staring at me," Dani whispered, wrapping her arm around his.

"They don't matter." He pulled her closer, encircling her waist.

As they turned up the slight hill towards the crown elites' tents, Katrin came into view. She slid in the muddy walkway as she hurried forward. "Oh, thank the gods."

Dani's face lightened in a smile. "Kat."

Liam dodged his sister as she embraced Dani, nearly falling down the hill.

The Dtrüa braced a foot behind her, arms around Liam's sister. "Is it a little ironic that your name shortens to my animal form?" She kept her voice low, pulling back to kiss Katrin's cheek.

Katrin glowed with joy. "More proof we were meant to be sisters." Her eyes grew glassy as she embraced Dani again. "I'm so thankful you're safe. How did you break the bond?"

"Someone broke it for me. It's a long story, but all that matters is Feyor can't find me."

Katrin cast a worried look at Liam, then back to Dani. "Matthias was just here. He said Feyor is attacking tonight?"

"Which is exactly why we don't have much time to clean up, and you should pack your bags and head for the pass before the battle starts."

Katrin glowered. "Like hells. At least Matthias is smart enough not to even suggest it. I'm needed here."

Liam shook his head.

She's lucky I don't have the energy to argue right now.

Dani wavered. "If it's manageable, I think I might sleep until the battle starts."

"That sounds like a wonderful idea." Liam encouraged them all to move back up the hill, and Katrin fell into step beside Dani, their hands entwined.

They fell silent as they walked towards Liam's tent, Dani's grip heavy on his arm.

How far did she run?

Katrin paused at the entrance. "I'll go get some fresh water." She eyed Liam. "You should—"

"I know, I know. I'm not completely incompetent." Liam brushed aside the flap, holding it for Dani.

She entered, clicking her tongue.

Everything ached, pushed beyond its limit after his training session and the rapid run towards Dani. But looking at her as she crossed the canvas covered floor, it was all worth it.

"My cot's straight ahead." He stepped to the side where his armor trunk sat still open, several pieces of clothing strewn on it and the chair beside. Embarrassment flushed through his cheeks as he scrambled to tidy it, despite knowing she couldn't clearly see.

Dani faced him, her brow knitting. "What are you doing?"

"Don't worry about it." He smiled, watching her as he automatically folded and replaced things where they belonged.

I've gotten too lazy with this new position.

Her head tilted, and she sniffed a few times, wandering to his cot and trailing her fingertips over his pillow.

It made his heart tighten to see her again, but paranoia made his stomach flutter. "It... doesn't stink in here, does it? Katrin always complains about..." He frowned down at his sweat-stained shirt, now splotched with mud as well. He lifted the bottom hem of it and sniffed. Grimacing, he scoffed and tore the shirt off, tossing it into the corner of the tent. "Never mind, don't answer that."

Dani chuckled. "It smells like you in here." She strode towards him, clicking her tongue again. Reaching out a hand, her touch found his bare chest and recoiled. "Sorry. I didn't realize you were..."

"Just the shirt. It... was kind of filthy." He caught her hand, encouraging it back to his chest. "And you don't need to apologize for touching me. Ever."

Her fingers flexed against his skin. "I missed your scent. I would've given anything for it while we were apart."

Everything lightened again, and he smiled. "Little odd, but strangely romantic of you." He stepped closer to her, untying the white pelt from her shoulders. He paused. "May I?"

Dani nodded, lifting her chin and sliding her hand up. Her fingers found the feline tooth he still wore, and she rolled her lips together in a smile before touching his face. "I should have told you something before I left."

Liam's brow knitted, his hand cupping hers. Her admission made him think of one of his own, and he kissed her palm. "I have things I should have said, too."

The months without her only confirmed it all.

The white fur over her shoulders slid off, and he tossed it onto his cot.

Dani's thumb grazed his mouth. "I want to—"

"I'm coming in!" Katrin shouted from outside the tent before the canvas flap opened. She walked in holding a water pail in one hand, the other covering her eyes in dramatic fashion.

"Oh, come on, Kat." Liam groaned. "We're not naked."

Dani let go of Liam, a sheepish smile spreading over her face. "Can confirm. Not naked."

"Unfortunately," Liam grumbled next to her ear before walking to his sister.

She smiled as she lowered her hand, holding out the pail to him. Her eyes trailed over his bare chest. "Not for lack of trying, apparently."

Dani giggled. "Would you believe it was because he thought he smelled bad?"

"He usually does, so, yes, I would."

Liam snatched the pail from her. "Thanks. I think I got it from here."

Katrin looked around him at Dani, chewing her bottom lip. "I should go help the medical tent prepare, anyway." She stepped around her brother, taking Dani's hands. "I just got you back, though, so you better be safe."

"You needn't worry." Dani tilted her head. "This time, I'm fighting on the right side of the snow. And my arrow dodging skills are better."

"I won't let her out of my sight, either." Liam carried the water to his cot, straightening the blankets.

"Go." Dani touched Katrin's face. "Be safe."

His sister nodded, bits of her hair falling free from the bun at the back of her head. "I hope you get some rest." She hugged Dani, kissing her cheek as she pulled away. Katrin gave a final look to her brother as she departed, though he chose not to guess at its meaning.

Retrieving the small stack of fresh linen he'd intended for cleaning himself after his training, Liam dropped one into the water, dunking it under the warm surface. He glanced at Dani, his chest tightening. "Come here." He held out his hand to her until she walked close enough for him to take hers and lead her to the foot of the cot. "Let's get you cleaned up."

Sitting, Dani ran a hand through her slightly longer hair. "How bad is it?" She touched her face, finding the cut on her cheekbone. Swallowing, she lowered her gaze, eyes lost in thought.

Liam knelt on the ground before her, hand resting on her knee. He wrung the cloth with one hand and lifted it to her cheek. "Not bad." He dabbed the shallow wound, already clotted, then cleaned around it. "I suspect you'll recover." He smiled as he brushed the damp cloth over the rest of her jaw, cleaning away the mud.

A smile spread over Dani's face. "I meant the mud, not the scratch."

Liam laughed, continuing up to her forehead. "Well, I don't like you with brown hair." He rubbed the cloth down a strand of her hair, frowning. "Might have to dunk your whole head after I finish everywhere else."

Dani made a face. "No wonder my hair feels so crunchy and smells like muck." She touched the locks again, causing dried flecks to fall to her shoulders. "Don't you have a bath?" Her lips twitched. "A really hot one, with bubbles?"

Liam laughed. "Sorry. This isn't that fancy inn in Omensea." He moved the cloth to her hands, cleaning each finger one at a time.

Her smile faded with an awkward laugh, and she huffed. "Gods, that seems like ages ago, now."

"Too long ago." He tangled his fingers with hers once they were clean, bringing her knuckles to his lips. "I missed you. Every day. Even missed our stupid little arguments we were putting on for show."

Dani rolled her lips together. "I don't want to do that anymore."

"Which part?" Liam brushed the cloth over his own cheeks before dipping it back into the water.

"The show. I don't want to pretend, but..." She sighed, blinking. "You're you, and I'm the enemy. I'd understand if you don't want to be with... you know."

Liam's heart pounded. "Dani." He dropped the cloth into the pail, freeing his hands to reach and hold both sides of her face. "None of that matters. I don't care if others look or question. If they stare." He lifted himself closer to her, between her legs on his knees. "You're not my enemy. You're so much more than that to me." He pressed his damp forehead to hers, feeling her breath on his lips. "I don't want to pretend anymore, either."

Her chin lifted, and her mouth met his. She inhaled through her nose, her knees pressing against his hips. Pulling away, she ran her hands through his hair. "I feared you'd change your mind again."

Holding her hand to his cheek, he shook his head. "I was an idiot before." He brushed some of the caked mud from her hair.

"Well, yeah, but..." Dani smirked, and he snorted. She delicately kissed his lower lip, the tip of her tongue touching its edge. "I was, too."

The sudden desire rising through him made it difficult to comprehend. "You?" He sought her lips again before catching himself only a hair's breadth away. "I don't remember you being an ass."

"An idiot, not an ass." Dani ran the tip of her nose up the bridge of his. "I had no idea what love was. What friendship was. I was so wrong."

A pleasant shudder passed through him, her words evoking the sensation he'd evaluated the past several months. It left him feeling powerful, yet weak at the same time.

His lips brushed over her skin, tongue playing along the drips of water still lingering on her jaw. Trailing to her neck, he nuzzled into her hair, working his way towards her ear. Grazing her lobe between his teeth, he hummed, making her spine straighten.

"I've never known love like this, either," he whispered, slipping his hand around her waist to pull her closer to him. "I love you, Dani."

The Dtrüa drew her face back, cloudy eyes dancing, unseeing, over his face. "How do you know? Even now, after all this time, when we were only together for... a blink. How do you know?"

"I know better now than I did before." Liam brushed his thumb over her lips. "It's... the feeling you leave in my chest, both when you're here and when you're not. That's what makes me sure of it."

Dani huffed a laugh. "I should have told you. I thought I was insane for feeling that way after only days. For loving you."

He smiled for what felt like the first time in months. "Glad I'm not the only one." He returned to her neck, trailing kisses towards the edge of her collar.

"I'm supposed to rest," Dani whispered, leaning into him.

He hummed again against her. "Want me to stop, then?" He ran his hands up the outside of her legs, fingers teasing beneath her tunic.

"No." Dani groaned. "But yes."

Liam chuckled. Rising, he lifted her chin to catch her mouth for a brief, deep kiss.

"Do you have military things to see to, or can you lay with me?" She chewed her lower lip, scooting further onto his cot.

"I'm pretty sure they all know where to find me if they need me." Liam followed her, crawling up over her, the ties of her leathers tickling his bare skin. "I already said I won't be letting you out of my sight." He supported himself with an elbow beside her head as he kissed her deeply again, unable to part without one more.

As he laid next to her, she pressed the length of her body against him. Dani breathed a deep inhale, draping an arm over him. Parting her lips from his, she nuzzled her face into his collar, kissing his skin. "I never wish to be away from you again."

He didn't care about the mud still caked in parts of her hair, holding her tight against him. "That's what I'm fighting for tonight."

"What *we're* fighting for."

Liam frowned, considering what she said. He winced. "Are you sure? These used to be your comrades. I wouldn't blame you if you didn't want to fight. It's different for you."

Dani paused, fingertips tracing patterns over his back. "I'm sure. They may have been my comrades, but I never had a choice. They only respected me out of fear. What they're doing is wrong. And I can give Isalica the advantage it will need."

Liam kissed her forehead. "Forgive me for worrying?"

Her cheeks moved in a smile. "I'll never ask you not to." She nuzzled closer, burying her face. "Besides, who else will keep you safe?"

He chuckled, shaking them both briefly. "Myself?" He kicked the blanket at the end of the bed up before tangling his legs with hers and pulling it over them. "Get some rest, beautiful."

Chapter 48

Dani shut her eyes, burying herself in Liam's scent. She'd dreamt of the moment he could hold her again for months, and now she struggled to miss any of it. "I can't sleep," she murmured, listening to the steady beat of his heart.

His chest rumbled, hands tightening around her. "Then we can just lie here. I'm perfectly comfortable." His thumb brushed over her shoulder, a light pressure that carried so much power.

A hollowness lingered in her chest, not filled by her return to Liam as she'd hoped.

Liam touched her shoulders. "What's wrong?"

"I don't know." Dani squeezed her eyes shut. "It's nothing."

He closed his hand over hers, staying quiet as if examining her. "Your heart is pounding. Did those idiots at the gate hurt you?"

"Just bruises, I think." She exhaled a slow breath.

Liam pulled her close to him again, nestling her head against his chest, chin resting near the top of her head. "We should have Katrin or Merissa check you out."

The Dtrüa shook her head. "No. I will heal." Memories flashed through her mind of the original changes she'd endured while becoming one of her people.

They aren't my people anymore.

The vacancy left behind by the bond felt like a void, desiring nothing but to be filled.

She held him tighter, nails digging into his skin as she breathed faster. "That isn't what's bothering me, though."

Twisting a strand of her hair around his finger, Liam kissed her head again. "Do you want to talk about what's bothering you?"

"I cannot explain it." Dani turned her face into his skin, trying to focus on his scent. "She said there would be side effects. Like this. Like this... hollow feeling in my chest." Whimpering, she fought the feeling of isolation washing over her. "I'm alone, now."

Liam squeezed her, holding her as if they could merge together. "You're not alone," he whispered. "You'll never be alone. You have me, and Kat, and Matthias. And I'm pretty sure Stefan likes you, he just doesn't talk."

Dani focused on his voice, breath slowing at his last statement. "Stefan talks. He told me this story from when he was a child, when his mother saved a young jaguar caught in a hunter's trap."

"Lies." Liam chuckled. "I've maybe heard him say three words."

She turned her face, pressing it to his chest. "Still haven't learned to listen, hmm?"

His deep breath swelled against her cheek. "Apparently, I'm no good at it." He shifted, pulling the blanket further over them.

"I'm sorry," Dani whispered, blinking the heat from her eyes as she touched his arm.

He shook his head. "I told you, you have nothing to be sorry for."

Her hand slid over his skin, finding the subtle ridges of the scars Tallos left on Liam's chest. "I have plenty to be sorry for."

"Not to me." He closed his hand over hers, bringing it to his lips. "I'll help fill this hollow in any way I can," he whispered. "You'll never be alone. I promise. And I'll be right here when you wake up."

Dani closed her eyes, turning her face into his skin again and breathing the teal smell she missed so much. Exhaustion eked through her muscles, and she nodded, relaxing into him.

The scents of the pine forest swirled around Dani, mere feet from where the scents shifted to the pale greens of a meadow, the earthy browns of the dirt already disturbed by the Feyorian army's march past. She tilted her head as Liam's teal scent drifted into her peripheral vision, his hands moving slowly over the mechanism of his crossbow.

Dani looked ahead into the open field, maw agape as she breathed. The air tasted like sweat and fear, and her tail lashed behind her.

Shouts echoed from the soldiers on the front line, far to the east.

Everyone around Dani and Liam kept silent, hiding among the pines. They clung to their weapons, bracing for the attack rolling past them like thunder through the clouds.

Feyor won't even see us.

"You still there?" Liam's voice was a near silent whisper.

Dani had covered her white fur in soot, darkening her shape to blend into the night. Enough so that even three feet from him, Liam struggled to see her. She snapped her jaws, clicking her teeth once for yes.

At least with the forest this dark, Feyor can't see, either.

"Are the drakes advancing yet?" Liam's scabbards tapped together on his back, where he'd secured them in a cross.

She clicked her teeth once.

The draconi smell wafted east towards the waiting armies, a muddy orange.

"Back of the line? Haven't heard them, yet."

She clicked her teeth twice.

They've gotten better at keeping them quiet.

"Shit." Liam turned, the foliage around him rustling.

More movement echoed after whatever sign he gave to the soldiers behind them.

"Stay smart, whiskers." Stefan's teasing tone whispered near her ear. His silent steps carried him away as she chuffed a response.

The string on Liam's crossbow clicked into place before his fingers brushed over her side. He crept forward, his steps uneven as he kept low within the brush. Once they left the darkness of the forest, the slivered moon would hopefully give him enough light to see by.

She looked at him, his scent creating the illusion of his face. Lowering her maw, she skulked ahead, paws silent on the soft summer grass. Moving out of range of Liam, she flicked her tail playfully at his face, hearing him sputter as he batted it out of the way.

The roar of battle grew louder, the trample of boots and clash of steel ringing through her ears. A wyvern shrieked in the sky above, shattering the silence the draconi had maintained. The lower growls of the drakes echoed through the valley.

Dani's heart leapt into her throat as the sounds overwhelmed her.

I'm not running away this time.

Breaking through the last bit of grass before the rest lay trampled by Feyor's advancing army, a familiar voice rose. Riez bellowed, his call announcing to the rest of the hidden Isalican troops to charge.

She let out a yeowl and lunged, claws tearing the ground as she barreled towards the enemy.

Feyor. The enemy.

Dani raced between the trees, vaguely aware of Liam's attempt to keep up.

A straggling Feyorian, running to join the fight, paused and faced her. He lifted a crossbow, its mechanism clicking as he took aim.

Liam's crossbow snapped to her left, the air whizzing before the Feyorian thumped to the ground, blood welling from the bolt in his neck.

Dani leapt over him, picking up the scent of a nearby drake. Glancing back for Liam, she raced towards the draconi.

Soldiers flanked its backside, guarding the massive beast.

She snarled and tackled one, claws finding the soft spots between his armor. He punched her head, his screams choking as her fangs sank into his neck. His comrade charged at her, and she ducked, but a crossbow bolt knocked him off his feet.

Blood tainted her vision, rising from the bodies in a crimson tide of metallic scent. It coated her tongue, dripping from her chin.

Liam's never going to look at me the same after this.

The drake bellowed and spun, tail lashing to the side and forcing

Dani to crouch. The scent blurred, taking a moment to reform as the creature stilled. Although she'd participated in the creatures' training for months, the concept of fighting one still made dread bloom in her gut.

Unless I needn't fight them.

The drake's giant maw could bite a human in half, and their backs could easily accommodate up to three riders. Their pearlescent scales were hard as stone, and would deflect most attacks unless perfectly aimed to pry beneath. She'd tried to explain it to the troops at Matthias's request, but her blind description would require their creativity in the battlefield.

The rider's scent materialized on the drake's back, the man barking commands.

The beast howled as something thunked into its hide, Liam's crossbow twanging. It jerked to the side, its rider shouting in surprise as the creature lumbered forward, charging at its last attacker.

Dani didn't have time to attempt communication, her stomach dropping out. Spurring forward, she sprinted after the draconi.

It barreled past Liam as he hit the dirt with a grunt. Another thud sounded, and the scent of the rider toppled from the drake's back when it reared on its hind legs in a rapid turn. Its tail collided with an Isalican soldier, its claws digging into the ground and sending up the smell of freshly tilled soil.

"Fuck." Liam rolled onto his back, the string of his crossbow snapping into place as the drake roared and thundered towards him.

Dani jumped over Liam, landing between him and the drake. She shifted to her human form, holding her hands in front of her at the charging drake. "Stop!"

"Dani! Move!" Liam batted at her legs, but she spread her stance.

The ground vibrated with each thundering step of the creature towering over her.

"Are you fucking crazy?!" Liam rolled, and the crossbow twanged, but the bolt whizzed past, hitting nothing. His swords scraped from their scabbards.

"Shek!" Dani put every ounce of authority she could muster into the command, born of a language the Dtrüa created to better communicate with the creatures.

The drake skidded, wafts of loam mixing with the musty orange as it tried to obey her order to stop.

She kept her hand outstretched as the beast neared, pushing its smooth scaled nose into her palm with a huff.

"Nymaera's breath." Liam sounded closer, having regained his footing.

The drake snorted at him, and she sidestepped to regain its attention. "Shek, taka."

The leather reins and bridle jangled as it shook its head.

The shout of the drake's rider rose, and Liam moved away from her. Metal clashed, but she focused on the enormous animal before her. Its thoughts pierced her mind, and she sensed its confusion. Its disquiet with the entire battle.

Dani gritted her teeth, channeling her Art. *You're safe with us. We need your help.*

The drake whined, a low hum that shook the rocks at her feet. His mind focused on the pain in his chest where Liam's arrow still penetrated his thick hide.

"What the hells are you doing?" Liam approached next to her.

"What I do best." She wiped the blood from her face with the back of her arm. Stroking the drake's face, she maneuvered to the arrow jutting out from its chest. *I can help you, too.* Gripping the shaft, she yanked it out.

The beast chuffed, shaking its neck in appreciation.

"You've got to be joking." But she heard his swords return to their sheaths.

The drake gave a low growl, whipping his head towards Liam, and to the soldier's credit, he didn't step away.

"I don't think he likes me very much."

Dani checked the bridle around his head, ensuring it was still secure. "You shot him."

"Doesn't look like it hurt him much."

"He's still going to hold it against you." Dani ran her hands along its side, finding the notch in its shoulder scales. "Dak."

The drake crouched.

"What are you doing?" Liam's tone suggested he already knew.

"What does it look like?" Dani hoisted herself up, climbing into the drake's saddle.

Liam's footsteps moved away. "You're crazy. A total badass, but crazy. And hot."

Dani laughed. "Remember that for later. No time right now."

"Right. Fighting. War." The clink of the straps of his crossbow sounded, and the drake growled and snapped. The crossbow hit the ground again, and the rumble in the drake faded.

"Easy, boy," Dani cooed. "Shhh."

"All right, no crossbow. Got it." Liam stepped closer. "You outran me enough as a cat. How am I supposed to keep up now?"

"You're going to join me." Dani held her hand out to him with a grin. "Get on, soldier."

"Serving me right up on its back, I see." Liam snorted as he made a wide circle around the drake's head, its neck turning to follow the whole way.

Liam breathed, his knuckles popping. "You can do this, Talansiet. It's just a big lizard."

Dani chuckled. "Sit behind me."

Someone shouted nearby, and the roar of battle grew with the pounding of her heart.

His hand touched her waist as he hoisted himself into the large saddle, his warmth pressing up against her. "Where to, madame dragon?" he teased in her ear.

"Ayke!" Dani's command made the drake stand tall again, and it growled, ready to obey. "This is how I give Isalica an advantage, but I need your eyes. Where are we needed?"

Liam's grip tightened, and he tapped her left shoulder. "Looks like they can use help near the east gate."

Dani used the reins in one hand to point the drake in the direction Liam instructed. "Vah."

It lumbered forward, and with a tap of her heel, it picked up speed. Stomping through the Feyorian soldiers, it thundered over the ground.

"Tell me when we're near the Isalicans." Dani put her hand on his, which squeezed around her waist.

"Hundred yards." He tapped his finger rhythmically on her abdomen. Four taps. "Fifty." With a tap, each representing another ten yards, she waited for the third.

"Ryke!" Dani tapped her left heel, and the drake spun, tail sweeping through the Feyorian line. Screams rose with the clatter of armor.

"Are we straight along the lines?" She shouted over the chaos.

The drake roared, its fangs gnashing into a nearby soldier, and she hoped it was Feyorian.

"More or less," Liam shouted, his grip tightening. "I'll guide you." He wrapped his arms entirely around her, hands touching her sides where he squeezed. "Left. Right." He indicated.

Dani tapped both heels twice and angled the drake according to Liam's instruction, sending it forward again in a rush.

"We're halfway through, keep going." Liam's voice echoed in her ear.

Liam gasped. "Spear!"

Metal sliced through the air and thumped into the creature. The drake shrieked, stumbling mid stride. It lurched to the side, legs giving way as it collapsed to the ground.

Liam wrapped himself around her as they flew forward, twisting to hit the ground first as the drake skidded to a stop, groaning.

Chapter 49

Chaos erupted in the medical tent, Merissa shouting commands to the small number of healers who'd survived the border assault. Each held their faces hard, unabashed by the coming screams. They moved in practiced rhythm, dashing between cots and basins of water.

"Don't get caught up with those who will die anyway."

The instruction made Katrin shiver. She remembered the last person who'd said that to her right before a dire wolf tore her in two. However, now they were within the barricade, and the only way an attack would make it to where Katrin stood was if they broke through the entire first and second line.

Through Matthias.

Her stomach clenched as she went to work soaking bandages, the first group of injured making their way in. Some holding their own flesh together, others missing limbs and carried by comrades.

I have to keep it together.

Merissa stood at the entrance, pointing those arriving towards the wings of the tent, based on their injuries. Fortunately, she'd spared Katrin from the more demanding triage wing, sending her those more likely to survive.

Gods know I can't decide who dies.

Wrapping what could go without healing as quickly as she could, Katrin sent soldiers on their way out the back flap of the tent faster than she thought possible.

The shouting and clatter of battle rose beyond her vision.

A deafening roar shook the posts of the tent, several gasps of surprise echoing around her. Dark shadows blocked the glow of the moon on the tent's canvas.

Katrin shifted out of her own light, hurriedly securing the bandage in place around a soldier's slashed arm. A quick brush of her fingers and summoning of her power banished the man's pain. "Get back out there."

Dani's voice tore into her mind. *Katrin, I need you.*

Katrin jerked up, startling a soldier who'd crept up behind her.

"Dani?" Katrin looked around the tent, the confused soldier shaking his bleeding head.

I'm at the front line with Liam near the eastern gate. We're all right, but I need you. If you can hear me, please come.

Panic radiated through her veins, but she gritted her jaw. "Someone will help in a moment." She touched the man's shoulder to guide him to a cot. "I'm needed somewhere else."

Tightening the strings at the back of her bloody apron, Katrin hurried for the open front entrance as Merissa directed a woman hobbling on one leg towards the other side of the tent. "I have to go."

"What?" Merissa's eyes went wide. "Why?"

"Dani needs me." Katrin dunked her hands in a basin of water, scrubbing them. "I'll come back as soon as I can."

Merissa's attention darted to a soldier carried between two others, who were less severely injured. "Don't get yourself killed, or Matthias will never forgive me."

Katrin gave her a reassuring smile before she ducked around the approaching soldiers, running into the night.

It took a moment for her eyes to adjust to the torchlight, the cacophony of soldiers roaring in pain and anger along with howls unlike anything she'd heard.

Her heart doubled in pace as she rushed between tents, dodging the Isalicans running down the main walkway. Slipping between the tents and the wooden barricade, she hurried towards the east gate, even though every instinct told her to run the other way. She lifted her skirt as she ran, tucking it into the sides of her belt. Checking the knife at her side, she unfastened the little thong securing it in place.

She slowed as she reached a narrow break between logs, just wide enough for her to squeeze through. Pausing, she closed her eyes and leveled her breath. The tickle of the Art flowed back into her, easy to access.

Heightened emotion always makes it easier.

In the darkness of her eyelids, blurry images passed in near blackness in the Dtrüa's vision as Katrin connected to her friend. Glowing orbs of orange streaked through the sky. Fire arrows soaring towards the Isalican encampment from somewhere beyond where Katrin stood.

Metal clashed, the now familiar sound of swords sliding against each other, though the blows sounded far different from when the crown elites spared.

"Dani, we have to move!" Liam's words sounded distant, the low whine of a creature in pain rumbling near her ear. The teal of his scent drifted through Dani's vision before being swallowed by the grey tang of blood and muddy orange of something else.

"I'm not leaving him!" Dani's tone made Katrin's chest ache.

Another gravelly whine and huffing like a blacksmith's bellows.

Liam's swords rang against an opponent's, and he grunted as something thumped. For a heartbeat, Katrin feared it was her brother, but then Liam's voice came again, closer. "He won't make it, Dani."

"Help is coming."

Katrin shook the visions from her head as she opened her eyes, the echo of Dani's voice reverberating through her as she looked back and forth across the barricade. Flames licked at the spiked walls, the shafts of the fire arrows that caused them becoming swallowed by the growing destruction. Only one part of the barricade she could see had been freshly assaulted, and she steeled herself as she turned towards it.

Thankful for the deep blue dress she'd chosen, Katrin blended into the shadows along the wall as she ran. Her lungs burned with smoke and the growing stench of death.

Casting an eerie glow across the battle, the flames of the burning barricade bounced off the soldiers' armor as they fought to keep all ground. Isalica's banners had pushed further into the field, stepping over a line of Feyorian bodies that looked viciously mauled.

She saw Liam first, wielding his swords against a pair of Feyorians who'd broken past the moving Isalican line. He stood protectively over an indistinct mass, firelight reflecting against pale pearlescent blue scales.

Dani knelt at the giant drake's head, her hand pressed where he bled black, seeping like tar over the glittering scales.

"This is insane." Katrin bounced on her toes, eyeing the Feyorian line. Inhaling sharply, she plowed ahead into the sticky trampled grass, hopping over dark masses that lay still.

Liam withdrew his sword in a smooth motion from the body at his feet, plunging it into the other soldier as Katrin circled wide to avoid the battle. His eyes darted to her, his sword raising.

"It's me!" Katrin squeaked, lifting her hands.

He froze, his eyes widening. "Katy girl, what in the hells..."

"I'm here to help."

Realization filtered over Liam's face, and he turned towards Dani, glaring. "You called my *sister* out of the safety of the medical tent for *this?*" Blood streaked his face, making him look sinister.

Dani held the shaft of a spear sticking out of a drake's neck. Blood stained her chin and neck, but determination steeled her face. "I needed her!"

"What difference does the drake's life make?"

Dani's jaw flexed. "All of it!"

"Shit." Liam spun, his sword meeting another soldier's Katrin hadn't even seen approach.

Squinting in the moonlight, her fear rose as the Isalicans retreated towards the barricade, icy scales glowing as several drakes neared the front line.

"Dani, we need to pull back." Liam growled, rounding the drake's head towards her.

"No! I needn't see to know this fight isn't going well." She tore from Liam's grip as he tried to lift her. "This is the *one* advantage we have. I'm not about to let it go." The Dtrüa's gaze flickered Katrin's direction. "Please heal him."

"The drake? You want me to heal this... behemoth?" Katrin suddenly felt sick at the task, the world already spinning. "Dani, I..."

"Will the two of you just *trust me?*"

Liam met his sister's eyes, but before he could say anything, he was forced around the drake's body as several Isalicans backed towards it. He waved them off, his shouts indistinct as Katrin's heart pounded.

The acolyte hurried to Dani's side, watching the cat-like eye of the drake lock on her. She froze only for an instant before she pushed her hands beside Dani's against the wound. "It's not about trust, you know that with me. I just don't know if I *can*." Her knees already felt weak, and she hadn't even started.

"Please try." Dani gazed at her, eyes hard.

The acolyte's throat seized, and she swallowed, the tang of the drake's blood already thick in the air. "All right. Just... please make sure he doesn't turn around and eat me after?" Katrin tried to put some joking in her tone, but it felt strained.

"He won't, I promise."

Chewing her lower lip, Katrin sucked in a breath and, with it, all of her power. The Art flowed readily into her veins as she closed her eyes, scouring the knowledge stored in her memories of the draconi. Her anatomy lessons at the temple would do little to help her know the proper way to stitch up the scales and stop the bleeding.

I don't even know where a drake's life-giving veins are.

Entering the calm that her power usually brought, Katrin sought the muscles and skin of the creature, exploring to connect whatever she'd read in the burned out library. Ultimately, she'd found very little on dragons, though recounts of Feyor's attempts to train the lesser draconi would now prove useful.

The drake chuffed, a trilling whine following as its tail curled in, encircling Dani and Katrin.

"I think I know what to do." Katrin shifted, pushing her hands more firmly around the head of the spear. "Pull it."

With a huff, Dani jerked the spear out of the beast's neck, and it roared.

The sound propelled Katrin into her concentration, and she pushed her palms against the frosty scales coated in hot blood.

Please work.

Katrin's body shook as she poured her strength into the creature, grabbing bits of its flesh and hurriedly knitting them together. The pain seeped through her own limbs, into her throat. But the Art obeyed, and she felt the muscle at her fingertips respond.

Once the flow began, it suddenly felt easier, as if the drake's soul assisted. So little of her own power drained, acting only as a guide for the animal as the wound sealed. The bleeding stopped, the flesh reforming.

The drake moved, sinuously uncurling as it rolled towards Katrin, forcing her to jump out of its way with a yelp of surprise. It cried out as the wound tore open, onyx gushing from it before Katrin threw her hands back over the injury. "Hold still, won't you?"

Its head swung towards her, as big as she was tall, and its eyes met hers. The glowing frost-blue irises matched its scales, and it let out a throaty rumble, holding still.

"Good... boy?" Katrin kept one hand on the wound, the other moving to stroke near the break in the scales that appeared to be its ear. The scales felt oddly soft, despite how they looked, like river smoothed stone. Leaning into her hand on the drake's injury, she wound her power tighter, rushing the healing as fast as she dared. Her stomach clenched as she watched those slitted pupils.

Finished, she stepped back, her boot slipping in the slick grass.

The drake lurched up, righting her with the side of its snout.

Another draconi screeched nearby, drawing the injured one's attention. The new one barreled towards them, Liam and Dani standing between it and Katrin.

Dani shifted out of her cat form, fresh blood around her mouth that she wiped away with the back of her sleeve.

The drake Katrin healed stood, stomping over the three of them while its tail took out a Feyorian behind them. It bellowed at its brethren, and the charging beast skidding to a halt.

The rider shouted commands, but the drakes ignored him as they exchanged a chortled conversation.

Huffing, the new drake whipped its head back to the saddled rider and grasped him in its mouth, ignoring his yelps as it flung him across the battlefield.

They're intelligent.

"Liam, we're taking this one." Dani ducked from under the first drake, hands gliding along its side as she ran towards Katrin. "You can have this one."

"What?" Katrin marveled at her brother as he moved without question, gripping the new drake's saddle, but pausing.

"How do I get it to crouch?"

"Dak."

With Dani's short utterance, the drake dropped his stomach to the ground, causing Liam to jump back in surprise before he hauled himself up.

Dani looked at Katrin. "Take this drake, he trusts you." She patted a spot near the animal's elbow. "Foot goes here. Shek means stand down. Ayke means stand. Dak means crouch. Uhh... What else do you need to know... Ryke means spin. If you want to steer left, use your right heel to push, and vice versa. Like riding a very smart horse. Get on."

"Shek, Ayke, Dak..." Katrin repeated, her head spinning.

The drake, who'd jogged back towards her, lowered itself to the ground. Blood still marred the scales around its neck, its lower lid blinking in a transparent film over its eye as it watched her.

Breathing felt impossible. "Aedonai be with me." Katrin touched her heart in gentle prayer, glancing at Dani as she climbed onto the second drake. She sat on its back in front of Liam.

Katrin just stared, unwilling to move closer to the mount offered to her. Her body jolted as it was pushed gently forward, the drake's scaled nose poking her in her lower back. "All right, all right." She turned to the animal, touching the sides of its grizzly maw. Staring into its eyes, she encouraged her power to greet its now familiar aura.

Who'd have thought draconi were so smart. Communicating...

The drake blinked again, its head tilting in recognition of her power. It huffed, its breath blowing her hair back from her face.

Before she could question herself any further, Katrin shuffled to its side and placed her foot as she'd seen Dani do, hoisting herself onto its saddle. "Shek?" She shook her head. "No, I mean Ayke."

The drake rose beneath her, and she grasped at the reins as she leaned forward to keep her seat.

Katrin stroked the leathery scales. "Uh, did Dani tell me how to get you to go?" She considered as she chewed her lips, then tapped her heels against the flank behind the drake's front legs, ignoring how far away the ground was.

The massive beast lumbered forward, obeying her command to turn towards the barricade.

Chapter 50

Matthias lifted his sword as a Feyorian soldier swung at him, blocking the attack. He spun his blade, disarming his opponent, and slashed across the man's middle. Backing up, he bumped into Micah's back. "We need to retreat further. They're gaining too much ground."

His friend growled. "Fucking wyverns are destroying the east barricade. How many jumps have you used?"

The prince caught another attacking blade, his muscles shaking with strain as he held it back. "Three." He huffed and pushed, kicking the enemy in the chest and sending him sprawling.

"Long ones?"

"Long enough. I have a couple left. Three if they're short." Matthias gasped as a crossbow bolt flew at them and yanked Micah to the ground with him.

"Was that another?"

"Nope. Just lucky." Matthias helped Micah to his feet. "Come on, we're getting surrounded. Fall back to the midline."

Micah nodded, rushing towards the battlefield's last blockade before the gates of their encampment. They leapt over bodies, ducking under the tail of a drake being taken down by a group of Isalicans.

Diving behind the spiked wall, Matthias twisted to defend from the running steps behind them. A Feyorian jumped at him, skewering himself on the prince's ready sword.

Matthias pushed the weight to the side, and the body slid off, leaving behind a wet sheen. He tried to catch his breath, standing.

They'd been fighting for hours. Blood and mud coated their faces and clothes, exhaustion tainting each stride. He gazed through the haze of torches and steel across the war zone, spotting three of his elites in the distance.

Hopefully Liam and Dani are safe.

Riez, Barim and Stefan fought a wyvern, along with several other soldiers. A massive bolas tangled around the creature's twisted wing, holes torn in the delicate membrane.

"We need to help them." Matthias rushed forward, but stopped when a second wyvern descended from the sky and grasped Riez with taloned feet.

It rose, wings beating like a drum as the others failed to save him. In their distraction, the first wyvern spun, taking out the other two with a heavy impact from its spiked tail.

"No!" Matthias gripped Micah's shoulder and breathed in his Art. Reality blurred, and he pulled himself backward through the battle as far as he could.

Inhaling, Matthias looked at Micah. "We need to move."

They stood well beyond the midline, not yet having taken their back-to-back stance.

"Now?"

"Now!" Matthias ran through the muck, boots sticking and weighing his steps.

Riez and the other two had been fighting north of the midline, which wasn't far, but chaos occupied the space between.

Matthias, with Micah close behind him, dodged attacks rather than returning them. He didn't look back, slipping in the mud and catching an enemy sword with his gloved hand. The blade bit through the leather, and he plunged his own into the woman's midsection.

She fell, and he tossed her sword aside.

"Never thought I'd..." He looked behind him for Micah, but the man wasn't there. "Kathira?" He spun, searching back the way they'd come.

His best friend lay in the mud, a bolt jutting out of his chest and another in his leg.

"Fuck." Matthias glanced at his other elites before racing back to Micah. Dropping to his knees, he slid to a stop near his head.

Micah choked, his eyes glazing over.

"I won't let you die." Matthias cringed, looking again towards where Riez and Barim were soon to meet the same fate.

His heart clenched.

I'm sorry.

Art washed through his body again, and he reversed the events.

Matthias, mid-run, gasped and spun. He jerked Micah to the side by his arm, a bolt flying where he'd been.

Micah yelped, one grazing his thigh, but righted himself. "You just did it again, didn't you?"

The prince panted, his sword arm shaking. "Five times. I don't know if I can do another, so stop trying to die." He rushed again, forcing his legs to run towards the other elites.

The wyvern crashed from the sky, making the ground vibrate with the impact as it struggled against the bolas tangled around its wing. Bones cracked, and Riez lunged, piercing the creature's wing where Matthias had seen it broken before.

I won't make it in time.

The prince shoved an enemy soldier out of his way, glancing back for Micah. He leapt over debris, boots slipping as he landed. Righting himself, the second wyvern dove towards Riez.

"Riez, above you!" He shouted as loud as he could, but the elite didn't hear him.

In the same fashion as before, the draconi captured the elite guard in his talons.

The other two fell to the first wyvern's tail.

Matthias's breath caught, and he stumbled.

I have to try again.

Matthias's head exploded in a migraine.

"You just did it again, didn't you?" Micah gaped at him, grabbing at the bloodied graze on his thigh.

I'm out of time.

"Six," Matthias wheezed. His limbs shook as he paused, spotting a riderless horse twenty yards to his right. He bolted for the mount, grabbing the horse's reins.

The ground shook with impact.

"Stay out of fucking trouble!" Matthias turned from Micah, galloping over the sea of dead bodies and broken weapons.

He only made it halfway before the second wyvern descended, but his vision blurred before he could witness their deaths yet again. The back of Matthias's head hit something hard, and he groaned, the horse struggling to its feet and trotting away.

The dark night sky spun above him, fire arrows streaking the blackness. The mud chilled his back, ears ringing.

"Matthias!"

Her voice doesn't belong on the battlefield.

Drakes roared, their bellows deeper than their flying cousins.

"Whoa, what the..." Micah's voice came from somewhere close, and Matthias groaned as he sat up.

His eyes focused on a drake, and his heart leapt into his throat.

The beast turned, its body blocking Matthias's vision of the Feyorian line. Its tail lashed, but passed over Matthias with a whoosh of air, and Katrin slid off its back.

I'm imagining things, now.

The prince shook his head, trying to clear his vision, but it didn't change. "Katrin?"

"How the hells did you get one of those?" Micah gaped at the monstrous beast, approaching cautiously as it eyed him.

Katrin rushed to Matthias, ignoring Micah. "Are you hurt?"

"You shouldn't be outside the walls." Matthias scowled, rising to his feet.

"And you shouldn't be laying on your back in the middle of a battlefield." Katrin looked gruesome, dark spatters of blood over her apron and arms, though her face was clean.

"I was trying..." His gaze drifted to where his men had fallen, and his eyes landed on Stefan crouching over a motionless Barim. He faced Katrin. "You need to get out of here. Feyor might win this."

"Katrin, can you take Matthias back to the camp?" Micah eyed the drake. "He's jumped at least six times. He can't do another. I'll go help Stefan and the others."

"No, I'm not leaving the fight to you." Matthias squinted, trying to still his swirling surroundings.

"Shut up and get out of here. You're going to get all of us killed trying to protect your stupid ass." Micah shoved his shoulder, causing Matthias to stumble into Katrin, who stabilized him.

Matthias growled. "Fuck. If you all die, I'm gonna kill you."

Micah gave him a sad grin. "And I'll haunt you." He gestured towards the drake, and Katrin's grip around Matthias tightened.

"Dak." The command in Katrin's tone seemed odd, but the drake purred as it crouched, her dirty hands trailing down his flank as she encouraged Matthias forward. "Help us." Command filled her tone rather than request, and the prince's double gave him a surprised glance.

"Yes, ma'am."

Katrin climbed onto the back of the beast first, then reached for Matthias.

He grumbled as Micah stepped up behind him, helping to hoist him up. His eyelids felt impossibly heavy as he sagged against Katrin's back, and she spoke another word that made the drake rise.

"Head northeast." Micah hissed as he put weight on his injured leg, tightening the length of leather already tied there. "We'll rendezvous at the entrance to the pass. But you can't stay here. We're going to lose the camp. I'll take care of the orders to retreat, just get our stubborn prince somewhere safe. Isalica needs him alive."

A wyvern screeched as it dove, but the drake lifted its massive head and howled in response, making the winged creature balk. It reared back, its wings filling with air as it beat higher, its rider cursing.

"Well, that's useful. Can I have one?" Micah eyed the creature and took a step forward. He froze when the drake gave a low warning growl.

"Might have to heal one. Or be a Dtrüa. Sorry, Micah. But I pray the gods be with you." Katrin's hand closed around Matthias's arm that wrapped around her middle. "You're going to have to hold on."

"I'm fine. Go." Matthias looked back as the drake started forward, watching Micah run towards Stefan, giving orders to a commander as he went.

I couldn't save them.

He cringed, leaning his forehead against the back of Katrin's shoulder. Heat burned his eyes, and he tightened his hold and whispered, "Are Liam and Dani safe?"

"They were when Dani insisted I take this drake." Katrin's voice drifted back to him in the wind as she turned her head. She held onto his arm, even though he knew if he fell she'd go with him.

The drake turned north, Katrin steering the creature towards the shadow of the mountains, and the din of battle faded beneath the steady thrum of clawed feet.

The sky brightened to the soft grey of dawn before the strips of clouds on the horizon colored pink and orange.

They turned to follow the mountain range towards the rising sun, the drake climbing the rocky slope with ease. It snorted as it broke over the line of a ridge, forcing them to lean forward while clinging to the creature's reins and saddle.

"Shek." Katrin stroked the beast's neck as he obeyed the command, stopping.

The drake swung its head back towards the battlefield, and Matthias dared look.

Fires dotted the landscape, smoke tainting the sky. The once lush field stood a mess of brown and black, movement still flurrying towards the camp's walls.

A wyvern dove from the sky, landing inside the encampment. It lifted its head in a shriek, batting away the Isalicans who ran to challenge it. The sunrise reflected on its scales, streaks of red blood coating its mouth and claws. Another joined it, the tents collapsing beneath talons.

To the west, Feyor's grey uniforms formed a line just outside the trees, a fresh battalion awaiting their orders.

Isalica's surrender horn blared in the distance, its tone melding with the cries of the draconi.

The prince closed his eyes.

To be continued...

The story continues with...

WINGS OF THE ETERNAL WAR

www.Pantracia.com

Cinders rain when a kingdom falls.

Even though Feyor's attack on Isalica's border has ceased, for now, Matthias's losses vastly outweigh his sense of victory. Grief consumes the prince, blinding him to the wickedness that has invaded his healer. He sends Merissa to Nema's Throne, unaware of the danger she poses to his home and capital city.

While trying to support her lover, Katrin discovers a light within herself only to have it mercilessly extinguished. The unexpected agony dissolves her strength, and being near Matthias only makes it worse. She abandons the encampment, severing all the bonds she'd created there, and leaves her prince in the dark.

Gaining a new role with her official pardon, Dani should be over the moon. But with her friendships strained and relationship with Liam on a precipice, all she wants is peace. Yet, when an old friend from Feyor brings unsettling news, she realizes peace may be impossible.

All must work together to prevent Feyor from obtaining what would be their deadliest weapon yet. Dragons. With a breath of fire, they could raze Isalica, unless the prince finds them, first.

Wings of the Eternal War is Part 2 of *Shadowed Kings*, and Book 9 in the *Pantracia Chronicles*.

CPSIA information can be obtained
at www.ICGtesting.com
Printed in the USA
BVHW030259190521
607684BV00001B/1

9 781777 526207